T0348210

WESTERN

Rugged men looking for love...

Starting Over With The Maverick
Kathy Douglass

A Family For His Boys
M. K. Stelmack

MILLS & BOON

Kathy Douglass is acknowledged as the author of this work
STARTING OVER WITH THE MAVERICK
© 2024 by Harlequin Enterprises ULC
Philippine Copyright 2024
Australian Copyright 2024
New Zealand Copyright 2024

First Published 2024
First Australian Paperback Edition 2024
ISBN 978 1 038 91051 6

A FAMILY FOR HIS BOYS
© 2024 by S.M. Stelmack
Philippine Copyright 2024
Australian Copyright 2024
New Zealand Copyright 2024

First Published 2024
First Australian Paperback Edition 2024
ISBN 978 1 038 91051 6

MIX
Paper | Supporting
responsible forestry
FSC® C001695

Published by
Harlequin Mills & Boon
An imprint of Harlequin Enterprises (Australia) Pty Limited
(ABN 47 001 180 918), a subsidiary of HarperCollins
Publishers Australia Pty Limited
(ABN 36 009 913 517)
Level 19, 201 Elizabeth Street
SYDNEY NSW 2000 AUSTRALIA

Cover art used by arrangement with Harlequin Books S.A.. All rights reserved.

Printed and bound in Australia by McPherson's Printing Group

Starting Over With The Maverick
Kathy Douglas

MILLS & BOON

Kathy Douglass is a lawyer turned author of sweet small-town contemporary romances. She is married to her very own hero and mother to two sons, who cheer her on as she tries to get her stubborn hero and heroine to realise they are meant to be together. She loves hearing from readers that something in her books made them laugh or cry. You can learn more about Kathy or contact her at kathydouglassbooks.com.

Visit the Author Profile page
at millsandboon.com.au for more titles.

Dear Reader,

Love has returned to Bronco, Montana. This time it has set its sights on Elizabeth Hawkins and Jake McCreery.

Elizabeth is a widowed single mother of five-year-old twins. She is at a crossroads, trying to decide whether to move to America to be closer to her family, or go back home to Australia and everything that is familiar to her daughters. The last thing she needs is a man complicating her life and making this decision more difficult.

Jake is a widower with three kids of his own. He is doing his best to raise his kids, although lately, he's had difficulty connecting with his tween daughter. His plate is full and there isn't room for anyone else in his life.

The kids take an instant liking to each other, so although Elizabeth and Jake are not looking for romance, they are open to friendship. Their kids have other ideas. With five little matchmakers determined to become a family, will Jake and Elizabeth take a chance on loving again?

I hope you enjoy reading *Starting Over with the Maverick* as much as I enjoyed writing it.

I love hearing from my readers, so feel free to visit my website, kathydouglassbooks.com, and drop me a line.

Happy reading!

Kathy

DEDICATION

This book is dedicated with much love to my husband and sons. I appreciate your constant support.

This book is also dedicated to my parents, who instilled the love of reading in me at a very young age. I miss you both every day.

CHAPTER ONE

ELIZABETH HAWKINS WALKED into the arena of the Bronco Convention Center and looked around. Although it was located in Bronco, Montana, half a world from the ones she'd spent her time working in back in Queensland, Australia, the surroundings felt familiar, and she was immediately at ease. As a member of the famed rodeo Hawkins family, she had spent most of her adult life traveling the rodeo circuit. Unlike her cousins who performed in the United States and three of her sisters who toured in South America, Elizabeth and her sister Carly were based in Australia. Her sisters Tori, Amy, and Faith had moved to Bronco and had urged Elizabeth to join them.

Tori had visited Elizabeth and her daughters in Australia last year. They'd had so much fun just being together, and Elizabeth had realized how much she'd missed having her family around. Now that her girls were approaching school age, she was faced with a decision. Should she move to the United States, where several of her sisters and her extended family lived, or should she stay in Australia and attempt to live the life she and her late husband, Arlo, had planned? The life they'd dreamed of? She didn't know, which was why she and her daughters were staying in Tori's old cabin on the outskirts of Bronco on an extended vacation—now that Tori had moved in with her fiancé, Bobby Stone. She needed facts in order to make an informed decision.

"What do you think?" Rylee Parker asked, bringing Elizabeth's attention to the present and the reason they were meeting today. Rylee was the marketing director of the Bronco Convention Center, and she'd been showing Elizabeth around.

"It's nice. The perfect venue to host a rodeo."

"Not just rodeos—although those are popular," Rylee said. "We're the preferred venue for everything from sales conventions to classic-car shows. What we're interested in hosting is something rodeo-related with you."

"Of course." It made good business sense for Rylee to capitalize on the Hawkins name. Her cousins—Brynn, Audrey, Remi, and Corinne—were big celebrities in the American rodeo world and lived in Bronco when not touring. Audrey, easily the best competitor on the woman's circuit, had recently married Jack Burris, one of the uber-famous rodeo Burris brothers who'd grown up in Bronco. The Hawkins Sisters had even competed against the Burris brothers in a Battle of the Sexes a couple of years back, an event that had given them and women's rodeo a higher profile in the United States. "What did you have in mind?"

"I have a couple of ideas, but I hoped we could brainstorm and come up with something new and fresh."

Before Elizabeth could respond, one of her daughters patted her thigh. Squelching a sigh, she looked down at Gianna, the older of her five-year-old twins by two minutes. Lucy and Gianna had once been so outgoing and confident, much like their charming father. Arlo, Elizabeth's beloved husband, had never met a stranger. Also like their father, Lucy and Gianna had been daredevils, willing to try anything. Elizabeth had found her heart in her throat on more than one occasion as she'd watched her little girls try to match the skills performed by older kids on the rodeo circuit. Arlo had always laughed and assured her that their girls could do anything. More than that, he'd always stood nearby, ready to catch them if they should fall. Gianna and Lucy were gifted athletes, and it was rare that Arlo had needed to save them. But his presence had been enough to allay all of Elizabeth's fears.

Sadly Arlo had succumbed to an unexpected heart attack two years ago and was no longer around to protect their little family or calm Elizabeth's fears.

Elizabeth swallowed hard, forcing away the unhappy memory. Although she had gotten over the agony that had accompanied his death, the occasional pang struck her at unexpected and inopportune times. Over the years, she'd learned to work through the pain, pasting on a smile and soldiering on. She was responsible for her daughters and didn't have the luxury of indulging her feelings. Her daughters had lost their father to a hidden health defect. They couldn't afford to lose their mother to grief. So no matter how desperately she'd longed to curl up into a ball and cry, she'd forced herself to carry on. *Fake it until you make it* had become her mantra.

"Are we done yet?" Gianna whispered.

Lucy moved closer to her sister. The two of them had become quiet after Arlo's death. Over time, with the love of their paternal grandparents and rodeo family, they'd begun to become the little girls they had been. Since they'd been in the States, the girls had begun to cling again.

"Not quite," Elizabeth replied. She'd wanted to leave the girls with one of her sisters or cousins while she met with Rylee, but the girls had kicked up a fuss. They weren't ready to let her out of their sight. Not that she blamed them. They were in an unfamiliar environment. Although people here spoke the same language for the most part, they did so with an accent, emphasizing just how far away from home they were.

"How much longer are we going to be here?" Lucy asked, her voice pitched even lower than her sister's.

"Not much longer. Do you girls want to sit on the benches and play with your dolls?"

Gianna and Lucy glanced over at the risers on the far side of the arena and then shook their heads.

Elizabeth flashed Rylee an apologetic smile. "Sorry."

"Don't be. I understand," she said. "I imagine they're still trying to get used to their new surroundings."

"Yes." Elizabeth stepped between her daughters, put her arms around their shoulders and gave them each a gentle hug. There had been so many changes in their young lives, requiring them to get their bearings over and over. Now they were in a strange country with a whole host of new relatives who kept coming around, wanting to spend time with them. Was it any wonder they were glued to her side? She was the only bit of familiarity they had. "If you want to reschedule our meeting to a later date, I'm willing."

Rylee waved her hand. "There's no need for that. I love kids. In fact, I often babysit my neighbor's toddler, so I can imagine how they're feeling right now. Your daughters are sweeties."

"Thanks for understanding. This isn't the usual way I conduct business."

"Since we're putting on a program for kids, it will be good to get their opinion. They can be our consultants." She stooped down and spoke directly to the girls. "Would you like to be our helpers?"

The girls grinned and looked up at Elizabeth.

Gianna gave a tentative smile. "Can we?"

"Absolutely," she said.

Gianna and Lucy nodded at Rylee. "Okay."

Elizabeth smiled. It was nice to know that Rylee understood her situation as a single mother of two young children. Although this was her first time meeting Rylee, she liked the other woman and believed they could become friends. "I appreciate that. But will it be okay with your boss? I don't want to cause any problems for you."

"Not at all. We have actually been talking about starting an on-site day care for employees. I don't know if you're interested, but there are a couple of day cares in town you might want to check out."

"My daughters have never been in day care. When my late husband or I weren't able to care for them, our friends on the tour looked out for them. When we were home, my in-laws were there with open arms."

"I'm sure that was wonderful."

"It was." If she moved here, she would lose that connection and those relationships. "So what did you have in mind for programming?"

"We were thinking about horse-riding camp. While there are plenty of ranches surrounding Bronco, lots of children in town don't have access to horses. Plenty of kids here have not even seen a horse close up. They don't know how to ride or care for them."

That statement was disappointing, especially given how many ranches were nearby. Elizabeth would do whatever she could to help remedy the situation. "My girls have been riding since they were two. They love being on horseback. This program sounds like something that would benefit a lot of kids. How would we make it work?"

"So you're on board?" Rylee flashed a hopeful smile.

"Yes. A pony academy sounds like it's needed in this town. But I'm not sure how long I'll be in Bronco. I don't want to make a commitment that I can't keep. It would be wrong to get the kids excited only to disappoint them."

"How about we start with a day and limit it to kids ten

and under?" Rylee said. "They can't be disappointed if they only expect one day."

"That's true. I can definitely commit to a day. If there's a lot of interest, I'm open to having a second day."

"That sounds good. Now we just need to come up with a catchy name."

"I suggest we keep it simple. Kids like to belong to clubs, so how about we call it the Pony Club?"

Rylee nodded. "That works for me. And it sums up exactly what the event will be about."

They firmed up the details and finished the tour of the convention center.

"I look forward to working with you," Rylee said when they were standing by the entrance.

"Same," Elizabeth said honestly. She took her girls by the hand and led them to the parking lot. Once they were in the car she inhaled deeply. She wasn't sure what the future held, but she'd taken a small step by agreeing to lead the Pony Club. She hoped Arlo would approve.

"COME ON—HURRY UP SO we won't be late." Molly picked up a boot and handed it to her brother, standing over him until he put it on.

"I don't need you watching," Pete said, shoving in his foot. He turned to look at his dad, who had been helping Ben to get ready. "Dad, tell Molly to stop bossing me around."

Jake McCreery blew out a sigh and looked at his two oldest children. At ten years old, Molly often acted as a mother hen. Generally Pete, two years younger, didn't mind her hovering. But today he was annoyed. At times like this, Jake missed his late wife Maggie's calm guiding hand. Although she'd died six years ago, giving birth to Ben, Jake still wondered how she would handle these dustups. *WWMD—What would Maggie do?*—had become his go-to phrase when things got rough. No doubt she would have the perfect solution that left everyone happy. But since she was gone, it was up to him to handle the situation.

"Molly, your brother is capable of getting ready on his own. Perhaps you should make sure you have everything you need."

Molly gave Pete one last exasperated look and then looked at Jake. "I just want to be on time to the Pony Club."

"I understand."

"All of our friends are going to be there."

Jake nodded. Even though they had plenty of horses of their own, he'd signed up his kids for the Pony Club. It would be good for his brood to be around other kids. Especially Molly. She often gravitated toward activities geared for older people where she would be surrounded by mother figures. Case in point, she'd been the youngest contestant in the Valentine's Day bakeoff at Bronco Motors earlier this year. Jake had been proud of her, of course, but he wanted her to spend time with other kids. She tended to act more her age around the girls in her class.

"Yeah," Pete agreed, his temporary pique with his sister a thing of the past. But then, Pete was too good-natured to hold a grudge. "Plus real rodeo stars are going to be there. With their winning belt buckles."

"And their horses," Ben piped up. He grinned, showing off the hole where his right front tooth used to be.

"Well, then, let's hit the road," Jake said.

Once everyone was loaded into the SUV, he headed toward the Bronco Convention Center.

Bronco, Montana, was two towns in one: the ritzy Bronco Heights and the middle-class Bronco Valley. Although there were differences—the obvious ones being the wealth disparity—for the most part the citizens got along well. Jake's ranch was about forty-five minutes out-side town, so he didn't make it here on a regular basis. But when he did, he enjoyed treating himself and his kids to ribs at DJ's Deluxe or shakes at Bronco Burgers.

The kids chattered happily about the club and what they hoped would happen. From the sound of it, they had ex-tremely high expectations. Jake crossed his fingers that they wouldn't be disappointed.

When they arrived, Jake parked and then stood back while the kids jumped from the vehicle. After Maggie's death, Jake had become very protective of his kids, afraid to lose another person that he loved. Disaster had struck once, taking his beloved wife without warning. For a while, Jake had seen the potential for disaster around every cor-ner, waiting to pounce on one of his children.

Ben was the third child, so by that time Jake should have had the father thing down to a science. He'd experi-enced the bumps and bruises, the fevers and crying jags twice before. Even knowing what to expect, he'd been a bundle of nerves with Ben, blowing every little thing out of proportion.

Luckily, the past six years had been uneventful. There had been no disasters, and over time, he'd begun to relax and had stopped expecting the worst to happen. Now a bump on the head was simply a bump on the head and not a potential concussion that required a trip to the doctor.

At the same time, his grief had faded. Even so, he still missed Maggie and always would. She'd been the best part of his life. He hated that she'd been cheated out of the op-portunity to watch her children grow up. Knowing that she wouldn't be there for birthdays and graduations broke his heart. But he couldn't wallow in grief. Not when he had three children depending on him.

There were several cars and trucks parked in the lot—a

clear sign that the Pony Club was going to be popular with the kids in town. Two kids who lived on a nearby ranch hopped out of an SUV and ran into the convention center. Apparently his three weren't the only ranch kids attending the club today.

Jake and his kids stepped inside. The sound of horses neighing filled the air. Without saying a word, the kids took off running. Not wanting to let them get too far ahead of him, he jogged behind them. When he reached the floor of the arena, he noticed several things at once. First, there were several kids—including Ben and Pete—clustered around rodeo star Ross Burris and talking a mile a minute as they pointed at the horses. Second, his daughter wasn't with them.

He looked around until he spotted her. She was talking to two little girls dressed in rodeo garb and paying no attention to the animals. Given that they had horses at home, that wasn't completely unexpected. Even so, he felt a twinge of guilt. It couldn't be easy for her to be the only female in the house. He tried to get in touch with his feminine side—whatever the heck that meant—but he knew he could never take the place of her mother. There hadn't been anyone to give her female guidance for six years.

Not that there weren't women eager to step into that role. Women had been trying to become a part of his family for years. Maggie had only been gone two weeks before they'd begun circling. Of all the things that had hurt and disappointed him, that had been the worst. He couldn't believe women who had known his wife for years, women who had been her friends, had suddenly thought that they could take her place in her family. *In his heart.* He hadn't looked at any of them the same way since.

Jake blew out a long breath, hoping to expel the negativity. Since his boys were in good hands, Jake made his way over to Molly. She smiled and waved excitedly at him.

"This is Lucy and Gianna," she said when he was standing in front of her. "They're identical twins."

He didn't recognize them. Perhaps they were new to town.

"Hello, Lucy. Hello, Gianna." He glanced at each girl as he spoke, hoping that he'd addressed them correctly.

The girls giggled, leaving him unsure if he'd gotten their names right. Although they were wearing rodeo costumes, their outfits were different colors. If he could get the names straight now, he would know which girl was wearing purple and which girl was wearing blue.

"They don't talk like us," Molly said, sounding amazed and impressed. "They have accents."

"Is that right?" he asked, looking from one girl to the next. They only stared at him. Then they moved closer together. The movement was nearly imperceptible, but he noticed it. He took a step away from them. The last thing he wanted was to make them uncomfortable.

"But to them, you're the one with the accent."

Jake turned at the sound of a woman's slightly accented voice. He took one look at her and gasped. Women were often described as *breathtaking*, although he'd never used that word before today. It fit her perfectly. She'd literally taken his breath away.

The woman was dressed in rodeo garb too. The fitted jeans emphasized her slender legs and curvy hips. Her fringed blouse floated over perky breasts and tapered down to her small waist.

He could listen to her sultry voice for days, but if he wanted the conversation to continue, he had to speak. Holding out a hand, he smiled. "I'm Jake McCreery. Molly's father."

"It's nice to meet you, Jake McCreery," the woman replied, taking the hand he offered. "I'm Elizabeth Hawkins."

Her brown skin was soft, and he felt the strangest tingling at the contact. It had been some time since he'd reacted physically toward a woman. He'd thought that part of him had died with Maggie. Over the past six years, nothing had changed that belief. At the urging of friends, he'd gone on the occasional date. Nothing had ever come of them. He'd laughed at jokes, had a drink or shared a meal, and had come home to his empty bed—never feeling a hint of the attraction he'd felt when he'd met Maggie. But maybe they had been the wrong person, because all of a sudden, his body was letting him know it was still in the game.

He checked her left hand and didn't see a ring. "Hawkins? That's a popular name in rodeo. Especially here in Bronco. Are you related to the Hawkins Sisters?"

She nodded, and her lovely hair brushed her shoulders. It was wavy, and his fingers ached to see if it was as soft as it looked. "Actually I'm one of them. My sisters just moved to Bronco after touring South America. And there's also my cousins."

"From the sound of it, rodeo is in your blood."

She laughed. "I don't know if you can say that."

"Your cousins and sisters are in rodeo. As are you. What more proof do I need?"

"You can say it runs in the family, but not so much in the blood."

"I don't see the difference."

"My sisters and I and many of my cousins are adopted. We're the same family, but we don't share blood."

"It's the love that makes a family," he said. "Not the genetics."

"I couldn't have said it better." Her bright smile touched his heart, and he smiled in return.

"Mummy, when are we going to start the club?"

Elizabeth checked her watch and then tapped the little girl on the nose. "In ten minutes, Gianna. Are you both ready?"

Ah, so Gianna was dressed in blue. That meant that Lucy was wearing purple. He'd gotten it wrong before. Jake made a mental note so he wouldn't make that mistake a second time.

"Ready," Gianna said.

"Ready," Lucy echoed, giving a little jump to emphasize the word.

"Do you need help?" Jake didn't know where that question came from. He was strictly here as a parent. Besides, he was sure the organizers had everything under control.

Elizabeth shook her head. "That's very kind of you to offer, but we've got it handled. Ross Burris and I will talk to the kids about life in the rodeo. After that we'll show the kids how to get on the horses and guide them on a quick trip around the arena. Finally we'll show them how to care for the animals."

"That sounds like a good plan. I'm sure the town kids will enjoy the new experience."

She tilted her head. Though there was nothing special about the move, she looked even more attractive. "I get the feeling that Molly isn't one of them."

"Nah. I live on a ranch outside town. We have horses, but my kids—Molly, Pete, and Ben—wanted to come."

She nodded. "There's something special about being around horses, even if you have one of your own."

"Plus there's the opportunity to meet rodeo stars."

She laughed. "That might apply to Ross Burris, but I live in Australia, so I'm sure none of the kids know who I am. Which is fine with me."

"Oh, so that's where your accent comes from. It's subtle—definitely not as pronounced as your daughters'—but it's there."

"I was born and raised in the States, but I moved to Australia about a decade ago. Over time I guess I picked up an accent."

"How long will you be in town?"

"I'm not sure. Definitely a few weeks more. This is an extended vacation to reconnect with my family. My sister lives with her fiancé, so she's letting us stay in her cabin. It's much better than a hotel."

Elizabeth's answer disappointed him, although he couldn't put his finger on why. He'd just met her, so why did he want her to stay around longer? The answer came immediately. He hadn't experienced anything remotely like the intense attraction he felt for Elizabeth with any of his dates. But then, perhaps her leaving was for the best. That way he didn't have to worry about this attraction turning into something that could result in pain. He'd had enough of that to last a lifetime.

"I hope you have a nice visit."

"So far my daughters and I are enjoying ourselves. It's been wonderful to see my family again."

"I bet. Thanks for letting my daughter hang out with your little girls. Molly is the only girl in the family. I think that she gets tired of just her brothers for company." He didn't know why he'd divulged that, especially to a stranger, but there was something about Elizabeth that encouraged sharing confidences.

"Molly is a sweet girl." She checked her watch and sighed. "It's time for me to get the event started. I need to corral my girls. They really enjoyed spending time with Molly."

"She was happy to do it. She's a little mother hen, so having two little girls around is right up her alley. But now I'll nab her and we'll join my boys." He gestured to Molly and then turned back to Elizabeth. "It was nice meeting you."

"It was nice meeting you too."

After Molly said so long to the twins, Jake steered her over to the boys. Pete and Ben were part of the group still gathered around Ross Burris. Ross had been born and raised in Bronco and was one of the famous Burris brothers. Although he wasn't as big a star as his brothers, Geoff and Jack, he'd done his share of winning on the rodeo circuit.

Ross told the kids to grab seats so they could get started.

Molly sat by her brothers, and Jake stood in the back, near enough to hear the presentation but far enough away not to be a distraction. Now that they were getting older, Molly and Pete liked to be on their own. They didn't want him hovering and watching their every move, so he tried to be as inconspicuous as possible. Besides, he wanted them to feel confident.

Thoughts of Elizabeth filled his mind, and he glanced in her direction. She was talking to a group of younger kids, holding the reins of her horse and allowing them to rub the animal's side. Her little girls were near her, showing off their costumes to a couple of other little girls who were duly impressed.

Jake couldn't seem to drag his eyes away from her. Just looking at her made his blood surge through his veins. With intelligent brown eyes, high cheekbones, and full kissable lips, she was truly beautiful.

"Any questions?" Ross Burris asked, pulling Jake's attention away from Elizabeth.

A little girl raised her hand. When Ross pointed at her, she asked her question. "Are you married?"

He smiled, unbothered by the query, although Jake was

sure it was not along the line he'd intended. Ross glanced over at an attractive woman sitting in the bleachers, taking notes. "As a matter of fact, I am. That's my wife, Celeste, right there."

The little girl nodded slowly. "Oh."

"My daddy isn't married," Ben added, unprompted. "My mommy died a long time ago. Daddy is never going to get married again. Me and Pete and Molly don't need a mom. We're fine just the way we are. Us four and no more."

Jake's heart sank as his son confidently parroted the words he'd heard all of his life. When Pete and Molly nodded in agreement, Jake wondered if he'd done the wrong thing by insisting they were fine on their own. In trying to protect himself and his children from pain, had he made a mistake by telling them repeatedly they didn't need anyone else?

If so, how could he remedy that?

CHAPTER TWO

"WE'RE READY TO go to the Pony Club, Mummy," Gianna said bright and early the next morning. It had taken the girls a couple of days to adjust to the sixteen-hour time difference, but once they had gotten used to being in American Mountain Daylight Time, they once more began waking up at the crack of dawn. It had taken Elizabeth a bit longer to adapt, but she was in the swing of things now too.

She and Arlo used to wake up early in order to enjoy quiet moments together, watching the sunrise and sipping coffee before starting their busy days. Elizabeth had tried to maintain that tradition after Arlo's death, but the dawn was too quiet. Too lonely. Now she only awoke with enough time to shower and dress before the girls began to stir.

Elizabeth set two bowls onto the small kitchen table before turning to look at her daughters. They were dressed similarly to the way they'd been yesterday, only this time in pink and green outfits. She'd left out short sets for them, but obviously they'd ignored them.

"Is that right?" she asked.

"Yes." Gianna and Lucy pulled out chairs and sat down.

Elizabeth set plates of Vegemite toast beside their bowls of Weet-Bix to round off their breakfast. She'd brought along some of their favorite foods for their vacation and was glad she had. Faith had cooked a typical American breakfast for them one day, and the girls hadn't been pleased at all. They'd taken one look at the plate of grits and bacon and turned up their noses. Since she remembered how strange some Australian foods had seemed to her when she'd first moved there, Elizabeth understood. If she and the girls decided to make a home in America, Elizabeth would do her best to help them adjust. Luckily, her friends and her sister Carly were willing to ship cases of their favorites to make the transition less painful.

"I told you that the club was only for one day. Remember?"

"But we want to go back. We want to play with Molly again," Gianna said.

"We like Molly," Lucy added before she took a big bite of her toast.

"I like Molly too," Elizabeth said, "but she's not at the convention center today since there is no Pony Club."

"Then where is she?" Gianna asked.

"I imagine that she's at home at this time of day," Elizabeth said.

"Then ring her and tell her we want to play again," Lucy said as if it was the most natural thing in the world. And to her, it was. They'd grown up in a close-knit rodeo community where getting together to play with their friends was simple.

Now that they'd made a new pal, Elizabeth wanted to nurture that friendship. She was willing to do whatever it took to help her daughters feel at home in Bronco for however long they stayed.

Elizabeth thought of the list of names, addresses, and phone numbers on the registration forms for the Pony Club. Jake McCreery's phone number would be in that file. Of course, it had been for camp use, not her personal use. Would it be crossing the line to call him to schedule a playdate?

Just thinking about Jake brought his image to her mind, and her heart skipped a beat as she recalled how attractive he was. He was about six feet, solidly built with ruddy skin, dark hair and expressive brown eyes. Dressed in well-worn jeans and a tan T-shirt that had clung to his broad shoulders, he'd stirred up longings in her that had lain dormant for two years. She hadn't been attracted to a man other than Arlo since she'd first laid eyes on him nine years ago. One look was all it had taken to fall madly in love. Now she was experiencing a similar attraction to Jake. She wasn't comfortable with the reaction, but she knew that it was easier to talk about controlling your feelings than it was to do it.

She'd enjoyed chatting with Jake and wished their conversation could have gone on longer, but she'd had a job to do. Perhaps that had been for the best. Her life was in flux. She was struggling to figure out her next move for her little family, so she didn't need to add another person to the mix. Besides, she didn't know whether she would even be in the United States two months from now, so it would be ridiculous to start something she wouldn't be able to finish.

She shook her head, trying to dislodge that foolish notion. Who said anything about starting a relationship? They'd only talked for fifteen minutes. Nowhere near enough time to get to know someone. Not only that, he'd given no indication that he was interested in anything other than killing time. He certainly hadn't done anything to make her believe that he was attracted to her.

"Why not?" Gianna asked.

"Why not what?"

"You shook your head? Why can't we ring Molly?"

Elizabeth bit back a laugh. That was what happened

when you had conversations with yourself. "I think we can ring her. But not until later. She might still be sleeping. Let's finish our breakfast first."

"Then you'll ring her?" Lucy said. Gianna might've been the spokesperson for the two, but Lucy always sought confirmation. Elizabeth had no doubt that her younger daughter would be demanding things in writing once she could read better.

"Yes."

Satisfied with Elizabeth's reply, the girls talked to each other as they ate. As someone who'd grown up close to her own sisters, Elizabeth was pleased that her daughters were good friends.

Gianna's and Lucy's lives mirrored Elizabeth's and her sisters' childhood in so many ways. Elizabeth and her sisters were third-generation rodeo performers. They'd been raised on the circuit in much the same way that Elizabeth was raising Gianna and Lucy.

Though they'd emailed, texted, and FaceTimed each other regularly, Elizabeth hadn't realized just how much she'd missed her family until Tori's visit. When they'd embraced, Elizabeth had broken down in uncharacteristic tears. Tori had been crying too. Tori had wanted Elizabeth to commit to moving back to the States, but Elizabeth could only promise to come for an extended visit. Tori's cabin wasn't the biggest, but it was cozy. Besides, she and the girls enjoyed each other's company and didn't need much space.

The girls finished their breakfast and then showed their empty dishes to Elizabeth before putting them into the sink.

"Good job," she said. "You're such good helpers."

The girls smiled, and then Gianna asked, "Are you going to ring Molly's daddy now?"

"Yes." Elizabeth found Jake's number and grabbed her phone. Since it was such a nice day, she went outside and sat on the porch step. After grabbing their dolls, the girls followed. They jumped into the white wicker rocking chairs, waiting for her to make the call.

Elizabeth dialed his number and then listened as the phone rang. Her heartbeat sped up as she waited for him to answer. Telling herself not to be ridiculous, she inhaled deeply so she wouldn't sound like a breathless teenager.

Jake answered on the third ring, and his baritone "Hello?" sent shivers down Elizabeth's spine.

Determined to ignore her body's reaction, she echoed his greeting before continuing, "This is Elizabeth Hawkins. I hope I didn't wake you."

His laughter was filled with mirth. "You're kidding, right? I have three kids. Getting them up during the school year may be next to impossible, but I don't have that problem in the summer. They're up with the sun."

"I wonder what the difference is," she said dryly.

"Oh, I think you can guess. Not to mention that I'm a rancher. Although I have a foreman who helps a lot with supervising the ranch hands, we meet most mornings to go over plans for the day."

"I got your phone number from the permission slip you signed when you registered your kids for the Pony Club. I hope it's okay that I used it."

"It is."

"Great. Please feel free to add my number to your contacts." She wanted to yank the words back the minute they slipped from her lips. It was presumptuous to assume he would want to get in touch with her in the future.

"Will do."

"I suppose I should get to the reason I called so you can get back to whatever you were doing."

"You mean it wasn't just to hear my voice?" His tone was warm and friendly. "I hoped you were calling to get my day off to a smooth start."

She laughed and leaned against the porch rail. Jake was just as easy to talk to as she remembered. "That too. But the other reason was to ask if you would consider letting Molly be a mother's helper a few hours a week. The girls really had fun with her yesterday. I'll pay her, of course."

"I'll have to ask her, but I can't imagine that she'll say no. She's always telling me that she's not a kid anymore, so she'll probably be thrilled to have a job. Not to mention that she was quite enamored of your little girls. She talked about them all the way home."

"Same here. And they woke up talking about her. Apparently she's their new best friend."

"I'll talk to her and get back to you. When is the best time to call?"

Elizabeth liked that he didn't speak for his daughter, didn't accept Elizabeth's offer on Molly's behalf. That one action spoke volumes about the kind of dad that he was. "Any time. My mobile is always on."

"Good enough. We'll talk soon."

She ended the call and then turned to Gianna and Lucy, who were looking at her expectantly. "Is Molly coming over to play with us?"

"I asked her dad. He's going to talk to her and then ring me back."

The girls looked at each other and then cheered.

"We don't know that she's going to come," Elizabeth cautioned. Ten-year-olds didn't generally hang out with five-year-olds. She might not want to do that, even if she was getting paid.

"She's coming," Gianna said. "She likes us."

Elizabeth smiled. There was nothing like the confidence

of a five-year-old. Even though it shouldn't have mattered one way or the other, Elizabeth hoped Jake liked her too.

JAKE HELD HIS phone for a moment after they ended the call. He'd thought about Elizabeth quite a bit yesterday. She'd been the last person on his mind before he'd fallen asleep last night and the first person on his mind when he'd woken up this morning. His preoccupation with her was as troubling as it was exhilarating.

He was attracted to Elizabeth. It wasn't something that he'd expected to happen, nor was it something that he welcomed. Not that he wanted to spend the rest of his life alone. But when he decided to open his heart again, he didn't want it to be with someone who might not be in the country next month. That would be pure foolishness. The best thing to do—the *smart* thing to do—would be to keep his distance so his attraction wouldn't grow. That way he wouldn't risk being hurt when she went back to Australia.

But that was the coward's way of thinking. Did he really want to live his life avoiding all risks? Playing it safe didn't sound appealing. He could miss out on a lot of good things that way. Admittedly, he'd been devastated when Maggie had died, but even knowing how much he would suffer once he'd lost her, he wouldn't trade one moment that they'd spent together for the world.

He chuckled to himself. Talk about putting the cart before the horse. There was nothing going on between him and Elizabeth. Nor had she even hinted about wanting something to develop. All she'd done was ask if his daughter could help her with her twins. That was it. Yet his imagination had them practically walking down the aisle.

"What's so funny?" Pete asked. His son was not light on his feet, yet Jake hadn't heard his approach. That was a sign that he was focusing on the wrong things.

"Nothing," Jake said.

"But you were laughing. If you know a joke, you should tell me so I can laugh too. Then I can tell my friends."

"You want to laugh, do you?" Jake grabbed his son and then playfully tossed him onto the sofa. From the time he'd been a toddler, Pete loved being tickled, so Jake obliged now. Pete laughed and rolled away, then began to tickle Jake.

"I want to play," Ben said, running into the room and jumping onto Jake's back. "Tickle me too."

"If you say so," Jake said. He flipped Ben onto the couch, then stretched his hands in his younger son's direction, wiggling his fingers. Ben giggled in anticipation. After a moment, Jake tickled Ben with one hand and Pete with the other.

Jake loved these spontaneous moments. After Maggie had died, he had tried to schedule family fun time. It had felt forced, and he'd thought he'd been doing something wrong. But these unplanned times created the closeness he'd longed for. They still had family game night and he took the kids on scheduled excursions, but these random moments of fun warmed his father's heart.

Maggie had been the glue that had held them all together. More than that, she'd been the heart of the family. When she'd died and the job had fallen to him, he'd felt incompetent. Grieving, he'd fumbled around, searching for a way to hold everyone together. Molly and Pete had been looking to him for guidance. They'd expected him to make things normal again. But he'd known that *normal* was a thing of the past and wouldn't be returning. Maggie was gone, and no one could fill her shoes.

No, if he ever married again—hell, if he ever seriously got involved again—it would have to be with someone really, really special. And since in his experience women like that were one in a million, what were the chances of that happening again?

"Grab his legs, Ben!" Pete yelled as he grabbed Jake's arms.

"Okay!" Ben said. He knelt on the floor and did his best to corral Jake.

After a couple of minutes of half-hearted resistance, Jake allowed himself to be overpowered. Eventually they all ended up on the floor, laughing uproariously. Jake held up his hands in surrender. "I give—you win."

Pete and Ben cheered and then stood with their hands raised over their heads. Pete shouted, "We're the champions!"

Ben nodded. "We're the best!"

"You should never try to beat us at tickling, Dad," Pete said. "We always win."

"I know. But I won't give up. Next time I'll win."

"What are you guys doing?" Molly asked from the doorway. She was dressed in a pink T-shirt and denim shorts. She used to goof around with them, but a few months ago she'd stopped. At the same time, she'd become interested in jewelry. She'd begged him to let her get her ears pierced, but he'd said no.

According to her, all of the girls in fifth grade had pierced ears. He didn't know whether that was true or not, but he'd told her that she shouldn't follow the crowd. The glare she'd focused on him had been searing. He might not have known the right thing to say, but he'd found the wrong thing that time.

There would come a time when he'd have to say yes, but not yet. She was still too young. *WWMD* hadn't helped. He and Maggie had never discussed what age would be appropriate to let Molly get her ears pierced.

"We were tickling Dad," Pete said. "Do you want to play?"

Molly frowned and shook her head. "No. That's a boy game."

Once again Jake was assailed by guilt. Molly's interests were changing, and he had to let her know that he understood. The problem was...he didn't. Not completely. He was a guy, and no matter how hard he tried, his imagination only got him so far.

But right now there was something he could do to wipe that frown from her face. "Do you remember the twins you talked to at the Pony Club?"

She gave him a *Do you think I have memory problems?* look. "Uh, yeah. It was only yesterday."

He decided to ignore her preteen attitude. "I talked to their mother. She said they really liked you. So she wants to know if you'll be interested in helping her with the girls a few hours a week. She said she'll pay you."

Molly grinned. "You mean like a real job?"

"Yes. I told her that I'd ask you."

"Yes. I want to. Of course I want to. I liked Lucy and Gianna a lot. They're only five, but they're fun to be around."

"I'll call her and let her know."

"Tell her that I can come every day."

"I don't think she'll need your help that often."

Molly was hugging herself and turning in circles, so Jake was certain that she hadn't heard his last comment. He and Elizabeth could work out the details later. The idea of talking to her again made Jake want to hug himself and turn in circles too. He made do with a smile.

"Can you call her now?" Molly asked once she stopped celebrating.

"Absolutely." Jake pulled up the most recent number on his call list and dialed it.

Molly held out her hand for the phone. "I should probably be the one to talk to her, since it's my job."

Jake nodded, tamping down his disappointment at being robbed of the opportunity to hear Elizabeth's voice again.

Molly held the phone to her ear. "Hi. This is Molly Mc-Creery. My dad told me that you want me to help with Lucy and Gianna." She stared at Jake and her brothers, her message clear: *Go away.* When they didn't move fast enough to suit her, she turned her back on them and walked over to the windows.

"Come on, guys," Jake said, dropping an arm over his sons' shoulders and steering them from the room. "Let's give your sister some privacy."

"We don't want to listen to her conversation anyway," Pete said, clearly offended.

"Yeah," Ben echoed. "We don't want to listen to her conversation."

Despite their protests, they were walking so slowly a snail could beat them in a foot race.

"Would you please hold on?" Molly said, giving them a meaningful look. Despite feeling put out, Jake was impressed by the way she was conducting business. He'd worn that expression and said those words countless times himself. This was the second time in as many days that he'd heard his words coming from the mouths of his children.

"You can walk faster than that," Jake said, nudging his sons.

Pete and Ben picked up the pace. By the time they reached the kitchen, they'd lost interest in trying to overhear the phone call. Pete opened the refrigerator and stared into it as if he hadn't finished eating breakfast less than thirty minutes ago. When nothing appealed to him, he closed the door.

After a moment, Pete and Ben headed for their room to play.

Jake was wiping off the counter when Molly ran into the room. She held out the phone to him. "Elizabeth wants to talk to you."

"Okay." His palms suddenly felt damp, and he rubbed them over his jeans. This was ridiculous. He wasn't some teenager about to talk to his crush. He was thirty-eight years old and a father. Nevertheless, he took extra pains to control his voice. "This is Jake."

"Hi. Thanks for allowing me to talk to Molly. She is such a sweet girl and very professional."

"That she is," Jake said proudly.

"Molly accepted my offer to be my mother's helper. My girls think they'll be having a playdate. And in a way they will, although I was careful not to refer to it that way to Molly. I'll be here the entire time, so you don't need to worry about supervision."

"When would you like for her to start?"

"How about tomorrow? I think I can hold the girls off until then." She laughed softly, and the sound illuminated a dark place inside him.

"That sounds like a plan."

She gave him directions to the cabin. He was familiar with the area.

Elizabeth insisted on paying Molly minimum wage. "After all, we want to teach her not to undervalue herself."

He liked the way Elizabeth said *we*. As if they were a team. He'd been alone on this parenting journey for six years, so even the illusion of having a partner was comforting.

"What time are we going tomorrow?" Molly asked the second he'd ended the call.

"Tomorrow around eleven. We'll drop the boys off at

karate first and then go over to Elizabeth's cabin. Does that work for you?"

She grinned. "This is going to be so good. Now I need to go pick out my clothes."

"What for? You're going to be playing with Lucy and Gianna. I'm sure whatever you wear will be fine."

Molly gave him a look that he was seeing much too often—the one that made it clear he didn't understand her at all. He hated that feeling, but he was coming to believe that it was true. The older his daughter became, the less he was able to relate to her. He wasn't going to turn into the stereotypical single dad who couldn't find common ground with his daughter. Underneath the attitude she was still his little Molly. He just needed to try harder.

"Do you want help?"

"Dad," she said, "I know how to pick out my own clothes."

"Right."

He was a bit disappointed at being brushed aside, but even that couldn't stop him from being excited.

He was going to see Elizabeth again tomorrow.

CHAPTER THREE

ELIZABETH CHECKED HER appearance in the full-size mirror, turning from side to side to make sure she looked her best from every angle. When she realized what she was doing, she laughed at herself and went into the main room where the girls were playing. This wasn't a date. She wasn't even leaving the house. She was simply entertaining a ten-year-old girl. The fact that said child was being dropped off by her handsome father was immaterial. Besides, she doubted Jake would give her more than a passing glance. She didn't get the impression that he was interested in romance. Given her situation, neither was she.

When Jake had told her that Molly was the only girl in the household, her heart had gone out to the child. With four sisters, Elizabeth couldn't picture being the only girl in the family. She supposed it would be lonely at times. She couldn't fathom not having a sister to share secrets with or talk to about fashion and boys. Elizabeth couldn't provide Molly with a female sibling, but she could give her two little girls to play with. Although Gianna and Lucy were friendly, they hadn't made a friend in Bronco yet. Until Molly. So this was Elizabeth's opportunity to help Molly and the twins at the same time.

There was a knock on the door, and Gianna and Lucy hopped up and raced through the room ahead of Elizabeth. When they reached the door, they stopped short of opening it. They knew the rule: they could peep out the side window, but only Elizabeth could open the door.

"It's Molly," Gianna said, tugging on the bottom of Elizabeth's shorts, urging her to move quickly.

Lucy applauded and jumped up and down.

"I know," Elizabeth said. She opened the door and stepped aside. The three girls squealed with glee as if they were long lost friends who'd been parted for years.

Gianna and Lucy grabbed Molly by the hand and tugged her into the cabin. Not that they had to exert much pressure. Molly seemed just as eager to come inside as they were to have her.

Elizabeth and Jake glanced at each other, sharing amused smiles. When their eyes met, Elizabeth's stomach went all topsy-turvy. What in the world was that? This was the second time her body had acted like a teenager around Jake. Arlo had been her one and only, so this reaction shocked her into stillness. The girls' excited chatter shook her out of her stupor, and she remembered her manners.

"Won't you come in and have a cuppa?" Elizabeth asked Jake, who hadn't crossed the threshold. "I mean coffee. I grew up in America, but I've lived in Australia for ten years. At times I have to remind myself to use American English."

"I understand," Jake said. "I wish I could stay, but I can't. I dropped the boys at karate before I came here. I need to get back before class ends."

Elizabeth held her smile in place to cover her disappointment. She'd hoped to have a bit of adult time. No, that wasn't entirely honest. She'd hoped to have a bit of *Jake* time. She'd been looking forward to getting to know him better. This playdate had seemed like the perfect no-pressure opportunity. "Okay. Maybe another time."

Jake checked his watch and then looked at her. "I suppose I have a few minutes. And a cup of coffee sounds good."

"Come on in. I'll brew some."

They stepped into the main room. Molly had made herself right at home and was brushing a doll's hair. Gianna and Lucy had brought several of their favorite dolls from home. Elizabeth's sisters and cousins had gifted them with more, so there was no shortage of dolls. At least fifteen were lined up on the sofa.

"We're going into the kitchen," Elizabeth said.

"We'll be fine," Molly said.

"I'm sure you will."

The girls didn't give her another look before returning their attention to their dolls. Apparently her presence was no longer necessary.

"Have a seat," Elizabeth said, gesturing to the kitchen table. She grabbed the coffee beans and began to grind them.

"Thanks. I appreciate you allowing Molly to come over today. When she was younger, she used to want to hang out with me and her brothers. Seemingly overnight she went from being one of the guys to moving to her own little island where we aren't welcome."

"Don't take it personally. She's a tween girl. It's only natural for her to develop other interests."

"I asked her if she wanted to bring a doll with her, and let me tell you…" Jake grimaced and shook his head ruefully. "The glare she sent me could have burned a hole in my chest. But now she's in there playing with dolls. I just don't get it."

"Tween, remember? She's in between being a little girl and a teenager. Besides, she's being a mother's helper.

She's keeping my girls entertained by playing dolls with them. It's a subtle distinction, but it's there."

"If you say so."

"Believe me, she doesn't need to bring toys with her. My girls have plenty. My entire family is doing everything in their power to convince me to stay in Bronco. To their way of thinking, everything is fair game. Including bribes. They believe if they win over the girls, I'll fall in line."

"I thought you were on vacation. Are you thinking about moving to Bronco?"

Elizabeth shrugged. She set the beans in the coffee-maker and let them brew. Although she preferred the sweeter, fancier Australian drink, she figured Jake would prefer the familiar American coffee. "I don't know. I'm at a crossroads in my life, so nothing is out of the realm of possibility. I want to do what's best for my girls. I'm just not sure whether that is moving to Bronco or going back home to Australia."

She glanced at Jake, and he nodded.

"Yesterday was the first day the girls didn't ask when we were going back home. Before we came here, I told them that we were going on a vacation. This isn't what they expected. They're used to ocean vacations where they can play on the beach and swim."

"There aren't many beaches in Montana."

"I know." She grabbed two mugs, filled them with cof-fee, and handed one to Jake. "Cream and sugar?"

He shook his head. "I take mine black."

Suppressing a shudder, Elizabeth added milk and sugar to hers. Not exactly a flat white, but this would do for now.

She sat across from Jake and glanced at him over her cup. Dressed casually in jeans and a blue shirt, he ap-peared totally at ease.

"Yesterday, I heard your son mention that you were a widower."

Jake nodded slowly. "Yes."

"I'm sorry for your loss."

"Thank you."

Elizabeth glanced at her hands. She inhaled deeply and slowly exhaled. "My husband, Arlo, died suddenly two years ago."

"I'm sorry."

"Does it ever let up?"

"The pain?"

She nodded, unable to speak.

He sipped his coffee, clearly thinking about how to answer her. "That's a good question. I don't know if the pain eases or if you eventually learn how to live with it. I have three kids, so I can't just wallow in misery. After Maggie died, I had no choice but to get on with my life the best way I knew how." He took another swallow of his coffee and frowned. "Sorry. I know that isn't much help. And probably not what you wanted to hear. I guess all I can say is that you have to keep going. Just put one foot in front of the other."

"Actually, that sums up how I feel. Making it from morning to night is a win for me. People seem anxious for me to remarry for my girls' sakes. And maybe for theirs too. Remarrying will be a sign that I'm no longer in pain, so they don't have to worry about me. They don't seem to believe that my girls and I are a complete family. A different family than we were when my husband was alive, and not the kind of family I'd dreamed of being, but a family nonetheless. And we are fine."

Jake nodded, then grinned wryly. "I won't bore you with the horror stories of the women who started coming around a couple of months after my wife's death."

"Yikes. Thankfully I didn't have that experience. Men were inclined to keep their distance and let me mourn the loss of my husband." They didn't speak for a minute, but the silence wasn't uneasy. And it gave them each a chance to deal with the sad emotions they'd dredged up. Any other time Elizabeth would have sat quietly, but she wouldn't get to know him better that way. And for a reason she wasn't quite ready to face, she wanted to get to know him better.

"Now that we've established there's not an ocean in the vicinity, what do you do for fun?" she asked, returning to the earlier, happier topic.

Jake smiled, apparently sharing her desire to change the subject. "Are you asking Jake the man or Jake the single father? Because my answers would be vastly different."

"Either. Both."

"Well, I'm a rancher, so I'm always busy, but when it's me and the kids we like to spend time outside. We love packing up sleeping bags and spending the night on the range under the stars. They still get a kick out of cooking hot dogs over a campfire. Especially Ben, who's only six and finally gets to hold his own fork."

"I can imagine how thrilling that is for him."

"He tries to keep up with Pete. He wants to be a big boy."

Elizabeth nodded. "I know how that feels."

He inhaled, and Elizabeth's gaze was drawn to his massive chest. She longed to run her fingers over it just to see if it was as hard as it looked. "I'm proud of him for wanting to do things for himself, but I'm sorry to see him grow up so fast. I miss the baby years. Given how hard it was to take care of him without Maggie—those early days and nights were rough—I should want to see him growing up." He shook his head. "This feeling is ridiculous."

"But completely understandable," she said. "My girls

were only three when we lost their dad. I don't have to tell you how hard those days were—even with lots of help from my in-laws and friends. Lucy and Gianna are becoming more independent, which is good. Even so, a part of me misses the days when I could hold both my little girls on my lap and just cuddle them. Don't get me wrong, we still do some of that. And every once in a while, they revert to some of their baby ways. But they're growing up so fast. I'm conflicted." She sighed and put her feelings aside. "So what does Jake the man do for fun?"

"Provided I have a babysitter?"

"Yes," she said. "In a perfect world, what does a night of fun look like?"

"I'm a bit of a foodie."

"Do you mean more than steak and potatoes?"

"At the risk of being forced to turn in my rancher card, yes. I love all kinds of foods. Whenever I can, I try out a different restaurant that serves authentic cuisine from different cultures."

"Do you prefer any particular kinds? Or are there foods that you avoid?"

"Nah, I'll try anything," he said. "Why veto something without giving it a try first? I don't want to miss a delicacy simply because it doesn't look like what I'm used to."

Elizabeth smiled. "I like your style."

Jake's watch beeped. He sighed, then lifted his cup and finished the rest of his drink. Standing, he pushed the chair under the table and put his mug in the sink. "I need to get going—I don't want to be late picking up the boys. Thanks for the coffee."

Time certainly had flown. She stood too. "I enjoyed the company."

When they entered the main room, Molly was sitting between the girls on a comfy chair. She was spinning a tale about a princess and her favorite pony. Gianna and Lucy were totally entranced and didn't look up when the adults entered. If today was anything to go by, this was going to work out wonderfully.

"Are you going to pick up Ben and Pete now?" Molly asked.

"Yes," Jake said.

"Okay. Bye." She smiled and then went back to her story.

Jake blinked.

Elizabeth sympathized with him. He'd just shared his mixed feelings about watching his younger son grow up. It was probably even more difficult with his one and only daughter. "She'll be fine."

"I know. She's had playdates before. I don't know why this feels different."

"Because it is different. She's at work." Elizabeth flashed him a grin. "Your daughter has a job. She's growing up."

He laughed. "And I'm being silly. What time do you want me to pick her up?"

"Whenever you want. I don't have any plans."

She opened the front door, and he hesitated as if unsure what to do. She suffered from the same confusion—which was ridiculous. This hadn't been a date, so there was no need to decide whether they should kiss. So why did she feel disappointed when he jogged down the stairs, hopped into his SUV, and drove away?

JAKE TRIED TO keep his mind on the road as he drove to the dojo in town. Yet no matter how hard he tried to concentrate, his mind kept straying to Elizabeth. Dressed in denim cutoffs and a blouse that she'd tied around her waist, she'd looked casual and glamorous all at once. She was too appealing for his own good, which was why he'd made up his mind to keep her at a distance. He'd intended to drop off Molly and leave, but when he'd seen the disappointed look on Elizabeth's face as he'd turned down her invitation for coffee, he'd known he couldn't stick with his plan.

He didn't regret the time he'd spent with her. It had been pure pleasure. She was even more delightful than he'd remembered. He was glad to learn that her time in Bronco might become permanent. But, he reminded himself, she could just as easily return to Australia.

Traffic was light, and he arrived at the dojo with three minutes to spare. He jumped from the SUV and made it inside in time to see his sons bow to the sensei. Once class was dismissed, the assembled kids raced over to their parents.

"Hey, Dad. Did you see us?" Ben asked.

"Sorry, bud. I missed the class. But I'll see you next time."

"It's okay," he said easily. "We just did the same things we always do."

"Just better?" Jake asked.

The boy shrugged and rubbed his nose. "You need to ask sensei about that."

Jake laughed. Ben was nothing if not honest.

"So is Molly still at her job?" Pete asked.

"Yes."

"What is she doing?"

"When I left she was telling Lucy and Gianna a story and playing with dolls."

"And she's getting paid for that?" he asked, his voice a cross between outrage and disbelief. "I can get a job doing that. Maybe their mom will let me help her too."

"You want to play with dolls?" Ben asked.

"No."

"Well, that's part of the job," Jake said.

"Never mind," Pete said, heaving a heavy sigh.

Jake nodded, hoping this was the end of it. Pete had never had a problem with Molly being able to do things that he couldn't before, so his attitude was perplexing. Hopefully this wasn't the beginning of the dreaded sibling rivalry. It was difficult enough dealing with Molly's changing interests and preteen snark.

The boys raced to the locker room to change into their street clothes. They returned a couple of minutes later, their gi tucked beneath their arms, folded as neatly as eight-and six-year-olds could manage. One of the first things their sensei had stressed was the importance of respect. That respect extended to their clothes. Each of the boys had taken his words seriously and never wore their gi outside of class.

Once they were buckled in the SUV, Pete asked, "What time are we picking up Molly?"

"Good question. How about we get her now?" Elizabeth wanted help for a few hours a week. Jake didn't think she meant all at once. Besides, this was Molly's first day at work, and he didn't want her to get tired. That last thought was a stretch. Molly thrived on having younger kids around to care for, so no doubt she was in seventh heaven.

He'd told Molly more than once that it wasn't her job to look after her brothers—it was his. She'd said that she understood, yet that hadn't stopped her from hovering.

As Jake drove, he listened with one ear to the conversation Pete and Ben were having about one of their favorite cartoons while taking in the surroundings. Though he lived in the area all of his life, he was still struck by the sheer beauty of nature in and around Bronco. The green grass, blue sky, and mountains in the distance were as soothing as they were picturesque. Just looking at them diminished his worries and filled him with a sense of calm.

Elizabeth's cabin was located on a beautiful plot of land. Or rather, her *sister's* cabin. The fact that she was staying in a borrowed home amplified the temporary nature of her visit. She was in town for vacation. When it ended as all vacations did, she would probably return to her home on the other side of the world. He reminded himself of his decision to keep his emotional distance from her—if not his physical distance—but somehow he didn't hear the warning. Despite everything, he didn't want to keep her at arm's length. He'd believed he'd buried his interest in women and his heart with Maggie. Now he was discovering that wasn't the case.

Too bad the first woman he was interested in lived in Australia.

He pulled in front of the cabin. Before he could turn off the engine, the boys had jumped from the SUV and were wandering around.

"This place is cool," Pete said. He bent down and then stood, a toad in his hand. Toads were rare in Montana, so Jake was surprised to see one. "They have lots of cool animals."

"Can we take it home?" Ben asked.

"No," Jake said instantly. If it was up to the boys, the house would be a menagerie. They wanted to keep every animal or bug they saw.

"Why not?"

"His friends and family live here," Jake said. "He'll be lonely if we take him away from them."

"We can find them and bring them too," Ben said.

"This is his home. He wouldn't feel comfortable in a strange place." Those words instantly made him think of Elizabeth. Even though she'd been born and raised in

America, she lived in Australia now. She'd given birth to her children there. How strange Montana must seem after all that time away. Perhaps she needed a friend to help her get acclimated. He shoved the idea aside. His life was busy enough. He didn't need to seek out more tasks to fill what little time he had.

"Okay." Pete set the toad back on the ground, and they watched as it hopped away, vanishing into the tall grass. The kids raced to the door and knocked on it loudly.

"I think they heard you," Jake said dryly.

The door swung open. He glanced up and straight into Elizabeth's large brown eyes. They twinkled with amusement. "Hello, boys. Come on in."

"Thank you," Pete said politely. Apparently Jake's lessons on manners were getting through.

"Thank you," Ben echoed. He looked into Elizabeth's face and smiled. "You're really pretty. Isn't she pretty, Daddy?"

Jake stuttered, temporarily unsure how to answer that question. The easy answer was *yes*. Because Elizabeth was gorgeous. "Remember what I said about commenting on people's appearance, Ben. It's rude."

"But I thought you meant we couldn't say bad things. We can't say good things either?" The boy sounded so perplexed that Jake struggled not to laugh.

"Thank you for the compliment, Ben," Elizabeth said.

"You're welcome," he said and then turned to look at Jake. "See, Daddy? She didn't mind me calling her pretty."

He could only sigh as Ben joined the other kids in the cabin's main room.

"You're going to have your hands full with that one," Elizabeth said, grinning.

"Don't I know it," Jake replied. The noise level coming from the front room rose several decibels with the addition of the two boys. Pete and Ben simultaneously questioned the girls about their day and showed off what they'd learned in karate.

"How about a snack?" Elizabeth asked.

That quieted the room.

"Can we have biscuits?" Gianna asked.

"What kind of snack is a biscuit?" Ben asked.

"The best kind," she said. "Don't you like biscuits?"

"For breakfast," Pete said.

"You get to eat biscuits for breakfast?" Lucy asked, amazed.

Elizabeth laughed and tugged on one of her daughter's long braids. "Biscuits are something different here than at home."

"Oh."

Elizabeth then looked at Jake's three kids. "What we call biscuits in Australia, you call cookies. So, would you like some cookies?"

"Yes!" Pete exclaimed, jumping to his feet.

"We love cookies," Ben said, coming to stand beside Elizabeth. He took her hand and swung it back and forth. There was a look of pure adoration on his face. Jake had never seen his son look like that at anyone, and his heart ached. Without a doubt, Ben would have adored Maggie. And she would have adored him right back.

"Then everyone go wash your hands," Elizabeth said, "and meet me in the kitchen."

If possible, the racket the kids made was even louder. Only Lucy seemed to lag behind.

"What's wrong, sweetie?" Elizabeth asked, stooping down so she could look into her daughter's eyes.

Lucy shrugged.

"Too much noise?" Jake asked. He squatted down beside Elizabeth so he too was at eye level with Lucy.

"Maybe," she said slowly.

"Perhaps I should get my kids and leave," Jake suggested to Elizabeth. He didn't want Lucy to feel uncomfortable in her own home. Clearly she wasn't used to such rambunctious kids as his boys.

"Molly too?" Lucy asked.

"Yes, she's one of my kids."

"I like Molly. I don't want her to go home." Lucy frowned as if in thought. "I suppose the boys can stay too."

"Are you sure?" Jake asked. "Molly will still be your friend even if we don't stay. You can play with her another day."

"I'm sure. The boys are okay. I guess I like them too."

With that proclamation, Lucy ran off to wash her hands.

"We can still leave," Jake offered.

Elizabeth shook her head. "There's no need to do that. Lucy might take a bit more time to make up her mind, but once she's reached a decision, she's comfortable with it. I want her to know that I respect her choice. I don't want to overrule her unless it's a matter of safety."

"In that case, I'm looking forward to having a biscuit."

Elizabeth laughed and punched his shoulder. They were still squatting, and their eyes met. And held. The amusement in hers gradually faded, morphing into something that resembled desire. She blinked, and the look was gone. That was probably for the best.

One side of her lip lifted in a sexy curve as she rose to her full height. She was about five feet eight, a few inches shorter than his six feet.

He stood as well and followed her into the kitchen. It was small, but with seven people inside it was positively claustrophobic. The kids didn't seem to mind. They were sitting around the table—Lucy and Gianna were sharing a chair, and Ben and Molly were sharing another. Pete had his own. He looked up and smiled. "We left a chair for you guys."

"Thanks," Jake said. The idea of sharing a chair with Elizabeth held more than a little appeal, but he wasn't sure she would feel the same. "I don't mind standing."

Pete shrugged as if it didn't matter one way or the other to him.

Elizabeth doled out the cookies to the kids and then looked at Jake. "What kind would you like?"

"I think I'll try a mint."

To be honest, any kind would do. He was happy just to be spending time with Elizabeth. He couldn't exactly call this a quiet moment, although there was a lot less noise now that the kids were filling their mouths with cookies and drinking the milk that Elizabeth had poured to wash them down, but it was still peaceful and fulfilling. He was learning to appreciate the small moments that he and the kids spent together. Life wasn't filled with the big, exciting moments that often formed memories. It was made up of the regular day-to-day interactions. These were the moments that set the tone for their childhoods and would give them the confidence they needed to navigate the future. These times determined whether his kids would look back and say they'd had a happy childhood.

"I think you're going to like it," Elizabeth said with a bright smile. He noticed that she smiled easily. He liked that about her. Although life had dealt her a raw hand, she hadn't let it make her bitter. But then, with two small children, she didn't have a choice other than to roll with the punches. Even so, he wondered what she felt in the still of the night. When she was alone in her bed, did she reach out for her husband's side of the bed, hoping to encounter his sleeping form, as Jake occasionally did, hoping to touch

Maggie? Did she have conversations with him in her mind? Did she ask herself what he would think of her choices?

When he realized he was standing there with his cookie in his hand, he took a bite. "Wow. That's good."

"I knew you would like it," Elizabeth said as she sat down.

"You should sit down with Mummy," Gianna said. "The chair is big enough for two people."

"And you always tell us not to eat standing up," Molly added. "You don't want to drop crumbs on the floor for somebody else to have to clean up."

What was it with his kids throwing his words back in his face?

He glanced at Elizabeth. Their eyes met and sexual tension singed the air. Without breaking their gazes, she slid to one side of the chair. Heart pounding, Jake crossed the room and eased into the chair beside her. Despite what Gianna claimed, the chair was definitely not made for two people.

Even though Elizabeth had moved over, their thighs still touched. The heat from her bare thigh worked its way through the denim covering his. Her sweet scent wafted around him, and the temptation to kiss her spouted out of nowhere. Knowing that would be totally improper, he took a second bite of his cookie. It was good, but not as good as kissing Elizabeth would be. But since that was out of the question, he needed to think about something else. "What kind of cookies are these?"

"They're biscuits," Lucy corrected.

"Right. I forgot. What kind of biscuits are these?" he asked.

"Tim Tams. They're Australia's most popular brand," Elizabeth said. She gave him a wicked grin as if she knew about his struggle. Perhaps she shared it.

Feeling a bit mischievous, he leaned a bit closer and was pleased when she inhaled and her eyes widened. Not wanting to attract the kids' attention, he replied, "I can see why. We might need to visit there so we can have more of these."

"You'll like it there," Gianna told him before turning to look at Molly. "If you come home with us, you'll be able to see our room."

"And play on our swings," Lucy added.

"Are we really going?" Molly asked, and Jake realized belatedly that none of the children had picked up on his joking tone. More than that, Lucy's and Gianna's words reminded him that Elizabeth and her little family were only going to be in the United States for a short while.

"I never like to say never," he said. "But we don't have any plans to visit Australia right now."

"It would be cool if we went," Pete said. "Then we could get a pet kangaroo. Or a koala bear. They have those in Australia. We read a book about them in school."

"I'll keep that in mind," Jake said.

"If you like Tim Tams, you don't have to go that far to get them," Elizabeth said. "They're sold in some stores here in the States. I'm not promising they have them here in Montana, though."

As the kids then began to talk about other things, Jake whispered to Elizabeth, "Thanks for the save."

"No worries. I sometimes forget how easily a joke can be misinterpreted. Before I know it, the girls are off and running with it."

"I'm usually more careful," he said.

"I understand," she said. "The first time I tasted a Tim Tam I nearly screamed. It was just that good."

Maybe. But it wasn't the delicious flavor of the treat that had distracted him. It was her. It felt so natural to be in her company. Hanging out with the kids. Like one big happy family.

What was he thinking? They'd hardly spent any time together. Their friendship—if they actually were friends—was too new. The last thing he needed was a thought like that.

He threw his napkin into the trash can. "C'mon, kids. It's time to go home." He had to get out of there before he said or did something stupid.

"Aww, but we just got here," Ben whined. The other kids chorused in with similar complaints.

"We can't monopolize Elizabeth and the twins' day," Jake said.

"I don't even know what that means, so how can I be doing it?" Ben asked.

Elizabeth laughed. It was a sweet sound that made Jake's pulse race. He could get used to that sound. Of course, he wouldn't let himself.

"It means that we need to leave so they can do what they planned to do for the rest of the day."

"Oh."

"Me too?" Molly asked. "Because I'm at work."

"You too." When she frowned, he hastened to add, "But if Elizabeth and the girls are free this weekend, they can come over for a cookout."

All eyes swung from him to Elizabeth. The kids seemed to be holding their collective breaths as they waited for her response. When Jake realized that he was holding his breath too, he forced himself to exhale. He was putting way too much importance on this spur-of-the-moment invitation.

"I would love to come," she said. "What do you think, Lucy and Gianna? Would you like to visit Molly's house?"

"Yes," they exclaimed without hesitation.

Elizabeth shifted her gaze back to Jake. Her radiant smile widened, and his heart thumped in response. "We would love to visit you this weekend. Do you need us to bring anything?"

"You can bring more of these cookies," Pete said. "They're really good."

Jake shook his head at his son. "Pete."

"What? She asked."

"I did ask," Elizabeth pointed out.

"That won't be necessary. Your company will be all that we need. How does Saturday work for you? I'll throw something on the grill for dinner."

"That sounds wonderful. We'll be there."

"Good." He smiled, for the moment quieting the voice inside him that warned he was getting too close to Elizabeth. "Then it's a date."

CHAPTER FOUR

IT'S A DATE.

The words echoed in Elizabeth's mind as she helped Jake hustle his kids out the door and into his SUV. There was a lot of commotion as the kids stopped walking to say *one last thing.* What should have been a two-minute goodbye took nearly five times that long as the children kept finding unique ways to stall. The noise and laughter weren't distracting enough to stop Elizabeth from replaying Jake's words in her mind.

It's a date.

She knew he hadn't meant the word in the traditional sense. Nobody took five kids on a date. Even so, she couldn't stop the tingling sensation that shot through her body each time she thought of his words. And she couldn't stop thinking of them.

It was strange. On the outside, everything seemed normal. She was sure nobody could tell how affected she was simply by looking at her. She smiled and laughed with the kids, making appropriate responses to their questions and comments. But on the inside? Butterflies were flitting around her stomach, crashing into the walls before turning and flying in the other direction.

Not that she should've been worried about Jake sensing her turmoil. He would have to know her better and longer to do that. Since they were still getting to know each other, she didn't have to worry that he could know that his simple statement had turned her into a ball of nerves.

Finally Jake corralled his three and got them into his SUV. Elizabeth stood between Lucy and Gianna beside the stairs. They waved as Jake drove off.

"See you on Saturday!" Molly yelled from the front passenger window.

"Bye!" Lucy and Gianna called. The girls waved until Jake's vehicle had driven out of sight.

"How many days until Saturday?" Lucy asked.

"You remember the days-of-the-week song?" Elizabeth asked. Even though the girls were too young for school, Elizabeth taught them at home. They could count to one hundred, print their first and last names, recognize their colors, and read basic sight words. They would be ready for school whether that was here in Montana or back home in Australia.

Lucy and Gianna nodded and then began to sing. As they recited the days of the week, they raised a finger with each day. By the time they reached Saturday, they each had seven fingers raised. Elizabeth laughed. That wasn't right. Of course, since they had started with Sunday, there was nothing they could do but have seven.

"Today is Monday. So let's try that again."

When they reached Saturday, they were each holding five fingers in the air.

"Five?" Gianna asked tentatively.

"That's right."

"That's a long time," Lucy whined.

"I know. But we'll have lots of fun between now and then."

"Doing what?"

"Playing. Going around town. And we'll visit my sisters and cousins. Doesn't that sound like fun?"

The girls exchanged glances. To them, Elizabeth's family were a bunch of strangers. They'd spent time with them on several occasions during this visit, but her daughters weren't of an age where they had much fun with adults. Even those bearing piles of gifts. Though Tori had come to Australia last year, the girls had been even younger then. Much too young to form a close relationship. In fact, they barely remembered her or her visit. Knowing her girls didn't feel close to her family hurt Elizabeth's heart. Before she'd moved halfway across the world, she'd spent a lot of time with her immediate and extended family. They'd been as close as a family could be.

Their bonds had been tested when Elizabeth moved to Australia ten years ago, but they'd held despite her absence. She and her family had picked up where they'd left off. But Lucy and Gianna didn't have a lifetime of shared memories to draw on. Their memories were of Australia and the friends and family, including Elizabeth's sister Carly, they had there. It would take time spent together for them to grow close to their American family.

But did Elizabeth intend to stay here, or was she going to take her children and go back home? Would growing close to her American family come at the cost of their relationships to their Australian family, who were their last links to Arlo? Those questions kept her awake some nights.

They weren't the only cause of her restlessness. Thoughts of Jake had also disturbed her sleep last night.

She would be lying if she denied being attracted to Jake. There was something about him that appealed to her on a basic level. Truth be told, a simple sexual attraction would be preferable. Those feelings were shallow and generally didn't survive long. But her attraction was also emotional. She didn't like it and fought her hardest to resist it. But there was something about his kindness and patience that reached inside her heart. She felt comfortable with him and looked forward to spending more time with him.

The very notion was a betrayal of Arlo's memory and all they'd shared. How could she possibly feel something—anything—for another man? Arlo Freeman had been her one true love. The first time she'd laid eyes on him she'd known that he would own her heart for all time. Even two years since his death, her heart still called out for him. The idea that she could suddenly care for Jake was un-imaginable.

Though she knew that was illogical, she couldn't stop believing it was wrong to like Jake and want to spend time with him. It wasn't as if they would be alone. Despite what he'd said, they weren't going on a date. She and the girls were visiting him and his kids on his ranch. The twins hadn't met many kids in Montana yet, so Elizabeth was happy they liked Jake's kids so much. Her girls weren't used to isolation. They needed other playmates.

"I like Molly," Lucy said, confirming Elizabeth's thought.

"I know," she said.

"Did you know her mum died?" Gianna asked.

"Yes."

"That's sad," Gianna added. "She died a long time ago. She's in Heaven now."

"I know."

"Just like Daddy," Lucy said.

"I miss Daddy," Gianna said. "I wish he could come back from Heaven."

"Me too," Lucy said.

And just like that, Elizabeth knew it would be unthink-able to even consider starting a relationship with Jake. It would further complicate their already complicated lives. They each had young children who had lost a parent. They might not still be mourning, but that didn't mean they were ready and able to welcome another person into their lives.

Adding new Hawkins relatives was enough of a change for Lucy and Gianna.

Elizabeth gathered her daughters into her arms and held them close, trying her best to let her love surround them and soothe their hurt. It could not replace Arlo's love or presence, but nothing could. Just as the Hawkins relatives would not replace their Australian family. The girls loved their grandparents and their uncle Nick, Arlo's older brother. And the Freemans adored them. Although they'd FaceTimed over the past weeks, Elizabeth knew it wasn't the same as spending time together. The distance between them made the impromptu visits they'd all been accustomed to impossible. At some point, the relationships would suffer and a link to Arlo would be broken.

Even so, none of them had protested when Elizabeth had informed them of her open-ended visit to America.

You need to do what you believe is best for you and your daughters, Arlo's mother, Grace, had told her. *Of course, we hope that means coming back to Australia to live. But you won't know for sure what you want unless you go back to America for a while.*

Elizabeth didn't know what she expected to happen by being back in America, but she certainly hadn't expected to become attracted to a man. A small part of her had hoped that being back home would be magical. That the answers to her future would come to her. She didn't need to know the whole plan. One or two steps would suffice for now. So far no part of the plan had been revealed.

One thing was certain—she didn't want to do anything to harm her children. She'd heard a million times that kids were resilient, but she didn't believe that was true. Lucy and Gianna had been devastated when Arlo died. But they'd been young and hadn't possessed the vocabulary to express the depth of their pain. They hadn't known the words to ask their questions or tell anyone how sad they'd been. What others had interpreted as resilience Elizabeth had recognized as confusion, hurt.

They had never known anyone who'd died, so they hadn't understood that Arlo would not be coming back from Heaven. Their paternal grandparents weren't rodeo performers, so when Elizabeth and Arlo hadn't been competing, they'd all spent time together. The girls had gotten used to not seeing their grandparents for extended periods of time while they'd traveled with their parents. But they'd known they would be together again. Long absences followed by happy reunions had been accepted as a natural part of life.

Although the twins now understood that Arlo was not coming back, they had no idea of the magnitude of their loss. Arlo had been a great father. Perhaps the best ever. He would have been an even greater one in the future if he hadn't been robbed of that chance.

"I miss Daddy too," Elizabeth said. "Do you want to look through the Daddy book?"

Arlo had always been big on taking pictures. The first time he and Elizabeth had gone out, he'd taken their picture. He'd said he'd wanted to document the first date with the woman he was going to spend the rest of his life with. He hadn't waited until they'd been doing something noteworthy to pull out his phone and snap a few shots. There were as many photos of them walking along the beach or cooking breakfast as there were of rodeo competitions and fancy events. Unlike most people, Arlo had actually printed his photos. As a result, they had numerous albums filled with memories. When the girls had been born, he'd doubled his efforts. There were many pictures of the four of them together doing everything from swimming or riding horses to sitting around watching kids' movies.

After Arlo's death, Elizabeth had taken over as family documentarian, trying to capture as many moments as Arlo had. She'd taken enough pictures to fill countless albums. She'd also devoted one album exclusively to photos of Arlo. Initially the girls had wanted to look through that album all of the time, touching Arlo's face in every picture. Over time, the request to look at the book had diminished until the album went months without being opened. Elizabeth couldn't decide if that was a good thing or not.

"No," Lucy said. "I just want to play. Can we stay out here for a while?"

Elizabeth nodded as she tried to ignore the crack that had suddenly opened up in her heart. She didn't want her daughters to mourn forever, but she didn't want them to forget Arlo either. They'd been so young when he'd died, and she knew that they had very few memories of him. She'd tried to keep him alive for them, but she knew eventually they would forget the feel of his strong arms holding them and the sound of his laughter. He would simply become a name and a face in the photographs.

Would Jake's presence—no matter how innocuous— hasten that process? Not that she needed to think too much about that. Because despite her many questions, she was certain about one thing. She wasn't ready to move on.

"Do you have enough hamburgers and buns?" Molly asked Jake. He looked up from his place at the kitchen table and met her eyes. Every once in a while, she seemed to forget that he was the father and she was the child. This was one of those times.

"Yes. You were with me when I went shopping, remember?"

She grinned sheepishly. "Oh, yeah. I forgot."

"Relax," Jake said. "Everything is going to be fine. We have plenty of food and drinks. Enough snacks for ten kids. We have whatever they might want."

"Not everything," Molly pointed out. "I wish we could have found some of those cookies they had. They were really good."

"I do too. But we have cookies of our own. Maybe Lucy and Gianna have never eaten those. Today could be their chance to try them, along with an old-fashioned American barbecue."

Her eyes lit up and she smiled. "I hadn't thought of that. We'll let them try some of my favorites."

As she raced over to the pantry and pulled out several closed packages of cookies. "I should have made some of my specialty cookies like I did for the Valentine's Day bakeoff."

"Your double fudge peanut butter cookies are terrific. Maybe you can make them another time," Jake suggested.

"Okay." She was wearing her favorite shorts outfit and new sandals. She'd brushed her hair until it shone. She blew out a breath. "I'll go check and see what the boys are doing."

"Why?"

"Because we're going to have company."

Jake stood up and held out his arm to his daughter. She paused and then came over to him. Dropping an arm over her shoulder, he gave her a quick hug. "I don't think Pete and Ben consider Lucy and Gianna their company. They might play with them for a little while, but mostly they are your company. The girls will want to do things with you."

"And what about Elizabeth? Is she your company?"

Jake froze, unsure how to answer. At once he was concerned about Molly's question as well as the unfamiliar tone of her voice. "I don't know. She's bringing her daughters over to play with you. I doubt Elizabeth will want to play with the boys, so I suppose she is."

"Then maybe you should put on a better shirt."

He looked down at his T-shirt. It was one of his favorites. "What's wrong with what I have on?"

"It's old and ratty. You wear it all the time. You should wear the shirt that Aunt Bethany got you for Christmas."

That shirt was made out of wool. "It's too hot for that."

"Then I'll find something better," she said. "You want to make a good impression on your company, don't you?"

Yes. And he'd thought he had accomplished that with this shirt. Obviously he'd been mistaken. Before he could reply, Molly dashed from the room. He pictured her rummaging through his closet, trying to find something she deemed appropriate for today, and he ran to catch up with her. The last thing he wanted was for her to grab a shirt and tie. Not that he was opposed to dressing up if the occasion called for it. Back when Maggie had been alive, he'd taken her to fancy five-star restaurants where a suit had been required. There was no way he was wearing anything approaching formal today. He didn't want Elizabeth to think he'd dressed up for her and get the wrong idea.

When Jake stepped into his room, Molly was reaching inside his closet. A second later, she pulled out two hangers and held them on either side of her so he could get a good look at them. She was smiling from ear to ear, clearly pleased with her choices. One—a dress shirt—was an instant no.

"Not the white one. It needs a tie, and I'm not going to wear a tie to a cookout. Besides, it's white. I don't want to get sauce on it."

Molly nodded. "That's true. I really like that shirt. I don't want it to get messed up."

"I like it too. You and your brothers gave it to me for Father's Day."

Molly shoved it back into the closet and then held out the other shirt to him. Not casual enough for a Saturday around the house. Especially since he expected to spend time standing over the grill.

"That's also a good shirt," he said.

"But you don't want to wear it."

He heard the disappointment in her voice, and his heart ached for her. He didn't want to dampen her enthusiasm. But he also had no intention of wearing that shirt.

"I think a T-shirt or even a pullover would be better for a casual afternoon at home. How about you help me choose one of those?"

"You'll wear the T-shirt I choose?"

He nodded. "Yes."

Molly smiled. "I can do that."

She opened the drawer and picked through the stack of shirts. After a moment, she pulled out an orange, yellow, and lime-green shirt that Jake had forgotten he had. A friend's son had been working as a salesclerk in a designer shop several summers ago. Wanting to support him, Jake had let the young man sell him an overpriced T-shirt. This one had been the least colorful of the selections. He'd bought it and immediately shoved it into the back of the drawer where it had remained for the past four years.

Until today. Well, there was no helping it. He'd told Molly that he would wear the T-shirt she chose.

"Thank you," he said.

Molly nodded and skipped from the room, closing the door behind her. When Jake was alone, he heaved a sigh and then pulled on the blindingly bright T-shirt. He looked in the mirror and winced. It looked even gaudier on. Luckily it was a sunny day, so he'd be wearing sunglasses.

Although he hadn't given his appearance more than a passing thought before Molly had started in on him, he suddenly felt self-conscious. He didn't want Elizabeth to think he normally wore tacky shirts like this.

Laughing at his foolishness, Jake went back downstairs. Ben and Pete were out back, chasing each other around the spacious yard and making enough noise for four kids. Jake wouldn't have it any other way. He loved the sound of their laughter. No matter how rough a day he'd had, knowing his kids were happy never failed to lift his spirits.

Jake was stepping into the front room when he heard a vehicle approaching. Despite telling himself this wasn't a date, his heart skipped a beat in anticipation. It made no sense to pretend he didn't find Elizabeth attractive. She was objectively gorgeous. More than just being blessed with good genes, she possessed a beautiful spirit. He liked the way she interacted with his kids, treating them with kindness and patience. Molly hadn't stopped talking about Elizabeth all week. No matter the topic of discussion, she'd managed to bring the woman into the conversation. In all fairness, she'd also mentioned Gianna and Lucy quite frequently, but her comments about Elizabeth stood out in his mind.

"They're here," Ben said, charging into the room. Jake had expected Molly to be excited, but he was a bit surprised to see that Ben was too. His kids had had friends come over to play, but they never got excited about their siblings' friends.

"Let's go say hello," Jake said. But he was talking to himself. Ben had already dashed outside.

Trying to slow his suddenly racing heartbeat, Jake stepped onto the porch. Elizabeth and her daughters were standing beside a black vehicle. Lucy and Gianna were laughing and talking with his kids. Apparently whatever shyness Lucy had felt around the boys before had vanished. Now the five kids were completely at ease with each other.

"We have swings and a tree house in the backyard," Pete said. "Come on—we'll show them to you."

The kids ran away, not giving him or Elizabeth a second glance.

"Well," Elizabeth said. "Talk about being forgotten. I guess I'm totally unnecessary now."

He laughed and descended the stairs. "Not to me. Welcome."

"Thanks."

"What do you have there?"

"The girls and I baked some bis—cookies for everyone."

Her miscue was a clear indicator that she was straddling two worlds. She had one foot in Australia and one in the States.

His life was so full right now that even if Elizabeth decided to stay in the States, he wouldn't have the time to properly date her. From the look of things, her life was just as busy as his. Two kids could take up just as much time and energy as three. She also had the added disadvantage of being in a place that was foreign to her kids.

"You didn't have to do that," he said.

"We were happy to do it. The girls and I enjoy baking together. Besides, they were practically bouncing off the walls this morning in their eagerness to get here," she said. "This was a good way to fill the time."

"Molly was the same way today. Actually she's been excited all week."

"I'm so glad to hear that. My girls miss Australia and their pals. Making new friends will help them feel more at home."

He held out an arm, directing her to proceed him up

the stairs and into the house. As she passed by, he inhaled and was treated to a whiff of her sweet scent. Her perfume was light with a hint of flowers. It suited her perfectly.

His eyes drifted down to her round bottom as she walked up the stairs. She was sexy without trying. Dressed in denim cutoffs that revealed her toned thighs and a yellow T-shirt with pink flowers on the front, she was a ray of sunshine. Distracted by the gentle sway of her hips, he missed a step and nearly fell. He grabbed the banister in the nick of time.

Elizabeth glanced over her shoulder, a mischievous grin on her face. "Still trying to get the hang of walking and talking at the same time?"

Laughter burst from him. "I've just about mastered it. It's remembering which leg to use first that has me confused."

She laughed and tossed her head, sending her curls cascading down her back. The dark tresses looked so soft that his fingers ached to touch them. Instead, he opened the screen door for her.

Elizabeth stepped inside and looked around. "You have a nice house."

"Thanks. It has its idiosyncrasies as many old houses do, but I love every creaking floor and slightly drafty room."

"It has character."

"That it does. Sometimes a little too much." He led her through the house and into the kitchen. She set her container of cookies on the table and then turned back to look at him. Every cell of her body exuded joy. And sex appeal. For a moment he was hypnotized by her radiance and couldn't move.

When he realized he was staring, he gave himself a mental shake. He was a grown man, not some lovestruck teen. So why was he gawking like he'd never seen a woman before, much less been alone with one? "Would you like a drink?"

"No. I'm fine."

"Then let's go outside where we can keep an eye on the kids. The weather's perfect for sitting on the patio."

"That sounds good to me," Elizabeth said as they went outside.

Jake and Maggie had planted several flower beds when they'd moved in, and he'd done everything in his power to maintain them. He kept the same flowers that Maggie had selected in the very same arrangement. The blooms weren't as glorious as when Maggie had been in charge, but he did his best.

"This is beautiful," Elizabeth said. "You must be one of the lucky ones who's been blessed with a green thumb."

"I don't know about that. What you see is the result of years of practice. Do you garden?"

"No. I learned long ago that I don't have what it takes to keep plants alive. Either I overwater or forget to water altogether. Years of practice won't change that," she said ruefully. "But I appreciate beautiful gardens. Yours is a work of art."

"Maggie studied landscape architecture," Jake explained. "She was good at finding the right combination of flowers."

"She was clearly quite gifted."

He nodded. He'd been so proud of his wife. For a reason unknown to him, he was glad that Elizabeth didn't possess Maggie's green thumb. The last thing he wanted was a poor imitation of his wife. Not only that, he was intrigued by the qualities that made Elizabeth different. He wanted to learn more about what made her tick.

"Can you tell me more about Maggie?" Elizabeth asked. "Unless that's none of my business."

She was direct. He liked that. "I don't mind talking about Maggie. At least not now. After she died, just thinking about her was painful enough to make my heart stop beating so talking about her was out of the question."

"I know what you mean."

Yes, she did. "Maggie was kind. And smart. I knew her from the time I was five, so I can't claim it was love at first sight. But once I knew what love was, I knew she was the one and that we would get married." He sighed. "Maggie loved being a wife and mother and making a home for all of us. She was happiest when we were all snuggled together on the couch watching a movie."

"How did she die?" Elizabeth's voice was soft, but he still heard the sadness in her words. Only a person who'd lost a beloved spouse could relate to the depth of pain he felt.

"Giving birth to Ben."

She gasped. "No. I'm so sorry."

"It was sudden. Everything was going fine, then Maggie began to hemorrhage." Jake sucked in a ragged breath. Even after all this time he was incapable of telling the story in a detached, unemotional manner. "They couldn't stop the bleeding. And just like that, what started out as one of the best days of my life turned into a nightmare. I couldn't celebrate my son's birth because I was mourning the loss of my wife. God forgive me...for one horrible moment, I—I actually blamed Ben for Maggie's death."

"Obviously, I never met your wife and would never dream of speaking for her. But as a mother, I would give up my life for my daughters in a heartbeat."

He nodded. "I would do the same for my children. It

was just so hard to accept that I'd lost the woman I loved more than everything in the world."

Elizabeth glanced over at Ben. He and Pete were chasing the girls around the yard, pretending to be monsters. Then as one, the girls stopped and turned the tables on Ben and Pete and began chasing them. No doubt they would all sleep well tonight.

"Ben seems like a happy child."

"He is. Of the three, he's the most easy-going. He rarely puts up a fuss and doesn't mind when the older kids boss him around. But then, as the youngest, there probably isn't much he can do about that, so he may as well roll with the punches."

Elizabeth laughed, and his stomach lurched. Even the most minor things about her aroused him. That wasn't good.

"Can you tell me about your husband?" he asked.

The light in her eyes dimmed as she sobered. "Arlo was the best man—the best person—I ever met. He never had a bad word to say about anyone, and nobody had anything negative to say about him. He was big and gregarious. The life of the party. People naturally gravitated to him. He was a rodeo star, but he never acted like a celebrity. He was down to earth. He absolutely loved our girls. He was the best father they could have had. The best husband I could have dreamed of. One minute we were making chicken parmigiana for dinner. The next he was gone. Dead from a heart attack. He had an undiagnosed heart condition. Now all we have is memories. The girls were so little when he died, they don't even have those."

Although she'd spoken matter-of-factly, Jake heard the misery in her voice, and his heart ached in sympathy. "Losing the person that you love sucks, doesn't it?"

"Yes. It took a lot for me not to be bitter. Arlo was such

a good man. I loved him so much. We all did. There are so many bad people in the world doing all manner of evil, and they're still alive when he isn't. Why was he the one who had to die? How is that fair?"

"The simple answer is that it isn't fair. Nothing in life is."

"I know. It would be great if it was. But…" She sighed. "Most of the time I accept the randomness of it all. I have to. I have two little girls who are taking their cues from me. I don't want them to be bitter, so I don't have a choice but to accept it. That's the only way to heal my heart."

"And has it healed?"

Before she could answer, the kids ran over and opened the back door.

"Where are you going?" Jake asked.

"Inside. Lucy and Gianna want to see our rooms," Molly said.

"Your room, or Ben and Pete's room?" Jake asked.

"Both of them," Pete said.

"Your room is dirty," he pointed out.

"So what? We don't care," Pete said.

"So do you care if Elizabeth sees your room?" Jake asked.

"Nope."

"Mine too," Molly told him. "*My* room is clean."

Jake turned to Elizabeth. "Would you like to see the rest of the house?"

"I'd love to." She winked at Pete, who smiled broadly. "Even the messy room."

Jake and Elizabeth waited until the kids came barreling back into the yard before getting up and making a detour to the kitchen. They poured glasses of lemonade for the kids and got them settled around the patio table with cut fruit before heading up the back stairs.

When they reached the second floor, Jake turned to Elizabeth. "Fair warning, the boys' room isn't just dirty. It's this side of a disaster area."

She chuckled. "I'm sure I've seen worse."

"I don't know about that," he said.

"You have to know how to pick your battles."

"A clean room isn't a hill I'm willing to die on." Pete and Ben's room was the first room they came upon. He stopped at the open and she peered inside.

She gave him a pained smile and patted his arm. "You have my sympathy."

"Thanks," he said dryly.

Molly's door was open, and they glanced inside it. He'd painted the room a pale green last year and bought her a white comforter with pink-and-green flowers. Molly was really proud of the way it looked. Her room was always spotless.

"This is so pretty," Elizabeth said.

"She loves it."

"How many bedrooms do you have?"

"Six. Maggie and I wanted to have a big family and we figured there would be less chaos if the kids had their own rooms."

"But Pete and Ben share."

"That's the way they want it. Ben is our traveling kid. Maggie and I prepared a nursery for him before he was born. He slept in there for maybe a week before I moved his crib into my bedroom. I needed to have him close to me. I couldn't rest if he wasn't. Losing Maggie made me afraid of everything. I got it in my head that Ben would die too. It didn't make sense, but it was my reality." Jake wasn't ordinarily this open about his feelings, especially with someone he just met, but there was something about Elizabeth that made sharing easy. He felt comfortable around her, as if they had been friends for a long time.

"Fear is often irrational," Elizabeth said. "Especially when coupled with grief."

"When Ben turned one, Molly wanted him to sleep in her room. To her, he was a living doll and she loved playing with him. So, I put the crib in there, and that's where he stayed for a while," Jake explained. "When Pete started school, he discovered that some of the other boys shared rooms with their brothers, and he wanted to do the same. So I moved Ben's bed in there. They've been together ever since. Poor kid has never had a room of his own."

"Maybe not, but he must enjoy being in demand."

Jake chuckled. "I suppose. To him it's perfectly normal. But if he ever wants his own room or Pete decides to kick him out—whichever comes first—there are plenty of empty rooms for him to choose from."

They continued down the corridor, pausing to look at the framed photos of the kids hanging on the walls. Jake opened three more doors revealing a guest room, although they rarely had overnight guests, and two rooms he used for storage. Then he reached his closed bedroom door. He hesitated. No woman other than Maggie had been in this room. Was he really going to allow Elizabeth into his personal space?

"Can't remember if you made your bed or left dirty clothes scattered around?" Elizabeth joked.

Her words made him laugh and removed all reluctance to allow her into his room. She wasn't looking to make a place for herself in his home. To her, this was one more stop on the tour.

"Unlike Pete and Ben, I always make up my bed. And my clothes are in the hamper."

"No stray socks lying around?"

"Not in here." He swung open the door and stood aside so she could go in. Ridiculously, his heart paused as he waited for her reaction. He'd tried to keep things the same as they'd been when Maggie had shared the room with him, but that hadn't been possible. Time had taken its toll on the furniture as well as the linen. Three years ago, he'd painted the walls and bought new furniture and bedding. He'd gone with oak furniture, cream walls, and navy curtains and linen. It was basic, but it suited his needs. Now he wondered if he should have taken his sister up on her offer to help him decorate with a bit more style.

"Nice," Elizabeth said.

"Do you really think that, or are you just being polite?"

"I mean it. It suits you."

Exchanging smiles, they left the room and went back downstairs. The kids had finished with their snacks and were playing on the swings.

Jake started a fire in the grill.

"Do you need any help with the food?" Elizabeth asked.

"I never say no to a hand."

She held up both of hers. "I've got two. Take your pick."

CHAPTER FIVE

THERE WAS SOMETHING so nice about working side by side with Jake to get a meal on the table, being part of a team doing whatever it took to accomplish a goal. They moved in tandem as if they'd been cooking together for years. Elizabeth had gotten used to doing household tasks alone, but now she realized how much she enjoyed having a partner. Cooking with Jake was comfortable—perhaps too comfortable—and she felt a hint of guilt that she brushed aside. She wasn't going to allow misplaced guilt to ruin today.

They reached for the cheese at the same time, and their hands brushed. Elizabeth's skin immediately warmed at the contact, and she felt a seed of desire sprout inside her. Their eyes met, and attraction blossomed between them.

Then Jake blinked and stepped away. "I'll go check on the grill."

Before she could think of a reply he was gone. Elizabeth blew out a breath. She didn't need this ridiculous attraction to complicate her life further. She gave herself a stern talking-to before joining everyone outside.

Elizabeth couldn't resist eyeing Jake while he manned the grill. Dressed in a bright T-shirt that had to be either a Father's Day gift or the result of a lost bet and faded jeans that emphasized his muscular thighs, he looked good enough to make her mouth water. Her heart thumped loudly at the sight of him. He was so attractive she couldn't stop sneaking glances at him.

And that was a problem. She knew that physical attraction was something that couldn't be controlled, yet she still felt as if she was being unfaithful to Arlo. Even knowing that Arlo wouldn't want her to spend the rest of her life alone wasn't enough to shake that feeling. But somehow she would.

"Is dinner ready?" Pete asked, running over. The other kids were behind him, expectant expressions on their faces.

"Yes," Jake said. "So everyone go wash your hands."

"My hands aren't dirty," Pete said, holding his palms out for Jake to see.

"You're kidding, right?"

"No." He pulled out a chair and sat down.

Jake looked at his son. "Go wash your hands."

"Come on, Pete," Molly said. "We're hungry. And your hands have germs. You just can't see them."

There was plenty of dirt that Elizabeth *could* see.

Pete frowned, but he followed the rest of the kids inside.

"What is it with boys and soap?" Elizabeth asked.

"I have no idea. I suppose we just like to rough it."

She laughed. "Is that what they're calling it these days?"

"That's the best I can come up with on such short notice."

Jake placed the platter of burgers and hot dogs on the table while Elizabeth brought out the side dishes. She was filling the last glass with lemonade when the kids came bounding back. Gianna and Lucy walked over to her and held out their hands for her inspection. She nodded and smiled. "Good job, girls."

Ben watched them for a minute. Then he shrugged, walked over to Elizabeth, and held out his hands. She inspected them and then smiled. "Good job, Ben. You're ready to eat."

He grinned, then sat down between the twins. There was a lot of talking as Elizabeth and Jake filled everyone's plate with their requested food. Once everyone had their food, Jake's kids picked up their burgers or hot dogs.

"They didn't pray," Gianna said to Elizabeth. She looked around the table. "Don't you pray before you eat?"

"Nope. We just eat," Pete said. He took another bite out of his burger.

"Are we going to pray, Mum?" Lucy asked, looking at Elizabeth.

Elizabeth raised her children to express gratitude before each meal. Clearly Jake wasn't rearing his children in the same way. Before she could reply, Jake answered.

"Of course," he said. He looked at Pete. "Stop eating so we can say grace."

Pete heaved a heavy sigh, but he dropped his burger onto his plate and bowed his head. Gianna, Lucy, and Elizabeth recited the prayer that she'd taught them from a young age. Once they were done, Gianna smiled and picked up her hot dog.

"We used to pray with Mommy," Molly said. "But we don't anymore."

"I don't remember that," Pete said slowly.

"Me neither," Ben added.

Elizabeth glanced over at Jake, who appeared pained. Wordlessly, he picked up his burger and took a big bite.

Deciding that Jake needed a moment alone with his thoughts and a change of subject, she tasted her burger. "This is delicious. You are definitely the grill master."

He gave her a smile, clearly grateful to talk about something else.

Once they'd taken a few bites and satisfied their initial hunger, the kids began to recount the activities of the day, talking over each other in their zeal. It became clear that the five of them had had lots of fun together. What was surprising was how well her girls had gotten along with the boys.

Jake didn't talk much during the meal, and Elizabeth wondered if he was okay. They'd discussed some pretty heavy topics earlier, stirring up some strong emotions. Hearing his sons say they didn't remember something about Maggie had to cut deep.

Once they'd finished their meal, Elizabeth said, "I guess the girls and I should get going."

"Already?" Molly asked.

"But we just got here," Gianna said.

"Yeah, they just got here," Ben added.

As one, the other kids began to beg to keep playing, explaining at great length and with loud volume the game they hadn't finished—the game they needed to finish.

Jake glanced at Elizabeth. She shrugged. It was up to him. She didn't have any other plans for the rest of the day and was content to stay awhile longer. As he'd pointed out earlier, the weather was perfect for sitting outside. But Elizabeth didn't want to overstay her welcome.

"How about we let you guys play for thirty more minutes," Jake said, picking up Ben and swinging him onto his massive shoulders. "Will that work for you?"

"Yes!" Ben exclaimed. He clapped his hands, clearly delighted to be on his father's shoulders.

"Can you pick me up too?" Gianna asked, patting Jake on his thigh.

"And me?" Lucy added. "That looks like fun."

"Sure he can," Ben answered before his father could. "Dad picks us up like this all the time."

Elizabeth's heart squeezed with pain at Ben's casual

words. Lucy and Gianna no longer had a father to carry them on his shoulders. Arlo used to carry them both at once, holding one giggling twin on each shoulder. They'd absolutely loved it. Thankfully Elizabeth had pictures of the three of them with wide smiles on their faces.

Jake lowered Ben, setting him on his feet, then looked at the twins. "Who is first?"

"Gianna, since she asked first," Lucy said.

Gianna giggled in anticipation and raised her arms. When Jake swung her over his head and set her onto his shoulders, she laughed loudly. Her smile was wide and bright enough to send Elizabeth's spirits soaring.

"Look at me, Mummy. I'm big."

"I see."

Jake walked around the yard, taking loping strides much to Gianna's delight. When he returned, he stooped down and lowered her onto the ground.

"Your turn," Gianna said, looking at Lucy.

"I don't want you to run with me," Lucy said, holding out her arms in front of her, preventing Jake from picking her up.

"I won't go any faster than you want me to," he said.

"Do you promise?"

"Cross my heart," he said, using a finger to make a cross on his chest.

"Okay." Lucy stepped up to him, trust written all over her face.

Jake lifted her carefully and settled her on his shoulders. He walked around the yard taking slow steps.

"You can go faster," Lucy said.

He sped up and then glanced at her.

"Faster," she ordered, and after a second repeated, "Faster!"

Laughing, Jake loped around the yard at the same speed

as he'd taken Gianna. Apparently Lucy wasn't afraid after all. Quite the opposite—she was having the time of her life. When the ride ended, Jake set her on the ground.

"Thank you," Lucy said, a wide grin on her face.

"My pleasure."

"Now you can start our thirty minutes," Molly said.

"How do you figure that?" Jake asked.

"Because you were playing with them. We couldn't finish our game. Now we can."

"I suppose you're right."

The kids raced over to the tree house and swings while Jake walked back over to the patio, his long-legged stride casual. It seemed to Elizabeth he was completely oblivious to how attractive he was. Of course, with three kids to raise on his own and no desire for a relationship, he probably didn't give his appeal a second thought.

So why was she so focused on it?

"Thanks for giving my girls pony rides."

He slid into the chair beside her. "You're welcome."

"I do what I can, including giving them pony rides, but there are some things only a man can do."

"I completely understand. I know my kids are missing a woman's touch. My sister, Bethany, helps out when she can, but she's an aunt. That's a totally different role."

"Molly told me about her. She's a wedding singer, right?"

He nodded. "Yes. And quite a gifted one. But then, I'm biased."

She grinned. "And you should be. Do you sing?"

He shook his head. "Not even in the shower. Trust me when I say that Bethany got all of the musical talent in our family."

"So I can't expect to be serenaded in the future."

The words popped out of her mouth before she could

stop them. Hopefully he knew that she'd been joking. The last thing she wanted was for him to think that she was coming on to him. Was she coming on to him unconsciously?

He laughed. "No. Sorry. You'll have to stick to the radio."

She relaxed, relieved that he could tell she'd been kidding. Leaning back in her chair, she sighed. "This has been great. I can't remember the last time I had this much fun."

He looked into her eyes. His were bright. Sincere. "Neither can I. So why are you in such a hurry to leave?"

"I'm not. You seemed a bit distracted while we were eating. I figured you were ready to get things back to normal around here. Maybe lower the volume a bit."

He chuckled. The sound reached inside her, making her heart go pitter-patter. He picked up his lemonade and downed it, then swirled the ice in the glass. "When you reach a certain number of kids, the noise level doesn't matter. Three kids or five, it's going to be loud. Especially when two of them are boys."

"I'll have to take your word for it." She smiled. "But one thing I have noticed is my girls are a lot more rambunctious today than they've been in a long time."

"Is that good or bad?"

"It's definitely good. They became a lot quieter after Arlo died, and they clung to each other. Their tight bond became even tighter."

"And that's bad?" Jake asked.

"In their case, yes." Elizabeth sighed. "They began to exclude other people. After a while, they rebounded, becoming more like themselves. Still... I often wonder if losing their father changed their personalities permanently."

"I believe not having a mother definitely changed my kids. Especially Molly. As a man, I can't teach her how to be a woman. The older she gets, the less I understand her. I have a feeling her teenage years will be even more challenging. Not to mention that she's taken on the role of mother to her brothers. I've told her repeatedly that she's not responsible for raising them, but it's like talking to a wall. I don't push her too hard because being a big sister is important to her."

Elizabeth frowned. "It's all so hard. I spend way too much time questioning myself and wondering if I'm making mistakes with the girls."

"Take it from me," he said. "Once you make a decision, stop debating it. Just stick with it. At least until you have proof that you're going in the wrong direction. Then turn around and start again."

"Is that what you do?"

"It's what I *try* to do. Sometimes I'm more successful than others. But practice makes perfect, and all that."

Elizabeth nodded. She liked his honesty and the way he didn't act as if he had it all together. He was muddling through, the same as she was.

By unspoken agreement, they turned the conversation to inconsequential matters. It was good to set aside the challenges of single-parenthood and talk about places to eat when she doesn't feel like cooking.

"DJ's Deluxe is hands down the best place to get ribs," Jake said. "You might not want to take the kids, though."

"If I want to eat out with the twins, what do you recommend?"

"Bronco Brick Oven Pizza. Or Pastabilities."

"Do you go there a lot?"

"Not really. But it's a nice change from my cooking. Of course, my mom is a great cook. My parents live in Bronco Valley and they have us over for dinner quite often." He grinned. "Nothing beats my mom's pot roast."

Time flew by, and those thirty minutes stretched into forty-five and then an hour. Jake gave the kids a five-minute warning so they could wrap up their game.

"Will Molly be free at any time next week?" Elizabeth asked. "She was quite a big help with the girls."

"She's free every day."

Once they decided on Tuesday and Thursday, Jake said, "Thank you again for doing this."

"There's no need for thanks. Molly is the one helping me."

"You're helping her too. She couldn't stop talking about how much fun she had. She wasn't only talking about Gianna and Lucy. She talked about you nonstop. Being around you is good for her."

"It was mutually beneficial."

He covered her hand with his. Once again electricity shot throughout her body. Their eyes met. Held. Elizabeth struggled to slow her racing heart. The blood pulsed in her veins and she couldn't look away to save her life.

Jake leaned closer and Elizabeth felt herself edging closer to him. They moved slowly as if pulled by a force neither of them could control. Then Jake blinked and jerked away. Realizing where she was, Elizabeth did the same.

Molly ran over then, the rest of the kids behind her. "We know our five minutes is up, so we decided to come before you called us again."

Jake stood and placed an affectionate hand on his daughter's shoulder. "Thank you for being so mature and cooperating with us."

Elizabeth inhaled deeply trying to slow her suddenly racing heart. She felt moisture on her forehead and swiped at it before anyone could see. It took a long moment, but she managed to regain control of her emotions. She stood.

"Can we come back again?" Lucy asked.

"Yes. You're welcome anytime." Jake turned from Lucy and looked directly at Elizabeth. "All of you."

Elizabeth's knees wobbled.

There were lots of hugs as the kids said goodbye. Once Gianna and Lucy were buckled into their booster seats, Elizabeth turned on the SUV. Before she drove away, she glanced at Jake and his children, feeling as if her life had just changed.

She wished she could be assured that change was a good thing.

JAKE WATCHED AS Elizabeth drove away, wondering why he suddenly felt as if he'd just lost an important person in his life. This bereft feeling didn't make sense. Elizabeth was barely in his life. They weren't a couple. They were only friends. He rubbed his chin. Could you count someone as a friend after only knowing them for a short time? He didn't know if there was a time requirement, but he felt that he and Elizabeth were friends. They were connected on such an elemental level that their relationship had even more depth.

He and Maggie had had a way of communicating that hadn't required words. They'd understood each other's moods and expressions. Their connection had been solid. He'd missed knowing someone completely, missed being known completely. Now he felt that same type of connection with Elizabeth. He didn't know how to feel about that. On one hand it felt like betrayal. On the other it felt right. Maggie wouldn't want him to mourn her loss forever. She'd been generous and loving. There was no doubt she would want him to have a happy life even if she couldn't be a part of it.

Intellectually he'd always known that. Since he hadn't been attracted to anyone before Elizabeth, he hadn't been forced to confront that reality. Or his feelings. Now, presented with the possibility of opening his heart to someone, he was confused and cautious.

"That was fun," Ben said, grabbing Jake by the hand and then swinging their joined hands. "I like Lucy and Gianna."

"Do you?"

He nodded. "Do you want to know why?"

"If you want to tell me."

"I like not being the youngest. I'm six, and they're only five. That makes me one of the big kids."

"Does it?"

"Yep." Ben gave their hands one last swing before letting go of Jake's and running across the yard. He hopped on the swing and immediately began swinging high, singing a song as he sailed through the air.

His children's easy acceptance of Gianna and Lucy was a good thing. If he and Elizabeth decided to pursue a relationship in the future, that was one problem they wouldn't have to deal with. Blending families was never easy. The thought alone made Jake's stomach pitch, and he ordered himself to slow down. He wasn't ready for a commitment. From what he could see, neither was Elizabeth. So why was the thought of getting closer to her so appealing?

Jake sat down and watched his kids play. He'd spent many evenings in this very chair over the years, feeling perfectly content. Now, though, he felt lonely. He'd enjoyed being with Elizabeth this afternoon—perhaps more than he should've. He missed her now—missed talking to her. The closeness of walking outside with her, of laughing with a partner. But, he remembered, she might be returning to Australia soon.

If that wasn't a warning that he needed to keep his distance, he didn't know what was.

CHAPTER SIX

"I REALLY LIKE the way you combed Gianna's and Lucy's hair," Molly said the following Tuesday. The girls were in their room gathering books for Molly to read to them. Elizabeth had brought several of their favorite books from Australia, but she'd read them so many times that even she was tired of them. So she'd bought a dozen new books for them yesterday. Elizabeth had planned to read one new book a night, but the minute Molly had stepped into the house, the girls had asked her to read some of them. When she'd agreed, they'd raced away to get their new treasures.

"Thank you."

"Do you think that you can do my hair the way you did theirs?"

"Then she will look just like us," Gianna said, returning to the room with a book in each hand.

"We could even be sisters," Lucy added, stepping beside Gianna. She was also holding two books. Apparently they intended Molly to read for quite a while.

"I can definitely braid your hair, but it won't look exactly like theirs," Elizabeth warned. She'd braided the front of her daughters' hair in neat cornrows that she'd pulled into two Afro puffs. Colorful barrettes and beads completed the style. "Your hair is a different texture. It won't puff up like theirs."

"But you can still braid the front?" Molly asked hopefully.

"Absolutely."

Elizabeth grabbed the comb, brush, and barrettes and then directed Molly to sit on the floor in front of her. Gianna and Lucy grabbed new coloring books and crayons from the table and sat nearby. Elizabeth parted Molly's hair down the middle and secured one section in a scrunchie.

Molly chatted happily as Elizabeth sectioned her hair and began to braid. "This is going to be so cool. I like different styles, but I don't know how to do any of them. Sometimes I wear a headband or put it in a scrunchie, but mostly I just wear it straight down."

"It can be hard to learn on your own. You do a good job, though. Your hair always looks nice."

As kids, Elizabeth, her sisters, and cousins had spent hours styling each other's hair. Many of them had been adopted and were of different races and ethnicities. Faith and Elizabeth were Black, Tori and Amy were white, and Carly was Latina, so they'd become experts at doing hair of different textures and lengths. Although Elizabeth and her relatives didn't resemble each other physically, their love for each other made it clear that they were family.

After she finished the braids, Elizabeth gathered Molly's hair into two ponytails. Her hair was straight, so there was no way Elizabeth could pull it into puffs. After a moment, she had an idea. She rolled Molly's hair into two buns and then added barrettes. They weren't exactly Afro puffs, but they looked good.

Elizabeth grabbed a hand mirror and gave it to Molly. "What do you think?"

Molly stared at her reflection, turning from one side to the other. Her smile grew wider with each passing second. Still holding the mirror, she reached out and hugged Elizabeth tightly. "I love it. Thank you so much."

"You're welcome." She returned Molly's embrace. Now she saw firsthand what Molly was missing by not having a mother around to teach her how to style her hair, about fashion, or a hundred other little things, and it broke her heart. Elizabeth could only imagine how Molly would feel attending mother-and-daughter events in the future. Would she choose to skip them altogether, or would she ask Jake's sister to accompany her? Perhaps Jake would be involved with a woman by then. Elizabeth felt a twinge of jealousy at that thought, although she had no right to feel that way.

"Do you guys like it?" Molly asked, turning to Lucy and Gianna.

"Yes. You could be twins with us," Lucy said.

"We used to be two twins, but now we're three twins," Gianna said.

Molly laughed. "There's no such thing as three twins. Three kids who look alike are called triplets. So that's what we are. We're triplets—aren't we, Elizabeth?"

Elizabeth smiled. "I suppose it would be all right if you called yourselves that."

"Can you polish my nails like theirs?" Molly asked.

Elizabeth and her daughters had weekly home spa days. Gianna and Lucy used to protest when it was time to get their nails trimmed. Once Elizabeth had begun giving them mani-pedis, that had all changed. Now they looked forward to having their nails filed and polished. Yesterday she'd polished their nails in spring colors—white, yellow, and three shades of green. She'd then used those same colors to paint sunflowers on two nails on each hand.

She smiled. There was still lots of polish left. And Molly looked so hopeful there was no way Elizabeth would refuse. "Of course."

"Yay." Molly hugged herself with glee. Gianna and Lucy joined hands and jumped up and down, celebrating with their friend.

"I'll go grab everything. While I do that, I need you to wash your hands."

Molly raced to the bathroom, and Gianna and Lucy followed right behind her. A minute later, they were back. The girls clustered around the coffee table in the small living room.

Elizabeth trimmed Molly's nails so that they were all the same length and then filed them into neat ovals. "Do you like the way I shaped them?"

Molly nodded, a wide smile on her face. She hadn't stopped grinning since Elizabeth had styled her hair. No doubt, she would fall asleep smiling.

As Elizabeth worked, Molly talked happily about life on the ranch. She spoke about her brothers, confirming Jake's statement that Molly was definitely a mother hen. She also expressed a desire to wear more trendy clothes.

"But Daddy doesn't know what they are. He doesn't know anything about clothes." She looked at her plain T-shirt and frowned. "Neither do I."

Elizabeth empathized with the girl even as she sympathized with Jake. It couldn't be easy for either of them. Elizabeth was lucky to be raising girls. She would be out to sea if she was raising a boy on her own. She could offer to help, but she didn't want Jake to think she was auditioning for the role of woman in his life. Besides, he'd mentioned that he had a sister. If he wanted, he could always turn to her for advice.

"I like your clothes," Gianna said loyally. "I think you look pretty."

"So do I," Lucy said. "You look really pretty."

"Thank you," Molly said.

Lucy and Gianna leaned close, watching and assisting as Elizabeth worked. With each finger she polished, they complimented her on her work.

"Now we just need to wait until the polish dries so I can paint on the flowers."

"How long will that take?" Molly asked. She was holding her fingers straight, being careful not to touch one to the other.

"About ten minutes or so."

"We usually sing while we wait," Lucy said, launching into the alphabet song. Gianna joined in when Lucy reached *E*. They sang the song three times before they tired of it. From there, they began to sing the kookaburra song, the Australian nursery rhyme Elizabeth had been singing to them since before they could walk.

Molly smiled when they finished. "That was very good. I would clap, but I don't want to mess up my nails."

"That's very smart of you," Elizabeth said. "I think we're ready for the flowers."

Molly squirmed excitedly.

Elizabeth worked freehand but managed to make the flowers look identical to the ones she'd painted onto the twins' nails.

"Now you need to sit very still and be careful with your fingers," Gianna advised Molly.

"We'll turn on the telly so we can watch something. And we'll remind you not to move your hands," Lucy said. She grabbed the remote and turned on one of their favorite Disney movies. It was in the middle of the program, but that didn't seem to matter to them.

"Do you like this?" Gianna asked. "It's not a baby show."

"I do like it. This is my favorite princess movie."

"Ours too," Lucy and Gianna chimed in together.

The girls sat next to each other on the floor, leaning against the back of the sofa as they watched the movie. Lucy and Gianna had seen it so often that they knew every word of dialogue. When the female lead broke into song, they joined in, singing with gusto. Molly looked at them and after hesitating briefly, she joined in. Her voice started out tentatively. Self-conscious. After singing a few of the lyrics, she sang louder and with confidence. Eventually all three of them were singing at the top of their lungs.

Elizabeth was glad to see it even if her ears would have been happier with a lower volume. She knew there came a point when children—especially girls—began to concern themselves with their peers' opinions of them. It was inevitable. She was happy that Molly still felt the freedom to be herself and could enjoy childish pleasures for a while longer.

Elizabeth turned her attention from the girls and went to work. The Pony Club had been a hit with parents and kids alike, and Rylee had contacted Elizabeth about holding a second session. Since the girls were occupied, it was the perfect time to reach out to Rylee.

She grabbed her phone and punched in Rylee's number. "Is this a good time?"

"It's the best. Especially if you're calling to tell me you're going to run the club again."

Elizabeth laughed. "I am. I'm pleased that there was a lot of interest."

"That's putting it mildly. Not a day goes by when I don't get at least one phone call from a parent asking if there will be a second event and wanting to sign up their children."

"I imagine sooner would be better than later. That way we can strike while the interest is high."

"Don't worry about that," Rylee said quickly. "I don't think interest will be waning anytime soon. As a matter of fact, would you be willing to hold it for three days? Or maybe even a week?"

Elizabeth thought a minute before answering. How

would that affect her daughters? She knew the girls had enjoyed themselves last time. But they were having a good time with Molly now. Even so, it would do them good to be around other kids.

Now Elizabeth had Molly's well-being to consider as well. Molly enjoyed being a mother's helper. She'd told Elizabeth that she had big plans for the money she was earning, although she had not shared what those plans were. If camp was only three days, Molly could still work for Elizabeth the other two days. That was a win-win.

"I can commit to three days right now. I'll need to check out a few things to see if a week is doable," she said.

"That sounds fair," Rylee said. "How about we talk in a couple of days?"

"That works. But I'm not sure if Ross will be able to attend."

"Don't worry about that. There are a couple of other rodeo riders we can contact."

"I'll also ask my sisters and cousins. If they're in town, I'm sure I can convince someone to help." That was one thing Elizabeth knew about her family—they were always willing to share the joy of rodeo with children.

Elizabeth ended the call at the same time the movie ended. The girls cheered, and movie forgotten, they looked at Molly's nails. She tentatively touched the yellow-painted nail. "It's dry."

"I told you it would be," Elizabeth said.

"I can't wait until everyone sees how pretty my nails are. They're going to love them."

"They look as pretty as ours do," Gianna said, holding up her hands and admiring her nails.

"You should let Mummy do them all the time," Lucy said. "You should come to our spa day."

Molly looked at Elizabeth, curiosity shining in her eyes. "What's spa day?"

"That's when Mummy does our nails," Gianna said. "We have drinks with fruit in them."

"And umbrellas," Lucy added. "Not real ones. Little paper ones."

"And we watch *Bluey* while our nails dry," Gianna said.

"I like having cotton balls between my toes," Lucy said with a giggle. "It tickles."

"Mummy does her nails like ours."

Elizabeth held up her hands for Molly to see.

"Could I come?" Molly asked, hope in her voice.

"Of course. We'll ask your dad to bring you."

"And I can have a fancy drink?"

"Absolutely. That's part of the fun. And I'll give you a pedicure if you want one of those too."

Molly laughed. Then she looked at her feet. She was wearing well-worn cowboy boots. "I do. I can't wait. That is going to be so much fun."

"Then it's a plan. I'll talk to your father about it when he picks you up."

Just mentioning Jake made Elizabeth's heart skip a foolish beat. She frowned, disgusted with her lack of control. This ridiculous attraction to him was an unwanted distraction that was taking up more and more of her time. She had a decision to make and didn't need to expend mental energy on Jake like she had last night. She was still miffed at herself for having dreamed about him yet again. It was as if the universe was trying to replace Arlo in her heart, something that she would never permit.

JAKE STOOD AT the back of the classroom and watched as his boys went through their drills. He'd dropped Molly at Elizabeth's before karate class had started, but there hadn't been time for more than a quick hello before he'd needed to leave. The degree of disappointment he'd felt at not being able to have coffee and conversation with Elizabeth again was more than the situation warranted. They'd just seen each other over the weekend and talked for hours. But that didn't change his desire to be with her today.

"Pete and Ben are doing quite well in class."

Jake barely managed to suppress the annoyance at the sweetly cloying voice. He pasted on a polite smile as he turned to face Cindy. Her eight-year-old son, River, was also taking karate. Cindy had been divorced for several months, and she'd made numerous changes to her appearance. She'd bleached her hair and teeth and begun wearing tight clothes. She'd also made it plain that she was on the prowl for a replacement husband. To her, Jake fit the bill. She dropped hints about going out every time she saw him. He always deflected, but either she didn't get the message or she thought she could wear him down.

She wasn't the first woman who had believed that. Maggie hadn't been gone for two months before several women began making a play for him.

Back then, his pain had made him blunt. Time had dulled the pain, and he was more diplomatic now. He didn't want to hurt Cindy. Until she had gotten the ridiculous idea of blending their families into her head, Cindy had been a friend of his. He used to look forward to talking to her while their boys took their lesson. Now? Not so much.

"So is River," he said.

"I imagine that Pete and Ben practice with each other during the week."

Jake shook his head and laughed. "Not as much as you would think. They like class, but getting them to practice their kata takes a bit of nudging."

"River doesn't have anyone to practice with," Cindy

said. "I was thinking that perhaps I could bring River out to the ranch and he could practice with Pete. They're the same age after all. Pete might prefer practicing with him instead of Ben. I could grab dinner at DJ's Deluxe for everyone and a bottle of wine for us. We could make a night of it."

"That sounds like a lot of driving just for a few minutes of practice."

Cindy opened her mouth as if to argue when one of the other mothers stepped up. She lived in town, and her son was a year older than Pete and River. An idea formed in Jake's mind. "Hey, Claire. Cindy is trying to find someone for River to practice with during the week. I live so far out, but you live in town. Maybe Daniel would like to practice with him."

Claire's eyes lit up. "Daniel would love to practice with River. Cindy, what time is good for you?"

Cindy glared at Jake, who managed to keep a self-satisfied expression from his face. He didn't want to hurt her feelings, but he wasn't interested in playing happy family with her. If she didn't get the message this time, he would be more direct in the future. He wasn't looking to add a woman to his life.

What about Elizabeth?

That unexpected thought came from out of nowhere, and he did his best to shut it down. Elizabeth wasn't like Cindy or any of the others who'd tried to use his kids to get close to him. She wasn't trying to shove her way into his life.

And if she did try? What would he do?

The answer came quickly—he had no idea.

Class ended and not a moment too soon. After the boys changed into their street clothes, they all hopped into the SUV and Jake headed out to the cabin to pick up Molly.

When they reached the cabin, the boys had jumped

out of the SUV and knocked on the door before he could tell them to stay in the car. They were not here for a visit.

"I hope we can have cookies again," Ben said.

"Biscuits," Pete said. "They call cookies *biscuits*."

"Whatever they call them. I hope we can have some more."

"Hey," Jake said. "This isn't a playdate. We're just here to pick up Molly."

"We were just picking up Molly last time too," Pete said. "And we got cookies then."

"Biscuits," Ben said and then laughed.

Jake was shaking his head when the door swung open. And there was Elizabeth, looking as stunning as always.

"Hi, Elizabeth," the boys said before running around her and stepping into the cabin. Immediately the laughter of five children floated through the open windows and door.

"Make yourselves at home," Elizabeth said dryly.

"Sorry about that," Jake said.

"No worries. Come on in."

"I may as well. The boys have already planted themselves in your front room."

"That's fine by me. They're welcome anytime."

He grinned. "Is it me, or are they making more noise now than they did on Saturday?"

"It's the small space. The walls magnify the noise."

"How about we take them outside and let them run around for a while?" he asked. "That is, unless you want us to leave?"

"Of course not. You're welcome to stay."

Ben walked up to them just then, a sweet smile on his face. Jake recognized the look. It was the one he wore whenever he'd been coaxed by Molly and Pete to ask for something.

"Elizabeth, can we have some of the cookies we had last time?"

"Of course. Do you want them now, or would you rather go outside and play first?"

Ben grinned at Elizabeth and held a finger in the air. "I'll be right back." He went back to confer with the others.

Elizabeth and Jake exchanged smiles. Clearly she was not new to the game.

"We want to play first and then have our Tim Tams," Ben declared when he returned. "You do have more, don't you?"

Before Elizabeth could reply, Gianna piped up. "Yes. Our aunt mailed more."

"That's Carly, my sister. She still lives in Australia," Elizabeth explained. "She sends lots of goodies."

"That's nice of her to send you a taste of home," Jake said.

She smirked. "I'm not so sure if it's as innocent as all that. It's her way of reminding me of everything we're missing while we're here."

"I take it that she wants you to move back to Australia."

"We're really close, so yeah, you could say that. We toured together so I know she misses me and the girls."

That was another reminder that Elizabeth's stay could have an expiration date. As if that knowledge was ever far from his mind. That was a big reason he needed to keep his distance. More than that, it was a reason he shouldn't let his kids get attached to her. He didn't want them to be brokenhearted when she went back home.

He frowned. Who was he kidding? The kids weren't worrying about what might happen in the future. The truth was he was trying to protect himself and keep his heart safe.

Jake and Elizabeth followed the kids outside and sat on

the wicker rockers as the kids chased each other around the yard. If they were playing tag, they were using rules known only to themselves. They seemed happy, so that was all that mattered.

"I spoke to Rylee today," Elizabeth said.

"About?"

"She wants me to run the Pony Club again. This time for three days. Maybe even a week."

"What are you going to do?"

"I committed for three days. I haven't decided about the other two." She glanced at him. "Would your kids be interested in coming again?"

"Definitely. They had a great time the first time around."

"That's good to hear." Her smile was radiant, and his heart skipped a beat. "Do you think five days would be too much?"

"No. It's summertime. Kids are looking for something to fill the endless hours of free time. Plus, at the Pony Club they get to see their friends again. Add in horses and you have a guaranteed winner."

"How will Molly feel if I run the camp for a week? She loves being my helper. I don't want her to miss out."

"She'll understand. And if it's not an imposition, she can always help you out at other times during the day. Or even on the weekend."

"It won't be an imposition at all. I know you think she's just playing, but she really is a big help."

Pride swelled in his chest. He knew that his daughter was a treasure, but it was good to know another person recognized it.

They sat in silence for a while, watching the children. After a few minutes, Molly ran over. "We're ready for our cookies now."

"Okay. I have a pitcher of lemonade to go with them," Elizabeth replied, standing.

Jake rose too.

Molly clapped, and Jake noticed her fingernails. They were polished different colors. "Whoa. Let me see your hands."

She grinned and held them out to him. "I forgot to show you. Aren't they cool? Elizabeth did it. Now my nails are just like Gianna's and Lucy's. We all have sunflowers."

"I see."

She preened. "They have spa day. Elizabeth said I can come next time and she'll do all of our nails. Our toenails too. And we'll have fancy drinks with umbrellas and fruit. Doesn't that sound like fun?"

He nodded, trying to keep his feelings from showing on his face. He didn't know how to feel about Elizabeth polishing his daughter's fingernails without his permission. Especially all of these different colors. It might be a small thing to her, but he was Molly's parent. She should have consulted him first. And she certainly should have spoken to him before she invited Molly to this spa day.

"I'll tell everyone to wash their hands so we can have our cookies," Molly said and then ran off.

His daughter hadn't noticed the change in his attitude, but Elizabeth must have. She turned to him, a concerned expression on her face. To her credit, she did seem remorseful. "I don't know what I've done, but I've done something to get on your bad side. Is it the manicure or the fact that I invited Molly to spa day with me and my girls? Why are you angry with me?"

CHAPTER SEVEN

ELIZABETH WATCHED AS Jake pondered her question. It hadn't been a particularly difficult one in her mind, so he must've been struggling to find just the right words so as not to offend her. "Jake, just say what you're feeling. I won't break. I'm stronger than I look."

"I guess it might be a combination."

"I'll simply remove the polish. No problem," she said. "Rescinding the invitation to spa day will be harder, but I'll handle it."

"And turn me into the bad guy?"

"Not at all. I'll explain to Molly that I should have asked you before I polished her nails."

"That would have been nice."

She sighed at the restrained anger in his voice. "It never occurred to me that it would be a problem. I've been giving my daughters mani-pedis for a while. It started as a way to trim their nails with the least amount of hassle. Over time it became one of their favorite things for us to do together. Mine too. Molly is the first person they invited to join us."

He blew out a breath. "Do you think I'm overreacting?"

"Does it matter what I think? You're her father, and what you say goes."

Jake shoved his hands into his pockets. "Don't take off the polish. She really seems to like the way her nails look."

"Of course she does. Most girls like having fancy nails. It makes them feel pretty and a little bit grown up."

"I'm being a jerk, and it has nothing to do with you," he said.

"Then why do I feel like it does?"

"One of the mothers at karate is using our boys to try to get close to me." His cheeks grew ruddy as he spoke. Clearly the entire situation embarrassed him.

"And you thought that I was doing the same with Molly? Are you *kidding me*?" Her voice rose on the last words. She looked over her shoulder. Luckily the kids were still crowded into the bathroom washing their hands. Even so, she lowered her voice. "Are you out of your mind?"

His expression was sheepish. "It sounds ridiculous when you say it out loud."

"That's because it is ridiculous. I'm not interested in a relationship with you, Jake."

Her words sounded harsh in her own ears, and she knew she could have been more diplomatic, but she didn't retract them. She didn't want there to be any confusion. Apparently he thought she wanted more than friendship with him and that she was sneaky enough to use his daughter in her plan. That he actually thought she could be so devious hurt her soul.

He winced. "I got it."

"Do you?" she asked. "Because my life is in flux. I don't need another complication. And that's what a relationship with you would be. I'm trying to decide whether to go back to Australia or start over here in America. That's change enough for me." She sighed. She might as well lay her cards on the table. "I like you as a friend. But if I'm being totally honest, I might even find you a little bit attractive."

"Just a little bit?" he asked with a wicked grin that made her heart skip a beat.

She ignored the sensation as well as his comment. "But

my situation remains the same. I might not even be in this country in a couple of months."

"As long as we're being honest, I find you more than a little bit attractive."

His words made her knees tremble, and she hoped he didn't notice the extra effort it took for her to remain standing. "Well, then."

What was she supposed to do with that bit of knowledge? The only thing she could do. Shove it aside and forget about it. She could only hope he would do the same.

"That's not the only reason I acted like a jerk. And it probably isn't the main one."

Elizabeth blew out a breath. "Then what is?"

"Because it's hard to see my little girl growing up. Watching her grow away from me. There are times when I don't understand her. Times when I can't give her what she needs. If her mother was here, she would know what to say and do."

Elizabeth nodded.

"I'm so proud of the young lady she is becoming. But seeing her new manicure only emphasized that I don't have the foggiest notion about what is important to her. I would never have thought about a mani/pedi as being something that mattered to her. And you've only known her for a little while, and you knew what she would like."

"I understand. It's hard to watch them grow up."

"I wish Maggie was here. Not just to help with the hard situations, but to see just how wonderful her kids have become. And she's not." Jake's voice broke on the last words, and Elizabeth's heart ached for him. She could relate to that grief.

"I feel the same way about Arlo. But holding on to the pain and anger isn't good for any of us."

"I know. That's why I'm trying to look to the future."

He moved closer and her heart began to thud. Their eyes met and the emotion she saw in his made it impossible for her to look away. The surroundings seemed to fade, making it feel as if they were the only two people in the world.

"Are we having our snack or not?" Pete said, running over to them and bringing an end to their true confession session. "We washed our hands."

"Coming right up," Elizabeth said, not sure if she was relieved or upset by the interruption. "Let's go, kids."

The group hustled into the kitchen and gathered around the table.

"Does everyone want the same cookies as last time?"

"Yes," they all said loudly.

Jake poured the lemonade, then stood aside as Elizabeth opened packages of Tim Tams. What she wouldn't give to eat a handful of the chocolate deliciousness now.

"Do you remember what everyone wanted?" he asked.

"Of course."

She felt his eyes on her as she passed out the treats. Once the kids had been served, she handed Jake several mint cookies.

"I'm impressed," he said.

"You should be." She looked around. As before, the kids had left a chair for her and Jake to share. The idea of sitting that close to him made her shiver. It had felt so good to sit beside him, his leg pressed against hers. Just recalling how good it had been to feel the heat from his body wrap around her made her shiver. Given the fact that she'd just confessed to being attracted to him, it would be best not to risk that kind of intimate contact again. "Come on— let's have our snack in the main room."

Jake nodded and followed her. Luckily he didn't try to make conversation as they ate. Instead they spent time alone with their thoughts. There was plenty for them to contemplate. Elizabeth was still reeling from admitting that she was attracted to Jake. She couldn't believe she'd just gone and volunteered that information. Not that it mattered. She had been honest when she'd told him she had too much going on in her life to consider a relationship.

Even so, she was thrilled to know that he was attracted to her. Not that anything could come from that. There were so many differences between them. A big one was their way of raising their children. She would never allow her daughters to keep their bedrooms as messy as he let Ben and Pete keep theirs. Gianna and Lucy made their beds each morning before they got dressed. They knew to toss their dirty clothes into the hamper and to put away their clean clothes. While neatness mattered to her, it clearly wasn't a big deal to Jake. It was good that the differences were appearing now before she and Jake got in too deep.

When the kids finished their snacks, Gianna and Lucy placed their dishes in the sink.

Molly did the same, then instructed her brothers to follow.

"Say thank-you," Jake said.

"Thank you," his kids chorused.

"You're quite welcome," Elizabeth replied.

"And on that note, we need to get going." Jake corralled his kids, led them out the door, and into his SUV.

Once the vehicle was out of sight, the girls turned to Elizabeth. "Can we watch the telly?"

"Sure."

When they were settled in front of the television Elizabeth grabbed her phone. Her mind was a mess, and she needed to talk. If she was back home in Australia, she would call Carly. But given the time difference, she couldn't. Luckily she had other sisters close by that she could talk to.

Taking one last look at her girls who were absorbed in their program, Elizabeth headed to the relative privacy of the kitchen. She was close enough to keep an eye on the girls but far enough away not to be overheard. Before she could punch in any of her sisters' numbers, her phone rang. When the name popped on the screen she smiled and answered.

"You must have ESP," she said to her sister Faith.

"Why do you say that?"

"I was about to give you a ring. Well, you, Amy, and Tori."

"Oh. Sister conference call. That must mean that the topic is serious. Should I add them in?"

Elizabeth hesitated. Faith had probably just called to catch up with her. If it was only the two of them on the line, they could do just that. If they added in Tori and Amy, she would end up discussing her feelings. But wasn't that what she wanted to do? Needed to do?

Besides, did she want to hide from her sisters? She'd been trying to hide from herself, and judging from her dreams about Jake, that wasn't working so well.

"Go ahead and add them. I could use all the help I can get."

"That sounds ominous," Faith said. "Hold on."

In less than a minute, Tori and Amy were on the line.

"What's up?" Tori asked.

"I just need a dose of sister common sense."

"Oh, it must be a man," Amy said.

Tori and Faith laughed.

"So who is it?" Amy asked.

"Talk about taking the bull by the horn."

"Why waste time?" she said. "You're going to tell us eventually. Besides, the girls will be demanding your attention soon, so there's no time to waste."

"I don't even know where to start," Elizabeth said. "I'm confused. And truthfully, I may be getting ahead of myself."

"So what? We're your sisters. It's not as if this conversation is going to go any further than us," Faith said.

"I know that." Elizabeth sucked in a breath and then blew it out. "I met a man."

Her sisters began to talk all at once, but she managed to hear Tori say, "About time."

"What's his name?" Amy asked.

"Where did you meet him?" This from Tori.

"Let her talk," Faith said.

"His name is Jake McCreery. I met him at the Pony Club." When nobody said anything, Elizabeth continued, "He's a widower with three kids."

"Wow. Three kids. Plus your two. Talk about a full house," Amy said.

"Nobody is talking about joining families," Elizabeth said, nipping that kind of talk in the bud. "We haven't even gone on a date yet. Nor has he asked me to."

"How long ago did his wife die?" Faith asked quietly, taking the conversation in another direction.

"Six years. She died giving birth to their youngest son, Ben."

"How sad," Tori said.

"That had to be hard on him," Amy said.

"I imagine it was," Elizabeth replied. From her experience she knew *hard* didn't begin to describe it.

"Has he been single since then? Maybe he isn't over his wife. If that's the case, you could be walking into a bunch of pain," Faith added.

"I don't know whether he is or not. Since I can't say I'm all the way over Arlo, I understand if he isn't. I know Arlo is gone and won't be coming back..." Before her sisters could comment she continued, "I'll always love him. He owns a piece of my heart that will never belong to another man. So I understand if a part of Jake will always love Maggie."

"So what's the problem?" Tori asked.

"Why does there have to be a problem?" Elizabeth countered as if she hadn't wanted to talk things out with her sisters.

"Because there's always a problem with love and romance," Faith said.

"It wouldn't be worth it if it came too easily," Tori said.

"There is no love or romance. I'm not in love with Jake."

"But you like him," Amy said.

"Is that silly? I don't even know him, but I dreamed about him."

"Aw." Tori sighed.

"I feel as if I'm losing Arlo. His memory is fading. This morning I couldn't remember the sound of his voice."

"It's been two years," Amy said softly. "You're entitled to move on. In fact, it's not healthy for you to keep living in the past."

"I'm not living in the past. But I don't want to pretend that my husband didn't exist. I can't act as if our love didn't sustain me."

"Nobody is saying that you should forget Arlo," Faith said.

"Arlo loved you," Tori said. "He knew you loved him. But he would want you to find love again. He would want you to be happy."

"I am happy. My girls make me happy."

"What about Jake? Does he make you happy?" Tori asked.

Did he? They had a good time together the other day.

She'd enjoyed talking to him today despite hitting a speed bump.

"He's easy to be with," Elizabeth settled for saying.

"That's not exactly an answer."

"He has his own issues. Women started pursuing him a couple of months after his wife died. Circling him like vultures."

"Talk about tacky," Faith said.

"And disgusting," Amy added.

"Yes. I offered to include his daughter in spa day. He thought I was using Molly in order to get close to him."

"Did he accuse you of that?" Amy asked, sounding offended on Elizabeth's behalf.

"Not in so many words. We talked about it, and he admitted that he'd jumped to the wrong conclusion."

"If you decide to have a relationship, no doubt you'll have more misunderstandings. I can't imagine it will be easy since you've both lost a beloved spouse. Plus you each have children to raise," Tori said.

Elizabeth sighed. "That about sums it up."

"I don't know what you're thinking," Amy said, "but I for one think that you should give the relationship a try."

"Even with all the possible landmines?" Elizabeth asked.

"Yes." Amy's reply came without hesitation.

"Why?"

"Lots of reasons," Amy said.

"Give me one."

"You deserve to be happy. So do the girls," she said.

"And Jake is the first man you've been attracted to since Arlo died," Tori added.

"And most importantly, a romance will keep you in Montana," Faith said. "If things work out with Jake, you'll settle down here and the four of us will be together again.

Who knows, Carly might even decide that she wants to move back to the States."

"That might be wishful thinking on your part," Elizabeth said. "Carly absolutely loves living in Australia."

"I notice that you didn't reply to any of the other things we said," Amy said.

"It's just so hard. I loved Arlo so much. I don't want to put him in the past. Getting together with Jake requires me to do that."

"Weren't you just saying something different?" Amy asked.

"I was. I know. Everything is so confusing. Whenever I think about Jake, I feel guilty. A relationship with him feels like the ultimate betrayal of Arlo."

"It isn't," Faith said.

"If you had been the one to die, would you want Arlo to mourn you for the rest of his life?" Tori asked.

"You better believe it," Elizabeth said, giving a watery chuckle. Her eyes were brimming with unshed tears, and she needed to lighten the moment. She didn't want to break down. She'd cried a river these past two years.

"You know we don't believe that," Tori said.

"I know," Elizabeth said. "It just feels different somehow."

"You can't ignore your feelings and hope they go away. You have to go through them," Amy said.

"We had such a good life. I can't believe that it's over. And my girls… Gianna and Lucy had the best father two girls could ever want." She gulped. "I just can't believe that they only got to have three years with him. They barely remember him."

"But you'll keep him alive for them," Faith said.

"But if I get involved with another man…"

"That won't change anything." Tori sighed. "I wish I was there so I could give you a big hug."

"Me too," Amy said.

"Well, what's stopping us?" Faith asked.

"Nothing," Amy said. "We're coming over."

"That's not necessary," Elizabeth said. "I'm fine."

"I'm sure you are. But it would be good to have a little time together. I'll stop and get us some takeout," Faith said. "I know that Gianna and Lucy would love to see us."

"If you insist," Elizabeth said.

"We do."

"Then come on over."

She hung up the phone and smiled. It was good to be here with her sisters. But would that closeness be enough to make her leave Australia and the only home the girls had ever known?

"So, ARE YOU going to get this one or not?"

Jake looked into the face of his ranch foreman. There was a confused look on Gerard's face.

"What one?"

"The steer."

Jake blinked then ordered himself to get back in the game. He glanced at the steer currently heading for a ditch a few feet away. "Yeah. I got it."

He spurred Lancelot into action, chasing down the stray steer and guiding it back to the rest of the herd.

They were moving the cattle from one grazing area to another. The cows were huge, and even riding a well-trained horse who knew when and how to move, Jake could get hurt if he didn't pay attention. And he was definitely distracted now. He had been all day.

The moment his alarm clock had gone off, he'd started to think about Elizabeth. As he'd fried bacon and eggs for the kids before his parents had picked them up to spend the day in town, he'd recalled how beautiful she'd looked the last time he'd seen her. He'd completely lost track of what he'd been doing as he'd fantasized about spending time with her.

And he was doing it again.

"You look like you have something on your mind," Gerard said as Jake rejoined him.

Gerard and Jake had been good friends since they were kids. Gerard had supported Jake in the miserable days following Maggie's death, listening as Jake raged against fate. He knew that anything he told Gerard would remain between the two of them. But he also knew that talking about Elizabeth now would only distract him even more.

"Maybe."

"And you don't want to talk about it."

Jake nodded. "I need to stay focused on this drive."

"Good enough." Gerard nodded and rode away.

Normally Jake loved cattle drives. There was something so peaceful about being on horseback and crossing the acres of his ranch. Today, with the bright shining sun in the clear blue sky, should have been next to heaven. But instead of enjoying it, he couldn't keep his head in the game. All he could think about was Elizabeth.

Finally they got the herd to the pasture. Gerard rode over to Jake. "We can take it from here. Your parents will be bringing the kids back in a couple of hours."

"Thanks." Jake turned Lancelot and they rode across the ranch until he reached the house and rustled up something for his dinner. His parents would feed the kids so that was one less thing Jake needed to worry about.

He was polishing off his steak sandwich when his mother called, telling him that the kids wanted to sleep over. "We'll bring them home first thing in the morning."

"Thanks, Mom."

"Enjoy your quiet time," she said before ending the call.

Jake leaned back in his chair and closed his eyes. He hadn't been this preoccupied since he and Maggie had first gotten together. She had been the only woman who could make his heart sing. Over time he'd learned to live without music in his life, learning to endure the silence.

Now Elizabeth was changing all of that. His body hummed whenever she was around. She was the first person that he thought of when he awoke, the last person that he thought of at night. Even now he was sitting here thinking about her when there were several other things he could be doing. Why was she relentlessly on his mind? She was only his friend. Friendship was fine with him. Did he want her to play a bigger role in his life? Maybe. But only if there was a place for him in her life.

He sighed. It was time to be honest with himself. Lying was a surefire way to make a mistake—something his children couldn't afford for him to do. Pretending he wasn't attracted to Elizabeth was a way of lying to himself. Admitting his feelings had lifted a weight from his shoulders. His ego had been boosted to hear that she was attracted to him. Even an old bachelor dad like him wanted to appeal to women. Well, not *women* exactly. Woman. Elizabeth Hawkins.

He liked their easy way of communicating. As a widow, she was uniquely qualified to understand his complex and confusing emotions. She could relate to wanting to get close but being afraid to move.

Guilt roiled his stomach. He shouldn't have been thinking that way about Elizabeth. It was as if he was putting her on the same level as Maggie. That was wrong. Maggie belonged in her own category. How could he feel as connected to a woman he barely knew as he had with his beloved wife?

Jake rubbed a hand over his face. Talking to himself was getting him nowhere. He was only going in circles. He'd gotten accustomed to the loneliness that came with being a single parent, but he still missed having someone to bounce ideas off. Someone who could suggest a solution he hadn't considered. That was what Maggie had always done for him. What they'd always done for each other.

But Maggie was gone. And he needed to talk to someone he trusted about his attraction to Elizabeth and the confusing emotions she awoke in him. He checked the time. No doubt, Gerard had just gotten home and was spending precious time with his own family. Jake didn't want to disturb him. But it was still early enough for him to call his sister, so he punched in her number.

Bethany answered on the second ring. "What's up?"

"I just felt like talking to an adult. Is now a good time?"

"Of course. I just finished learning a new song." Bethany was a wedding singer extraordinaire and in great demand. Jake hadn't been exaggerating when he'd told Elizabeth that his sister had enough talent for two people.

Bethany and Jake had always been close. They'd grown even closer after Maggie's death. Back then, he'd depended on her—perhaps more than he should have. When he'd been shrouded by grief, she had been a comfort and a shoulder to lean on. She'd stepped in and cared for the kids when he'd been paralyzed by sorrow. If not for Bethany, he wouldn't have made it through those rough early months.

But he'd never faced a situation like this one.

Now that Jake had someone willing to listen, he didn't know how or where to start.

"It must be serious if you can't find the words." Bethany's voice was a mixture of amusement and concern.

"You could say that."

"It can only be one thing. You met a woman."

He knew that his sister was astute, so he shouldn't have been surprised that she'd put her finger on his problem right away. But he was. "I won't bother to ask how you guessed that."

Bethany's whoop was a sound of complete joy. "It's about time."

"What makes you say that?"

"It's been six years since you lost Maggie. I know that you loved her with your whole heart, but nobody expects you to be alone forever. It's okay for you to move on. That's what she would have wanted for you."

"You've told me that before."

"I know. But this is the first time that you seem to be taking my words to heart," Bethany said. "So who is this woman?"

"Her name is Elizabeth. Elizabeth Hawkins."

"Is she related to the Hawkins rodeo family?"

"Yes. She competes in the rodeo too but in Australia."

"Wow. She's a long way from home."

"I know." He explained how she'd come to Montana.

"Is she staying in Bronco?" Bethany asked.

"That's the question. I wish I knew the answer to it."

"Have you asked her?"

"We talked about it briefly. She doesn't know what she plans to do in the future. She's taking it day by day." Jake sighed. "Elizabeth is a widow with twin five-year-old daughters."

"Oh. When did her husband die?"

"Two years ago. She's trying to figure out her next move."

"Something that you know all about," she said.

"All too well."

"And if she decides to stay? Then what?"

"I don't know." Jake looked up at the ceiling as if the answer would somehow magically appear there. It didn't. "I know that Maggie is gone, but it feels wrong to even think about sharing the rest of my life with someone else. Helping to raise another woman's children and letting her help me to raise Molly, Pete, and Ben in Maggie's place."

"She wouldn't be taking Maggie's place any more than you would be taking her husband's. You'll each have to make your own places in the kids' lives if you decide to make a go of it."

"Should I even try?" he asked.

"That's not a question I can answer. Nor should I."

"Point taken."

"But I will say that you're lucky to have found someone worthy of taking a chance with."

"I'm sorry that things didn't work out for you and Rexx." Rexx had been the bass player in Bethany's band and definitely not worthy of her.

"That whole relationship was a mistake from the beginning."

There was something about the tone of her voice that gave Jake pause. She didn't sound like herself. He immediately sprang into big-brother mode. "What's wrong?"

"Nothing."

"Don't tell me nothing. I can tell that something's wrong," he said. "You've listened to my troubles for six years. If I needed anything, all I had to do was call. Surely you can let me do the same for you."

Bethany sighed. "I'm good, Jake. Really."

Jake knew that she was holding something back, but he couldn't force her to tell him. Nor would he try to. He respected her too much for that. She was entitled to have her own secrets. "Okay."

"What do the kids think of Elizabeth?"

"They like her. They've talked about her nonstop since they met. She hired Molly as her mother's helper."

"Considering the way Molly tends to mother Pete and Ben, that's right up her alley," Bethany said. "How does she like it?"

"She loves it. Molly is so proud to earn her own money. And she really likes being around Elizabeth's daughters."

"I'm sure. Pete and Ben are good kids, but Molly needs other little girls to play with. Living on the ranch can make getting together with her friends that much more difficult."

"I'm a rancher," Jake said somewhat defensively. "I can't move to town and still make a living."

"I'm not accusing you of doing anything wrong And I certainly don't expect you to sell the ranch. I'm sure Molly doesn't either. But the fact remains that she is the only female in the house. Being around Elizabeth and her daughters must be nice for her. That's all I meant. And I think you know that."

"I do."

He was quiet for a while.

"What aren't you telling me? What's bugging you?" Bethany asked.

"She polished Molly's nails and styled her hair to match Gianna's and Lucy's."

"That's a good thing."

"I know," he said. "It just made me feel… I don't know how to explain it."

"It made you feel like you're failing in some ways because you're a man."

"Yes. It never occurred to me that she might want a manicure. And I'm not talking about a plain manicure. Her nails are all different colors. Elizabeth painted sunflowers on a couple of them."

"I bet Molly was over the moon."

"She was."

"Most dads don't think of things like that, so don't beat yourself up over it. Heck, it never occurred to me, and I'm a woman."

"Thank you for saying that. It makes me feel a little bit better."

"Good. And you should know there will be times in the future when you're not going to think of things. Not just for Molly, but for the boys too. You can't know everything that matters to them."

"Maggie would have."

"No, she wouldn't. Maggie was a woman. Flesh and blood just like you and complete with flaws. You have built her up in your mind to mythical proportions, but she didn't have magical powers. She didn't see or know all."

"So, you're telling me what?"

"Two things. First, go easy on yourself. You're a good dad."

He smiled. "What's the second thing?"

"Remember Maggie the way she was. Otherwise no woman will ever be able to compare. Give Elizabeth a real chance."

Jake nodded even though his sister couldn't see him. He'd asked for her advice. Now he needed to follow it. "I will."

CHAPTER EIGHT

"THIS IS GOING to be so much fun," Ben said as he raced across the sidewalk to the doors of the convention center.

"Wait until we catch up," Jake called even though Molly and Pete were hot on Ben's heels. The kids were so excited to attend the Pony Club again. They'd been awake for hours and had asked him repeatedly when they would be leaving. Judging by how fast they were running, they couldn't wait another second.

Jake jogged the last few steps in order to catch up with the kids. It was unlikely they would be in any danger, but he didn't want his kids to run amok. And while he didn't worry about other people's opinions about most things, he didn't want to look like a bad father. Especially in front of Elizabeth, whose girls had to be the best mannered kids he'd ever met.

He laughed to himself at that ridiculous notion. He wasn't auditioning for the role of Lucy's and Gianna's stepfather. He had his hands full with just three kids. It took supreme effort to give each of them individual time and attention. He couldn't see how it would be possible to divide his time five ways. Given his failure to recognize Molly's changing interests, the last thing he should have been considering was taking on more girls.

"We know where to go," Pete said.

"I know. But let's stay together."

Pete huffed out a breath, but he stayed with the group.

When they reached the arena, the kids spotted their friends. Before Jake could stop them, Pete and Ben dashed away to join them. He saw a couple of girls who were in Molly's class.

"Hey, isn't that Emma over there?" he tried, but he couldn't remember the name of the other little girl.

"Yeah. And Jessie." Molly waved and continued to look around. Then she smiled. "I see Elizabeth and Lucy and Gianna. I'm going over there."

She stepped away, and he followed. Molly stopped and stared at him. "I don't need you to go with me. I'm not a baby."

"I know that. I just wanted to say hello to Elizabeth. After all, she's my friend too."

Molly narrowed her eyes for a moment as she considered his words. He didn't know if she was focused on the fact that he called Elizabeth his friend or whether she thought he was using Elizabeth's presence as an excuse to follow her. She nodded. "Okay."

Elizabeth's back was to him, and he took a moment to study her. She was wearing a rodeo shirt covered with sponsor patches and jeans that her round backside filled out nicely. The fringed pink shirt was tied at the waist, emphasizing its small size. Her pink cowboy boots had fringe around the top, adding style and fashion. She might've been dressed to ride a horse, but Jake just thought she looked hot.

She turned just then, and their eyes met. He was close enough to notice her chest rise with her quick intake of breath before she smiled. Her eyes sparkled with pleasure, and his heart leaped in response. When Molly reached Elizabeth, she ran straight into her arms. As they hugged, Jake smiled. Elizabeth said something that didn't reach his ears, but whatever it was made Molly laugh.

When Jake reached the floor, he walked over to Elizabeth, wishing that he could give her a hug too. Of course, that was out of the question. They didn't have that type of relationship. Even so, his arms ached to hold her.

"How are you?" Elizabeth asked. She stepped closer, and her sweet scent teased his senses.

"How do I look?" he countered, suddenly feeling playful.

She paused and gave him a once-over, starting with his booted feet and letting her gaze travel over him until it reached his black cowboy hat. "Honestly? You look like you've been wrestling with three kids who were eager to get to the Pony Club."

The laugh that burst from his lips was loud and quite unexpected. A couple of parents turned to look at him. "That bad, huh? I hope nobody else noticed."

"Only someone who has been dealing with excited twin girls for hours would notice, so you're safe."

He shook his head. "You look too good for me to believe that."

She laughed. "It's the lighting in here. And makeup."

Her words gave him the excuse he needed to study her face. She didn't appear to have an ounce of makeup on her glowing brown skin. She removed her cowboy hat, brushed her wavy hair over her shoulder, and then replaced the hat.

An attractive woman walked over to them. "Sorry to interrupt, but I just wanted to let you know we're ready whenever you are."

"Thanks," Elizabeth said. She looked at Jake. "This is my sister Faith. Faith, this is Jake, my new friend. His daughter, Molly, is my mother's helper."

Faith smiled and held out a hand. "It's nice to meet you, Jake."

"Likewise." He shook her hand and then looked back at Elizabeth. "I'll get out of your way so you can get started."

"I'll talk to you later," she promised.

Something to look forward to.

Jake nodded and walked away. He spotted Pete and Ben with a group of kids, and he took a seat in the middle of the arena where he could keep an eye on them. Elizabeth walked up to a microphone and asked for quiet. In an instant, you could hear a pin drop.

She welcomed the campers, then called the kids by name to form groups. The session would last for three hours each day. Several parents had left, and Jake knew that he could run out to Bronco Feed and Ranch Supply. He didn't often have time to himself, and there were many errands he could run while the kids were otherwise occupied. Instead of taking advantage of the free time, he stayed seated. Elizabeth was enchanting, and he enjoyed looking at her.

She was quite gifted, and the kids were hanging on her every word. She helped each of them with the horses, kneeling down in front of one little girl of about seven who appeared to be afraid. The girl backed away, and Elizabeth stood. Before the child could bolt, Gianna walked over and took her hand. Then Lucy went over to the horse. Either the twins were quite persuasive or the little girl's ego would not allow her to fear something that two younger kids didn't. Regardless, after a moment, she reached out and touched the horse.

Although he had absolutely no reason to be proud—he had nothing to do with the twins or how they were raised—he was filled with pride. Jake glanced at Molly, who also watched the scene. She seemed a bit lost, as if unsure of her role. He'd explained to her that she would be a camper and not Elizabeth's helper, but he wasn't sure she'd understood what that difference entailed.

Elizabeth walked over to Molly and put a hand on her shoulder. She said something, and Molly nodded and smiled. Then Molly began talking to another girl, helping her to become comfortable with the horses. Obviously Elizabeth had understood Molly's feelings and known how to make her feel needed. His daughter blossomed with Elizabeth's attention.

Maybe he needed to reconsider his stance about adding a woman to his family.

"I LIKE BEING your assistant like Lucy and Gianna," Molly said, smiling up at Elizabeth.

"I like having you as my assistant. You're doing such a good job," Elizabeth said.

"I tried to do my hair the way you combed it the other day, but I couldn't. And the little braids came out. So I had to do it the old way."

"If it's okay with your father I can comb your hair after camp today."

"Why wouldn't it be okay with Daddy? He never says anything about my hair."

Elizabeth didn't want to mention the discussion that she and Jake had had the other day about Molly's nails, so she hedged. "I know. But he may be busy with the ranch after club ends. We want to be considerate."

"I get it now. I suppose we have to talk to Daddy about it," Molly said. "Can you do it? He won't say no if you ask."

Elizabeth wasn't so sure about that, but when she glanced down at Molly's hopeful face, she couldn't do anything but agree. "Sure."

"And when is spa day? Some of my nails are starting to chip. I saw Emma and Jessie in town the other day, and

I showed them my nails. They liked them so much. They wanted to know if you could do their nails too, but I told them no. It was only for me and Lucy and Gianna. I told them they needed to ask their own moms."

Their own moms. Was Molly starting to view Elizabeth as a surrogate mother? Or had Elizabeth read too much into that comment? After all, given that Emma and Jessie had mothers, that was a true statement. "We'll talk to your father about doing your hair and nails. Maybe we can show him the designs before we do them. Just to get his opinion."

Molly's nose wrinkled, but she didn't say anything.

Elizabeth patted her shoulder. "Well, let's get back to work. There are lots of campers depending on us to show them what to do."

In addition to teaching the kids about horses and giving them short rides around the arena, Elizabeth talked about her life on the rodeo. There were lots of questions, and she happily answered all of them. By the time the day ended, she was talked out. The campers moaned and groaned when she announced that parents had arrived, but she reminded them that they would be meeting again in two days.

Although Jake was sitting on the bleachers as he had throughout the session, Molly didn't go over to him. Instead she hung by Elizabeth's side, playing with Gianna and Lucy. Once everyone was gone—including Faith, Tori, and Amy, who'd waved and indicated they would call her later—Elizabeth led the girls over to where Jake sat with his sons.

He stood up as they drew near. Gianna and Lucy ran over, and Gianna grabbed one of Jake's legs. "Can you carry me on your shoulders again? And Lucy too?"

"Wait a minute," Elizabeth said. "Did you even say hi before you asked for a favor?"

"Oops. Hi, Jake. Do you want to carry me on your shoulders?"

Jake gave Gianna a lopsided grin that made Elizabeth's stomach tumble. "Of course I would like to give each of you a ride. Who wouldn't?"

Gianna shrugged.

"Elizabeth wants to ask you something," Molly said.

"Is that right? Well, I'm all ears."

Pete burst into laughter. "That would be funny. You wouldn't have any hands or legs if you were all ears."

Ben gave his brother a quizzical look before walking over to Elizabeth and grabbing her hand. He gave her a snaggletoothed smile. This sweet little boy was finding his way into her heart. "Hi, Elizabeth. Club was fun. We should do it every day."

"Ben," Molly said sharply, "Elizabeth was trying to talk to Daddy."

"Sorry," he said, his smile just as wide as before. Clearly nothing bothered him.

"Is it something you want me to ask in private?" Elizabeth asked Molly. "Or can everyone hear?"

"It's not a secret," Molly said. "I don't care who hears."

"In that case… Jake, would it be okay if I combed Molly's hair in a different style? I have a couple of ideas that she might like."

His brow wrinkled in confusion as if unsure why she was asking him this question. Then his face cleared as he must have recalled their previous conversation. "Of course. That would be fine."

"And Elizabeth wants to show you how she wants to do my nails on spa day. I told her you don't know anything about fingernail polish, but she still wants you to see the design. To be considerate."

Regret was visible on Jake's face, and Elizabeth realized that he had actually meant it when he'd apologized. He hadn't simply been trying to get past an unpleasant moment. That raised him a few notches in her book.

"Molly is right," he said. "I don't know much about nails. Do whatever you think would be best."

Elizabeth smiled. "I have so many ideas for our next spa day."

"Why don't we get to come to your house like Molly does?" Ben asked.

"I'm working," Molly pointed out. "Besides, you're a boy. We're doing girl stuff."

"Can you guys come over to our house?" he asked. "That way we can do regular kid stuff."

"Yeah. I want to play in the tree house and on the swings," Gianna said.

"Me too," Lucy chimed in.

"You can come over today, right, Dad?" Pete said. "We aren't doing anything fun."

"Maybe Elizabeth and the girls have plans."

"No, we don't," Lucy said. "We can come over today, right, Mummy?"

Elizabeth glanced hopelessly at Jake, then looked at her daughters. "It's not polite to invite yourself to someone else's house."

"I didn't," Gianna said. "Pete invited us."

"So he did. In that case, if it's okay with Jake, it's okay with me."

"Say yes, Daddy," Molly said, and the other kids added their pleas.

"Sure. I can throw something on the grill again."

"I feel as if I should add something. Fruit salad or some kind of dessert."

Jake shook his head. "That's not necessary. Your company will be enough."

"Are you sure?" Elizabeth asked.

"Positive. If it makes you feel better, you can cook next time."

For five kids? "Or I'll get takeaway."

Once the kids decided they wanted a "girl car" and a "boy car," they ran outside to the vehicles and piled in. Elizabeth had a vague idea of how to get to his ranch, but she felt more comfortable following his lead.

The girls whispered to each other on the ride, talking too quietly for Elizabeth to catch more than a word or two every now and again. Not that she tried. How much mischief could three little girls dream up, especially when two of them were only five?

Elizabeth let her mind wander as she drove. Naturally it found its way to Jake. He was beginning to occupy her thoughts more frequently, popping into her mind seemingly at will and at the most inopportune times. One minute she would be concentrating on the task at hand and the next she would find herself smiling, thinking of something he'd said. Or the way he moved. He didn't so much walk as he sauntered. She couldn't count the number of times she remembered admiring the perfect way his shirt fit his muscular chest and shoulders. She'd spent way too much time imagining how good it would feel to be wrapped in his strong arms. How heavenly it would feel to be kissed by him.

Elizabeth felt her temperature rise, and she fanned herself with her free hand. She shouldn't be thinking this way about Jake, especially while driving. Truth be told, she shouldn't be fantasizing about making out with him at any time. She had two daughters to raise and major decisions to make. The last thing she needed was to add a further complication to the mix. She should be trying to clarify her thinking, not muddying up the water.

Even with the self-discipline she'd developed from her years on the rodeo circuit she didn't have the power to keep from daydreaming about Jake. As her sisters had so aptly pointed out, she was a living and breathing, flesh and blood woman. The desires and needs that had been dormant for the past two years were awake and demanding attention. She was relieved to no longer be numb, but she would prefer her feelings come on gradually and not hot and heavy as they were doing. But you couldn't always get what you wanted.

Jake signaled and turned into his driveway, so she did the same. They parked, and the kids scrambled from the cars. Talking as if they hadn't seen each other in ages, they ran to the porch. Then they turned away from the front door.

"We're going to play on the swings," Molly announced. As one, the kids raced back down the stairs and around the house to the backyard. Their happy laughter floated to the front of the house.

"I like that sound," Elizabeth said to Jake.

"So do I." He unlocked the front door, and they went inside and headed straight for the kitchen.

"My girls have changed a lot since they've gotten to know your children."

"I hope the change is positive."

"It is. I think they're becoming who they would have been if they hadn't lost Arlo. They're more carefree. Lucy isn't as quiet as she'd become. I love to see it."

"Maybe that's a sign that you should move to the States."

"I don't believe in signs," Elizabeth said.

"What do you believe in?" he asked.

"Oh. That's a good question." She paused. "I believe in facts. I believe that hard work pays off."

"I can agree with that." He opened the freezer and pulled out a box of frozen burgers and a couple packages of hot dogs.

"I hope we haven't put you in a bad position."

"You haven't," Jake said.

"If you have the ingredients, I could make potato salad. That is, if your kids eat it."

"They aren't picky. I haven't had potato salad in longer than I can recall, so I would love some."

They gathered the ingredients, then Elizabeth set the potatoes in a pot of water to boil. While the potatoes cooked, she chopped an onion. At the same time, Jake prepped the meat for the grill. The kitchen was spacious, yet on more than one occasion she found herself close enough to Jake to touch. Although she managed to resist the temptation, she wasn't above breathing in his scent whenever he was near. He smelled so good. Like clean male and fresh air. It was enough to weaken her knees.

"Let's sit outside while the potatoes boil," Jake said.

"That sounds good to me," Elizabeth said, following him to the patio and then taking a seat at the table. She leaned back and then glanced over to where the kids were playing. It was a relief to know there was another adult looking out for her daughters. Jake could be thinking the same thing right now about his kids. Two adults were definitely better than one.

"We work well together," Jake said, saying what she'd just thought.

"We do."

"I think we might play together well too."

She glanced over at him. He was looking at her, a gleam

in his eyes and a smile tugging on his lips. She leaned onto her hand. "Do tell."

His eyes widened as he realized how suggestive his words might have sounded. "That didn't come out quite right."

"Then say what you meant."

"I think it would be fun to go on a date. Just the two of us. We can go to dinner. Or a movie. Or both. You could bring Gianna and Lucy over here, and I could get my sister to babysit."

"That sounds nice," Elizabeth said. "But I can get one of my sisters to keep Gianna and Lucy. We wouldn't want to overwhelm Bethany with five kids. Besides, my sisters are always telling me that they want to spend more time with my girls. I think this is part of their plan to convince me to stay in Montana."

"In that case, definitely call one of them."

"I guess I don't have to ask where you stand on my dilemma."

"Is it a dilemma?" Jake asked. He sobered, setting all joking aside for the moment.

"Maybe *dilemma* isn't the right word. But it is a big decision. I don't want to make the wrong one."

"Instead of thinking in terms of right and wrong, why not think of it a different way?"

"If you know another way, please let me know."

"How about looking at it as a now and later decision?" he said. "Look at it as a question of what you do now. Remember, it's not an unchangeable decision. If you decide to stay and it doesn't turn out the way you want, you can always go back. And vice versa."

She shook her head. Why hadn't it occurred to her to look at it this way? All her life she'd been accused of making mountains out of molehills. Making problems bigger than they actually were. Yes, deciding whether to move to the States or go back home to Australia was a big decision, but it wasn't etched in stone. She could reverse course if warranted.

"No?" Jake asked. "You can't see it that way?"

"What? No. It makes perfect sense."

"Really? You were shaking your head as if you disagreed."

Elizabeth laughed. "I was shaking my head because it's so simple. I don't know why I didn't think of it."

"You're too close to the situation to see it clearly. I'm an outsider, so I have a different perspective."

"Well, thank you for your advice. I'm feeling relieved."

"Keep me around and I'll give you all kinds of good advice."

Elizabeth smiled. Keeping him around was tempting. And not just for his advice. She liked the way he made her feel.

"So are you up for a date?" Jake asked.

"Yes. Just tell me where and when."

"The *when* is easy. How about Saturday night? That is the traditional date night. Unless the babysitters are busy."

"I'll check with my sisters and get back to you."

"Good enough. We have the *when* covered. Now about the *where*."

"I'm easy."

"There are a lot of good places to eat in town," Jake said. "If it's okay with you, I would prefer to avoid the family restaurants and go somewhere a little more upscale."

"It's more than okay. I would prefer an adult-only location," she said.

"In that case, I'll make reservations at Coeur de l'Ouest."

"Ooh-la-la. French name. I take it that's one of Bronco's best?"

"It's the fanciest one in town. I'm sure you'll enjoy it."

"It sounds wonderful. I don't get to dress up often. I miss it."

Jake leaned in close and whispered, "Keep this under your hat, but there are times I actually enjoy wearing a suit and tie."

She pretended to lock her lips. "Your secret is safe with me."

CHAPTER NINE

"YOU LOOK SO PRETTY, Mummy," Lucy said on Saturday night.

"Thank you." Elizabeth bent over and kissed her daughter's cheek. When she'd packed for this vacation, she'd included two of her favorite dresses even though she hadn't believed she would have the opportunity to wear either of them. Happily she'd been wrong. Tonight she'd had a momentary debate, trying to decide between the little black number that hit her mid-thigh and the red one-shoulder pencil dress. The girls had seen the dresses lying on her bed and immediately cast their votes in favor of the red one.

"I don't know why we can't come on the date," Gianna said, poking out her bottom lip. "We like Jake."

"And he likes you too. But Aunt Faith has brought pizza for you. You're going to have lots of fun."

"Can we have a lamington for dessert?" Lucy asked.

"Yes."

"I guess that's okay," Gianna said slowly.

Elizabeth and Faith exchanged smiles at the twins and their long-suffering attitude. Elizabeth had no doubt the girls would be perfectly content eating their dinner and watching a movie with Faith.

There was a knock on the front door, and her heart skipped a beat. She'd been expecting Jake, so there was no reason her pulse should be racing. No reason she should suddenly be hoping that he liked red.

"I'll get the door," Faith said.

"Thanks," Elizabeth said, taking the opportunity to check her appearance in the mirror before following her sister out of the bedroom.

Faith greeted Jake and welcomed him into the house. His deep voice floated across the air, reaching Elizabeth as she stepped into the main room. She took one look at Jake and smiled. He was attractive in jeans and shirts—even that blindingly bright T-shirt he'd worn the other day—but dressed in a navy suit, light blue shirt and red tie, he was positively dashing.

"Hello," she said, pleased that she'd managed to keep the breathlessness from her voice.

"Hi." Jake crossed the room and placed a kiss on her cheek. The contact was brief and totally appropriate, yet her response was anything but. Her heart skipped a beat and her stomach flip-flopped. Out of nowhere she pictured herself grabbing him by the lapels and laying a hot kiss on him. That was just for starters.

Oblivious to her thoughts, he held out a bouquet of pink roses. "These are for you."

"Thank you."

"Hi, Jake," Gianna said, coming to stand beside him. "Why can't me and Lucy go to dinner with you and Mummy?"

Before Elizabeth could remind Gianna that they had already discussed this, Jake replied. "Because this is an adults-only date. Just like you and Molly have your play-dates. I don't get to come to those."

"But we didn't tell you to stay home," Gianna pointed out. "You can come next time."

Jake chuckled. "Molly might not agree. She likes it being just you and her. Besides, your mother and I want to talk about grown-up stuff."

"Is Molly going?" Lucy asked.

"No. She's at home with her brothers. Her aunt is babysitting them."

"Aunt Faith brought us pizza. And Mummy made lamingtons for dessert."

"What are lamingtons?"

"You don't know what that is?" Gianna asked, her voice soaked with disbelief.

Jake shrugged. "I guess not."

"I'll tell Jake all about them later," Elizabeth said. "We need to get going. Can I have a hug goodbye?"

"Yes," the girls said, rushing over to her.

Elizabeth stooped down and hugged each of her daughters, holding them close before letting them go. To her surprise, they went over to Jake and held out their arms to him. He hesitated for a second, as if touched by their actions, before squatting down and giving them each a tight hug. He rose, a smile on his lips.

"Bye, Mummy. Bye, Jake," the girls said and raced into the kitchen.

"Have fun, you two," Faith said. "Stay out as late as you want. We'll be fine."

"Thanks," Elizabeth said and then turned to Jake. "I'm ready when you are."

He held out his arm, and she took it. Elizabeth had seen Jake's muscles, but even so she was surprised by the strength of his biceps. Tingles shot from her fingers, tripping up her arms to her spine where they danced merrily up and down. It had been years since she'd felt anything remotely like this, and she knew she was in trouble. She'd never been able to separate the physical from the emotional—had never wanted to—and now she was afraid. Sexual attraction was bad enough. Falling in love with Jake could be the worst thing to happen to her right now.

But she was worrying for nothing. Her heart was a long way from getting involved with him.

They stepped outside, and he led her to a sedan. Her confusion must have shown on her face because he smiled and explained. "I don't always drive a truck or SUV. I keep this car in the garage for special occasions. The kids don't ride in it, so it's clean."

He opened the passenger door for her, and she sat down. Once she was settled, he closed her door, circled the vehicle and got inside beside her. His broad shoulders brushed against hers, and the car suddenly felt intimate. She was worried for a bit that things might be awkward between them. After all, this was their first time alone without the kids as a buffer. What if they didn't have anything to talk about?

"Would you like to listen to music?" he asked, his hand hovering over the radio knob.

"I wouldn't mind," Elizabeth said. "So long as it isn't the Wiggles. We saw them in concert last year, and the girls haven't stopped talking about it yet."

"You think that's bad? Wait until they become preteens and discover boy bands. You'll long for these days."

"I take it Molly has reached that age."

"She's only easing into it, so she's not listening to the music nonstop. But I don't know how much longer my luck will hold out. She'll be a teenager soon."

"I remember those years. Being a teenager was so dramatic. Everything was really intense. My feelings were so big." Elizabeth laughed as she recalled her early teen years. "I don't know how my parents survived."

"I can't imagine you being an overwrought teen."

"Believe it." She breathed a sigh of relief as she realized she'd worried about nothing. It was easy being alone with him. She turned in her seat and looked at him, momentarily struck by his strong profile. "I wasn't just moody. I was artistic and moody, which is…shall we say, an interesting combination. I actually sat in my room and wrote some really bad poetry. I even put a couple of them to music and strummed along on my guitar."

He laughed, a rich sound that made goose bumps rise on her arms. Talk about dramatic. Apparently some things hadn't changed with time. "Were these poems about boys?"

"Do you even need to ask? There's something about unrequited love that inspired the creative part of me."

"You wouldn't by chance have recorded any of those songs."

"I did," she said. "But thankfully those recordings no longer exist."

"That's too bad. I would love to hear one. You know, to better understand the kind of music you wrote."

"I don't remember any of the songs, but I can set the mood for you. Picture a girl with long braids dressed in a rainbow T-shirt, cutoff denims, and cowboy boots sitting on her bed. Got it?"

"Yep."

"Now imagine her playing a guitar, singing overwrought and cheesy lyrics featuring words like *broken heart* and *new start*, *crying* and *sighing*. *Pain* and *insane*."

"Please tell me those words weren't part of the actual lyrics." His lips twitched, and she could tell that he was trying to hold back his laughter.

"I was young. And intensely emotional."

"That's a word for it," he said, grinning.

"Don't tell me that you skipped that phase where you felt every emotion deeply. Where you didn't just fall in love, you wallowed in it."

"I thought I hadn't, but now that I know people actually

wrote odes about their feelings, I have my doubts. Maybe I missed that part of my development."

"It's not too late," Elizabeth told him. "You can still write poetry."

"I don't think I can rhyme as well as you did."

"There's always free verse."

He gave her a goofy grin. "Has verse been arrested?"

That dad joke was only slightly funny, but Elizabeth couldn't stop the chuckle that burst from her. "That was really terrible. You definitely don't have what it takes to write poetry."

"You're saying I'm not cool enough?"

"And probably not enough angst."

Their laughter mingled.

"How else did you express your emotions?" Jake asked. "Or do I want to know?"

"That was about the most creative. Of course, I did the requisite scribbling of the boy of my dream's name on the cover of my notebook. And practicing writing *Mr. and Mrs.* whoever it was I loved at the time."

"I did the same thing for my crush," Jake said. "I nearly failed world history because instead of taking notes, I was jotting down Sandy's name. Oh, and drawing her portrait."

"So you were an artist?"

"Not really. Hers was the only picture I drew. To be honest, it didn't look a thing like her."

"What happened to Sandy?"

He shrugged. "I have no idea. One day I looked at her and—poof—the attraction was gone. There was no zing. She went from being special to ordinary overnight."

"I know. What's that about? You go from thinking you'll absolutely die if you don't see that person to looking at them and feeling…nothing."

"Ah, true love ran its course."

Elizabeth nodded. "Funny how that works out."

"Yeah. Until the real thing comes along. Then you know you will never be the same." His voice was wistful and a bit sad.

They reached the restaurant, and Jake pulled up to the valet, exchanged his key for a ticket, and led Elizabeth inside. She looked around. The decor was exquisite. Enormous crystal chandeliers dangled from the high ceiling, casting refracted light around the room. The candlelight flickering on the pristine white tablecloths and over silver cushioned chairs set the perfect ambience.

She smiled. "You weren't kidding when you said this restaurant was fancy. It's positively beautiful."

"This is nothing. Wait until you taste the food. It's even better than the dining room looks."

"I know I'm going to enjoy myself."

Jake gave his name to the maître d', who checked his tablet and then led them through the dining room to a table beside the window. There wasn't a bad table in the restaurant, but Elizabeth was pleased to have a view of the mountains. After sitting in the plush chair, she stared out the window at the snowcapped peaks. There was no denying that Bronco was scenic.

When they'd first arrived in town, the girls had commented on how different the United States looked when compared to Australia. After a week, they'd stopped complaining about the differences, but that didn't mean they'd stopped noticing them. She knew children could be flexible at times, but she didn't want to lean on their ability to adjust any more than necessary. She didn't want to make their lives more difficult than they had to be. For a while she'd feared that was what she'd done by coming to America. But after meeting Jake's kids, Lucy and Gianna seemed so much happier here in Bronco. They were finally making themselves at home, which was a great relief.

"What's good?" Elizabeth asked, turning her mind back to the present.

Jake's brow furrowed. "I suppose I should have mentioned this before. They have a fixed menu."

"Oh."

"I hope that's okay."

"It's fine," she said and then smiled. "That takes away some of the decisions."

"I take it that you're tired of making those."

"You could say that."

"The server has a menu with tonight's meal if you want to look at it."

She shook her head. "No. I love surprises. I'll look at this as adventure eating." The aromas filling the air were tantalizing, and she knew she would enjoy whatever was served.

"You are so easygoing. I love that about you." His mouth fell open as if he realized what he'd said. A hint of panic surrounded him as if he feared that she might take his words out of context. He needn't have worried. She understood what he meant.

"Right back at you," she said, injecting her words with lightness, hoping to put him at ease again. This was too nice a night to ruin. She might not be looking for love, but she wasn't immune to his appeal—and he had appeal to spare. It was everything from his gorgeous face to his well-defined chest to his muscular thighs. Suddenly she felt warm all over. She lifted her glass of ice water and took a long sip. The water was cold enough to make her teeth chatter, but it did little to douse the flames inside her. Her mind might know that she wasn't interested in a romance, but her body was rejecting the message.

Elizabeth leaned her chin into her palm and looked at Jake. "Tell me more about yourself."

"What do you want to know?"

"Whatever you want to tell me. You told me your parents live in town now. Did you grow up in Bronco or move here later? What do you like about the town? What do you like about being a rancher? Give me your best sales pitch."

He laughed, and the sound made her stomach do a ridiculous little flip-flop. "So you want me to sell you on Bronco."

She shrugged. "I'm looking to add to my knowledge so I can make an informed decision. I've lived in Australia for a decade, so I know pretty much everything I need to know about Queensland. But it's been a while since I've lived in America. And I've never lived in Bronco. All told, I don't think I spent more than a week in Montana, so my knowledge is limited."

He rubbed his hands together and grinned. "Then sit back and prepare to be wowed."

"I'm all ears," she said and then laughed when she recalled Pete's bad joke. Clearly father and son shared the same sense of humor.

"Let me answer your first question. I did grow up in Bronco Valley."

"I keep hearing people talk about Bronco Heights or Valley, but I'm not sure what the difference is. Maybe you can explain it to me."

He tapped his fingertips together and her eyes were immediately drawn to his long, lean fingers. They were tanned and she noticed a couple of nicks on his knuckles. Suddenly she imagined his fingers caressing her body.

"Bronco is really two towns," he explained, pulling her attention back to his words. "Bronco Heights is where the wealthier people live. You know, big houses on big lots.

Bronco Valley is home to the middle class. There may be a big difference in bank accounts, but the people in the Valley and the Heights generally get along well together."

"So there aren't cliques."

"I didn't say that. People may associate with some of their neighbors and not others. They have their friend groups. But those groups aren't defined by wealth or neighborhood. Nor are they opposed to other groups. They're based on shared interests."

She nodded slowly. "That's good to know."

"Is that a plus for the town?"

"If I'm keeping score, then yes," she said. "But it's the same way back home, so that doesn't give Bronco an edge."

He rubbed his chin. "Oh. You're a tough sell."

"Surely you want to earn your win. You don't want me to just give it to you, do you?"

"I don't know who told you that. I'll take victory any way I can get it."

"So, no oversize male ego for you?"

"I have three children. Two of them are boys. They make fun of me like it's their job. It's hilarious to them. In case you haven't noticed, they're brutal. They don't hold anything back. If I didn't have thick skin, I'd be in tears every day. You can't have an ego of any size and be a parent of boys."

Elizabeth laughed. "That is so true. Even with girls. Gianna and Lucy love me with their whole hearts, but they are still at an age when they haven't learned diplomacy. Trust me, I know when my hairstyle doesn't *accentuate the positives*, should I say. And I know when I've eaten too many onions because my breath stinks."

He laughed with her and then continued, "Back to my sales pitch. You already know about the restaurants that we have."

"Yes. I've eaten at a couple. They were good."

"I don't suppose I'll get points for mentioning the rodeos we have."

"Considering that my family competes in them and that I might as well?" She shrugged. "Maybe. It has been quite a while since I've seen my sisters and cousins compete. It would be interesting to participate with them."

"Oh. An unexpected point," he said, one side of his mouth lifting in a sexy grin. "I'll take that."

She held up a finger to stop him from gloating. "Of course, Carly and I often compete in the same rodeos back home, so there is no advantage here."

"Sure there is. You only have one sister in Queensland, but you have three sisters and several cousins here. Bronco has numbers."

She nodded. "I'll give you that one."

The server brought their meals, and they stopped talking long enough to sample everything. Elizabeth closed her eyes, and a hum slipped through her lips.

"Well?" Jake asked.

She opened her eyes and looked directly at him. "You already know the answer. It is absolutely delicious. Probably the best thing I've ever eaten in my life."

"Another point for Bronco."

"Oh, yes. I wasn't even thinking of that."

"You might not be keeping score, but I am."

Elizabeth laughed. Although she would never admit it, Jake's presence was a point in Bronco's favor. No man in Australia appealed to her, and she didn't expect one ever would. Of course, she hadn't expected to meet anyone here either. Despite her intentions to avoid romantic entanglements, she was drawn to Jake. The feeling of disloyalty was fading, but it wasn't entirely gone. It still had a hold on her emotions, although it was losing its grip. At some point she would have to overcome that feeling, whether or not she and Jake decided to have a relationship. If only she knew the way to get rid of it.

"I'll keep that in mind," she said.

As they ate, they talked about everything under the sun. Jake was quite amusing, even with his corny dad jokes, and Elizabeth laughed more than she had in years. He regaled her with stories of growing up with a sister. They had been good friends even back then, but often had blowout disagreements. Luckily neither of them held a grudge and they had maintained their closeness.

The meal was spectacular, and each bite was even tastier than the one that preceded it. The flavors were layered and complemented each other. Although Elizabeth wasn't much of a foodie, she appreciated the way each course had been designed to build upon the previous ones. But as magnificent as the meal was, it came in a distant second to Jake.

When the server set the dessert in front of her, Elizabeth sighed. "I can't believe this delicious dinner is coming to an end."

"It has been good."

Elizabeth tasted her cake. "This is so good. A fitting end to a wonderful meal."

"Speaking of dessert. What is a lamington?"

"It's one of the most popular Australian desserts. Basically it's a little bit of heaven."

"Can you bring it down to earth for those of us who haven't been to Australia to enjoy one?"

"Yes. Sorry. It's a square of sponge cake coated in chocolate sauce and rolled in coconut. The girls love them. It can be a bit messy to make, but it's worth it."

"It sounds good."

"It's better than good. I'll make some for you and the kids. Then you'll be hooked."

He nodded. "I can get with that."

"You've cooked for me and the girls a couple of times. How about I make an authentic Australian meal for you and your kids?"

"I think they'll love it. I know I will."

"When is a good time?" she asked.

"As soon as you want. Tomorrow. The next day. We eat dinner all the time. Practically every day."

She rolled her eyes. His dad jokes had gotten worse throughout the meal, yet they amused her to no end.

"Do you want us to come out to the cabin, or would you rather use my kitchen? That way the twins could play on the swings and in the tree house."

"That would be nice. Your kitchen is bigger and your table seats more people. We'll be more comfortable there."

"Then it's a date. How about Monday?"

She nodded. "That sounds good."

They finished their dessert, and Jake paid the bill. "Are you up for a walk before we head back to the cabin? It's such a nice night."

She nodded. "I'm enjoying myself immensely, so yes."

The night was slightly cool but still pleasant. There were very few streetlights out this way, and the darkness cloaked them in intimacy. Elizabeth paused, then turned in a slow circle. "I love looking at the sky here. It's so deep and dark. The moon and stars seem so much brighter."

"One more point for Bronco," Jake said.

"I can't believe you're still keeping score."

"I told you, I'm in it to win it."

"You're determined, I'll give you that."

"When the prize is getting you to stay in town, most definitely."

Elizabeth's heart skipped a beat. It had been a while

since a man had gone out of his way to win her over. Jake was definitely giving it his all.

He reached out and took her hand into his. His palm was callused, evidence of hard work, but his touch was gentle. Electricity shot from her fingers throughout her body. Goose bumps popped up on her arms and she shivered.

"Cold?" Jake asked. Before she could answer, he released her hand and draped his arm around her shoulder. He pulled her close and the warmth from his body wrapped around hers.

Elizabeth drew in a breath, inhaling his intoxicating scent. Coherent thought fled and it was all she could do to put one foot in front of the other without stumbling.

They walked in silence for a few more minutes before they returned to the car. The ride to the cabin was relaxing, and they chatted companionably. As they got closer to the cabin, Elizabeth's anticipation grew. Her nerves jangled, and she wondered how the night would end. How would they say good-night? Would he kiss her?

Her desires were wreaking havoc on her emotions. She hadn't kissed a man other than Arlo since their first date nearly a decade ago. She hadn't wanted to. Now she was actually contemplating it. More than that, she wanted it.

Elizabeth was ready to admit that her attraction was more than physical. It was becoming emotional. Surprisingly, the admission came with only a small side of guilt. That was a step in the right direction. Another step and she'd consider the possibility of falling in love.

Not that she had decided that Jake was that man. There were so many things she needed to figure out, not the least of which was where she and the girls were going to live.

She looked up and realized that Jake was pulling up to the cabin. He turned off the engine. Instead of getting out of the car, he glanced over at her, a slight smile tugging on his lips. His eyes were filled with mischief. "So."

She looked back at him, waiting for him to say more. When he didn't, she echoed him. "So."

"I had a really great time."

"So did I."

"Good enough to do it again?"

"You mean go to dinner at Coeur de l'Ouest?" She knew that wasn't what he meant, but she needed a minute to gather her feelings.

He chuckled. "We can do that again, sure. But that's not exactly what I meant. I was talking about going on a date again."

"Are you talking about dating? Or going on a date?"

"I hadn't thought about it like that. But… I'd say dating. How do you feel about that?"

"I like the idea." Had she actually just said that? The answer had burst from her before she'd had the opportunity to mull it over. Perhaps that was for the best. After all, Jake had asked how she *felt*, not what she *thought*. She had enough going on in her brain without trying to crowd in more. Maybe going with her feelings was best in this instance.

"So do I." He nodded and then opened his door.

That was it? She wasn't certain of the kind of reaction she had been expecting, but that wasn't it.

He opened her door and held out his hand, helping her to get out. She took his hand, and sparks flared at the contact and her anticipation grew. Though her reaction was ridiculous, she had to admit that she liked the sensation. Jake was a man worthy of her attraction. He was a good father to his kids and was kind to her daughters. He showed Gianna and Lucy the same patience and concern he gave his children, yet somehow he managed not to overstep. That was a tight line to walk, and he traveled it quite well.

They reached the cabin and paused. The breeze blew, shaking the leaves on the trees and rattling the wind chimes. She inhaled, and her lungs were filled with the sweet fragrance of flowers. With a sky full of stars, the setting was incredibly romantic. The perfect place for a first kiss. She wanted it. Did Jake?

"I'm not exactly sure what to do now," Jake said, his soft voice breaking into her musing.

"Neither am I," she admitted.

"I want to kiss you, Elizabeth. But I'm worried about… well…messing up things between us."

His confession chased away her nervousness. The tension in her body vanished, and she relaxed. "There's only one way to find out."

A cocky grin flashed across his face a second before he reached out and pulled her into his arms. His head lowered and he pressed his lips against hers in a searing kiss. The electric shock that she'd experienced when they'd held hands was nothing compared to this. It was as if she'd touched a live wire with wet hands. Her entire body tingled from the top of her head to the toes of her feet. Even her hair seemed to vibrate with excitement. Being held against his hard, muscular body felt like heaven.

He deepened the kiss, and she opened her mouth to him. As he swept his tongue inside, her pleasure multiplied. Multiplied again. Elizabeth closed her eyes, allowing herself to enjoy sensations that she hadn't experienced in years. She knew she should pull back—this was a first kiss after all—but the feelings rocketing through her body felt too good and she didn't want to stop. And as Jake didn't seem inclined to end the kiss either, it went on and on.

Finally her mind regained control of her emotions, and

she pulled back. Kissing Jake had felt so good. She knew it would be easy to let the fire burning inside her turn into a raging inferno, sweeping her away.

But could that lead her even closer to the kind of complication she wanted to avoid?

CHAPTER TEN

JAKE FELT ELIZABETH easing away and forced himself to release her, reluctantly ending the kiss. It had been forever since he'd held a woman in his arms, an eternity since he'd experienced pleasure this intense. Despite the years that had passed, he still recognized when a woman wanted to slow things down. Though he was loath to admit it, that was a good plan for now. This was their first kiss. He hoped it wasn't their last—he would be ready for the second one to start soon—but he knew they needed to keep their wits about them. After all, there were other people to consider. Their children had each lost a parent. If he and Elizabeth decided to pursue a relationship, they needed to be sure that it would last so their kids didn't get hurt. They had to be sure they were making wise decisions. Thinking clearly would be harder to do under the haze of lust.

Leaning his forehead against hers, Jake breathed out a long sigh. There was no reason to hide his feelings. They were probably obvious to Elizabeth. "That was some kiss."

"Yes it was." Although her face was hidden in the shadows, he heard the smile in her voice. That husky tone made him want to pull her back into his arms for their second kiss, but he resisted. Hopefully there would be time for that again in the near future.

"So." He dragged the word out over several syllables. "I suppose we should say good-night now."

She nodded and unlocked the front door. She stepped inside and then turned and looked at him. "Coming in?"

It was tempting. "I'd better get going. Bethany is waiting up for me."

"Okay."

"I'll call you tomorrow."

"I'll look forward to it."

Jake waited until Elizabeth closed the door behind her before getting into his car and driving away. Thankfully traffic was light, and he made good time. As he drove, he replayed the date in his mind, recalling every detail. Every move Elizabeth made, every smile she turned in his direction was etched in his memory. The sound of her laughter had illuminated the dark spot in his heart that had developed over the years. As the night had progressed, he realized that spot had faded into nothingness.

Just looking at her had been pure joy. Her red dress had fit her body so perfectly it must have been made for her. It had clung to her body, caressing her curves and leaving nothing to the imagination. In her heels, her shapely legs seemed to go on forever. Jake didn't like to use the word *perfect* to describe a person because he knew that everyone had flaws. Even so, Elizabeth was as close to perfect as a person could get.

Although he generally drove in silence, he'd left on the radio. A pop song he remembered from his high school days started to play, and he hummed along. That song was followed by another familiar one. He turned up the volume and tapped the beat on the steering wheel. By the time he pulled into the garage and got out of the car, he was singing. When he realized what he was doing, he nearly tripped. He couldn't recall the last time he'd hummed, much less sung. Apparently Elizabeth brought music back to his life.

His singing turned into laughter, echoing around the vast backyard. That had to be the corniest thing he'd ever thought. Yet it was true. Elizabeth made him so happy that he was singing out loud.

He unlocked the back door and stepped inside. It was way past the kids' bedtime, but that never mattered to Bethany. Whenever she babysat, she let them stay up as long as they wanted, which meant he usually found them sprawled on the living room floor, fighting sleep.

Jake was surprised to find Bethany alone on the couch, reading a mystery. The television was on, but the volume was turned down so low she couldn't possibly hear it.

"Hey," she said, looking up. She used a bookmark to save her place and then set the book on the table beside her. "How was your date? Tell me everything."

He inhaled and then smiled. He and Bethany hadn't talked about their dates since they were in their teens. For him, there hadn't been much to talk about until he and Maggie had started going out. "I'm kind of beat. I think I'd rather go right to bed."

"Really?" She sounded disappointed.

He couldn't keep a straight face any longer and felt himself grinning. "No way. I find myself in a talkative mood."

She picked up her paperback and tossed it in his direction. Laughing, he caught it and set it on the coffee table.

"You know I'm going to pay you back for that, Jake."

"When I least expect it, I'll expect it," he said, parroting the familiar threat they said to each other as kids. Of course, they'd very rarely followed up on it. "Where are the kids?"

"In bed asleep, where they've been since bedtime."

"Really? Generally you ignore that rule."

She shrugged. "I had a bit of a headache and needed some quiet."

"Why didn't you say something? How are you feeling now? Can I get you an aspirin?" He leaned in closer and studied her. "You do look a little green around the gills."

"I was a little queasy, but I'm fine now. And don't try to change the subject." She patted the cushion next to her. "Sit down and tell me everything."

"Are you sure you don't need some ginger ale or maybe some tea?"

She picked up a glass from the table beside her, then gestured to the half-eaten sleeve of saltines. "I have everything I need. Tell me about your date. And don't leave out a single detail."

"In that case…" He sat down and cleared his throat dramatically. "I had a great time. Dinner was perfect. The restaurant had wonderful ambiance. The view was second to none. The food was delicious, and the service was impeccable."

"I see." Bethany smiled and then turned in her seat so that she was looking at him. "Okay. Now get to the juicy parts. Did you kiss her good-night?"

"Are you kidding me? You want to jump to the end of the evening? Don't you want to know what we talked about?"

"Later. But first…" She wound her hand in a circle. "The kiss?"

He felt himself smiling as he remembered the sensation that had rocketed through him as their lips had touched. Describing the feeling as *electric* was underselling it by half. But he didn't have a good enough vocabulary to do it justice. Even an hour later his lips still tingled as if every nerve ending had been turned up to eleven. Nothing had ever felt as good. He couldn't wait to do it again.

"From the look on your face I'm going to go out on a limb and say the kiss was good."

"Better than good. It was like nothing of this world." He heaved out a sigh. "I don't know how to describe it to you."

She laughed and held her hands out in front of her as if trying to stop the words from coming out of his mouth. "That's okay. I want details, but not *those* details. Just knowing that she rocked your world is enough."

"Are you sure? Because I can be more specific," he said. When Bethany covered her ears and began to hum, Jake laughed. "I guess you don't want the blow-by-blow."

"Let's rewind back to the beginning of the date. What was Elizabeth wearing?"

He closed his eyes, and Elizabeth's image appeared in front of him. Beads of sweat popped out on his brow as his temperature rose at the memory. "She had on a red dress that fit her like a second skin. Well, maybe not that tight, but it was really sexy."

"I get the picture. She looked good."

"Let's just say that red is now my favorite color."

She shook her head and laughed. "You are so predictable."

"I get the feeling that's not good."

"It is good," Bethany said quickly. "I just bet that whatever color she wears on your next date will become your new favorite color."

"I fail to see the problem with that."

"There isn't one." Her smile faded and her expression grew serious. "It does my heart good to see you this way."

"What way?"

"Happy. Playful. You always put on a good front for the kids, but I still can see the sadness in you. It's diminished over the years, but there was always a hint of it. Like a shadow. No, like a ghost hovering around you. It's not here tonight. You seem truly happy."

"I am." Jake heard his words and realized he was telling the truth. He actually felt happy inside. The smile wasn't for Bethany. He wasn't being jolly in order to keep the kids happy. He wasn't faking it until he could make it. He had made it to the other side of his grieving. It had taken a while, maybe longer than it should have, but he was healed. More than that, he was ready to take a chance on love again.

"HOW WAS TONIGHT?" Faith asked. She handed Elizabeth a glass of lemonade and then took a sip of her own.

Elizabeth leaned against the back of the sofa and placed her bare feet on the coffee table. She'd washed her face, brushed her hair, and changed into a pair of shorts and a T-shirt. She was completely relaxed and eager to relive the date with Faith. No doubt Tori and Amy would expect a recap tomorrow. She'd enjoyed herself so much that she relished the idea of talking about tonight as many times as possible.

"It was wonderful," Elizabeth said with a contented sigh. "It was the most fun I've had in years. Pure bliss."

"Pure bliss, eh?" her sister looked at her. "Tell me everything. Don't leave out a single thing."

Elizabeth launched into a detailed retelling of the evening. Faith nodded every now and again, but instead of it being a dialogue, it was more of a monologue.

"What do you think?" Elizabeth asked after she'd told her sister about everything, including that hot kiss. *Especially* that hot kiss.

"I think you sound happier than you have in years."

"But?" Although Faith hadn't said anything negative, Elizabeth sensed her sister had more to say. Faith generally spoke her mind, so this reticence was a surprise. "Don't feel like you have to hold back. I'm not fragile any longer. I won't break if you tell me what you're thinking."

"I'm not the right person to ask about romance. At least not now."

"Why? What's going on now?"

Faith sighed. "I'm not in the best frame of mind when it comes to relationships. I don't have a lot of warm feelings for men these days."

Elizabeth nodded. "I know things haven't worked out for you in the past. But I still believe there's a wonderful man waiting for you. He's probably just around the corner."

"You always were the optimist. I can't believe that after all you've been through that you still have that kind of faith and willingness to put yourself out there."

"Hold on. I think we're talking about two different things. I was hurt after Arlo died, but that didn't make me stop trusting men. My relationship with Arlo was the best thing that happened to me. Losing him was devastating. My reluctance to get involved has nothing to do with thinking someone will break my heart."

"I know. I like Jake. He seems like the real deal."

"I think so too. And I have a feeling that sooner rather than later the right man for you is going to come along and you're going to fall head over heels for him. He'll feel the same way about you."

Faith scoffed. "I'm not sure if that's a blessing or a curse. I thought you loved me."

"You know I love you. You also know I only want the best for you. And just to be clear, that was a blessing."

"Then I'll take your words in the spirit they were intended."

"Thank you."

Faith stood. "And on that note, I'm going to head home."

"You know you're welcome to stay the night here."

"I know, but I'll pass. It would be a bit tight."

"We could have a sleepover like we did in the old days. Those were always fun."

Faith laughed. "With you talking my ears off? I wouldn't get a bit of sleep all night."

"Probably not," Elizabeth admitted.

"Unlike when we were kids, I need my sleep."

"All right. If you're going to be all adult about it. Text me when you get home."

"Will do."

They walked to the door together. Elizabeth opened it and then turned to her sister. "Thanks again for watching the girls for me. I appreciate it."

Faith took her hand and gave it a squeeze. "It was my pleasure. I love every minute I get to spend with my nieces."

Elizabeth smiled. "I'm glad you're all getting to know each other."

Faith got into her car, waved, and then drove away. Once she could no longer see the taillights on her sister's car, Elizabeth closed the door and went to check on the girls. As usual, Gianna's thin blanket was twisted around her legs. Elizabeth straightened it and then brushed a kiss on her daughter's forehead. Lucy was half-in and half-out of her bed, so Elizabeth lifted her and placed her on the middle of the mattress. She kissed Lucy's forehead and then tiptoed from the room, closing the door behind her.

When she was in her own room, Elizabeth changed into her favorite cotton pajamas and hopped into the bed. She doubted that Jake would be sleeping, and before she could talk herself out of it, she grabbed her phone and shot off a quick text to him.

Just checking to see if you made it home okay.

That wasn't entirely true, but he didn't need to know that she couldn't stop thinking about him. Couldn't stop wishing she could be in his arms right now.

Jake's reply came immediately.

Yep. I've been here for a while. I'm waiting for my sister to text that she got home. I tried to get her to stay the night, but she preferred to sleep in her own bed.

Elizabeth read his text and smiled before she replied.

I'm glad I didn't wake you.

She wasn't sure what else to say. She hadn't reached out with any particular topic in mind. She'd just wanted to get in touch with him. No, it was more than that. She actually wanted to hear his voice. Her phone dinged, signaling a new text.

Do you feel like talking? That would be a lot better than texting.

She smiled, relieved they were on the same wavelength.

That sounds great.

A few seconds later her mobile phone rang, and she answered it before it could ring a second time.

"Jake?" Her voice sounded breathless, as if she'd been running as opposed to sitting in her bed.

"It's good to hear your voice. I was tempted to call you, but I didn't want to risk waking you up."

"I'm normally asleep at this time," she admitted, "but not tonight. Like you, I'm waiting for my sister to let me know when she's home."

There was a brief silence, but it wasn't uncomfortable. In fact, it was quite relaxing. It was nice not to feel compelled to fill the silence with conversation. Though they were in their separate homes she still felt connected with him.

Elizabeth often missed the activity and the excitement of being with Arlo. With the girls around, she was able to keep busy. Filling her day with activity kept the loneliness at bay. But in the quiet of the night when the girls were asleep, Elizabeth was alone with her thoughts. For a while she'd been consumed with sadness. Eventually that sorrow had faded into melancholy. Now even that was gone, leaving behind acceptance.

Tonight she was filled with contentment. Perhaps because she was sharing the night with Jake.

After a while they began to talk again. They didn't speak about anything of consequence, but they didn't need to. Keeping the connection alive was the important thing.

They talked for about twenty minutes before Jake sighed. "I suppose I should let you go to sleep. Would it be okay if I called you in the morning?"

"Of course. Are you still bringing Molly over tomorrow?"

"Yes. But I thought we could talk before then. That is, if you don't mind."

"I don't mind at all." She actually relished the idea of starting her day with an adult conversation. "Especially since I'll get to talk to you again."

"Then I'll talk to you in the morning."

After they said good-night, Elizabeth held her phone. Their relationship had shifted tonight.

She just hoped that she was ready for the changes that shift would bring.

CHAPTER ELEVEN

ELIZABETH GRABBED THE bags of groceries from the back seat, then headed for the steps. "Come on, girls."

"Why can't we just go in the backyard and get on the swings?" Gianna asked, looking over her shoulder. She was halfway between the car and the side of the house.

Lucy, standing beside her sister, nodded. "We want to play."

"Because we need to say hello first. We don't just go into someone's backyard and start playing. That's rude."

"But that's where everybody is," Gianna said. "Can't you hear them?"

Elizabeth nodded. The wind carried the children's laughter over to them. She knew Molly, Pete, and Ben would be glad to see the twins and would immediately welcome them into their game. They'd spent a lot of time together and now treated each other like old friends. Dare she say like family? Should she insist on standing on formality? Clearly her girls felt at home here.

"Fine, go on back. But be careful. And say hello before you start playing."

Those last words had been spoken to the air because the girls had run away the minute Elizabeth had given her approval. Shaking her head, Elizabeth climbed the stairs. Before she could ring the doorbell, she heard her name being called.

"Let me help you with that," Jake said, jogging around the porch and up the stairs.

"Thanks." Elizabeth handed over two of the three bags she'd been carrying.

"Am I holding the secret ingredients for an authentic Australian dinner?"

"I don't know how secret they are. I'm making some of the most popular foods from home, and the recipes are available everywhere. The girls were supposed to help me carry everything, but they abandoned me the second we got here."

"They love the swings. They hopped on the minute they stepped into the yard."

She shook her head. "I told them to say hello first."

Jake shrugged as they walked into the kitchen. "They did. All in one smooth motion."

"I suppose that's something."

"They're kids." He set the bag on the table and then pulled aside the curtain. "Look. They're having a great time."

Elizabeth set down her bag, then glanced through the window. Gianna and Ben were swinging and laughing as each tried to go higher than the other. Lucy was standing at the top of the ladder, waiting for Pete to slide so she could have her turn.

"Where's Molly?" Elizabeth asked.

"She was out there a minute ago."

The back door opened with a crash. Molly burst into the room. She was breathing hard as if she had just run across the enormous yard.

"Hi, Elizabeth. I didn't know you were here yet."

She turned and smiled at Molly. "We just got here."

"Daddy said you're going to cook some real Australian food for us. Can I help?"

"That would be wonderful."

"I can't wait to eat Australian food. All Daddy ever makes is boring regular food."

Jake laughed, clearly not at all bothered by having his food be dissed so spectacularly. But then, hadn't he already admitted that his kids were brutally honest, emphasis on *brutal*? "That's the only kind of food I know how to make."

"You should get some cookbooks so you can learn to make new foods," Molly said to him before turning back to Elizabeth, who managed to keep her amusement from showing on her face. "I told him that before, but he didn't listen to me."

"The food we'll be cooking is easy to make. But it's delicious. If everyone likes it, I'll write down the recipes so you can make it anytime you want."

"I know we're going to like it. We liked the biscuits a lot."

Elizabeth smiled at Molly's use of the Australian term. "Let's wash our hands and get started."

Molly and Elizabeth washed their hands at the kitchen sink. They stepped aside when they were finished, and Jake grabbed the soap.

Molly was wiping her hands on a paper towel. She stopped and looked at her father. "Why are you washing your hands? Elizabeth and I are the ones who are going to cook. Not you."

A look of disappointment flashed across his face before it was replaced by a smile that didn't quite reach his eyes. "I thought I might stick around and help. That way I will know how to make it later."

"Elizabeth said she would write it down. Plus, I'll know how to make it."

"Molly, you might not always want to cook," Elizabeth said. She didn't want this to turn into a battle. The day was supposed to be fun. More than that, it hurt her heart to see Jake so disappointed. Elizabeth knew Molly didn't mean to be cruel. She loved her father too much to deliberately hurt him. She just had her own idea of how the day should go. "It will be good if your father knows how to cook these dishes too."

Molly frowned, clearly not happy with the turn of events. Jake could read her feelings too. "How about I go see what the others are doing?" he asked. "If you need my help, you can just call me."

"Okay. Bye," Molly said.

Elizabeth gave him a smile. Even though she had been looking forward to Jake's company, if he was giving his daughter this opportunity to learn how to make these dishes without him, Elizabeth certainly wasn't going to get in the way. Besides, she empathized with Molly. She probably didn't get many opportunities to have time alone with a woman. Elizabeth would never try to replace Molly's mother, but she could help when she could.

Molly watched her father walk out the door and then turned back to Elizabeth. Her face was glowing with excitement. "What are we making?"

"We're going to make meat pies, peas, and mashed potatoes. For dessert we'll make Pavlova. How does that sound?"

"What kind of pie has meat in it?"

"Only the best kind."

"What's a Pavlova?"

Elizabeth dug her mobile from her purse and went to one of her favorite food blogs. When she found a good image, she handed the phone to Molly. "This is a picture of a Pavlova. Isn't it pretty?"

Molly's brow wrinkled. "That looks really hard to make. Maybe we need Daddy's help after all."

"No way," Elizabeth said. "It looks hard but it's easy. Trust me, okay?"

Molly thought for a moment. Then her face cleared up and she smiled. "Okay. I trust you."

Elizabeth showed Molly how to cube the beef. When they were done, Elizabeth put the meat in a pot to brown. Then they moved on to the next step.

As they worked, Molly peppered Elizabeth with questions.

"Am I cutting the onions right?" she asked.

"You're doing a great job."

"I wish they didn't make me cry so much."

"I can do them," Elizabeth offered.

Molly shook her head. "I want to do it."

"Rinse your hands. That should help."

Molly washed her hands and rinsed her eyes. She grabbed the knife and began to work again. "I want to be a good cook like you."

Elizabeth didn't point out that Molly hadn't eaten much of her cooking. Maybe in her mind all mothers were good cooks. "You're off to a great start."

"Do you think I'm too young to have a pink streak in my hair?"

Where had that come from? The question was too off-topic to be a spur-of-the-moment query. Perhaps Molly had already asked Jake and he had said no. Elizabeth didn't know. One thing was certain—she wasn't going to get drawn into the middle of a parent-and-child dispute. "I don't know. What does your father say?"

"I didn't ask him. He doesn't know anything about hair. Not like you do. Just look at the way he wears his. It's all boring."

Elizabeth thought Jake had attractive hair. His haircut could be described as *traditional* but never as *boring*. But then, Elizabeth didn't want to put a pink streak in her hair either. Maybe in Molly's eyes Elizabeth's hair was boring too. "Do you want a pink streak?"

"Maybe. Sometimes. I saw this girl on TV with a blue streak. But blue is for boys."

"How old was the girl?"

"Maybe fourteen or fifteen."

"I suppose that might be the right age, then," Elizabeth said, taking the coward's way out. But really, she didn't know what was considered appropriate in Montana. She didn't want to set up Molly for ridicule. Or worse, judgment.

Elizabeth had never been conservative. She believed people should do what made them happy as long as their actions didn't hurt anyone else. If she was Molly's mother, she would let her dye her hair any color she wanted. Heck, she'd take her to the salon and have it done professionally. But that was *her*. When she recalled Jake's reaction to Molly's manicure, she had a feeling he wasn't the type to approve of a pink streak.

"You're probably right," Molly said.

As they worked, Elizabeth marveled at Molly's focus. She was determined to do everything exactly as Elizabeth instructed. Every once in a while, she would pause to let Elizabeth check her work, holding her breath all the while. Elizabeth made a point of praising Molly even when she corrected her.

Molly jumped from one topic to another. She asked Elizabeth's opinion on everything from music to TV shows to books. When Elizabeth replied, Molly nodded as if storing Elizabeth's words in her mind, planning to make them her own in the future. As a mother, Elizabeth knew she had a big influence on her daughters. They parroted her words back to her on occasion. More than once, she'd heard them addressing their dolls in the same tone and using the same words as she used with them.

It was clear that she had the same influence on Molly. She wasn't entirely comfortable with that knowledge. She wasn't Molly's parent or even her stepparent. Should she have that type of impact on Molly's thinking? She wasn't sure. But since she'd stepped on the proverbial landmine in the past, she would be more cautious this time. She would talk to Jake and let him decide how she should proceed.

Once the beef was simmering and the tables and counters were wiped, Elizabeth turned to Molly. "This is going to take a while, so we need to start on the Pavlova."

"Are you sure it won't be hard to make?"

"Positive. But it's important that we follow the directions carefully. We'll need egg whites for the meringue, but it's important that not even one bit of yolk gets in. Otherwise it won't fluff up."

"Maybe you should do that part."

"No way. We're a team. We can do it together." Elizabeth showed Molly how to carefully separate the whites from the yolks, then they worked together to complete the task.

"Your dad can scramble the yolks for breakfast tomorrow," Elizabeth said, sealing them in a container.

"Okay," Molly said. "I'll tell him."

When the egg whites reached room temperature, they added sugar and beat them. When the meringue was finished, they set it in a preheated oven.

"This is where we need a little luck," Elizabeth said.

"Why?"

"Because if there's a lot of noise and bumping in the kitchen, it might fall. It will still taste good. It just won't be as pretty."

"We shouldn't let anyone come in the house, then," Molly said.

"That's a bit extreme. They might need to go to the bathroom. We'll just ask them to tiptoe. When it's done, we'll let it cool in the oven. I'll keep watch on it while we're outside so you don't have to worry about that."

"Okay."

"Now let's go outside. The girls have been looking forward to playing with you. I can talk to your dad for a while."

"You won't do anything without me, will you?" Molly asked.

"No. I may come in every thirty minutes or so to stir the meat, but that's it. When it's time to do anything else, I'll let you know."

Molly grinned. She took two steps, then paused. Then she ran over and gave Elizabeth a quick hug before running out the door. Elizabeth stood frozen as unexpected emotions coursed through her. She hadn't expected to feel this strongly for Molly. Not that she didn't want to care for the little girl. Of course she did. But Elizabeth couldn't put herself in the position of being a surrogate mother when she wasn't sure how long she would be in Molly's life. Judging by Molly's behavior, that ship might have sailed.

Elizabeth and Jake's relationship was still in its infancy. It might not progress any further than it had. Elizabeth didn't know everything about romance, but she knew that one hot kiss didn't a relationship make.

Despite all that, this turn of events wasn't necessarily bad. Elizabeth had plenty of room in her heart, plenty of love to give to a motherless child or three. Giving and receiving love was never a bad thing.

Elizabeth stepped outside and looked around. She'd expected Jake to be sitting on the patio, but he was playing in the yard with the kids. He was pushing Gianna on a swing while watching Lucy do her version of a cartwheel across the grass.

"That's good, Lucy," he called when she stopped and looked at him. "You're a great tumbler."

"Thank you," she said, then launched into another one.

"Look at me, Daddy," Ben yelled, standing on the top of the slide. "I can go upside down."

"I'm watching."

Ben grinned and then slid headfirst. His hands shot out and hit the ground a half second before his head would have slammed onto the grass. He sat up, then grinned at Jake, who gave him a thumbs-up.

Molly was standing beside Jake and talking a mile a minute. No doubt she was telling him all about her adventures in cooking. The only person who wasn't trying to attract Jake's attention was Pete, who was tossing a ball into the air and catching it in his glove.

Jake looked over at Elizabeth and smiled before turning his attention back to the kids. She didn't know how he did it. He seemed so relaxed and at ease, as if dividing his attention between all these kids at once was second nature. There were times when she felt overwhelmed just dealing with two.

Since Jake had everything under control, she decided to take a few minutes to herself and sat down on the patio. After a while, Molly sat on a swing beside Gianna and Ben grabbed a glove and began to play catch with Pete.

Jake took a look around, ambled over to the patio, and sat next to Elizabeth.

"You have skills," she said.

"What skills might those be? The way I sat down? Clearly I'm the boss of the chair."

Elizabeth giggled and punched him in the shoulder. "I

was talking about the way you handled the kids. They were all over the place, but you managed to give all of them attention. How did you do it?"

"I'm used to it. Pete was on his own, and up until a few minutes ago you had Molly."

"I guess that's fair."

"Molly said she had a lot of fun with you. She also told me that you're a much better cook than I am."

Elizabeth laughed. "I hope she feels that way after we eat."

"Trust me, you can do no wrong in her eyes. She's very fond of you."

Elizabeth smiled. "The feeling goes both ways."

Ben and Pete called for Jake to join their game of catch.

"Do you want to play?" Jake asked Elizabeth.

"Sure. But be warned, I haven't thrown a ball in years."

"It's like riding a bike."

"No, I don't think it is. You use your legs for one and your hands for another."

"You're cute," Jake said. "I meant it's not something you forget how to do."

"I would love to join the game. That is if the boys don't mind."

"That's not going to ever be a problem. My boys think you're the best. And so do I."

Her heart skipped a beat, and she smiled. She was coming to think the same about all of them.

"Are you going to play ball, Elizabeth?" Molly called from her swing.

"I'm going to try."

Pete and Ben cheered and instantly claimed her for their team.

"I want to play," Molly said, running over.

"Me too," Gianna said, hopping from the swing.

"What are we playing?" Lucy asked. "And I want to be on Jake's team."

"They don't have gloves," Pete said.

"That's true," Jake said. He walked over to Elizabeth. "Do they know how to play baseball?"

She shook her head. "Nope."

"How about we play a different game," Jake suggested.

Pete groaned. "Why?"

"Gianna and Lucy don't know how to play." Jake dropped an arm over his oldest son's shoulder and whispered loud enough for Elizabeth to hear, "To be honest, I don't think Elizabeth knows how to play either."

"What are we going to play instead?" Pete asked.

"How about hide-and-seek."

Pete, Ben, and Molly cheered while Lucy and Gianna just looked confused.

"Forty-four homes," Elizabeth said.

"I love that game," Gianna said. "Who is going to be it?"

"I'll be it," Jake said. He walked over to a huge tree in the middle of the yard, leaned his head against the trunk, and began to count slowly.

Pete and Ben took off running. Apparently they had a good place to hide.

Molly took each of the girls by the hand and ran across the lawn. She turned and looked at Elizabeth. "Aren't you coming? This is a great spot. I hide here all the time, and Dad never finds me."

"Sure."

The yard was large, and there were plenty of big trees they could hide behind. Molly ran past those without a second glance, so Elizabeth followed. Finally they came upon some buildings on the edge of a fenced pasture and crept inside one. It was dark and damp.

Lucy and Gianna giggled.

"Shh," Molly admonished quietly. "You don't want Daddy to hear us."

"Right," Gianna said in what Elizabeth imagined was supposed to be a whisper but fell far short.

Elizabeth inhaled and immediately wished she hadn't. She was a rodeo performer, so she was used to being around stock. It didn't smell like live animals in here, and she just hoped Molly hadn't led them to some animal cemetery.

"Ready or not, here I come!" Jake yelled, his voice carrying from the distance.

Lucy laughed and immediately covered her mouth with her hands. Molly opened the door a bit and then peered outside. She then turned back to look at them. "Daddy is going in the other direction. When I say *go*, run as fast as you can to the home base, okay?"

Gianna and Lucy nodded. Molly glanced over at Elizabeth, who nodded as well. After a minute, Molly turned and whispered, "Go."

The girls took off, sprinting as fast as their little legs could go. Elizabeth ran more slowly, intentionally lagging behind so that the girls would beat her.

Jake's back was to them, and he didn't turn around until they were nearly at the tree. When he spotted them, he ran in their direction, attempting to cut them off. As expected, the girls reached the tree in time to tag it. Elizabeth sped up as she tried to outrun Jake. Her fingers were tantalizingly close to home base when Jake's arms wrapped around her waist. In one smooth motion, he lifted her and spun her around.

"I got you," he said, triumph in his voice.

Elizabeth glanced up at him, a smile on her face. He looked back at her, a devilish grin on his. His eyes sparkled with mischief before they darkened with desire. Suddenly longing filled her, replacing every hint of playfulness.

"Oh, Mummy. You're out," Lucy said, mournfully.

"Sorry that you lost, Mummy," Gianna said. "But yay, Jake. You caught Mummy."

"I thought you would be able to run faster than that," Molly said. "Or I would have waited until Daddy was farther away."

"That's all right," Elizabeth said. "It's just a game, and games are supposed to be fun."

"I'm having fun," Gianna assured her.

"Me too," Lucy echoed. She looked at Jake. "Why are you still hugging Mummy?"

Molly glanced at them as if realizing for the first time that Elizabeth and her father were still entangled in each other's arms. Being in Jake's arms felt so natural that moving had never crossed Elizabeth's mind.

"I just wanted to be sure that she could stand on her own. She did run a long way," Jake said as he released her. "Remember, your mother isn't as young as you guys are."

"You'll pay for that," Elizabeth whispered.

"I look forward to it," he whispered back. Then he spoke louder. "Now I need to try to find Ben and Pete."

"You'll never find them," Molly said. "They have a good spot."

"Do you want me to help you find them, Jake?" Gianna asked, walking over and taking his hand. "I'm good at finding people. We play this game at home, and I win when I'm it."

"I would love your help," Jake said. He led Gianna to the tree house. "Let's look up there."

Slats had been nailed against the trunk, forming a ladder. Jake climbed the lowest three rungs and peered inside the tree house. He jumped down and looked at Gianna. "They aren't in there."

"Where can they be?" she asked.

At that moment, Pete and Ben came running from the other direction. They were laughing, and the sound reached Jake and Gianna.

"There they are, Jake," Gianna said, taking off running. "Come on so you can tag them."

Jake nodded and jogged toward his sons.

"Faster!" Gianna cried. "They're going to beat you."

Jake sped up, but it was too little too late. Pete and Ben touched home base seconds before Jake got there. Lucy and Molly joined Pete and Ben's celebration.

"It looks like Mummy is the only one you caught," Gianna said, giving his hand a sympathetic pat.

"That's okay. I don't mind," Jake said.

"That's good because you never win," Pete said.

"Are you losing on purpose?" Molly asked, suddenly suspicious.

"Are you winning on purpose?" Jake countered.

"Yes," she replied without taking a breath.

"Maybe you could try losing on purpose so I could win," Jake said.

She giggled and shook her head. "Nope."

The kids ran over to play on the swings, leaving Jake and Elizabeth alone. She leaned against the tree trunk and grinned at him. "Pretty sneaky. Turning the pressure back on her. Molly didn't notice you didn't answer her question."

"I've had years of practice. But I don't know how much longer that trick's going to work."

Elizabeth laughed as they walked across the lawn. She went inside and checked on the beef before joining Jake on the patio. "That was fun. Even though you caught me."

"It was." He gave her a long look. "Did you let me catch you?"

"Dinner won't be long."

He grinned. "Smooth. But not so smooth that I didn't notice you didn't answer my question."

"I guess you'll never know." She laughed and leaned back against her chair. "You know, you have a new fan in Gianna. She really likes you."

"What's not to like?"

"Good point. My daughter has excellent taste."

They laughed and talked quietly for a few more minutes before Elizabeth checked the time. "I need to call Molly in so she can help with the next steps."

"Thank you for letting her help you. It really means a lot to her."

"Of course. I enjoy her company. I'm just sorry that she pushed you aside that way."

"Are you apologizing for my daughter's behavior?" He laughed. "I don't see how you could possibly be responsible."

"I'm saying that I'm sorry if your feelings were hurt."

"They were a little bit. But I understand. Molly wanted to have some female bonding time with you. She didn't want me horning in on her fun."

Elizabeth grinned at him. "I wouldn't have minded you sticking around."

"It's better this way."

"How do you figure?"

"When I want to have some time alone with you, I'll remind her of today."

"When will that be?"

"As soon as we can manage."

She smiled as she contemplated spending more time in Jake's arms. Her lips tingled as she anticipated more hot kisses. If she could sneak one now, she would. But there were five sets of eyes who could look at them at any moment. She stood and waved to Molly. Then she grinned at him. "I'm free when you are."

"Now?" Molly asked, running over. Lucy and Gianna were behind her.

"Yes. We need to finish the meat pies and the Pavlova. The peas and potatoes will be easy."

"Easy-peasy," Gianna said, and then she and Lucy laughed at her play on words.

"Okay," Molly said. She looked at the twins. "I'll be back to play with you later."

"See you later," Gianna said, then she and Lucy ran off to play with the boys.

Elizabeth and Molly returned to the kitchen.

"Now we're about to do the best part," Elizabeth said as she took out the pastry sheets. "We could make our own puff pastry, but it's a lot of work and the store-bought ones are just as good."

She set the muffin tins on the counter, then showed Molly how to cut the pastry sheets to size. Molly was nervous as she did the first two, but once she had the hang of it, she relaxed and began to ask questions about Australia, which Elizabeth did her best to answer.

"When you guys go back, can I come and visit?"

"I would like that, but of course, we would need to ask your father."

"He could come too. Plus my brothers. It would be a lot of fun, and it wouldn't be fair if they had to stay home." Molly looked directly at Elizabeth. "You do like Pete and Ben too. Right?"

"I do. Your father and brothers would be welcome to come for a visit with you."

They placed the crust in the tins. Elizabeth removed the

Pavlova and then set it on the dining room table where it would be out of the way for the time being. Then she put the pie crusts in the oven to brown.

"I think it is so cool that we'll each have our own pies. I might eat two."

"We're going to make twenty, so there will be enough for seconds. There should be some left over for tomorrow too. While they're cooking, let's peel the potatoes and boil the water."

"Dad makes mashed potatoes from the box."

Elizabeth squelched a frown. She wasn't a fan of those, but she understood the need to cut corners on occasion. There were only so many hours in the day and too many tasks for a single parent to complete. She just preferred to save time in other areas. Food was her love language, and she wanted people who ate at her table to savor every bite.

"Then he will love the ones we make for him," Elizabeth said, handing a vegetable peeler to Molly and keeping one for herself.

"Cooking is a lot of work," Molly said sometime later. They had peeled and cut the potatoes, filled the pie shells with meat, covered them, and set them back in the oven.

"It is. That's why I like to make enough food to have as leftovers the next day."

"That's smart. You know a lot of things that Daddy doesn't."

"Maybe. But your dad knows a lot of things that I don't know," Elizabeth said. "Plus he does a good job of taking care of you and your brothers."

"He won't let me get my ears pierced."

"Oh." That was a nice neutral response. Hopefully it would keep the conversation from veering into criticism. That thought was so ludicrous that Elizabeth could only shake her head. Of course Molly was going to complain about her father. She wouldn't have brought up the subject otherwise.

"He doesn't think I'm old enough."

"I see." Another noncommittal response. Like the first, it didn't end the conversation.

"Lucy and Gianna have pierced ears. How old were they when they got their ears pierced?"

"They were babies. But every family has their own rules. Just because I allow my girls to do something doesn't mean that your father is wrong to keep you from doing it. Do you know what I mean?"

"Sort of." Molly frowned. She understood, but that didn't mean she liked it.

"Good." Desperate to change the subject, Elizabeth redirected Molly back to their cooking project. But after they'd mashed the potatoes Molly picked up the conversation about earrings. "Since you know it's okay for kids younger than me to have their ears pierced, you should tell Daddy. Maybe he doesn't understand. You know, he's thinking about it like a dad, which is the wrong way. He should think about it like a mom would."

"Have you asked him?"

"Yes. He just said no. I think he thinks I'm too little." Molly spoke slowly. Thoughtfully. "I'll go with you when you tell him that I'm old enough. We can show him Gianna's and Lucy's ears too."

"I think it would be better if you ask him. He might not like me butting into a family matter."

"Daddy likes you. He won't listen to me because I'm a kid."

Elizabeth blew out a breath. There didn't seem to be a way out of this. Not without hurting Molly's feelings. "Okay. We can ask him after dinner."

Hopefully Jake wouldn't get upset and toss her out on her ear.

CHAPTER TWELVE

"DINNER IS READY," Molly announced proudly as she stepped onto the patio, a wide smile on her face. "Wait until you taste what we made."

"I know it's going to be extra good because you and Mummy made it together," Gianna said, beaming at her.

Molly nodded. "Thank you."

"I can hardly wait," Lucy said. "I'm starving."

They had eaten sandwiches and fruit for a late lunch, but that had been a while ago. The kids rushed over to the door. Molly held her arms out, blocking their entrance.

"You're in the way," Pete said. "How can we eat if we can't get in the house?"

She didn't budge. "Here are the rules. Number one. Walk very quietly. No stomping or running. Number two. No loud talking. We don't want the Pavlova to fall."

"The what?" Pete asked.

"The dessert," Elizabeth said. "And don't worry, Molly. It has set, so it will be fine."

"Well, they should be careful just in case."

"We'll be very quiet. Won't we?" Jake asked, making eye contact with each kid. He held Pete's gaze just a bit longer. The children nodded in agreement. "Good. Open the door, Molly."

Molly opened the screen door and then stepped aside. She gave each of her brothers a meaningful look as they passed her. Gianna and Lucy tiptoed in an exaggerated fashion as they went into the house.

Once everyone had washed their hands, they took their places at the dining room table.

"The table looks very nice," Jake said.

"Molly set it," Elizabeth said quickly. She smiled at Molly, who grinned proudly. "Since she worked so hard to cook this delicious meal, it's only right that the table look nice."

"I love meat pies," Lucy said. "My stomach can't wait to eat one."

After a quick blessing, Elizabeth began serving the meal, placing a meat pie on each plate. Jake followed, adding mashed potatoes and peas.

Molly held her breath while her father and brothers took a bite of their pies.

"This is really good," Pete said. "I never heard of a meat pie before, but I like it."

"Me too," Ben said.

Molly beamed and then took a bite. "I like it too. When we go to Australia, I'm going to eat them all the time."

"When are we going to Australia?" Pete asked.

"I want to come too," Ben added, looking around. "Am I going?"

"Hold on a minute," Jake said, looking from Elizabeth to Molly and back again. "Who said anything about going to Australia?"

Elizabeth felt Jake's eyes on her. She needed to straighten things out before the conversation got out of hand. "Molly and I were talking about Australia. I told her that all of you are welcome to visit anytime."

"So, you've made up your mind." Jake's voice held a hint of disappointment.

She should have known he would jump to that conclusion. "Not at all. Molly and I were just having a general conversation."

The smile he flashed her made her heart skip a beat. It felt good to know he wanted more time with her. Especially since she felt the same way about him.

"I see." He nodded. "It is a good idea. One that we should consider. Especially if the food is this good."

After that, Jake's kids spent the rest of the meal asking Lucy and Gianna what it was like to live in Australia.

When it was time for dessert, Molly stood. "Wait until you taste the Pavlova."

"Oh, we love Pavlova," Gianna said, rubbing her tummy.

Elizabeth had stored the dessert in an airtight container in the kitchen before Molly set the dining room table after it was done. Now she removed it and placed it on a tray. After putting fruit on top, she handed the tray to Molly, who carried it into the dining room. There was much oohing and aahing when she set the dessert on the table.

"You made that?" Pete asked, both skeptical and impressed.

Molly nodded. "Elizabeth helped."

Elizabeth and Jake exchanged amused smiles at the way Molly had framed her answer.

"Since you made it, you should get the first piece," Elizabeth said as she sliced the dessert.

"Can I have the second?" Ben asked.

"Sure," she said. "And don't worry. There's plenty."

Once everyone had a piece they began to eat. Unlike with the meat pies, Molly didn't wait for others to taste their food before taking a bite. Others soon followed suit. Nobody spoke for a moment. Then the silence was replaced with groans of pleasure.

"You are the best cook, Molly," Ben said. "This is the best Pavlova I've ever had."

"It's the only Pavlova you've ever had," Pete pointed out. "But it is really good, Molly."

The compliments continued in between bites. When the last bit of dessert was gone, everyone leaned back in their chairs with satisfied smiles. Molly's smile had grown broader as the compliments had gotten more effusive. Now she was practically glowing.

"Since Elizabeth and Molly cooked, the rest of us will do the dishes," Jake said.

"Okay," Gianna said. "We know how to wash dishes."

"Yeah. We're big girls, so we help Mummy all the time," Lucy added.

Elizabeth watched with pride as her daughters hopped up, set their utensils on their plates, and walked carefully to the kitchen. After a moment, Pete and Ben did the same.

Molly reached for her dishes, but Jake stopped her. She glanced at him, a quizzical expression on her face.

He grinned. "You cooked, remember?"

"So, what do I do now?"

"Relax." Jake stacked Molly and Elizabeth's plates on his.

"Let's go sit on the patio," Elizabeth said.

"Okay." Molly looked at Jake. "When you're finished in here, Elizabeth wants to talk to you."

"About?"

"About getting my ears pierced like Lucy and Gianna."

"That's not exactly how we were going to talk about it," Elizabeth said, looking at Jake and trying to gauge his mood.

He shook his head and set the dishes back onto the table.

"Don't say no, Daddy. Please." Molly clasped her hands as if in prayer.

He pulled out the chair beside her, sat, and took her hands into his. "I wasn't going to say no. If you want to get your ears pierced, I guess it's okay."

"Really?" she asked, hope dripping from her voice.

"Really."

Molly shrieked and then jumped up, throwing her arms around Jake's neck. "Thank you. Thank you. Thank you."

The other kids came running to see what the commotion was about.

"What's going on?" Pete asked.

"Daddy said I can get my ears pierced."

"Is that all? I thought it was something important," Pete said, shaking his head.

"It *is* important," Molly said, looking annoyed at her brother.

"You can wear earrings like me and Lucy," Gianna said.

"I don't know what kind I want," Molly said. "There are so many pretty earrings to choose from."

"When are you going to get them pierced?" Gianna asked.

"I don't know." Molly looked at Elizabeth. "Will you go with me and Daddy?"

Elizabeth looked over at Jake before answering. He nodded his approval. "Yes. When do you want to go?"

"Can we go tomorrow?"

"Yes. If it's okay with your dad."

"It is," Jake said.

Molly smiled and hugged her waist. "This is so exciting."

The younger kids grabbed the glasses and napkins and carried them into the kitchen. Too excited to sit still, Molly followed them.

"I hope you know that I didn't bring up getting her ears pierced. That was all Molly," Elizabeth said.

"I do. Molly has talked about it for a while. To be honest, I didn't have a good reason to say no. I was trying to keep her from growing up too fast. She already acts like a little mother around here. But since Gianna and Lucy have pierced ears, I guess it's fine."

"We'll get her some nice, age-appropriate earrings."

"I know you will." He smiled and appeared to be about to say something. Instead he rapped his knuckles on the table. Elizabeth would rather he say what was on his mind as opposed to keeping it to himself.

"What is it?"

One corner of his mouth lifted in a sexy grin. "I should have known you could tell that I had something on my mind."

"I do. So just tell me, and we'll deal with the fallout."

"There shouldn't be any fallout. This is something good." He smiled. "Our kids get along great with each other. And my kids adore you. Not to be vain, but your girls like me too. And I know that you really, *really* like me."

Elizabeth punched his shoulder. "Oh, you do, do you?"

"Yes. And I really, *really* like you too. So let's spend more time together. Not just the occasional dates when we can get babysitters. I would like to see you more, even if that means all seven of us and not just the two of us. It's not fair to ask you to drive out here all the time, so I'm willing to pack up the kids and come to the cabin."

Elizabeth shook her head.

"You don't want to see me more?"

She laughed. "No. Yes."

"Which one?"

She inhaled and then blew out the breath. "Yes, I want to see you. No, it's not necessary for you to bring the kids to the cabin. I don't mind driving. Besides, there's so much more room here. We can improvise at the cabin every now and then, but I do prefer to eat together. Besides, my girls love playing in the tree house and on the swings."

"If you're sure."

"I am."

After Jake and the younger kids finished cleaning the kitchen, everyone went back outside to enjoy the evening.

Pete and Molly were trying to teach the younger kids how to walk on their hands. Every time one of them landed on the ground, Elizabeth winced. The kids only laughed and tried again.

"Don't worry. Kids bounce," Jake said.

"I hope nobody's dinner comes back up," she said.

"We finished eating forty minutes ago, so that won't be a problem."

"Has that much time passed? I really should get the girls and get going."

"What's the rush? The kids are having a great time. I don't have to tell you how much I'm enjoying your company."

"In that case…" Elizabeth leaned back in her chair, letting the cool breeze blow over her body. She closed her eyes and a peace settled over her. She could get used to this.

"Owww!" The screech followed by crying filled the air, and Elizabeth's eyes flew open. Jake was already on his feet, and she jumped up and raced behind him. They reached the kids in seconds.

"Sorry, Ben," Gianna said. "I didn't mean it. It was an accident."

"What happened?" Jake asked. His voice sounded shaky and louder than usual.

"Me and Ben crashed," Gianna said. "And my feet hit his face."

Jake lifted his son's chin and studied his face carefully.

His hand trembled. "No blood. Shake it off, bud. You're a tough rancher."

Ben turned and took two steps away. He squared his shoulders as if trying to stop crying.

"What? He's not a tough rancher. He's a little boy." Elizabeth said sharply. She walked over to Ben, stooped down and held out her arms. Still sniffling, he went into her embrace and leaned his head against her breast. She kissed his forehead and rubbed his back. "It'll be okay."

Ben sighed and snuggled closer.

"Does Ben need a doctor?" Gianna asked in a quivering voice. Her eyes filled with tears.

"No," Elizabeth said quickly. "I can take care of him."

"I didn't do it on purpose," Gianna repeated, wiping a tear from her face.

Lucy took her sister's hand and patted it. "It's okay, Gianna."

"I know you didn't mean to hurt him," Elizabeth said. "And Ben knows that too."

He looked over at Gianna and echoed Elizabeth's words.

Elizabeth looked at her girls. "Why don't you two go and swing for a while."

"Okay, Mummy," Lucy said, leading her sister away. Gianna glanced over her shoulder, and Elizabeth gave her an encouraging nod.

"How about some ice for your face?" Elizabeth asked Ben. He stared up at her and nodded against her breast. She looked at Molly and Pete who hadn't moved. Clearly they were concerned about their brother. "We'll be right back."

Elizabeth stood, wrapped her arm around Ben's thin shoulder, and steered him toward the house. When they reached the kitchen, she grabbed a dish towel and filled it with ice. "This is going to be cold, but it's going to help. Okay?"

Ben sniffed and nodded. Elizabeth pressed the towel against his red cheek. The color was starting to fade, but he might have a little bruise in a couple of days.

"Hold that against your face, okay, sweetie?" she asked.

"Okay. Can I go back outside?"

"Of course."

He slipped his hand into hers and gave her a wide smile. When they stepped onto the patio, he leaned against her side. "Can I sit on your lap for a minute? You know, to help me feel better."

"If you think it would help," she said.

He nodded. Elizabeth didn't think he was still in pain, but she knew a little bit of affection went a long way. She sat down. Holding the ice pack in his hand, Ben scooted onto her lap and leaned against her. Elizabeth smiled to herself and wrapped her arms around him. She sang softly to him, and he smiled at her. A feeling of contentment filled her as she rocked the little boy in her arms.

MOLLY LOOKED AT her brother in Elizabeth's arms, her eyes narrowed and her lips pinched. Then she looked up at Jake. "I know how to take care of Ben."

"Yes, you do. But he wanted Elizabeth." Jake managed to keep the hurt out of his voice. He'd felt the sting of rejection as his son bypassed him in favor of Elizabeth. *He* was Ben's parent, not Elizabeth. But then, he hadn't offered Ben comfort and Elizabeth had. Not wanting to baby his son, he'd offered strength. In retrospect, that had been the wrong approach.

Afraid his child had been seriously hurt, he'd forgotten to ask *WWMD?* He'd simply reacted.

"Why?"

"He likes her." That was the best answer he could come up with. When Molly's frown only deepened, he knew he had a problem on his hands and that he had to do his best to solve it before it grew. "But that doesn't mean he doesn't need you."

Molly looked at him. This time her expression was not as easy to read, leaving him at a loss for words. No doubt she was dealing with the same mixed emotions that he was. She'd loved spending time with Elizabeth and had even shoved Jake aside so the two of them could be alone. She hadn't seemed bothered by the fact that her brothers liked Elizabeth too. But that was before Ben had turned to her. Did Molly look at Elizabeth as a threat now as he had for a few rough moments? Maybe. But Jake was an adult and could recognize when he was being ridiculous. As much as she liked to think of herself as a mini adult, Molly was only a child and didn't possess that ability.

Jake held out his hand. She looked at it for a minute before she took it. "Let's go for a walk."

"Where?"

"Nowhere in particular. I just didn't get a chance to spend much time with you today. You were with Elizabeth."

"We were cooking," she pointed out.

"And you did a great job. But a little Dad-and-Molly time would be good too."

She heaved out a breath. "If you say so."

They walked in silence for a couple of minutes. He searched for something to say to make the situation better. "Tell me about the earrings you want to get. You said something about flowers and butterflies."

"Yes. They come in a lot of colors. How many can I get? Can I get a jewelry box like Gianna's and Lucy's? They brought them from Australia. Do you think they sell that kind in Montana?"

He shrugged. He had no idea since he'd never seen

them. "I don't know. But if not, I'm sure we can find a nice jewelry box for you."

That seemed to satisfy her.

"I'm better now," Ben called. Molly and Jake turned as he ran over to them.

"Let me see your face," Molly said.

Ben turned to the right and to the left. "Elizabeth put ice on it. And she let me sit on her lap. She sang me a song and told me a story. Now I can play again. Here she comes."

Jake turned as Elizabeth approached. She was smiling, and he breathed a sigh of relief. He was glad that her annoyance had passed. His had too.

"I'll go keep an eye on Ben so he doesn't get hurt again," Molly said and then walked away, making a big point to ignore Elizabeth. Clearly Jake hadn't gotten through after all.

"Okay," Jake said. Elizabeth didn't seem to notice Molly's attitude, and he didn't point it out.

"So much for our quiet moment," Elizabeth said, coming to stand beside him. She bumped his shoulder with hers. The twins ran over to Ben. Gianna said something Jake couldn't hear, and then Ben and Gianna hugged.

"I hope you didn't mind taking care of Ben."

"Of course not." She gave him a perceptive look. "I hope *you* didn't mind. It's clear Molly did."

Elizabeth had picked up on the attitude after all. "She's used to taking care of him."

"And you? Did I step on your toes?"

He blew out a long breath. "To be honest, I was a bit jealous there for a minute."

"Why?"

"I guess because I've had Ben to myself for six years. I've been both father and mother to him. Having him reject me was a bit of a shock to my system." He gave a self-conscious smile. "I'm embarrassed to admit all of that."

"Don't be silly."

"That's what I told myself."

"That's not what I meant. I mean it's silly to be embarrassed by how you feel. We all have negative emotions. I probably would feel the same way if my girls preferred someone else to me." She took his hand and gazed into his eyes. Hers were filled with compassion and understanding. "We need to be honest about how we feel. Even if it's an emotion we aren't proud of. And we're going to have to understand how the other feels."

"You're something else, you know that?"

"I hope you mean that in a good way."

"Only the best way."

She smiled at him, and his heart thudded in his chest. He appreciated her kindness, but he would be lying if he denied the impact her body had on him. They were close enough for him to inhale her sweet scent with every breath. He wondered if he could sneak a kiss without one of the kids seeing.

The more he was around her, the more he wanted to be with her.

Ben and the twins ran over then. Ben grabbed Elizabeth's hand and smiled at her. "What are we going to do now?"

"It's time for me and the twins to go home."

"I wish we could stay here all the time," Lucy said.

"Not me," Gianna said. "I miss home. And I want to see Grandma and Grandpa."

Lucy thought for a moment. "Yes, me too. But I wish we could come here all the time on vacation."

Jake glanced over at Elizabeth. Hearing her daughters talk about missing home and their grandparents had to be tugging on her heartstrings. Every time he thought that she might be leaning toward staying in Montana, something happened to pull her back toward Australia. He understood how difficult her decision must be. He also knew it would be wrong to try to convince her to stay. She was already being pulled in different directions. He didn't want to add to her pressure.

That didn't mean he would stand idly by and hope for the best. He'd never been the type to let luck or fate rule his life. He would show Elizabeth how he felt. Hopefully that would be enough to keep her here.

CHAPTER THIRTEEN

ELIZABETH LOOKED AROUND the main dining room of the Library, a restaurant in Bronco Valley, and sighed. It seemed as if everyone in town was attending the bridal shower for Winona Cobbs, one of the most popular people in Bronco. Elizabeth smiled as she thought about the ninetysomething-year-old woman who was about to take the plunge. Talk about a leap of faith.

"Isn't this just the best?" Amy said to Elizabeth. She spread her arm out, encompassing everything from the pink-and-white balloons forming high arches to the enormous bouquets of flowers perfuming the air to the trays overflowing with every hors d'oeuvre known to man. That gesture also took in the fountains of pink drinks and the five-piece band playing songs from the fifties. Clearly no expense had been spared. Given the bride's advanced age, Elizabeth would expect no less.

Although Elizabeth was a relative newcomer to town, she'd been invited along with her sisters. She recognized some of the guests and had been introduced to the others. Naturally Winona's daughter, Daisy, was in attendance as well as her granddaughter, Wanda. They were talking to Winona's great-grandchildren, Evan and Vanessa.

"It definitely is the biggest bridal shower I have ever attended," Elizabeth replied. She and her sisters were sitting together at one of the numerous tables. They'd played some of the traditional bridal shower games as well as a few Elizabeth had never heard of.

"That's because everyone is so happy that Winona and Stanley have finally gotten past their jealousy and quarreling. Now they're finally getting together for good, and everyone wants to be a part of it," Tori said.

Elizabeth didn't know much of the backstory, but to her way of thinking, it wasn't important. The past didn't count. What mattered was these two people were getting their happy ending.

Winona had been circulating and came upon them in time to hear Tori's comment. She looked at Elizabeth and her sisters and tossed her long purple print scarf over her shoulder before replying, "I can't tell you how much I regret making Stanley wait so long before agreeing to marry him and setting a date. Looking back, there was too much quarreling. I should have done more to assure him that he had nothing to be jealous about. He is my one and only."

Winona met each of their eyes before continuing. "In my defense, I still had the scars from my relationship with Josiah all those years ago. I know we were more or less just teenagers ourselves, but even so…" She sighed. The man she was referring to was her former love—and the father of her child—rancher Josiah Abernathy. They had fallen for each other decades ago, but when he'd gotten Winona pregnant, it had been a scandal that had rocked their ranching community. "I loved him and I felt betrayed when he lied and told me our baby had been stillborn. But now, I've found my daughter again, and all of that is behind me. My scars are healed, and I'm ready to start the next chapter of my life."

"I'm sure he's just happy to finally make everything official," Elizabeth said.

Winona nodded and then looked at her intently. After

studying her a moment, she took Elizabeth's hand. "The past is present. The present will pass."

Elizabeth didn't know what the older woman meant. Before she could ask for clarification, Daisy came over and whisked Winona away.

"What was that about?" Elizabeth asked her sisters.

"She claims to have second sight," Amy said, "so maybe she was doing some type of fortune telling. And to be fair, she has given similar fortunes to other couples in Bronco."

"Really?"

Faith shrugged. "Winona is a bit odd, but she means well. And she's completely harmless."

"Okay," Elizabeth said. She had her own quirks, so who was she to judge?

The sisters rose and began mingling, talking with other partygoers. Although Elizabeth didn't know all of them, it didn't take her long to notice that a certain theme ran through every conversation. No matter the topic, they inevitably got around to talking about Jake.

"When is the big date?" a smiling woman asked. She'd been part of a larger group Elizabeth had met earlier, and she struggled to recall the other woman's name.

"What big date?" Elizabeth answered. After trying out a few names—Candy? Mandy? Brandy?—she gave up and decided to just talk.

"You know. You and Jake McCreery. Everyone has seen you around town together. It's common knowledge that you and your girls have been spending time with him and his kids at the ranch. Marriage is the next logical step."

"Jake and I have not discussed marriage once," Elizabeth said emphatically.

"Have you guys touched the pearl necklace yet? That will definitely speed things up a bit."

"What pearl necklace?" Elizabeth asked, then immediately regretted it. She didn't want to prolong this conversation. "Never mind. I'm not interested in speeding up anything. I like things just the way they are."

"I'll tell you, just in case you change your mind. The necklace has magical powers. At least when it comes to matters of the heart. It helps get couples together. It could work with you and Jake," the woman said. She winked and then walked away.

"What are you frowning about?" Faith asked, coming over to Elizabeth and handing her a plate with meatballs on it. They returned to their table and sat down.

Elizabeth exhaled and forced a smile. She didn't want to be a Negative Nelly at such a happy event. She recounted the conversation between bites of the tasty hors d'oeuvres.

"You and Jake have been spending a lot of time together. Naturally that will stir up talk. I'm sure Randi isn't the only person thinking you're about to take a trip down the aisle."

"Why?"

"Because Bronco is a small town. There's not much else to do here," Tori joked.

"I'll have to deduct a point for that."

"What does that mean?" Amy asked.

"Inside joke that Jake and I share."

"Inside joke. Hmm," Tori said.

"You seem really happy with Jake," Faith said. "Are you? Can you see yourself making it work with him?"

Elizabeth fantasized for a moment about being married to Jake. Spending their days and nights together would be wonderful. Then reality hit. "Can you imagine being the mother of five children? It is hard enough with just two. It's not as if any of them are teens and for the most part self-sufficient."

"At least none of them are in diapers," Faith said.

"There is that, I suppose," Elizabeth said with a laugh before she sobered. "I've lived my life on the road. So have my girls. Jake and his kids are rooted to the ranch. I can't ask them to suddenly change their lives and travel the rodeo circuit in Australia any more than I can ask Gianna and Lucy to live on a ranch in America."

"I thought you wanted to settle down when the girls start school."

"I do. Now that Arlo is gone, roots are more important than ever. That feeling of having a home. A place where you belong," she glanced at her sisters. "But school isn't compulsory in Australia until they're six."

"Does that mean you're going back?"

Elizabeth pushed her empty dish into the middle of the table and then rubbed her forehead. "I don't know. That's where our roots are. The place that has always been their home. Arlo's family is there. They can help the girls remember him. But you are all here. And the girls are making friends now. We're all happy here." She sighed. "I thought I had time to plan my next move, but time is slipping away and I haven't decided anything. I have to do something. I can't remain in limbo forever."

"Don't think you have to make a decision soon based on needing to vacate the cabin," Tori said. "You're welcome to stay there as long as you need."

"Thanks. I don't want to inconvenience you."

"You aren't."

"Well, you can worry about that later," Amy said, putting her arm through Elizabeth's. "This is a party. Let's have fun."

"That sounds like a plan I can get behind," she said, shoving away her troubling thoughts. A celebration of love was no place for worrying about her problems.

AFTER A NIGHT of troubled sleep, Elizabeth woke up early the next morning. She took a quick shower and then dressed in shorts and a favorite T-shirt. She and the girls were going to spend a quiet day here in the cabin. That was good since she wasn't in the frame of mind to interact with other people. She needed time to hunker down with her little family.

She was setting breakfast on the table when Gianna and Lucy barreled into the kitchen. They were wearing sundresses she'd bought for them at the mall in Wonderstone Ridge when they'd gotten Molly's ears pierced. The three girls had each gotten four matching dresses.

"Don't you both look pretty," Elizabeth said.

"Thank you," Gianna said.

"Is today a special day?"

Arlo had liked to create their very own holidays. They'd celebrate by eating treats and creating special banners. He also invented games that the girls always won. Although her heart had not always been in it, Elizabeth had kept the tradition alive. Now the girls created their own random holidays.

"Nope," Lucy said. "We just like these dresses."

"Daddy said we look like princesses," Gianna said. "Didn't he, Lucy?"

Elizabeth's heart stuttered. She knew the girls didn't have specific memories of Arlo. They'd been so young when he'd died. Elizabeth often told them stories about him and reminded them of how much he'd loved them. How proud of them he'd been. Had they decided to make up a story of their own? Creating a memory of their father telling them how pretty they looked in dresses he had never seen them wearing?

"Did he?" Elizabeth asked, going along with them. She

knew her little girls missed their daddy and wished he was around.

Lucy nodded. "But he said they were too pretty to wear on the swings."

Goose bumps rose on Elizabeth's arms. "When did he say that?"

"When we bought them," Gianna said, digging her spoon into her cereal.

"You were right there when he said it," Lucy pointed out. "Don't you remember?"

Elizabeth's heart hammered and she felt her mouth go dry. "*Jake* said that."

The girls nodded. "Yes."

"Jake is not your daddy."

"We know. But Ben said that it was okay if we pretend that he's our daddy. And we said he could pretend you're his mummy."

"When did this all happen?" Elizabeth tried to sound calm, but panic leaked into her voice.

Lucy shrugged. Time was a developing concept for them. Not to mention totally unimportant. "You did make him feel better after Gianna kicked him."

"I didn't mean to," Gianna was quick to point out. "It was an accident."

"I know. But it happened," Lucy said and then grinned at her sister. "But he still loves you."

"And I love him," Gianna said. "You must love him too, Mummy. You let him sit on your lap that time you fixed his face."

"You even sang the feel better song to him. You only sing that to me and Gianna," Lucy said. "So it must be okay for him to say you're his mummy."

Elizabeth marveled at their logic. It was all so simple to them.

"Ben's mum died and our daddy died. He needs a mum and we need a daddy," Gianna explained. "So we're going to share."

"Is that right?" Elizabeth managed to say.

Gianna looked directly at her. "You always say it's nice to share."

There was nothing she could say to that, so she only nodded.

The girls nodded and then resumed eating. When they talked, it was about their favorite pictures in their new coloring books. Clearly choosing a new father and volunteering her services as mother to Ben was not a big deal to them. But for her it was gigantic. Not because she didn't like Ben. He was a sweetie and had carved a place in her heart.

Things were spinning out of control. First the gossips in town were having a field day talking about her and Jake. Now this. It was one thing when hers was the only heart at risk. And Jake's. But now their children were part of the equation. They were all becoming attached to each other. Worse, they were claiming her and Jake as parents. If things didn't work out, their children would be hurt. They'd lost parents once. They didn't need to experience that pain a second time.

She needed to talk to Jake. They needed to get a handle on the situation while there was still time. Getting their families together had seemed like a good idea at the time. The kids all got along well, and everyone was happy. Of course, everyone was happy when things went well. They would be in a world of hurt if things went bad. Even if there wasn't a bad breakup, they would all be heartbroken if she and the girls returned to Australia. But that wasn't reason enough to stay in Bronco.

The thought of denying Gianna and Lucy half of their

heritage and keeping them apart from half of their family—the part that could tell them about their dad—nagged at her. Staying in Montana would be like erasing Arlo from their lives. Excluding his way of life from their future would be a horrible thing to do to them.

She liked Jake. No—her feelings went much deeper than that. She was falling in love with him. At another time that knowledge would fill her with joy. Now it only distressed her. Because she had to put on the brakes until she knew the right thing to do for all of them.

JAKE ENDED THE phone call and smiled. Elizabeth was bringing the girls over. It was an unexpected surprise, since they'd planned to spend the day apart. She'd told him that she'd fallen way behind on housework and needed to catch up. He also had piles of dirty clothes begging for his attention. Even so, when she'd said she wanted to come over, he instantly changed his plans. The laundry could wait.

The past few weeks had been clarifying. He realized that he'd met the woman he wanted to spend the rest of his life with. After losing Maggie, he didn't think he would ever find love again, so he hadn't even bothered to look. Love had found him anyway. He was in love with Elizabeth. He hoped—believed—she felt the same. They would find a way to make a relationship work—here in Bronco or in Australia.

It would take work to blend their families. Five kids living under one roof meant five different personalities finding a way to get along. Sure, it was working now, but it wouldn't be long before Molly was a teenager. Then Pete. Those years would bring their own challenges. Even so, Jake was up for it because he knew the good would always outweigh the bad.

When Elizabeth and the girls arrived, his kids ran out to greet them before they had even gotten out of the car. Then, as expected, they all ran into the backyard to play.

"Hi," he said to Elizabeth once they were alone. He pulled her into his arms and kissed her deeply. They'd agreed that they wouldn't expose the kids to any public displays of affection because it might be confusing for them. But the kids weren't around to see. Besides, he believed it was time to let the kids know they could become a family. Hopefully Elizabeth would agree.

"Hi," she said, pulling away and ending the kiss much sooner than he would have liked.

He looked into her face. She wasn't smiling, and his stomach plunged to his toes. "What's wrong?"

"We need to talk."

Like everyone in a relationship, he hated the sound of those words. "I can see that something is bothering you. Whatever it is, we can work through it together."

She shook her head. "*Together* is the problem. I think we're getting ahead of ourselves, Jake. We need to take a step back."

"What do you mean 'take a step back'?" Clearly he was alone in his belief that they were on their way to becoming a family.

She looked somewhere over his shoulder. "We've been spending a lot of time together. Too much time together. The kids are getting attached. We need to be sure of our feelings and what we want before we move to the next level."

Jake could only stare at her. Elizabeth was saying *we*, but he had a feeling she was talking about herself. *She* wasn't sure if her feelings were real. *She* was having doubts about the future. *She* wanted to step back from him.

He considered trying to convince her that his feelings

were real and that they belonged together, but he wouldn't. You couldn't talk a person into loving you. Either they loved you or they didn't.

Maybe she wasn't over her husband yet. It wasn't out of the question. Arlo had only been gone two years. It had taken him three times that long to get over Maggie and open his heart again. It would be wrong not to give Elizabeth the time she needed.

He loved Elizabeth and would do whatever it took to make her happy. If that meant stepping back and giving her space, then he would. That was the noble thing to do. The right thing. He just hoped it wouldn't take her six years to get over her grief.

"So what do you want to do?" Somehow he kept his voice calm.

"Take a break." Her voice was soft, but he heard the pain and conflict there.

He'd expected her to say those words, but hearing them was still a dagger to his heart. "If that's what you need, I'll do it."

She nodded, clearly relieved that he hadn't argued. "Okay. I'll get the girls, and then we'll be gone."

"What should I tell Molly? Do you want her to stop being your helper?"

Regret crossed her face. "I think we can take a week or so off. I'll still pay her, of course."

"That's not necessary. I'll just explain that we decided to take a break. She'll understand."

"I hope so." She sounded so sad, he wondered why she was doing this. Taking a break obviously wasn't making her happy.

They stood there for a few seconds, looking at each other. It was as if neither of them wanted to face the reality that this was goodbye. The sorrow was coming off Elizabeth in waves. Then, as if she realized there was nothing more to say, she turned and walked into the backyard to gather her girls. Molly, Pete, and Ben returned with them.

"Let's go, girls," Elizabeth said, opening the back passenger door.

Gianna and Lucy looked at the car and then ran over to Jake. They each give him a tight hug. He held them tight before releasing them. They might not have been children of his body, but they were daughters in his heart.

"Bye, Jake," they said. Then they turned and ran back to the car. They waved one last time before they hopped into the vehicle.

He stood there, unable to move, watching as the three of them drove out of his life.

CHAPTER FOURTEEN

"WHY DID THEY leave so fast?" Pete asked, looking down the driveway as Elizabeth's car disappeared from view.

"Yeah, they just got here," Ben said, kicking a rock.

Jake looked at his children. He waited for Molly to chime in, but she didn't say a word. She only tugged on her T-shirt.

"Elizabeth and I decided not to see each other for a while," he told his children.

"Does that mean Gianna and Lucy won't come over?" Ben asked. "And that we can't go over to their house either?"

"Yes."

"Aww. I like them a lot," Ben said sadly.

"I know," Jake said softly.

"When will they be coming back?"

"I don't know," he said honestly. He was just as sad as his son, but he needed to be strong for them.

"I'm going to miss them," Ben said.

"Me too," Pete added. His voice was low, and Jake had to strain to hear it. "I like having them around. Lucy and Gianna are like little sisters. And Elizabeth felt like a mom."

"I know you said we're better on our own, but I like when Elizabeth is here," Ben said. "She makes me happy. So do Gianna and Lucy."

Jake brushed his hand over his youngest son's hair. "It

is better having them around. I hope they'll come back soon. But in the meantime, we'll be all right."

"It doesn't feel all right," Ben said, wiping a tear from his face. "It feels really bad."

Jake pulled his sons into his arms, doing his best to comfort them. After a minute, the boys pulled away. They trudged to the backyard, but no laughter followed them. Only silence.

"It's my fault," Molly said once her brothers were gone.

"What is?"

"Elizabeth leaving us."

"This isn't your fault."

"I was mean to her. I like her, but I was jealous that Ben liked her better. I should have been nicer. I didn't even say bye to her that day."

"That was a long time ago. Elizabeth knows that you like her. And she likes you too."

"Then why is she leaving us?"

"This is something between Elizabeth and me. Believe me, it has nothing to do with you."

Molly's brow wrinkled in thought. "I still need to apologize for being mean to her."

"Okay. And you'll see that she never held that against you."

"I'll apologize at the Bronco Spring Sing."

The Bronco Spring Sing was the brainchild of the high school chorale teacher. The Bronco Summer Family Rodeo had been a huge success in recent years, and so she thought it would be a good idea to showcase other talented Bronco residents, especially students of all ages. The Spring Sing was scheduled for this Saturday afternoon. He and Elizabeth had planned to take the kids together. But that was before they'd decided to take a break. "We don't know that she'll be there."

"But she has to come," Molly cried. "We're singing a song together."

"Who is?"

"All of us. Me and Pete and Ben and Gianna and Lucy. We've been practicing for a long time. You have to let us go."

"Of course I'll take you and your brothers. But I can't promise that Gianna and Lucy will be there."

"Can you ask her? Please?"

Jake shook his head. Molly's pleading just about broke his heart, but he'd just promised Elizabeth that he would give her the space that she needed. He couldn't turn around a few days later and tell her to bring Gianna and Lucy to the Spring Sing where they would see each other again. He would do his part and take his kids. Hopefully Gianna and Lucy would convince Elizabeth to bring them.

Then he would have the chance to see Elizabeth again, if only from a distance.

ON THE MORNING of the Bronco Spring Sing, the kids woke up early. After practically swallowing their breakfast whole, they ran upstairs where they stayed until it was time to leave. They hurried downstairs and ran to the SUV. Molly was wearing a pink floral sundress that she'd gotten when she'd had her ears pierced, and the boys were wearing blue striped dress shirts and khaki shorts.

They talked among themselves as Jake drove to town. They were getting out of the SUV when Elizabeth pulled into the parking spot next to him. The kids waited until Gianna and Lucy were out of the car before grabbing each other in a group hug.

"We want to sit together," Molly said, her glance encompassing Jake and Elizabeth.

"Yeah," Gianna added. "We missed everybody."

"My heart was sad before, but now it's happy again," Lucy said.

"Mine too," Ben added. He walked over to Elizabeth and gave her a big smile. "Aren't you happy to see me again?"

She nodded. "Yes. I'm happy to see all of you."

Ben took that as his invitation to hug Elizabeth, and he wrapped his arms around her waist. Her arms went around him, and she brushed a kiss on his head. Pete nudged Ben aside so he could get a hug.

"I missed you, Jake," Gianna said, coming over and embracing him.

"Me too," Lucy said, wrapping her arms around him.

Jake's heart swelled with emotion, and he swallowed hard before answering. When he spoke, his voice was rough. "I missed you both too."

Molly hung back for a second before she approached Elizabeth, who held out her arms. Then she rushed over. "I'm sorry I was mean to you that time, Elizabeth."

"I know," Elizabeth said. Still holding Molly in her arms, she leaned back and looked into her face. "Don't give it a second thought, okay?"

"So you forgive me?"

"I never held it against you. But yes, I forgive you."

Molly sighed and leaned against Elizabeth for a minute. Then she pulled away and looked at the other kids. "We need to go inside."

As one, the kids followed Molly.

When Jake and Elizabeth were alone, he gave her a serious look. "I hope you know I didn't set any of this up."

She nodded. "I know."

"You asked for space, and I intend to give it to you." No matter how it broke his heart.

"I appreciate that."

"You're looking good," Jake said. Whether she was wearing a simple blouse, skirt, and sandals like today or the red dress she'd worn on their first date, looking at her made his pulse race. He might've been giving her the space she needed, but that didn't require him to hide his attraction to her. He wanted her to remember their fun times, wanted her to remember how good their kisses had felt.

She smiled and brushed her hand over her white denim skirt, drawing his eyes to her slender body. "Thanks."

"Are you okay with sitting together?" he asked. "If not…"

"It's fine."

He opened the door to the convention center and gestured for her to go ahead of him. A sign in the entrance directed them to a midsize room, so they walked down the hall together.

She turned to him. "What is this Bronco Spring Sing?"

"I don't know any more than you," he said. "This is the first time it's been held. I've decided to just go with the flow."

"That's probably best. My girls were so determined to come today." She lifted her arms and let them drop to her sides. "So here I am."

The first two rows were filled, so they took seats in the third row. Elizabeth looked around. "Where are the kids?"

"I suppose they're backstage."

"Why would they be backstage?"

"You don't know?"

She shook her head, sending her hair flying over her shoulders. Suddenly he had an intense desire to pull her into his arms and bury his face in her hair. He fisted his hands so he wouldn't give in to that temptation. "Know what?"

"They're performing in the show."

"Really? What are they singing? When did they decide all this?"

"I don't know the answers to either of those questions. I just know they're going to be singing together."

The seats around Elizabeth and Jake quickly filled and before long nearly every chair in the room was occupied. The master of ceremony took the stage and welcomed everyone to the inaugural Bronco Spring Sing. She then introduced the pianist. The first performer was a girl of about twelve who sang a solo. When she finished, the crowd cheered. She grinned and bowed before skipping from the stage.

There were several more participants, each of whom sang with boundless enthusiasm and varying degrees of talent.

Finally, Jake's and Elizabeth's kids took the stage. Jake's chest puffed with pride before the kids even sang a word. The girls looked sweet in their matching dresses, and the boys managed to remain unruffled. Elizabeth glanced over at him. The bright smile on her face gave him hope. Surely she could see that they belonged together.

"What is the name of your group?" the emcee asked, placing the microphone in front of Gianna's face.

She took the microphone. "My name is Gianna Freeman."

She passed the microphone to her left, and the crowd chuckled.

"And I'm Lucy Freeman."

The emcee shook her head as each child took the mic, said their name, and then passed it along. Molly was last. After introducing herself, she handed the microphone back to the emcee who placed the microphone in a stand, adjusted the height, then stepped away. Molly organized the kids into a semicircle, then counted to four. After they had sung the first lines of the lyrics, Elizabeth gasped.

Confused, Jake turned to look at her. "Are you all right?"

She nodded. "They're singing 'Waltzing Matilda.' Arlo used to sing it to the girls every night. It was a Freeman tradition. His parents sang it to him when he was a boy. Now Lucy and Gianna taught it to your kids."

Jake covered her hand with his, listening as the kids sang the next verses. When they finished the tune, the kids joined hands and bowed. Jake jumped to his feet, whistling loudly through his fingers as the rest of the audience applauded. He might've been biased, but theirs was the best performance of the afternoon.

Once the last act finished their song, all of the participants returned to the stage and bowed together. Then they scattered in every which way.

Jake glanced at Elizabeth. She still seemed to be emotional and lost in her thoughts. "I'll round up the kids and bring them all back here."

She nodded. "Thank you."

ELIZABETH WATCHED AS Jake crossed the room, weaving between clusters of children. Their kids had split into several groups and were goofing around with their friends. Gianna and Lucy, ordinarily glued to each other's side, were actually standing in separate groups. That little bit of progress gave her joy. Elizabeth wanted her girls to be close yet independent.

Elizabeth's eyes traveled around the room until she located Ben, Pete, and Molly. Over the past weeks they had made their own places in her heart. She'd missed them terribly these past few days. She'd grown used to Pete's jokes,

Ben's affectionate hugs, and Molly's curiosity. There was no way she could walk away from them.

Gianna went over, grabbed Jake's hand, and smiled up at him. He said something to her that made her laugh.

Elizabeth had missed Jake so much. She'd missed how contented she felt around him, missed how much he made her laugh. She'd been tempted to call him so many times this past week, just to hear his voice, but stubbornly she hadn't.

But she wasn't the only one who'd missed him. Gianna and Lucy had missed him too. Several times a day they'd asked when they could go back to the ranch. They'd wanted to play with Molly, Pete, and Ben. Wanted Jake to give them pony rides. Her daughters loved the McCreerys. In their minds, they were a family. It didn't matter to them that they didn't share a drop of blood. Given the fact that most of the Hawkinses didn't share genes, Elizabeth knew biology wasn't the most important thing. Love is what a family was made of.

She smiled as she recalled the five children singing "Waltzing Matilda." Lucy and Gianna had to have taught the others the song. Listening to them sing this song was what Elizabeth had needed to put her mind at ease. Her girls remembered Arlo. They remembered home. They wouldn't lose touch with their Australian heritage if they moved to the United States. They were carrying it inside them. It was a part of them and always would be. Not only that, they were sharing their heritage with their friends.

Elizabeth's eyes filled with tears as she realized that they had found a new home in Montana with Jake and his kids. This wasn't the outcome she'd expected when she'd decided to visit America, but it was the best one ever. Tears of relief streamed down her face. She wiped them away, but more took their place. Her emotions were too strong. She had no way to control her feelings or to stop her tears.

Jake walked up to her. When he saw her tears, he paused, and his smile faded. He stooped in front of her chair and took her hands into his. She read the concern in his eyes. Wasn't that just like him? She'd pushed him aside, yet here he was, worried about her. If that wasn't love, she didn't know what was.

"What's wrong?" he asked.

Her emotions were getting the better of her, and all she could do was shake her head. She took a deep breath in an attempt to get a hold of herself but was unsuccessful.

"You don't have to say it." Jake's voice brimmed with sorrow and disappointment. "You've made up your mind to leave town. Hearing that Australian song made you miss home."

She shook her head. The song had affected her, but not in the way he thought.

"Then you're officially breaking up with me for good?" His tone was even sadder and filled with heartbreak.

Finally she was able to speak. "Wrong again."

"Then what?" His voice was quiet, but she heard the fear and desperation there.

She couldn't bear the pain he was feeling. She cupped his face. "I love you, Jake. And I love your kids. I don't want to live another day without any of you."

He blinked. "What?"

"You heard me. I love you."

"I love you too." Their eyes met. His were intense. Filled with strong emotion that made her heart leap. "I love you so much. I'll live wherever you want. As long as we're together."

"I've decided. The girls and I are staying in Bronco."

"Really?"

"Yes." She glanced over at the kids. They were sitting at a long table, nibbling on cookies and sipping red punch from clear plastic cups. "Our kids are already a family. I think we should make it official."

He laughed and his eyes lit up. "Are you asking me to marry you?"

She shrugged. "I wasn't, but I will if you want me to."

He grinned. "Actually my ego would prefer that I do the asking."

She smiled. "If that's the way you want it."

"It is."

She folded her hands on her lap and sat up straight. "I'm ready."

"I'm not going to do it now. Not like this." He gestured to the surroundings. The room was nice for a concert, but it was not exactly romantic.

"I hope you aren't going to make me wait too long." Now that she realized how she felt about Jake and the kids, she wanted to get the future started.

"No. I would only be hurting myself." He stood and pulled her into his arms. Then he lowered his head and kissed her deeply.

Tingles shimmied down her spine, and she kissed him back with all the love in her heart. He deepened the kiss, and she allowed herself to be swept away before she reluctantly pulled back. "We don't want to stir up more gossip."

"Speak for yourself," he said then pressed a kiss on her lips, lingering for a moment before breaking contact and leaving her longing for more.

Laughing, she pulled away from his arms, creating a slight distance between us. "Stop. People in town already believe we're engaged or soon will be."

"Really?" He raised his eyebrows.

"Yes. Apparently gossip about us is running rampant. I'm told that's normal in small towns."

He laughed. "I don't think there's any more gossip here than any other place."

"I beg to differ. No one gossiped about me on the rodeo tour." He opened his mouth to argue, and she pressed her fingers against his lips, preventing further discussion. "I would prefer that we avoid being the topic of more gossip in the future."

"So would I." He looked over at the children at the table. "We should tell the kids first anyway. You know, so they can get used to the idea of being a family."

She nodded. "Okay. But let's not tell anyone else until it's official."

"I like the idea of this being our secret for a while longer."

"In that case, I guess we should wait until we're at home to tell them. I don't know about Molly, Pete, and Ben, but Gianna and Lucy haven't learned the art of whispering yet."

Jake laughed. "I wouldn't expect any of them to be able to keep quiet when we tell them the news."

"In that case, let's go home."

Jake caressed her cheek, and she leaned into his hand. "Home. I like the way that sounds."

So did she.

Two weeks later...

"How many scoops of ice cream do you want?" Jake asked. They had brought the children for ice cream at Cubby's for a treat after a hot day filled with fun activities.

"I would love three," Elizabeth said with a grin. "That way I won't have to choose between my favorite flavors. But the sensible part of me that wants to model self-control will have to be content with rocky road and butter pecan. Sadly, chocolate chip will have to wait for another day."

Although this wasn't her first time getting ice cream here, Elizabeth was still delighted by the shocking bubblegum-pink paint on the building.

"Very mature of you," Jake said.

"I know. I'm proud of myself."

"If you want, I'll get a pint of chocolate chip to go."

She folded her hands in front of her chest and batted her eyes. "You're my hero."

"That's what I plan on being from this day on."

Elizabeth looked around. "Where are the kids? I thought for sure they would be shouting their orders at us."

"Wait here."

"What do you mean? We have to find them before they get into some sort of mischief."

Jake kissed her briefly. "I have everything under control. Just take a seat at the booth in the front and wait for us. I'll be right back."

Shaking her head, Elizabeth did as Jake had directed.

These past couple of weeks had been wonderful. As expected, the kids had been delighted when she and Jake had announced that Elizabeth and the girls were staying in Bronco and that they would all be a family soon. Ben had immediately hugged her and told her he was glad to have a mother like all the other kids at school. Pete had asked if he could call her *Mom* instead of *Mum*. Molly and the twins had asked if they could be in the wedding even though technically Jake and Elizabeth weren't engaged. It had been loud and chaotic, and she had loved every second of it.

In a moment, Jake was back with the kids. They were walking with their hands behind their backs and grinning from ear to ear. They ran and sat in the booth next to the one where Elizabeth was sitting.

"I have something to ask you," Jake said. His smile was broad, but Elizabeth noticed a bit of nerves. He inhaled and cleared his voice. "But first, I want to tell you how much you mean to me. There was a time, not too long ago, when I believed my chance at love had come and gone. I didn't think I would ever be able to love a woman with my whole heart. Needless to say, I was wrong. You mean the world to me."

He approached her booth and took her hands into his. His were trembling as much as hers were. "I couldn't pull this off on my own, so I have five helpers."

He nodded at the kids who stood beside him, grins on their faces. Molly pulled a handwritten sign from behind her back. The word *Will* was written there. Then Pete held a sign with *You* on it. Ben's sign read *Marry* and Gianna's sign read *Us*. Finally Lucy held up a sign with a question mark written on it.

Elizabeth clasped her hands to her chest. Though she'd known Jake had intended to propose to her, she hadn't expected anything this sweet. But then, the children were a big part of their lives, and it was only right that they be part of the proposal.

Jake knelt in front of her and held out a small, velvet box. He opened it to reveal a princess cut solitaire.

"Well?" Ben said. "Are you going to marry us?"

Elizabeth smiled. "Yes. Yes, I am going to marry all of you."

Smiling, Jake slid the ring on Elizabeth's finger. Then he kissed her gently. The kids swarmed them and wrapped them in a group hug. A family hug.

It had taken a while, and for a time Elizabeth hadn't believed it was possible. She had found love again. All seven of them would live happily ever after.

* * * * *

Don't miss the stories in this mini series!

MONTANA MAVERICKS: THE ANNIVERSARY GIFT

Welcome to Big Sky Country, home of the Montana Mavericks! Where free-spirited men and women discover love on the range.

Starting Over With The Maverick
KATHY DOUGLASS
May 2024

A Lullaby For The Maverick
MELISSA SENATE
June 2024

MILLS & BOON

A Family For His Boys

M. K. Stelmack

MILLS & BOON

M. K. Stelmack writes historical and contemporary fiction. She is the author of A True North Hero series—the third book of which was made into a movie—The Montgomerys of Spirit Lake series and the Ranch to Call Home series with Harlequin Heartwarming. She lives in Alberta, Canada, close to a town the fictional Spirit Lake of her stories is patterned after.

Visit the Author Profile page
at millsandboon.com.au for more titles.

Dear Reader,

At last, the third and final story in my miniseries A Ranch to Call Home—Grace and Hawk's story. You briefly met them in the first book, *A Family for the Rancher*, and what polar opposites! Feisty and impulsive, Grace has held a high-powered life in the city, while Hawk, reserved and sacrificing, has struggled to keep together the multigenerational family ranch deep in the foothills of southern Alberta. I loved bringing these childhood friends back together—they really are made for each other!

A special thanks to Don and Myriam Wilson. As residents at the Calgary Stampede OH Ranch, they graciously instructed me in the ways of cowboying and ranching in southern Alberta, including its history and traditions. Myriam's tour into the back pastures brought us into view of a special herd— wild elk! Any mistakes are mine only.

And thanks, as always, to you for kicking back with my book in hand. If this is your first experience with me, hello—come see me on my website, mkstelmack.com. And if you are reading me again, you've made my day.

Take care, y'all!

Best,

M. K.

DEDICATION

To the ranchers of the foothills,
for keeping the tradition alive.

CHAPTER ONE

GRACE JANSSON TOUCHED her house key to the lock, and from inside came a distinct thud and scrambling. A break-in. She'd lived for fifteen years in Calgary, a major city a short two-hour drive away, and never once had been a victim of property crime. Yet two months into her new life in the remote foothills of Southern Alberta and some perp had selected her for a home invasion.

Or maybe an animal. Maybe she'd left the back door unlocked, and a deer or raccoon had pushed its way in. She had swept out deer droppings and carried out a swallow's nest when she'd moved in.

A chair scraped across the floor. A long scuff mark across her newly polished wood floor. Definite human activity.

She whipped out her phone to call the police. A piercing howl broke from inside, followed by yipping, and then a smashing and tinkling of fine crystal. Her mother's vase.

The little, thoughtless stinkers. The tenor of their voices gave away their youth. Probably not much older than her toddler-aged nephew and six-year-old Sadie.

Inside, abrupt silence fell and then the pounding of feet. Oh no, they weren't.

She raced to the back of the house, her feet slipping on the slushy March snow in time to spot a small boy dart out the back door. He caught sight of her and, not stopping, called over his shoulder. "Saul! Hurry!"

The second boy burst out, but Grace was there to grip his unzipped jacket. He froze, and then screamed, "Amos!"

Amos tore back and grabbed the hand of who must be his twin. The familial likeness to each other and to their father was too much.

"Hey, listen—"

Amos used the edge of his hand to chop on her grip. Ineffective, but it hurt. Well, if he saw her as the enemy, she might as well play the role. She pulled Saul against her, taking him into both arms. He didn't resist.

"Leave me alone," she said to Saul's defender, "or I will feed your brother cookies while you watch."

He stepped back, but his scowl remained. "You don't have cookies. We checked."

"Including the cupboard above the fridge?"

Amos looked over at his brother, whose shoulders sagged. "It was too high. I couldn't reach," Saul said. His near-black hair curled at the ends, just like his father's.

"That's okay," his brother said. "Who puts cookies there, anyway?" His hair was even curlier and longer, and right now, hair length was the only way she could distinguish the twins. They both wore the same blue shirt jackets, blue jeans and snow boots.

"Someone," Grace said, "who battles her impulses. Now, can we agree that if I release your brother, you will both come inside like gentlemen and partake of cookies and juice?"

"And then we can go?"

"And then I will release you into your father's custody."

"Dad's not around."

"Then, to whoever is taking care of you."

Saul dipped his dark head. Dirt smudged his neck, and Grace resisted the temptation to rub it off. Amos fixed Saul with a warning look.

"Please tell me someone is taking care of you."

"Uh," Amos said, "you better just call Dad."

He seemed to assume that she had his father's number, as if everyone would know who he was, and probably in this community, everybody did.

She knew that the boy's last name was Blackstone, that he was twin to Saul, that their father's name was Hawk Blackstone and that her new home was the old homestead of the Blackstones' before Hawk and his parents moved to their present location on the adjoining quarter more than ten years ago, leaving The Home Place to gather dust and bird nests, it would seem. Word from her father was that Hawk's parents had moved into town when Hawk had brought his bride there to live.

She also knew things Amos didn't. Like how she and their father had once been good friends until fifteen years ago, but that in the past six weeks or so since she'd formally occupied the place, neither had renewed contact. Which only went to show that back when she was eighteen to his twenty, she was right to think that he would move on.

But she had his number. Mateo, her sister's husband and Hawk's former employee, had insisted she have it in case she ever needed help. As Mateo recited it, Grace had finished it for him. Hawk had not changed it in the past fifteen years. He didn't care for change. Her complete makeover of his fourth-generation home place over the past year probably had him grinding his teeth.

"I intend to call him, but right now, let's assess damages."

The twin whirlwinds had ransacked the place she'd originally planned as her weekend home, but now was her full-time residence and location of her bed-and-breakfast. Kitchen cupboard doors were flung open, potato chips strewn across her granite countertops, and there was a huge sticky spot on her tiles from spilled juice. All six of the specially upholstered chairs restored from the original were missing from around the dining table.

The boys had dragged them into the living room, which had sustained the worst damage. A dozen or so of her quilts, productions created over the course of the past fifteen years, her comfort and her pride, were now stretched and bridged between furniture, stuffed under chairs and strewn across her floor.

"Do you realize," she said to the boys captured in her hands, "that if you two were adults, you could end up in jail for this destruction?"

The eyes of both boys widened, and Grace mentally kicked herself for scaring them. That was Hawk's job, not hers. She could play the stern but forgiving neighbor.

"This was our place first," Amos argued, "but then you moved in."

"Because I'm the owner. I get to do that, according to the law."

Amos twisted at her grip on his wrist, but she held on. "It's still our place."

"In that case, why did you wreck your own place?"

"It's not wrecked. Everything is just…moved."

Saul's hand in her other grasp twitched. "There is the glass thing."

At the base of the bureau, bought by her great-grandfather, lay her mother's crystal vase shattered into a million pieces. And gone with it, the hands-on reminder of the years of bouquets she and her sister and her father had brought home to her. The dandelions and weeds with stems so short her mother had tamped them in with a damp towel. The sunflower cut from the garden for her birthday. The dozen roses on Valentine's Day. The Mother's Day bouquets of tulips or daisies bought from saved allowances. Gone.

Gone like her mother. Broken glass. Broken neck. Both accidents. In both cases, she hadn't been there to prevent them.

"You're right, Amos. Most everything was just moved. By you two, and you two are going to move it all back." With her help. She couldn't see them ever properly folding a quilt.

Saul pointed at the remains of the vase. "And that?"

"That I will take care of." She'd sweep up the worst now, and would likely find bits here and there for weeks, months after. That was the nature of breaking something this precious. You could never be sure of finding all the pieces. "But first, I'm calling your father."

AT FIRST, Hawk ignored the incoming call from a private number. Creditors and collection agencies had sneaky ways of contacting him. He tapped End Call and turned back to loading cartons of eggs into his grocery cart. Now that his father had moved back from Ridgeview after his mother's passing last year, he household easily went through a dozen a day. His father suggested they buy chickens, like when Hawk was a kid. "It will teach the boys responsibility, like it taught you."

Responsibility hadn't come from tending chickens; he'd been born to it. As an only child, it had been on him from the time he could spell his last name to uphold the Blackstone legacy. Outside of the twins, he had done a poor job so far.

"And where are those boys of yours?"

Hawk looked up from his eggs. Irina Sandberg. She and her teenage granddaughter, Amy, lived across from the old

Blackstone homestead. He did a hard mental check. From where Grace Jansson lived.

"At home with Dad. I thought it would go easier." Last time, with the boys, he had spent as much time taking out bags of candy and boxes of sugary cereal as packing in the items on the list. And a good thing. Easter chocolate and candy lurked at every twist and turn.

"And how is Russell?" Irina and Russell had known each other all their lives, and she and his mom had been fast friends.

His phone buzzed. Again, the private caller and again, he cut it off. "Good, good. You know Dad."

Irina, slim and level with the third grocery shelf, stood with a bag of potatoes and a carton of milk and a ham in her shopping basket, yet she carried it on her arm as if it were a tiny purse. She seemed to expect him to elaborate, but he didn't know what to say that wouldn't give away his secret worries about his dad's health.

"He keeps busy. With the horses and the boys."

His phone buzzed from the same number. He would let it go to voice mail. Maybe they'd leave him alone if given the opportunity to leave a message.

Irina tapped the bag of coffee beans, also in her basket. "Tell him to come over for coffee anytime."

It might be a good outing for his dad. He had not been himself these past weeks. He would stop one job, start another. Perhaps he needed to get out of his head for a while. "I'll let him know, Irina."

His phone pinged a notification and then rang again. "You might as well get that," Irina said, sidling away, "if you want any peace."

She was probably right. He swiped up on his phone screen. "Hello?"

"Hawk Blackstone?"

The lesson he'd learned was never to give the caller your identity. "Who's this?"

"Grace. Grace Jansson. Do you remember me?"

Well, it wasn't as if he could have avoided her forever. He forced out a steady exhale. "I do."

"That's good, because I have visitors you might know. Amos and Saul."

Why had his dad taken the boys there? "You should say hello at least," his father had complained in February when she moved in.

"Same distance for her to come here as for me to go there," Hawk had countered. A whole half mile.

His dad had let it go, as he had a lot of things lately.

"I see."

"So." Grace drew out the one word long enough to have said ten. "I thought that, as their father, you might be interested to know that your children are wandering about the country on their own."

What? "They're supposed to be—" What did it matter now what should be? "Are they okay? They have hats, jackets?"

"Fully equipped, but hungry. The conscripts are disassembling the fort they made of the living room before they receive their rations of cookies and juice. But they are unscathed after their skirmish with enemy forces."

When they were kids, he and Grace, sometimes with her younger sister, Haley, and her childhood friend-now-husband, Mateo, had played out elaborate scenarios of forts under fire, besieged castles, ransacked temples. Two minutes into their first conversation in more than a decade, and it felt as if he and Grace had never parted.

Except they had. "Is the enemy holding them for ransom?"

"One demand. Pick them up in person. Come alone."

"Give me an hour. I'm in Diamond Valley right now."

"That's only thirty minutes away."

He needed to find out what was going on with his dad first. "I have an errand I was hoping to take care of."

"Fine. Any longer, and I will cut their hair." Amos erupted in the background with a panicked cry.

"Can you put Amos on the phone?"

"I thought you'd never ask."

There was a shuffling and muttering, and then, "Dad?"

"Amos. I'm coming to get you, but you and Saul need to stay put. Promise?" He didn't like to bind them at age five to their word, but he couldn't have them turn into runaways, either.

"Promise."

With Amos's buy-in, Saul would also comply. "And, Amos...why did you run off on Grandpa?"

"We didn't. I said we were going for a walk and he said okay, so we did. We got permission. We did nothing wrong."

Sometimes Hawk envisioned Amos making that same defense before one authority figure after another in his future.

Amos's voice dropped. "Hurry. I've seen the scissors."

For a second, Hawk contemplated delaying his arrival, just to see if Grace would inflict the arduous ritual on the twins, first encounter with his boys notwithstanding. Once when she was ten to his twelve, she had pulled out the electric trimmer from the barber's kit from the bathroom vanity and waved it at his bushy head. He had agreed to a one-inch trim, but she had put on the wrong attachment and plowed a buzz cut from tip to crown before she realized her mistake. To stop her tears, he told her it suited him fine in this hot weather and to just give his whole head an army cut. She actually had the gall later on to tell him it had all worked out for the best, hadn't it? And because it was only hair, he'd agreed.

"Sit tight. Be good. Keep your promise." A little late for the first two orders, but wasn't three the lucky charm?

He called the land line to the house. His dad had a phone, but the two were rarely together.

"Hello?" His dad sounded as steady as ever.

"Hey, Dad."

"Hawk. You left town yet?"

"About to."

"I see we're nearly out of milk. Do you mind picking some up?"

His dad didn't seem troubled that he hadn't seen the boys in a good hour. "Dad, are you—"

"I was putting together some milk and cookies for the boys when I saw we're getting low."

Hawk walked down an empty aisle to gain a little privacy. "Dad, are you aware that the boys walked on their own all the way over to The Home Place?"

"A walk? Saul asked to go on one a while back. I didn't think they'd go so far. I guess it will be a while before they are back."

What was the matter with him? "Dad. They are five. You can't leave them alone outside. There's still snow on the hill. The same hill bears and cougars take."

There was a long pause and Hawk could hear his father breathe deeply. "I'll go get them," he mumbled.

"No, stay there. I already arranged with Grace that I would pick them up."

"Grace? You talked with her?" His voice brightened.

"She called me to say she had the boys."

"Well, that's good," his dad said. "Be sure to thank her for me."

That was appropriate if Grace had penned a wandering

calf, but he was talking about his grandkids. Something was definitely wrong with his dad. Of all the other things going wrong in Hawk's life, this one scared him the most.

FIFTY-EIGHT MINUTES after talking to Hawk, a black crew cab truck rolled past the window where Grace and the twins sat at the kitchen table, and parked on her new gravel pad next to the house. The first occupant of her guest parking spaces, though not the one she'd expected.

"Dad!" It was about the tenth word Saul had said to Amos's ten thousand. And after taking his twin's lead during the entire visit, even letting Amos select the cookies to eat, he was the first out the kitchen door, Amos right behind.

She reached the door in time to see Saul vault into Hawk's arms. Hawk stood, holding Saul, his free hand opening to take Amos's. The arrangement happened so quickly and naturally that it must be habitual.

The three looked like they belonged in a picture gallery of country living. Hawk, lean and strong in his cowboy hat and jeans, and, tilted into him, the boys with their dark swirls of hair and bit of baby chubbiness.

She felt like an outsider, and, well, she was. No one from the community had dropped by since she had moved in.

Yes, she could've come to his place. It hadn't stopped her nearly three years ago when she'd come to tear a strip off Mateo after he'd deserted her sister, Haley. Back then, her sole purpose had been to persuade Mateo to leave the Blackstone Ranch and return to Haley. The only words she and Hawk had exchanged were to convey her dismay over the sale of The Home Place. She had left, determined to find a way out for Hawk. Her father had come up with the solution when he bought the place and turned management over to her. Hawk had got much-needed cash, and she, thanks to her dad, had prevented her favorite piece of land from falling into stranger's hands. And no, she was not a stranger. At least, not to the land.

Hawk walked with the boys toward her, across the snow-pocked grass. Maybe, just maybe, the snow might melt in time for her first guests booked for the Easter long weekend two weeks from now.

"Thanks for watching over the boys," Hawk said.

"My pleasure." It was. She had next to no experience with kids, outside of her nephews and niece, almost three-year-old Jonah and his baby brother, Jakob, plus six-year-old Sadie. Young kids, but the responsible adults in their lives had never made the mistake of actually leaving her alone with them. "I've never taken care of kids on my own before."

"I'm sorry this was your introduction. Amos, Saul, what do you say?"

"Thanks for the cookies," Amos said.

"Thanks," Saul said to Hawk's shirt collar.

"And what about making a mess of her place?"

"But we cleaned it all up," Amos said.

"Except for the vase," Saul said and received a glower from Amos.

Hawk's lips thinned, and Grace spoke hurriedly. "That old thing? Don't worry about it."

Hawk held her gaze, and she forced herself to shrug and smile. The last thing she wanted was for Hawk to feel indebted to her, especially over an accident. She was the last person on earth to judge someone for careless impulses.

"Boys, what do you have to say for yourselves?"

Saul turned his head to Grace. "I'm sorry for wrecking your place."

"Me, too," Amos conceded.

"Apology accepted."

With his load of boys, Hawk turned to the truck. "Thanks again."

That was it? No small talk about the spring winds, the cost of doing business, how she was settling in or who was not taking care of his kids when he wasn't around?

She couldn't let it go.

"Wait." She came down the porch stairs. "I have one more demand before I release the kids." Saul looked worried; Amos, curious.

"They have to try out my play pit." She pointed to a clump of poplars, among which she'd set a barrel, stumps, a hammock, a rope lashed between trees. "Fifteen minutes, and then they have to give me their honest opinion."

"Come on, Saul," Amos said.

Saul looked at his dad. "You can choose," Hawk said. "You can stay with me or go with your brother. I'll be here, either way."

"Go with Amos," Saul whispered.

"And there are toys in the storage bin," Grace called after them. "It's for guests with kids," she added for Hawk's sake. "I'm opening a bed-and-breakfast. In time for the Easter long weekend. I'm calling it The Home Place."

If he recognized the name as the casual reference the Blackstones made to the old homestead, he only gave a careful nod. "Easter is in two weeks? It's still the middle of March."

"You haven't seen the chocolate bunnies in the store?"

"That's no guide. Christmas goes up in October."

He had a point. "This year the moon has decreed that Easter comes at the end of March."

"Okay."

"I remember us playing in the trees when we were kids, so I added some equipment."

"Okay."

"I would show you around inside, but there's no taking eyes off those two."

"Yeah." He dragged his hand down his face. "Thanks again."

She noted the strain around his eyes, the tension across his shoulders. Back when they were kids, she would have nudged his shoulder, needled him until he let loose with whatever was bothering him. Usually horse related. And then she would impart advice or try to fix it herself. She couldn't stand to see him upset.

And she still couldn't. "That's three times, Hawk. I know you appreciate what I did. The question is, why did I have to do it?"

He gave her a wary look.

"Look, it's me you're talking to. I'm not about to sic child protective services on you. I can see that the boys think the sun rises and sets on you, but come on, Hawk. What gives?"

He looked at his boots. "Miscommunication between Dad and me, that's all."

There was a mountain more, but experience had taught her that Hawk could avoid questions like birds dodged vehicles. "Your dad lives with you now."

"He moved back when Mom passed a year ago."

"I heard," she said. Hawk's mom had been an endless source of iced tea and clean clothes and warm smiles for Grace during her summer stays. The Blackstone and the Jansson ranches were five hours' drive apart, but Grace had never experienced a second of homesickness under the care of Hawk's mom. Grace had bawled for days when her dad told her that cancer had taken Angela. "I am sorry."

"Yeah, it's been hard on dad," Hawk said.

"I guess it's good having him around. An extra hand, right?"

"It's under control," Hawk said.

That comment was odd. "I didn't say—"

He sighed and rubbed his temple. "Look, Grace, I know you mean well, but we haven't really talked for nearly fifteen years. Why start now?" He took a step away from her. "Amos, Saul, time to go."

In other words, mind your own business. Something she'd never been good at, but he had a point. He didn't want her in his life, and she had no reason to be.

"What did you think of the play pit?" she asked the boys as they rejoined their dad.

"It's cool," Amos said and Saul smiled. He had a different smile, both happy and uncertain. As if asking for permission to feel joy.

"Can we come play here tomorrow?" Amos said.

"No," Hawk said, swinging Saul into his arms. He took Amos's hand. "What do you say?"

"Please don't thank me again," Grace told Amos. "Or else I will give you that haircut here and now."

Amos clamped his mouth shut. Hawk turned his dark eyes on her. "I'll take my chances with the haircut, and say it again. Thanks, Grace."

She had got his thanks more times than enough, but not a single answer to what was happening in his life. Seeing him so stressed had stirred up her old desire to set things right for the man she had once considered her best buddy.

A dangerous impulse she had to resist. She had never been any good at going half measures. When Hawk had angled for more than friendship fifteen years ago, she had made a clean break from him. She couldn't pursue her legal career and a life with him. All-in or all-out. She had flung herself into her career, and her driven personality had won her cases but not the support of her coworkers. Hawk was right to slam on the brakes to any renewal of their friendship.

"I should be the one thanking you," Grace muttered to Hawk's retreating truck.

CHAPTER TWO

"YOU CAN TELL your husband I finally met his old boss yesterday," Grace said as she studied quilt patterns on her laptop, her phone on speaker beside her at the dining table. She usually had no problems envisioning her next quilt, but she was struggling this time around. She lacked a theme.

Haley gasped and Grace thought it had to do with her news, but her sister's next words set that to rest. "Jonah, let Mommy pour the milk."

"I do it, I do it!" Her nearly three-year-old nephew's insistence drilled into Grace's ear, even with the phone an arm's length away.

"I think Mateo and I made too big of a deal about Jakob drinking from a sippy cup on his own," Haley muttered to Grace. "Jonah now figures that he needs to outperform his six-month-old brother."

"Boys," Grace said, "and their messes."

"You talk as if it's lived experience."

Grace described her encounter with Hawk's twins that had Haley gasping again, this time with laughter. Grace didn't mention the vase.

"How is Hawk?" Haley asked, laughter still in her voice.

"Oh, you know him. Hasn't changed a bit."

"Uh, you were going off to university when you last saw him. I'm sure he has changed."

"It hasn't been that long. I saw him three years ago when I came down here to talk to Mateo."

"Yes, thank you, sister. That was so helpful."

"You two are married now, aren't you?"

"Please don't overestimate your role in that outcome. Okay then, three years. I haven't seen him in that time either, but Mateo has. He says that he looks as if he's carrying the weight of the world on his shoulders."

Hawk hadn't smiled, hadn't engaged in small talk and had moved as if dragging cement blocks. "He's definitely carrying a load."

"Does he just have the one hired hand?"

"I don't know. He didn't say."

"Mateo said that his father lives there now, so I guess he helps with the boys."

"He wasn't yesterday. I don't know what happened. Hawk didn't say. He didn't say much. Mostly thank you and goodbye."

"I'm sure selling his breeding stock is eating at him. I think Mateo would hand it all back to him tomorrow, if Hawk asked, but—"

"Wait, what did you say? He's giving up his breeding stock?"

"You know that. Mateo bought a colt a year ago."

"One colt. One. Hawk has got—what?—fifteen, twenty horses. He's still breeding them." Grace hovered over a complicated pattern for a spiral quilt. But was it challenging enough?

Haley was silent, too silent.

"Okay, what's going on?"

"I don't know. But he himself brought up the idea to Mateo when they talked last month. He has a mare ready to foal, and I think the understanding was that maybe Mateo would take it over."

"No. Hawk loves breeding horses. That was the whole

point. Doesn't he have this awesome reputation? Why would he give it all up?"

Haley sighed. "You know, Grace, not everybody can lead the supercharged, successful life you do. Jonah, drink at the table."

If only her little sister knew how wrong she was. But hey, thirty-four was a wonderful age to launch a new career. Maybe she could get a sideline with quilts. Run classes or something. "Money, then? I thought his problems were solved once he sold the home quarter to Dad."

"That was three years ago this fall. Expenses could have piled up again." Haley sighed. "Look, Mateo and I are just speculating. Mateo doesn't want to press, because he thinks it's not his business. You, however…" Grace's sister let her voice trail off.

"How is Hawk's business mine?"

"Because you two were besties growing up. And now that you're there right beside him, I don't know why you haven't gone over there yourself."

Grace closed her laptop window. "Because I have no reason to. Because I'm trying to mind my own business." And because Hawk didn't want her meddling in his affairs. "And anyway, I'm the new kid on the block. He should come see me first."

"That doesn't sound like you. You have made a career out of getting into people's business."

And that had turned out horribly. Not that Haley or anyone knew. They all thought she was on a sabbatical from the law firm and would return in September and manage the bed-and-breakfast from there with local help. She would have to manufacture another lie to stave off questions she couldn't bear to answer.

"I'm launching another one, as you know. One built on

letting people escape from their business for a little while. Anyway, how are our niece and baby nephew doing?"

She was referring to Brock and Natalia's children. Natalia was married to Brock, her dad's hired hand, really the son he'd never had. They all lived on the Jansson Ranch with their four-month-old, named Daniel, and Sadie, Brock and Natalia's niece. Sadie was adopted by them, after her widowed father died in a drowning accident.

Haley was not to be deterred. "Tell me you're not the least bit curious about Hawk's life and I'll drop it."

"Of course, I'm curious, but that doesn't mean I'm going over there to snoop around."

Haley let out a sigh. "It's not snooping, Grace. It's remembering that you two were the best of friends until life happened. And he could really do with a friend right now."

But what kind of friend would she be?

After the call, Grace walked over to the kitchen window, the one facing Hawk's home place. They were more or less a straight half mile apart. A long slope coming off the prominent ridge to the west blocked the view, the same slope that the twins had walked to get to her place, or they had come along the flat road. Either way pointed to their determination. Amos's, at least. Saul had likely gone along because his brother told him to.

Yes, she was curious. But after yesterday, she was also worried. Curiosity she could ignore. Worry was harder. And more dangerous. *Worried* had got her fired from her job and forced her to retreat out here in the dead of winter. Renovations were already well underway then, so there was power and a new furnace.

She loved this part of the world. It affected her bone-deep: its wind, its sweeping curves, its timelessness. But it was also where her mother had died. A death she could have prevented if she'd kept her word.

Her mother had come to the Blackstone Ranch to visit with Hawk's mother for a week. Grace, in her third year of university, was supposed to drive out for the day from Calgary to go horseback riding with her mom while Hawk's mother attended to local volunteer commitments. Except, then her mother called to tell her to pack an overnight bag, that Hawk's mother had invited Grace to stay the night, that they would have a big supper and that Hawk would be there. It would be just like old times. Grace had come up with an excuse fast to back out completely, wanting to avoid the awkwardness between Hawk and her from her solo visit there two summers ago.

But her mother had divined the real reason. "Oh, Grace, can you not move on from that? He has."

She had really not wanted to go then. Yes, she expected Hawk would get over her and date other girls. She just didn't want to see that in action.

Her mother had been disappointed. She had hoped they could camp out at the old Blackstone place. She had been trying to persuade Angela to convert it into a bed-and-breakfast. Maybe with trails behind the house up to the ridge. With Blackstone horses. She could have used Grace's powers of persuasion. Grace had said that the homestead wasn't going anywhere, and perhaps another time?

Except there hadn't been one. Her mother had gone riding alone. And ended up on a rocky ledge with a broken neck and the horse with two broken legs.

It might never have happened, if Grace had not broken her promise because she simply had wanted to avoid discomfort. She should've faced it head-on.

She was now. She'd driven out here the day after getting fired from the firm and woke up the next day committed to fulfilling her mother's dream of turning the place into a bed-and-breakfast. In less than two months, she'd sold her city condo and landed her first of three bookings. But Hawk was one confrontation she must avoid for the good of all.

Yesterday had already shown that, with him, she couldn't resist poking her nose where it didn't belong. Despite their friendship…sure, she would stick with that term…melting away, she didn't trust that once involved, she could maintain her distance.

THE FOLLOWING MONDAY MORNING, the local county office emailed Grace the links to the application for her permit. Pages and pages of paperwork, all to judge whether she could have a horse trail that already existed and just needed upgrading.

There was no use arguing the point. She had achieved junior partnership in five years because she quickly learned which battles to pick. That afternoon, she wrapped herself in winter gear and headed out to tramp along the trails. The sooner she roughed out the basics, the sooner she could start filling in the blanks.

It was slow going in the lingering snow among the trees, and then when she emerged from the trees, the ceaseless foothills' winds snapped against her lined jacket. Grace tightened her scarf and checked her phone fitness app. She had walked three-quarters of a kilometer, or as the app happily informed her, .447 of a mile.

"I hope you appreciate what I'm doing, Mom." No, she wouldn't blame her mother. She kind of liked to set herself against the wind, feel it scour her face.

The trail thinned from here to the ridge, if memory served correctly. At the top, there was the main trail that ran along the twenty miles of the ridge, with a view of the Rockies to the west. She could see the short, thin spire of the cairn to mark the spot where her mother had fallen to her death.

After busting through wind-packed drifts, Grace took a breather behind a familiar boulder. Every creature knew this rocky outcropping provided the best shelter for rabbits, coyotes, calves. And for a boy and girl resting from their play.

She looked down and across to the Blackstone spread. The cattle were in the corrals. Black Angus mostly. A rider cut away a cow from the herd. Cow and horse walked to an open gate. Hawk. It could be him. The cow walked easily into a smaller pen containing a shelter. Probably a cow ready to calf. The old cycles of ranch life.

She hadn't forgotten all that, despite the decade and a half of city living. She'd grown up on a farm, and that sense never left, even if her family wasn't there to remind her. In a couple of months, right where she stood now, the same cattle would graze.

That was another issue to deal with in her report. She would need to speak to Hawk as a local rancher. Get him to sign off on his cooperation. No time like the present.

Maybe she could sweeten his compliance with a deal to rent horses from him to use on the trail rides.

She turned to head down the ridge to the Blackstone Ranch and dropped to the ground. Pain shot through her ankle.

She struggled to her feet, but her ankle screamed, and she retreated to the boulder.

"Great," she said aloud. "Now what?"

HAWK SPOTTED GRACE making her way up the hill, her red parka inching across the snow swept pasture. What she was doing? The wind was bad enough. Mix that with the snow. She should be down at The Home Place.

Then the red spot ducked behind the boulder. Twelve minutes passed before it emerged, moved and then returned to the boulder. A quarter of an hour passed. Hawk drew out his binoculars from inside his coat. His father's trick. Good for eagle watching and finding lost calves.

Grace had taken off her boot and was examining her ankle. As he watched, she hobbled a couple of steps and then collapsed back down.

Nathan, his hired hand, was forking hay to the cow.

"Can you take it from here?"

The nineteen-year-old scanned the calving pen with the five cows. "Depends on how long they take."

"I won't be long. Back in an hour or two."

He saddled Wildrose, and they reached Grace in less than a half hour. She could've watched his progress the entire way, but she didn't speak until he reached her.

"You used your binoculars, didn't you?"

"Not much red out here this time of year."

She pointed at her outstretched leg. "Did your binoculars show I wrecked my ankle?"

"You seemed to favor it."

"You come to rescue me?"

She made it sound as if he was trying to be a hero. Far from that. He was just being responsible. "If that's what you want."

"Yes. I want very much."

He swung down. "You need help to get up?"

"Considering it's my left ankle that's broken or sprained or whatever, and that's the one that I use to mount, then yes."

That meant putting his hands on Grace, wrapping an arm around her waist to support her. Brief contact, but when it came to Grace, hot enough to burn. "You can mount her on either side. I'll bring her closer."

"Or," she said, "since you bothered to come all this way, you could lend a helping hand over to the horse."

Exactly as he feared, she clutched him the instant he was within reach and he had to put his arm around her. She hopped and teetered along, bumping up against him. Even through the thickness of their jackets, he could feel her curves. It was going to be the longest fifteen feet of his life, unless—

He lifted her in his arms.

She gasped, her face right there next to his. Her blue eyes were wide with surprise, her cheeks pink from the wind. But there was a brightness in her expression, as if this was all just fun and games. "Hawk, what are you doing?"

Trying to put as much distance as he could between them, ironically. In answer, he set her down on the right side of Wildrose.

Grace took her cue, put her foot in the stirrup, and swung herself up. Wildrose didn't shift, good horse that she was.

"Are we riding double?"

"I'll walk."

He started off, leading the way back.

"Aren't you worried about twisting your own ankle?"

Better a twisted ankle than sitting close to her. "I know what I'm doing."

They angled down off the ridge. He could have her back at her place within the half hour, and then he would be back in the saddle. All was quiet, except for the rattle of the harness, the hoofs on the ground, his own tread on the snow. But he could feel her sighs, the little breathy noises. Grace was building up, like a wind before a storm.

And then she hit. "Aren't you curious about why I was hiking around up here?"

"Your land, your business."

"When has that ever applied to this part of the world? Everybody is up in everybody's business."

"I'm not."

"You know, I believe that. But I am more than happy to share."

He marched on, his eyes on Grace's earlier tracks.

"As you know, there is quite a nice network of trails through here. I thought to run rides along here for my guests."

Where would she stable the horses? Keep the feed? "That's a whole new operation."

"Yeah, but Mom wanted it."

The Blackstones hadn't mentioned Miranda in years, definitely not in the year since his mom had died. It was as if the cairn was only a heap of stones. "She planned to talk your mom into converting The Home Place into a bed-and-breakfast with trail rides."

"First I heard of that."

"I don't think she got the chance," Grace said softly. "Anyway, now I have the chance to carry out Mom's vision. I'm halfway there with the bed-and-breakfast. Now the trail rides."

They had reached a flat spot just before the trail entered the trees, a good place to talk. A good thing, because he had a thing or two to say. "My cattle run through here."

"I know. That's why I thought we need to talk first. My application passed first reading at the county, but now I need to meet with ranchers to find out their level of support."

"I'm not supporting anything that interferes with the cattle."

"I didn't say it would."

"How could a bunch of city folk traipsing up and down the hill not affect the cattle?"

"There are several scenarios."

He waited. Let the lawyer in her worm her way through this.

"A fence, for instance."

"Through bush and into rock. And then what about the elk and deer?"

Grace didn't even pause, as if she had already known what his objections would be. "No fences, and the guests ride at designated times."

"And who is going to teach time to the cattle?"

She gave him the same bleary-eyed look he no doubt was giving her. "It's not as if the cattle are in the same place all summer. They start off here in May and June, but by July you will have driven them north of the river. I could run trail rides then, during the peak periods for me, and there won't be any conflict."

A fair argument. The county had granted her request for a bed-and-breakfast. The Home Place had already undergone the biggest change possible. Gone from being a home to a place of business. The only other bigger change was when his dad's grandfather had come up here from Montana to cowboy on a ranch of an absentee Englishman and put down his own claim. Back then, The Home Place amounted to a one-room cabin with a ribbon of smoke rising from the chimney. A picture of it sat on the mantel with his great-grandfather outside on his horse. "That might work."

She gave him her special smile, the one where her left eye scrunched up into a half wink, as if they were sharing a secret. "See? That wasn't so hard."

He walked on. It was too cold for these boots. "I haven't agreed. I'll have to think it over."

"Of course," she said. "I would have fallen off of the horse in shock if you'd agreed on the spot. There's one more thing."

With Grace, there always was.

"I was wondering if I could rent horses from you for the rides. I can pay for the gear, and for your time, of course."

"How many do you need?"

"I'm not sure. Three or four, likely."

He only had two horses he trusted to have untrained riders on. She was riding one, and the other was due to foal in July. "I don't have any to spare."

"If I bought some, would you be interested in boarding them?"

And have Grace coming over on a more-or-less regular basis. His dad and the boys would be thrilled. As for him— "I'm not, but thanks."

"Why don't—" She cut herself off. "All right," she said. She was backing off, exactly as he wanted her to, only he felt a little empty. It came as a relief when she spoke again.

"I want to make the trail a kind of memorial to Mom. Are you okay with that?"

Memorial? "How do you plan to do that?"

"Not much, I suppose. Have it named on my website. Maybe a sign at the front, a plaque. Just something to show she came from around here."

Miranda's dad had been Diamond Valley's pharmacist, and all the family had returned to Montana when he'd retired. Only Miranda hadstayed in Alberta. There was a picture of her and his mom on the mantelpiece, and over the years, he had more or less slid that image of her over the sight of her when he'd found her after her fall. "I always wish her well when I find myself up there," he said.

That sounded stupid, and he was about to explain himself when Grace murmured, "Thanks for doing that."

He gave a quick nod and resumed his walk. Ten more minutes through the trees and they would be at the back fence of the homestead, then back to the cattle.

"How are Amos and Saul?"

"Good."

"Home with Russell?"

"With their aunt." He didn't bother adding that the aunt was the boys' mother's sister. Gemma was, well, a gem for taking the boys. Except that she led a busy life, too. He glanced at his phone. He would barely make it back in time before having to run into Ridgeview to pick them up. He picked up his pace. Hopefully, Nathan could handle the cows.

"I like your boys, Hawk." Grace spoke almost dreamily. "They're...interesting."

"How so?" Hawk had never heard that word attached to the twins. It usually didn't get any more complimentary than "energetic."

"I don't know. It's hard to explain. They look a lot alike and they are inseparable, but they both have their own distinctive personality." She sighed. "I can see that they are a lot of work, and I can see how they are worth every minute of it."

Hawk swallowed. It was what he thought when he was about to give up on the ranch, on the day, on cooking a meal. The kids were worth it. He choked out a quick thanks.

"Stop thanking me," she said. "It's not a compliment, just an observation."

They reached the creek at the back of The Home Place. It was still frozen, and only a horse's length across, but one misstep was enough. He turned to Wildrose. "Take your time."

The mare did, probably because she was loyal enough

to follow Hawk off the edge of a cliff. She wasn't cutting horse quality, but Wildrose was just as special to him.

As they came up to the other side, Grace did what he had intended and rubbed Wildrose on the neck. "Good job keeping me in the saddle."

He stopped at the graveled parking space in front of the house. "You need to get off here. I don't want to pick stones out of her hoofs." Which meant doing what felt much like chewing on the gravel at his feet. "I'll carry you across."

"Why, Hawk, I do declare," she said in a faux Southern belle accent.

He did not look at her while he carried her to the door, her arms looped around his neck, pretty sure she was looking up at him with that half-wink smile. He set her down and stepped back as if she were on fire. She teetered on her weak ankle.

"The clinic's open until nine," Hawk said. "I've run the boys in a few times when they have had a fever. Amos needed stitches once."

"Why am I not surprised with that boy? I'll take a painkiller and ice it, and see how I'm doing tomorrow."

He nodded and turned, eager to make his escape.

"Hey, Hawk. Thanks for being my cowboy in shining armor."

Back when they were kids, she used to poke him and he'd automatically say, "That hurt," even when it didn't, even when they grew older and he wished she'd lay more than a finger on him. Fifteen years later, she was poking with words, and it still didn't hurt and he still wished for…more. The first time alone together, and he had her in his arms. Twice. Armor was exactly what he lacked around her.

He counted it a minor victory that he kept walking and let her have the last word.

CHAPTER THREE

AMOS AND SAUL rode up on a pony, just as Grace was about to start the egg hunt for her five child guests on Easter Sunday. The parents of both families looked on as she, with an Easter bunny puppet as an MC, prepared to give the countdown. The older kids, eleven and ten, crossed their arms to show their disdain for childish pursuits, even as they eyed viable locations for caches amid the remaining snow banks and open grass. The three younger ones bounced like bunnies, baskets swinging.

"Just a minute," Grace said, and approached the twins. "You two run off on your grandpa again?"

"Not Grandpa. Amy," the one in front said. They were again dressed identically in jackets and boots with fresh matching haircuts. She would have to rely on their behavior to tell the difference. He dismounted and the other followed. The first one to get off handed the reins to Grace, as if the pony was now her problem. Amos, then. "We're going back, so we're not running away."

"And we didn't come alone," Saul explained. "We came with Greta, and once she kicked a cougar."

Amos had his eyes on the kids and their baskets. "What's going on here?" He spoke in the high-handed way of an adult.

The right thing to do was place a phone call to Hawk, and get the boys picked up. She was still kicking herself for flirting with him two weeks ago. She had enjoyed teas-

ing him far too much. What would she have done if he had
taken the bait and flirted right back?

He had sent her a simple text confirming that he agreed
to trail rides based on their conversation, and she had sent
her acknowledgement via text, too. Yep, both of them were
keeping at arm's length, instead of, well, her being in his
arms.

But the boys looked so wistfully at the pastel balloons
and baskets. They were lonely and bored, and they had
come over to see her. Who was she to refuse the black-
haired, booted delinquents? Grace looped the reins over
the railing. Greta had gray around her mouth and likely
didn't care to go one step farther.

"Only if you answer one question and no lying."

They shrugged their agreement.

"Are you Amos?"

"Yes. How can you tell?"

Because Amos rode up front in their little duo. And
Saul kept a careful watch. "I have my ways."

She lifted Easter Bunny and spoke in a falsetto voice.
"All my eggs have fallen out of my basket when I was
running away from a coyote," she explained in a high,
breathless voice. "Would you help me find them? I have a
prize for the one who finds the most." The puppet pointed
to a basket on the top step, dominated by a huge chocolate bunny.

Amos turned to Saul. "If one of us wins, we split it with
the other, okay?"

Saul regarded the basket, the competition and, finally,
his brother. "We have to share with Dad and Grandpa, too."

Amos shrugged his agreement, and the boys entered
the competition. Grace, via Easter Bunny, explained the
range of where the eggs might have fallen——not beyond

sight of the adults—and that time was a factor, before setting them loose.

"Those two boys look like the real deal," one mom gushed. She wore jeans and a puffed vest, and held a cappuccino. Grace knew not to deprive her urban guests of boutique coffee.

"They are," Grace said, "neighbors from up the road."

"Aren't they a little young to be out alone?" the other mom said. "I mean, shouldn't they at least be wearing helmets?"

Grace's phone rang, and she stepped away to take the call.

"Hello. Um, I was wondering… This is Amy Sandberg, and it's about two boys, Hawk Blackstone's boys. He gave me your number, in case. I am supposed to be, actually I am—"

Grace couldn't let the girl fumble along any further. "I know them. Amos and Saul. They are here, safe and sound. They came on a pony."

"Oh, thank you, thank you. I'll come get them right away."

Amos was engaged in a round of rock-paper-scissors with the two older kids, Easter Bunny's rule for deciding eggs spotted at the same time. Amos gave a fist pump as he won the round.

"Actually, I have an egg hunt happening right now. And there's juice and snacks after. How about I bring them and the pony back in an hour or so?" Her ankle was fine, after two weeks of tender care.

"Uh, it's just that Hawk will be back by then. He went out with Russell. That's why I'm here."

"Perfect. There'll be someone home when I bring them by." If Amy thought she could get the boys back without having to provide an explanation to Hawk, that wasn't happening. Yes, the boys were born jail breakers, but their antics needed to be nipped in the bud.

By Hawk, of course. She would simply return the boys, like a good neighbor.

Amy heaved a sigh. "All right. I—I'll call Hawk."

"Sure," Grace said. "Good idea." See how well that would go for the poor girl.

Saul took the prize, having more eggs than he could count and six more than the next closest, the older girl. The kids got to keep the chocolate-covered eggs they'd found. Grace had a sinking feeling she would pick up shiny wrappers for weeks. She and the crows.

The guests piled into their vehicles soon after with promises of coming again. Little did one mom know her husband had booked a romantic getaway just for them, for their anniversary weekend in July. The lure of trail rides snagged him.

Now, she just had to figure out how to get horses before then.

The walk back over the hill with the boys proved illuminating. She discovered they attended kindergarten on Tuesdays and Thursdays all day, after which they stayed with their aunt and played with their cousins until Hawk picked them up. Their cousins were girls, and bossy. They hung out with their grandpa other days, usually. Not lately, Saul had contributed. The babysitter was okay but hung out with Nathan, the hired hand. That's what she was doing today, when they left. Amos had apparently told her of their traveling plans, but conceded that he hadn't waited to get her attention, which had been on Nathan.

They were coming down the backside of the hill, the Blackstone spread before them when Saul pivoted the questions to her. "Do you live by yourself in the house?"

"Yes, unless I have guests."

"You don't have kids?"

"No."

There was a moment of silence while they absorbed her childless state. It was unusual for women her age not to have children in the rural areas. In Calgary, no one would've blinked an eye.

"Aren't you lonely?" Amos asked.

And here she'd been thinking they were the lonely ones. Maybe she had projected her own feelings on to them. She missed the bustle and camaraderie of the law office, the staff birthday celebrations and the after-hours drinks. She missed the sense of belonging, that her presence mattered.

"Sometimes it's quieter than what I'm used to."

"We could keep you company," Saul said.

"Since you don't have kids of your own," Amos explained, "and we don't see Mom much, anyway."

She turned to face them. "I'm your neighbor, not your mother. I'd like you to come visit me, and then you go to your home. That's it. Are we clear on that?"

The boys nodded, their expressions like kicked puppies. She sighed. "And neighbors keep open doors for each other. You are always welcome at my place. Okay?"

Happier nods this time. Hawk appeared from the horse barn, his mouth in a harsh, flat line.

"Looks as if I have to thank you again." His eyes were on the boys.

Saul looked abashed, but not Amos. "Saul won top prize. Look, a big chocolate bunny, and we got eggs, too! I am happy to share." Amos was clearly trying to talk his way out of trouble.

"All of which I'm confiscating," Hawk said, "as it was obtained by illegal means." He gestured to the candy, and the boys relinquished their winnings. "You take Greta inside the barn. Amy and Nathan are already there to watch while you two brush her down. And then he'll show you how to clean out her stall."

Heads down, Amos and Saul did as they were told. Amy came out of the barn and took the boys' hands. Hawk was still tight-lipped when he turned to Grace. "I'll drive you back." He sounded as thrilled to be alone with her as before.

She was rounding the hood of his truck when the front door to the house opened.

"Grace, is that you?" Russell appeared on the front step. She hadn't seen him since she was eighteen. During her whirlwind drive out for a couple of hours three years ago, he had still been living in Ridgeview with Angela. His hair was mostly white now, and he was thinner. But his smile was just as wide.

"As you live and breathe," Grace said. "How are you doing, Russell?"

"The better for seeing the prettiest girl I know. Come in and have a coffee."

Hawk sucked in his breath. "She has to get back, Dad. I'm dropping her off."

Why was Hawk trying to hurry her off? "Not before I have a coffee with you, Russell. Do you still make it strong enough to risk a heart attack?"

"Not quite," Russell said, holding the door wide. "I'm still around, aren't I?"

Once she was inside, Russell closed the door, right on Hawk following them in. Deliberate?

Inside, the place wasn't exactly neglected but somehow looked unfinished. There was a set of couches but no coffee table and no throw rug on the floor. The kitchen counter had a box of crackers and a jar of peanut butter and three rolls of paper towels at different stages of use. The dining table had letters and envelopes, as if Hawk ran the operations from there.

Behind her, Hawk opened the door. He pushed papers to the far end of the table, and tossed flyers onto letters from the bank. "Have a seat," he said, his voice grim.

His anger with the kids didn't explain his attitude. They'd run off before and he hadn't been that upset. What was up?

It STARTED OFF well enough. Hawk sat silently while Grace and Russell chatted together. There was a slight blip when Russell asked Grace twice if she took cream and sugar, but she answered a little more loudly the second time. Good, let her think his dad was deaf.

"And how's your father? Why hasn't he come down this way?"

"I ask him that myself."

"It must be at least twelve, thirteen years. Since before Miran—" He broke off, shook his head.

Grace took his hand. "Yeah, I know." Hawk felt thankful for Grace the second time that day. "Dad tells me you two go way back."

Russell grinned. "You don't know the half of it." And then he called up old times, and the tightness in Hawk's chest ease. His dad was as good as ever when he talked about the past.

But it being the way of all conversations, it didn't stay in the past, and during a lull, Grace asked, "So what do you do these days to keep yourself busy?"

His dad blinked and frowned in confusion, just as he had when they had gone on the drive into the mountains that morning. Hawk had wanted solid one-on-one time to gauge his dad's mental acuity. His father recognized where they were, but for the names of neighbors he had known all his life, Hawk had to prompt the answers. His father wondered at the new fence at the Sandbergs', even though they had augured in posts last fall and driven by it once a week since then. He forgot Amy's name. And then had wondered if she was old enough to take care of the kids, even though she had driven herself over.

All signs of dementia, but until that was backed up with an official diagnosis, strangers like Grace didn't need to know. "I keep him busy enough," Hawk said.

Russell's tension eased. "Yep, always something. And the boys. They keep me busy."

"They got away on you a couple of weeks ago."

Russell looked up as if she were about to tell a good story. "Oh?"

Grace paused. "When they walked over to my place."

"Walked to your place? You live in Calgary."

Hawk avoided the look of uncertainty Grace shot him. "She moved into the old home place, Dad. Remember I sold the quarter coming up three years ago to Knut?"

"But aren't you a lawyer?"

It was Grace's turn to look uncomfortable. "I am, but I'm on a bit of a sabbatical. I am living down here full time now."

"I see. Well, the old place needs some fixing up."

Hawk cut in again. "I guess you haven't been there in a while. Grace has fixed it up nice." Not that he would know.

"You should come by, Russell. I don't think you'd recognize it."

"The wiring is no good. You will have to fix that."

"It's all fixed," Grace said.

"Good," Russell said. "Good." He passed his hand over his temple. "You don't mind, I'm going for a bit of a lie down."

Sunday naps had always been part of the Blackstone

lifestyle, so Hawk was spared another of Grace's quizzical glances as his father disappeared down the hallway to his bedroom.

But that didn't mean he escaped her interrogation. "Something's going on with your dad."

"What do you mean?"

She gave him the scrunchy left eye, but without the smile. "Russell. He's not himself. Do you know that?"

"He's tired. Mom's passing hit him pretty hard." His dad had started to decline right after. That's why he'd encouraged him to move back, and living on the ranch had seemed to give his dad a boost of energy. But during winter, he had lapsed.

"I'm not talking about his nap. There's more to it. How could he forget that I live here now?"

"I'm not really prepared to talk about Dad with you."

"I'm not sure that you're really prepared to talk about him even to yourself."

She was wrong there. During the entire drive today with his dad, he had also been talking to himself. *Hawk, time to be the caregiver. Get him help.* "I'm not blind to what's going on."

"Then, why did you leave him with the boys the other week?"

He had asked himself the same question more than once since then. "I guess I wanted to believe it was all in my mind. What happened made me realize I couldn't ignore the signs. As you saw today, I adjusted."

"Same outcome. The boys sneaked away on her, too."

"Easy enough to do when your babysitter has her eye on the hired hand. She as much admitted that herself, and that there'd be no repeat, either."

"Ah, teenage romance. First love is the most powerful." She spoke lightly, nostalgically.

Grace had been his first love; he hadn't been hers. She had broken his heart back then, but he was all grown up now. Had loved again and lost again. This latest loss, he still paid monthly support for. "Stupidest, too."

She looked out the window. "True enough."

He didn't want to sit in the past with her, and he didn't want to talk about the present with his dad. He couldn't change one, and he had no idea how to deal with the other.

"Have you talked to your dad?"

"Grace, it's none of your—"

"Business," she finished, turning back to him. Unshed tears stood in her eyes. "I know it. I don't have any claim on you or your kids. But look, Hawk. I care. I care about your dad because he's a good man. And I care about your boys because they're good people, too."

That was Grace. That was why he had once loved her with the strength and foolishness of an untested heart. Because she was a power unto herself. Like the winds that would come off the ridge and knock off your hat and cut to your very bone. All around you, all the time. If Grace cared, there was no force that could turn her.

"Fair enough," he said.

She swiped at her eyes. "Okay, then. So, I was thinking. Since the boys are bound and determined to come visit me, and since I told them that they could, why don't we set up exact times for it to happen?"

"You don't have to do that."

"Hawk, I just said that I cared for them. As neighbors. As my mom's friend's grandkids. I'm not doing you a favor. I'm asking if you would share your boys with me for a while every week."

Of course she wasn't taking on the boys as a favor to him. "All right."

"And you can drop off your dad, too, if he wants."

"He can manage on his own, still."

"I'm not saying that. I'm saying that I am more than happy to host your family. I can do Mondays and Wednesdays since the boys are busy Tuesdays and Thursdays."

"How do you…? Never mind. The boys didn't know that they were up against a legal mind."

Grace bit her lip, looked out the window again. "Yep. They didn't know." There was an odd strain to her voice.

"Missing work?"

She shrugged. "Sometimes. So, Mondays and Wednesdays?"

Grace didn't want to talk about it, and he wasn't about to push her. None of his business.

"I'M ON THAT website of yours. How do I pay for a room?" That was the first thing out of Grace's dad when she picked up his call, that evening.

She was piecing together scraps at her quilting table, hoping for something to click into place. No luck so far.

"What? Are you coming down?"

"Not if I can't figure out how to pay. What's the point of booking online, if there's no way to pay?"

"Dad, I don't have a booking page. What you're looking at is the contact page. You leave me your email and phone number, and then I will contact you. It's a way for me to screen people."

"Oh. I see." It was as much of an admission of fault as she was likely ever to get from him. She had honed her argumentative skills at his knee. Haley said the two of them were constantly bickering because they were the same—brutally honest.

Usually. Grace had withheld her termination from her family, primarily because she couldn't bear the inevitable honesty from her father. He would either scold her or he would take her side and threaten to storm her old office. Exacting and loyal. Great, troublesome qualities.

"When would you like to come down?"

"When will you have me?"

"Weekdays are better. I have openings then."

"Meaning you want to keep your weekends free for proper guests. I can pay."

"Dad, you are not paying to stay. You already paid for the house you'll be sleeping in. Now, pick a day."

"Natalia said that I can come any day, but just to give her a week's notice."

"Natalia has you on that short of a leash?" Grace and Natalia had hit it off right from their first meeting in Natalia's collectible store in Spirit Lake.

"I want to bring along Sadie, but Natalia needs to let her teacher know."

Grace thought of Amos and Saul mixing it up with Sadie and smiled.

"Let's plan for you to stay for a Tuesday and Wednesday. That way, you can be here all day Wednesday when I have Hawk's boys."

"You taking care of Hawk's boys?"

"On Mondays and Wednesdays. Just for the next little while."

"Don't you have things to do?"

"They are five. I can bring them along on errands, and I always have chores to do around here. They escaped over here twice already, convinced the place is still theirs. It's just easier to host them than to fight them."

"Since when did you have a problem fighting anyone on anything?"

"I fight if the cause is good."

"You've taken a shine to them."

"I'm just being a good neighbor. And I like to keep

busy." Between the boys and guests, she certainly couldn't complain about loneliness anymore.

"A couple of weeks back, you told Haley you hadn't spoken to Hawk the whole time you were down there, and now you're taking care of his kids. Sweet deal for him."

"I made the offer. I don't mind. They are...fun." Why did she keep defaulting to that word? They were fun, but not the way partying with friends and coworkers had been. More like the fun of projects, of making a quilt—long, complicated, fulfilling and never turning out quite the way you expected.

"What's going to happen when you go back to the city?"

"Oh, that's not for months. It's not a permanent arrangement, anyway. How's life with a newborn? Sleeping through the night yet?"

"I don't know about them, but I am. I'm out in the bunk quarters." Brock had lived in the attached quarters until he and Natalia had married. Then Knut had insisted they switch places. With Haley and Mateo less than a mile away, his days were full of family.

Which begged the question he was dodging. "Why visit now, Dad? After all these years?"

"Because you haven't been there all these years. Now I have a reason to pay a visit."

"You could have visited Russell and Angela. You had an open invitation from them."

"Right, then. Let's say it's about time."

If he wasn't going to say it, then she would. "It's about Mom, isn't it?"

Her dad's sigh was audible through the phone. "You know how I put together all those pictures a year or so ago?"

Her dad had taken over the living room for months, sorting through old pictures, archiving them on the computer and handing over flash drives to Haley and her, with all the pictures labelled and in neat folders.

"I think there were a few missing pictures. And I'm coming down to take them."

Grace could buy that. Her mother had wanted to transform the place into a B and B, and her dad had helped make it happen for her when he had purchased the land. "I guess you can see mom's dream come true."

"You have more to do with that happening than me. I bought the land to help out you and Hawk."

Grace started at how casually her dad linked their names together, as if they were a couple. "Help me?"

Her dad's voice grew distant, as if he'd turned away from the phone. "Oh, you know, I didn't buy it for my health."

"Are you saying you bought it for mine?"

"It's helping you, isn't it?"

Something in his voice suggested that he knew about her work situation. Or she was overthinking this.

"Anyhoo," her dad glided on. "I might stop in and see Russell while I'm out there."

Should she tell her dad about Russell's likely dementia? Russell deserved some privacy, but the two men were old friends. "When's the last time you and Russell talked, Dad?"

"I dunno…around Christmas, I guess. Why do you ask?"

"Just making conversation, is all."

"That's all we did, too. Talked about the old days, mostly."

The old days were Russell's strong suit. Her dad had probably not noticed that anything was amiss four months ago. "Okay, I'll let Hawk know that you're coming down, and you two old codgers can get together."

Her dad grunted at her derogatory term. "I can always count on you not to hold back what you're thinking."

Except she had lied by omission twice. About her firing at the firm and Russell's likely dementia. And if she had learned anything from her legal career, the truth eventually wormed its way out.

CHAPTER FOUR

HAWK DROPPED THE boys off with Grace on the Wednesday following Easter Monday. She'd had a guest staying over on Easter Monday and wanted a couple of days to prepare for them. As he drove away, Hawk looked in his rearview mirror. Grace was pointing out something to Amos and was holding out her hand to Saul. And Saul took it.

More easily and naturally than he did his mother's. The boys had not seen their mother since Christmas, three months ago. She had been relieved when he had obtained sole custody. She had told him as much.

"It's probably for the best, right?" she had said in her soft, questioning way, which had once made him want to give her certainty and take away her fears. Instead, he had only given her trouble. Outdoor living, and then worst of all, kids. Not the one he had talked her into, but two.

The babies had thrown her into a state of shock she had never recovered from. He had put it down to the over-whelming work of newborn twins, and chronic sleeplessness, but when Eva lay in bed through dirty diapers and empty tummies, he'd had to admit that his wife was in full-blown postpartum depression. He urged her to seek help, even arranged for health services to call her, but admitting to her state seemed too much for her. That's when Mateo stepped up, and together, the two men had taken charge of the twins.

One day when Amos and Saul were seven months old,

he came in from outside, and the house was unusually quiet. Eva sat in the living room in front of the playpen. Hawk checked on them, as per habit. They were happy enough, clean, sitting up, facing each other.

"Hawk," she said. "I can't do this anymore."

He began to say how he knew it was tough, but it would get easier, and then— She had held up her hand, palm raised.

"Hawk. I don't know much about myself. But I hate my life. I hate this place. You're a good man, but I hate being with you. And these babies... I will never love them. I have tried, but they were your idea. Take them."

She left the next day.

He didn't blame her in the end. There had been warning signs. She had always been reluctant about the ranch, but he'd thought that his love for the ranch would be infectious. He thought he could fill the unidentifiable emptiness in her life.

Grace had reminded him that he was about to ignore the warning signs with his father. He couldn't put off the hard conversation any longer.

He found his father in the barn, looping rope. Over the years, his father had handled hundreds of miles of rope, but in his hands now, the process was slow, extra deliberate.

"The boys are with Grace," Hawk said.

"Okay."

"It'll give us time to talk."

His dad didn't answer but kept winding rope, as if he had arthritis in his hands.

"I was noticing," Hawk began and stopped. "I was wondering if you are finding things harder than usual."

"Everything gets harder at my age," his dad said. Something he often said since turning seventy on his last birthday.

"I suppose," Hawk said. "I guess I meant things you used to find you could do without thinking. Like, I don't know, making coffee or dealing with numbers."

"I can make coffee. I can count. What are you getting at?" His dad sounded irritable. Mood swings were another sign of dementia.

"You seem to have trouble doing ordinary jobs, and I'm wondering if you'd like me to make you an appointment with a psychologist to figure out what's going on."

"A psychologist? You think I'm crazy?"

"No, Dad. It's just that with age come changes."

"I am an old man. Aren't I allowed to slow down?"

According to websites Hawk had visited last night, people with normal aging memory loss worried about their mental state, while those with dementia denied any problems.

"You don't have to do another minute of work, for all I care."

"That's what you already figure. That I'm good for nothing."

"Dad, that's not it."

"Then, why don't you let me be with the boys?" His dad's eyes were wide with accusation—and hurt.

Hawk stared down at his boots. Old and wrinkled and soft, bought the year the boys were born. "Because last time you had them," he said, "they wandered off."

"One time, one time only, and you take them away."

"You didn't know they had wandered off, that's the problem. What if Grace hadn't been there?"

His dad hung the rope. The loops were uneven, but his dad either didn't notice or didn't care. "But she was there, and that's the point. The boys weren't in any danger. She takes good care of them."

He made it seem as if Grace was always around.

"I am sure she does."

"She's nothing like—" his dad frowned "—that first wife of yours."

Hawk knew it was cruel, but he had to make his father see. "What was her name, Dad?"

"Why? Don't you remember?"

"I do," Hawk said. "I'm not sure that you remember."

"You can't expect me to recall everybody."

"But she was your daughter-in-law for three years. We had Christmases together. There is a picture in the house of all of us together."

Fear flashed across his father's face. And then anger. "I don't have to put up with this." He turned and walked away. "I'm going inside. To make coffee by myself."

Okay, Hawk thought. *Don't push it.* But it was a classic catch-22 situation. He had to let his father come around to the idea himself, because he couldn't forcibly drag him in for a diagnosis, but the nature of the disease prevented his father from recognizing the symptoms.

Hawk prayed his father would come to his senses soon.

THE BOYS TURNED out to be quilters. Well, Saul was. They had wandered into Grace's quilting room, and Amos had latched on to the sewing machine, while Saul had taken up the scissors. She had hung up a few wall quilts, and they had sat—actually, sat—and stared at them. Saul, especially, had studied the patterns and refused to budge, despite Amos's urgings that they go outside. Saul decided he'd rather build quilts, and without his playmate, Amos joined him.

Grace inwardly winced at their hatchet job, but gave them free rein. She could fold fabric later to straighten out the squares. Saul might have spent all day on this art project but, after lunch, had allowed Amos to drag him outside. They wanted her to drop them off early to show her the pen their dad kept them in. What?

"Of course," she had said. "I'd be delighted."

It was a cattle pen on a slope above the corrals where the boys could see everything and be seen. There were bales and toys and an old saddle, hockey sticks and balls in an old metal water trough. And rope. Scraps from around the ranch.

Off in the real corral, Hawk was leading a yearling horse. Was it any relation to Risky Business, the mare that Mateo had bought almost three years ago from Hawk and now showed to good profit?

She waved, and he raised his hand. "Do you want to go see your dad?"

"Nah, we can see him from here," Amos said.

"Rule is," Saul explained, "is that an adult lets us in, and we have to stay here until Dad or Grandpa says we can come out."

"What if you have to pee?" Grace said.

Amos pointed to a spot at a fencing panel. "Dad said to aim between the rails."

Grace sucked in her lips to suppress a smile. "As long as you got a plan."

"Yeah, we always got a plan," Amos said. "You can go now, Grace." He climbed the railings without a backward glance.

Saul stayed behind. "You said we can keep building a quilt?"

"I did. And we will. I promise." Making a quilt with them had not ignited her creative spark, but she had seen it in the boys' eyes, the value of making something out of nothing. And that had thrilled her in a way she had not experienced before. Was this what mothers felt?

"Will we get it done before you leave?"

"I'm not sure what you mean."

"Dad said that you're going back to the city."

Of course. Hawk assumed she had a job to go back to. He had probably heard through Mateo that she was on a sabbatical. Now Hawk was part of her great lie.

"Who knows what the future holds?" Grace said. "I promise you we will finish the quilts long before I leave. In fact, after we make a quilt for you and Amos, we can make another one for whoever you want."

"Grandpa," Saul said. "His has holes so big I can put my foot through them."

"Sure. For Grandpa. You good to play with Amos now?"

Saul smiled. "Yep. You can go."

"I'm going to talk to your dad, but I'm keeping my eyes on you two."

Grace reached the corral fence as Hawk rounded the inside with the yearling. He looked as if they were on a stroll. "All right for me to come in?"

He glanced at her hikers. "As long as you don't care what your boots pick up."

Except for a few replacement boards, this was the same fence from her summers here. She fell into step beside Hawk, the yearling on the other side. The roan gave her a little side-eye, but Hawk, buffered between them, continued on.

"She's a beauty," Grace said. "Light on her feet."

"Gets that from Mama. She has a bit of the Indian pony in her."

"Huh?"

"The secret ingredient to my stock. Picked her up from a horse sale up north. A three-year-old then, and broken to ride but not to cutting. But man, she was fast."

Hawk's face relaxed and his mouth almost twitched

into a smile. He pointed with his chin up to the play corral. "Had enough of them?"

"I think they had enough of me. Amos wanted to show me their outdoor pen, and I had to admit that I was curious about where their dad kept them corralled. But as soon as we got here, he shooed me off. Saul did, too, once I promised we would continue on the quilts next time."

"Quilts?"

"Yeah. I've been making quilts since—since Mom passed. It started off as a kind of therapy, and then it just became a kind of passion. Saul, especially, has a real eye for pattern."

"That right?" Hawk said, a shot of pride in his voice. "He always gives things a careful look over."

"He wants to make a quilt for Russell. I was wondering... Do the boys have clothes they've outgrown?"

"Four boxes in their closet. Have at 'er. You short on cloth?"

"Funny. I wanted to make the quilt special. And hold the boys' interest before they turn into horsemen, like all the Blackstones before them."

Hawk's face clouded over. "I hope so." The filly leaned over and nuzzled Hawk's belt. Hawk pushed away her nose. "Go on with you." Then rubbed her neck.

"Kind of a mixed message there, Hawk."

"She needs to know it's okay to make mistakes."

"What's her name?"

"Palette, Pal for short. After her mama, Paintbrush. Dad's choice." Hawk's face tightened, and Grace guessed where his mind had gone.

"How is he?"

"I tried to talk to him this morning."

"I take it that didn't go well."

"He doesn't think there's a thing wrong with him, other than being old."

"Why am I not surprised? Stubbornness is hereditary among the Blackstones."

"An excellent trait to get through trouble. Dad is using it to avoid trouble."

They walked together, their strides matching. "Do you want me to talk to him?"

"Not yet. I'd like him to think it over. It might be hard, coming from you."

Grace tried not to take offense, but— "What do you think I'm going to be, cold and callous?"

"No, I think that you're going to be direct, and my dad doesn't need to hear from somebody he hasn't seen in a dozen years that he's probably got dementia."

Hawk's breath hitched on the last word, and Grace's heart went out to him. How would she feel if her cantankerous dad, the man who was never at a loss for words, suddenly couldn't remember where she lived? If she and Hawk had not gone their own ways so long ago, she might have reached out and taken his hand. As it was, she said, "Okay, I get it."

"You know, we wouldn't be walking this horse today if it wasn't for Dad. He got us into the cutting horses."

"I didn't know that. The horses always seemed to be around."

"Oh, we always had horses. But mostly just quarter horses for riding. But one time, Dad went south to Arizona to a horse show, and he rode a horse that came straight from Metallic Cat."

"That's the futurity stallion, right? Mateo and Haley bring it up about Risky B."

"That's because she carries his DNA. Anyway, Dad got on a trained cutting horse. The trainer gave him a few pointers and then just told him to give the horse full head. Dad said later that it was like riding a tiger. He said he never had a better high. And he swore he was going to bring cutting horse stock to the Blackstone Ranch. Grandpa was still alive then, and them two got into the biggest fight, Mom said. Well, Grandpa did. Dad never raised his voice once. He just kept saying how it was going to be. And then he went into the Blackstone account and cleaned it out. Went down south and bought that horse."

Grace sucked in her breath. "Kitkat Wrapper. I remember her. Your dad wouldn't let me near her."

"Yep, her. She came here as a three-year-old, and Dad brought up a trainer for the summer. Converted a corral into an arena, and when the trainer left, Dad kept it up. She paid off, and then we bred her with good stallions. Some of them were good, really good."

"Where are the rest?"

Hawk pointed over to the small pasture adjoining the barn. "That's it."

Grace counted. "Five? But when I was out three years ago, there were easily fifteen."

"Twenty-one, to be precise." Stiff regret marked his voice.

"What happened?"

"Horses are expensive to keep, especially when— There were bills to pay."

His ex-wife's bills. How could she have abandoned her own children and then expected Hawk to pay for her up-keep? *Stop it, Grace. None of your business.*

"You wouldn't rent horses to me because you don't have any?"

"That's about the size of it."

"I suppose I should be glad it wasn't anything personal."

He didn't comment.

"Okay, was it also personal?"

Hawk looked up to the ridge. "Ah, Grace, when has it not been personal?"

It was her turn to seek answers from the lofty ridge. She was really trying to hold back, to keep their affairs separate, to only do what a neighbor with time on her hands might do. But this was Hawk. The one she had spent the best summers of her life with, when they were as inseparable as the twins were now. She had broken with him completely because she knew she couldn't take him in small pieces. Nothing or the whole cake. The very fact that she was walking beside him right now, and not beetling away, proved that her stiff resolve was ice cream on a hot day.

Hawk cleared his throat. "Anyway, it's not all bad. We produced Risky B, and she was the best from her line so far."

Grace forced herself to focus on Hawk's effort to steer the conversation in a safer, less personal direction. "Was?"

Hawk gave a little smile, and Grace's heart skipped at this sudden glimmer of happiness. "I think this one here's the best yet. I got this feeling."

"What does your dad think?"

"Dad keeps calling her Risky B." Amos let off a holler, and they looked up in time to see him jump off a stack of square bales and hit the ground. Saul ran over, making ambulance noises, and helped Amos to his feet. "Wish Dad was as easy to fix."

Grace gave up. "You're right, Hawk. It is personal between us. There's no going back to our summers again, but we are more than neighbors. Your best horse belongs to my sister and her husband, and she asks me about your state of mind—"

"What?" Hawk pushed up on his cowboy hat, his face flushed. "Haley thinks you know how I'm feeling?"

"Exactly my point. As much as we might throw up fences between us, there are five-year-olds, horses, nosy family and our own memories to knock them down. So how about we not fight it but deal with who we are and where we're at?"

Hawk scratched the filly behind the ears. "What did you have in mind?"

She glanced up at the ridge and back to his dark eyes, watchful and glinting.

"Okay, this is the thing. I feel as if we're family." She rushed on. "Not like brother and sister."

"Given our history, we are definitely not that."

His voice was rough, suggestive of— No. "Anyway, our mothers were best friends, and we lived in each other's homes during the summer, and then Mateo marries Haley, and then he buys your best horse, which is like—I don't know—buying a piece of you, and then I'm living on your land."

"Your dad's land now."

"That's what I mean. It's all mixed up for good, and so we need to figure us out. And until we do, you're not selling any more horses, especially to Mateo. We'll figure something out."

"Not sure you can tell me what to do."

"Hawk, didn't I just do that?"

He smiled, as if they were kids planning a camping trip. "We're one messed-up family."

Wasn't that the truth?

GRACE'S TWO ADULT guests emerged from their car, stretching, and shouting to each other, despite standing beside each other. It was amazing how quickly Grace had become used to the profound quiet of the country. The slamming of their car doors was like bullet shots. Or maybe it was her nerves. Ever since the online booking request had popped up last week, Grace had braced herself for her former colleagues.

"This place is absolutely amazing," Keira said, spinning slowly in all directions. She was the office manager at the firm and had helped assign interns to Grace in the case that turned out to be her last one. Grace had stopped at Keira's office on the way out with her moving box and had apologized for pressuring Keira into favoring her above the needs of the other lawyers in the firm. Keira had merely wished her well and asked her to stay in touch. And when Grace had assumed that Keira was just being nice, had called her three weeks later to ask how she was doing.

As soon as The Home Place opened, Keira had booked a room. And then she had sent a message last week to say that Rachelle wanted to tag along. Grace had swallowed her bile and agreed. Only two weeks after her Easter opening, she wasn't in the position to turn down clients.

"I kind of like it myself," Grace said. "Welcome."

Rachelle surveyed the place with a cynical smile. Why had she come? Rachelle and Grace had been hired within months of each other eight years ago, and they had become instant rivals for favor in their boss's eyes. They both entered a rivalry the years had not diminished.

The last case had been especially vicious, as Rachelle played all kinds of tricks to undermine Grace's work. But in the end, Rachelle had won. Won, because she was right. Grace had bullied staff and manipulated colleagues to the greater glory of her own case without regard for the firm. Her boss had been right to expunge her toxicity.

But Rachelle's victory still stung. She would take Rachelle's money and bite her tongue, as a delightful host should. And for Keira's sake. She didn't need a reenactment of workplace tension on her miniholiday.

She waited for them on the steps and Keira folded her in a tight hug. "I miss you," she whispered in her ear. "I especially miss your croissants."

Grace laughed and squeezed her friend back, absorbing her positive energy.

She looked over Keira's shoulder at Rachelle with her cynical smile still in place. Grace released Keira. "Hello, Rachelle. Welcome to The Home Place."

"Oh, I wouldn't have passed up this opportunity for the world." Without a word of invitation, she waltzed right in.

Keira's smile faded. "I'm sorry," she whispered. "I know she's not your favorite person."

If only to ease the worry lines on Keira's face, Grace would take the high road. "No problem," she said. "That's all in the past."

Rachelle was standing before the wood stove, her wheeled overnight bag at her feet. Grace had splurged on the pioneer woodstove replica from Natalia's store. Functional, but as Rachelle was proving, also eye-catching.

"Does this actually work?"

"Sure does," Grace said. "I'll be cooking your pancakes on it tomorrow morning."

Rachelle wrinkled her nose. "None for me. I'm strictly keto."

Grace had specifically asked about dietary references on her registration form, and Rachelle had filled in "None." "Then, an extra helping of eggs for you."

"I can eat meat as well. Steak or, if you don't have that, bacon."

Grace fixed a smile on her face. "I'll whip you up something special, Rachelle. Rest easy. How about I show you your rooms?"

When they arrived at the top of the stairs, Keira had her bag in tow, while Rachelle didn't. If she expected Grace to carry up her luggage, she was going to have to sleep in the clothes on her back and spend the day with fuzzy teeth.

"This is your room, Keira."

It was the larger of the two, with a queen-size bed. Russell and Angela's old room. Keira skimmed her fingers over the star-patterned quilt. "Did you make this?" Keira said. "It's absolutely gorgeous."

Mostly sage green, it was bordered in fabric she had specially ordered. "Thank you. I'm fond of it, too. There's an armoire over here," Grace said. "Three electrical outlets."

Rachelle gave a little snort. "Electricity. Yay."

If Rachelle only knew how much brainstorming had been done with the electricians to figure out a way to wirethe place and still meet code, she wouldn't be so sarcastic. No, check that. Not as sarcastic.

"And your room, Rachelle."

She took them farther down, past the bathroom. "A shared bathroom?" Rachelle questioned. "And the shower is downstairs?"

"I'm working with a home old enough to be a heritage site," Grace said. "The plumber and I had to be inventive."

"I think you should have negotiated a better deal," Rachelle said.

Grace couldn't have done better, but she registered Keira's pleading look and only said, "Perhaps so."

Grace opened the door to Rachelle'sbedroom and got the comment she expected. "Small."

"You are right, and that's reflected in the lower rate. But I think the view is first-class."

Rachelle moved to the window, and Grace braced herself for another criticism. How would the view of the greening ridge and a glimpse of the creek somehow not meet her standards? Instead, Rachelle gave a genuine smile.

"Well, would you look at that? A real-life cowboy."

"Let me see!" Keira joined Rachelle at the window, and sucked in her breath. "Oh wow! He's totally how you would picture them. Like at the Stampede."

She turned to Grace. "Do you know who he is?"

Grace dutifully peeked out the window. Sure enough, Hawk had emerged from the bank of trees on horseback. He was looking down, his cowboy hat covering most of his face, his hand loose on the reins as he approached the creek that ran behind her place. He wore a jacket shirt and work gloves, and yes, he looked exactly like he could star in a Western.

"Yeah, I know him. He lives up the road. We're neighbors."

Keira got right to the point. "Is he available?"

"I don't know. The topic hasn't come up."

"You've talked with him, and you haven't found out?" Keira squeaked.

Hawk let his horse edge to the creek crossing, and the horse stepped in. "That's so...incredible," Keira whispered.

Rachelle turned to Grace. "He's coming here. Right?"

"It would seem so. If you two want to make yourselves comfortable, I'll just go out—"

Keira waggled her finger at Grace. "No way are you keeping him to yourself." She paused. "Unless you already have plans—"

Grace waved her hand. "No, we're just— Our families are friends."

"Well then," Rachelle said, heading for the stairs and Hawk, "what's that about all's fair in love and war?"

No, no, no. If Rachelle and Keira talked to Hawk for two minutes, it would come out that she wasn't employed by the firm. She could already see the disappointment in his eyes.

She had to steer Hawk away. She caught up with Rachelle and Keira on the front steps. Hawk had crossed the creek and was coming up across the small pasture where the old paddocks had once stood.

"That horse," Grace said quickly, "sometimes gets spooked. You better let me check with Hawk first."

"Hawk? His name is Hawk?" Keira breathed. "That's so…perfect."

Grace intercepted Perfect Name at the edge of the paddock. "Hey, there."

He looked past her to Rachelle and Keira. "I've come at a bad time."

"A little bit. My guests just arrived and we were about to go out for dinner."

It was four in the afternoon, and his cool gaze said as much. "All right, then. I just wanted to stop by and put my signature on the consent for the trail."

"Okay, that's great." She did not want to pass up this opportunity. He was hard enough to track down, and he had come all this way.

"I can come by another time," Hawk said.

"No, no, I'll just go back in and grab the paperwork."

Hawk looked past her. "Meanwhile, it looks as if I'll be entertaining your guests."

Rachelle and Keira were fast closing the distance, Rachelle a few steps in the lead. Whether she liked it, Hawk was about to get pulled into her old work life.

"Hawk, I'd like you to meet my guests, Rachelle and Keira."

"More than that," Rachelle said, reaching up her hand to Hawk's. "We used to work together at the same firm."

Hawk removed his work glove and leaned down to take her hand. Rachelle hung on for a few seconds longer than she needed to, and Grace fought the urge to whack her hand loose. Keira gave a little wave and giggled.

Hawk's lips twitched. He had attended enough Calgary Stampede events to know exactly the effect he had on the urban bunnies. He glanced at Grace and his smile broadened. Nothing pleased Hawk Blackstone more than to see her riled up.

"Welcome to my part of the world," Hawk said. "Staying long?"

"Only until tomorrow," Rachelle said and added with a seductive purr, "but we're here all night long."

No way was Grace hosting a one-night stand under her roof.

"Grace says you live close by," Rachelle said.

"I do," Hawk said. "I live up the road with my family."

"With his twin boys," Grace said. "I take care of them twice a week. They are absolutely adorable. Anything to help Hawk out."

Grace knew she sounded catty, but she was doing this for Hawk's own good. Neither of them was suitable. Rachelle was too domineering, and Keira was...well, too submissive.

Keira took the hint and dropped her gaze. Rachelle, of course, saw it as a challenge. "Oh, how old?"

"Five."

"Really? I have a five-year-old niece."

"You do?" Keira said. "I never—" Rachelle shot her a look, and Keira shrugged.

Hawk had his laughing eyes on, and Grace knew he would grin all the way back home.

"So," Hawk said to Rachelle, "you said that you used to work with Grace. You at a different firm now?"

Rachelle blinked and turned to Grace. She could feel heat rise to her cheeks, to the top of her skull and beyond, into a little cloud of guilt above her. Rachelle took it all in, and spun back to Hawk.

"I'm at the same firm. It's Grace who has moved on. Have you managed to find a position elsewhere yet?"

Grace could feel Hawk's eyes cut to her. Could feel all sets of eyes on her. "My position is here right now," she mumbled.

"And what a great place to land in," Keira rushed in. "This is such beautiful country. And the views! And it even smells different. So…fresh! I kept telling Rachelle that on the drive here."

Be quiet, Keira. You're only making it worse. Or from Rachelle's smirk, better.

"Well, I've interrupted enough," Hawk said. "I'd better be getting back." He tipped his hat to Rachelle and Keira, something he and Grace used to do as kids when they were spoofing Westerns.

He gave her a nod, his expression unreadable. She couldn't tell if he was disappointed or angry for leading him on about her so-called sabbatical. Right after her big talk last week about how they were all one big happy family-like group. He'd opened up to her about Russell and then came to sign papers as a gesture of trust and hospitality, and in return, she had lied to him.

"I'll come by later," Grace said. "If that works."

"Sure," he said. "I'll be around."

It was a polite thing to say, but she could tell from the stiffness in his back that she had a lot of explaining to do.

CHAPTER FIVE

GRACE ENDED UP cooking supper for Rachelle and Keira, because the prima donna openly asked Grace to. Keira had rushed to say that guests were served breakfast only, but Rachelle had laughed and said, "Yes, but we're friends. Right, Grace?"

When it was just Keira coming, Grace had planned to cook a meal and they would have a long evening together of gossiping. Somewhere deep in a bottle of wine, Grace would apologize again for her office antics.

"Right," Grace said. "I'll fire up the barbecue and throw on steaks. Grill up some veggies. Will that do, Rache?"

"Wonderful," Rachelle said. "Will the marinade be gluten-free?"

"It'll be everything free," Grace said, "because there will be no marinade."

"Wonderful," Rachelle repeated. "How about we eat at seven?"

And on it went. Would Grace add an extra towel in the bathroom since the ones there were a little small? Would Grace check for the visiting hours at the local distillery? Would Grace open another wine bottle?

When Rachelle disappeared upstairs to use the bathroom after dinner, Keira sidled up to Grace in the kitchen. "I'm so sorry that I invited Rache out here. She's a diva at work, but I didn't know how much she has it out for you."

Grace scraped Rachelle's meal into the garbage, nearly

half a steak. She was not used to eating Grace's proportions, Rachelle had explained.

"It's okay, Keira. I'm more worried that she's ruining your time here. I handled her for nearly eight years, remember?"

"But she's coming on real strong, even for her."

"Rachelle and I were at each other's throats from day one, and I regret that, once again, you are caught in the middle." Grace could hear a toilet flush from upstairs and hurried on. "Listen, Keira, I want to apologize again for how I treated you during that last case. I was always a little pushy, but I went overboard. I don't regret all the work I did for my client, but I regret expecting you to favor me over the needs of others in the office."

Keira raised her hand as if to brush aside the apology, but then she lowered it and took a deep breath. "Yeah, it was…hard. Whatever I did, someone was unhappy. And that meant that I was always unhappy. It's…better now, I admit. Seeing you two together now brings it all back."

Grace felt sick to see Keira's dejection. "Look, I'm the problem. So I'm going to remove myself."

At Rachelle's step on the stairs, Grace called out. "Hey, I was just telling Keira that I have to run over to Hawk's. I need him to sign paperwork, and it's got a ticking clock on it. But here—" she signed the back of her business card and handed it to Keira "—your ticket to half-price drinks at the bar in Ridgeview, the big one with the Western front, Bar None Saloon. Saturday night, there's always a band, and it's shoulder to shoulder real cowboys."

"Really?" Keira said.

"Really. I know the owner." Grace knew the owner because she'd enlisted him into her network of local businesses. "And don't worry about drinking. I will drop you off and pick you up."

Keira turned to Rachelle, like a kid to a mom. "Can we? It'll be fun."

Rachelle crossed her arms. "When will you pick us up?"

"Twenty minutes after you call to say you want to be picked up."

"I suppose we could." She glanced over at her suitcase still parked in front of the woodstove. "I gave blood yesterday and I'm not supposed to lift anything for the next twenty-four hours. Would you mind?"

"Certainly," Grace said. Anything to get them on the road so she could try to set things right with Hawk.

GRACE FOUND HAWK leaning on the pasture fence for the five horses. When he turned at her greeting, his jaw was a hard line and his dark eyes strained. The earlier humor with Rachelle and Keira had vanished.

She drew her hand down her blond ponytail to calm her nerves. "I drove the girls to Bar None for a night on the town," Grace said. "I came out so we could finish our conversation." And confess to her lies.

"Bar None, eh?"

"Yeah, Emmett took it over from his dad, built a dance floor. There's live music every Saturday. Good bands, too. I've gone a couple of times." Back when the winter nights closed in early on her, alone in the half-renovated, memory-heavy home. She rattled on to cover for her nerves, "Emmett was there once, and we came up with the idea of a kind of passport of discounts and freebies for visitors to use at local, participating businesses."

"Emmett always was good at roping people into his schemes." Hawk sounded bitter. Why would—

Grace connected the dots. "Oh, that Emmett."

"Yeah, that Emmett."

A girl always remembers her first kiss, except the aftermath of Grace's was far more memorable. At eighteen, she was still without her first kiss. She and Hawk had driven to the bar on her last night at the ranch before returning to the Jansson Ranch and then to her first year of university. When Emmett had shown interest in her, she sneaked out with him to his truck. A rap on the glass from Hawk had interrupted them.

"Still want a ride home, or you made other plans?"

She had gone back to the ranch with Hawk, and they had their first and last fight together out here in the middle of the horse pasture under a flashlight beam. Why had she kissed a stranger when he had brought her to the bar? Why did he think they were on a date? How could she not have tried with him? She remembered her answer, the one that shut the fight down for good. *Because we are friends, and friends don't kiss.*

He had walked off into the darkness and she'd gone back to the house. She left the next day, with Hawk already fixing fence in the far pasture. Grace covered with a story about how they'd said their goodbyes the night before. Once gone, she couldn't find a way to heal the rift, and her mother's death had kept her away.

She followed Hawk's gaze out to the horses covered in blankets. The yearling held tight to his mother's side. Never too old for Mama's warmth. Did Amos and Saul miss their mom that way? What was it like to have a mom who wasn't there for you?

"We need to figure out what to do about the cows coming into your yard," Hawk said without preamble. "The fence got so rotten we took it down and let the cattle into the yard, but that won't work going forward."

"I can put it back in."

"For my cattle? That isn't fair."

Except if Mateo was right, Hawk was cash-strapped.

Between the sale of her condo and her decade of savings, Grace had money, even after all the renos. But she knew Hawk wouldn't accept money straight out. "How about you provide the muscle? That's more than the materials. Fair enough?"

"All right. I'll be turning the cattle out in the next few weeks, so the sooner I can get at it, the better."

She was adding to his workload, but— "And that horse pen attached to the fence… Do you think you could tighten up the wire, put in a few new posts for the trail horses?"

"You found horses, then?"

"Not yet, but I'm sure something will turn up in the next couple of months."

Hawk grunted. "And if it doesn't?"

Grace hated his pessimism. When they were kids, he had talked about how he was going to have a hundred horses and people working for him and go to shows across North America. "Then I will have a place for them when it does. You draw up a shopping list and I'll order it."

"We can load it on my truck. Saves the delivery charge. And I run the boys into town every other day, anyway."

"They weren't with you today."

"At their aunt's in town. Her daughter's fourteenth birthday."

"And five-year-olds were invited?"

"It was the family party. No doubt she'll have her own friends' party, too. But Gemma and her husband are big on family."

They would be the sister or the brother to Hawk's ex. Another piece of information she filed away. When news of Hawk's wedding had reached her, she had not recognized the bride's name. Eva, her dad had said, had moved with her family from Calgary to Diamond Valley to open a jewelry store.

The cattle were in the sprawling pasture next to the horses, and in the quiet, she could almost hear them chewing their cud. Nathan moved among them with his dog, Doxie Sue.

"Your hired hand seems to fit right in."

"Not bad for a stray."

She settled her shoulder blades against the pipe railing, pulled the cuffs of her sweater over her hands to warm them in the freezing spring evening. "I got to hear this story." She didn't really, but anything to avoid owning up to her lie.

"Not much to it. Amy brought him over, and he says he's looking for work. Willing to work for room and board, and a bit of spending money. We agreed to try each other out, and if either didn't like the arrangement, off he'd go. That was November."

A stranger with unscheduled access to the twins. "But you don't know his background. I mean, with kids."

"He's from Montana and that's paperwork I frankly don't have the time for. Besides, he came with a dog."

"You're telling me that if he's good enough for a dog, then he's good enough to have around kids?"

"She's one smart dog." Hawk rolled his shoulders. "You come here to investigate my help?"

No, but she liked to lean on the fence and talk things over with Hawk. "My dad's coming down on Tuesday. Is it okay if I bring him over to see Russell?"

"Did you tell him about Dad?"

"I don't think I'll have to. Dad will see it for himself. I don't know if he'll say anything to your dad, though."

"Avoiding the truth seems to run in the family," Hawk said, squaring to her. "Does a friend lie?"

Well, here it was. "No, she doesn't, unless the truth is embarrassing. It was kind of my fault."

He looked ready to listen, then his jaw tightened right up again. "None of my business."

"How about you make it yours for a few minutes? I've got no one else to talk to about it."

"What about Haley and your dad?"

"I haven't told them. What about *embarrassing* didn't you hear? On top of disappointing Dad. He tells everyone about me being a hotshot lawyer, and now I'm a glorified homemaker."

"Nothing wrong with that," Hawk said. "Both our moms were that, and neither of us think any the less of them."

"You know what I mean."

"I don't think I do, but go ahead. Convince me." Some of the tension had gone from his body. If her minor tragedy distracted him from his genuine worries, so be it.

"I have developed a bit of a reputation for being a bull-dog in civil law matters."

Hawk's mouth twitched. "You don't say."

She glared. "Do you want to hear this or not?"

"You're the one who wanted to talk it out." His mouth was about to split into a smile. She should hate him for enjoying himself, but it was enough that he was.

"Anyway, city council approved my client's small six single-home development in north Calgary. It had taken two years to gain that approval, during which a car accident had taken his wife, leaving him with seven-year-old twin daughters."

Hawk made a sympathetic noise in his throat.

"You know where he's coming from. He had mortgaged his assets to the hilt. He had sold their home to pay for mounting costs, and moved into a tiny one-bedroom apartment. They ate spaghetti most nights."

Grace stopped. There were so many parallels between her former client and Hawk that she had not noticed before.

Single father. Twins. Hard luck. She had always thought that she had fought for the man because his cause was just. But three years ago, she had argued against Hawk selling the Blackstone home place, and their father had bought it out of regard for some convoluted ancestral link between their mother and related Blackstones in Montana. Grace had pushed for a solution, but her dad had saved the day. Fighting for her client was fighting for Hawk when she hadn't the power to save him on her own.

"The suspense is killing me," Hawk interrupted her thoughts.

"The city was stonewalling him with paperwork. He couldn't afford my fee, he said, but neither could he afford any more delay. His story hit home for me. Maybe it was the death of his daughters' mother. Sudden, like Mom's. Their lives had changed forever. So I took on the case." She wouldn't admit to the part of how her client's case reminded her of Hawk. That connection was too raw, yet.

"I discovered one council member directly interfering because the developer's homes would ruin her view. I became...intense. I snatched legal interns from their work on other lawyers' cases, and shifted my caseload to colleagues with promises of help and then didn't keep my word. And yes, sleep deprivation made me snippy."

"Remember that time you pulled an all-nighter waiting for a cougar?"

"I protected us."

"Against nothing. Except I got you as mean as a cougar all the next day. So yeah, I sympathize with the staff."

"I thought it was worth the trouble in the end. My client won damages from the city and we had forced the council member to step down amid allegations of personal interference. I bought pizza and beer for the entire office, and while they were kicking back, my boss called me into his office.

"I expected him to congratulate me. Which he did, and then he handed me my notice. I sat there stunned as he explained how I had thrown his entire firm into chaos. I won the case, but had lost the goodwill of the firm. His duty was to the firm.

"'Maybe,' he said, "'you should find an occupation more suited to your temperament.'"

Hawk grinned. "And here you are, a B and B owner in God's country."

"Yeah, look at me. I sent him and his wife an invitation to come visit at my good-guy price as a way to reach out and try to get back in their good graces. George and Hilda were family friends. He brought me on as a favor to my dad, and I've disappointed them…and my dad. That's the real reason I don't want him finding out."

"What if George and your dad talk?"

Grace dragged her hands down her face. "The terror is real, believe me."

"You want to go back?"

"I don't know where I want to be, but this is as good a place as any to find out where that is."

"So, ask me." His voice was low, dogged. "Ask me for the favor you really came over to get."

"All right. I'm hoping that you don't tell Dad about my job and, by extension, don't tell your dad either, in case it slips out."

"You're going to have to tell your dad at some point."

"I told him I was on sabbatical until September. I've got the summer to figure things out. I guess I want to buy time and get something going for myself so he won't worry that I ruined my life."

"Can't you just look for work at another firm?"

"I can, but—" She swallowed. "I can't swear that I won't do the same thing all over again. And besides—word gets out. I'd practically have to go independent."

"You could set up somewhere else in Calgary."

"I sold my condo."

"Whoa. You really pulled up stakes. But the longer you delay, the bigger the lie in the end. That and I'll have to keep up the lie in front of Mateo and Haley."

"Are you saying you want something in return?"

"No, I don't want anything." He spoke with such finality, it hurt.

"Will you do it?"

"I won't tell Knut."

Grace let out her breath.

"But Mateo is a different story. If he asks me directly, I'm not lying to him. I've got too much riding on my dealings with him to harm it with a lie to save you from putting off the inevitable."

"That's fine." She would just have to make sure that she didn't give Mateo any reason to ask. But wait—

"Too much riding on what dealings?"

He turned back to the horses. In the growing dark, the horses were silhouettes. Outrage and loyalty rose inside her, the same emotions she had felt when listening to the developer's case. If she would lose her job over a guy whose circumstances were something like Hawk's, how far would she go to help the real Hawk?

She touched her hand to his arm. "Talk to me."

HAWK FELT THE pressure of her hand on his arm like the heat of the sun, despite chilly evening. There had been a time when he had thrived with her around. A cloud had hung over him for years after she had left and never come back, even for a visit.

Now listening to the story of her firing had brought back what he had missed about her. The same Grace pushing the envelope for whatever cause she had set her mind on. Cougars or city hall, she never backed down.

"You might as well tell me, because all I have to do is call up Haley and ask her."

She had him there. She always had him. "I'm thinking of selling the horses."

"All of them?"

"Yes."

"But Blackstone Ranch isn't Blackstone without the horses."

Trust her to cut to the heart of it all. "Didn't you say that our families' businesses cross over, anyway? Mateo would have them, is all."

"But you agreed not to sell the horses."

"You telling me not to doesn't equate to me agreeing, Grace."

"Fair enough, but Haley told me Mateo would rather look for another solution, rather than take your horses."

"Then I would owe him," Hawk said. "And you have no idea how tired I am of owing people money." He had never said that aloud before. Even with Mateo, he had kept it mostly to business. But one conversation with Grace in the near dark, her hand on him, and he was coming apart. He shifted his arm along the railing, stretching the space so her hand might easily slip away. Instead, she edged closer. "It's that bad, eh?"

The automatic halogen light at the barn switched on, and suddenly the two of them were lit up. He bent his head under the sudden glare, the sight of her hand on his arm filling his vision. "It's not good."

"I thought that by selling the home quarter, you would've got back on your feet."

"Other bills came up."

"Like the ex?"

People thought Eva had taken him to the cleaners. He had sidestepped all that, but it was too much for Grace to think that way, too. "Of all the debts I have, I don't begrudge a cent to my kids' mother. She and I made an agreement, and I'll stick to it."

"Even if it means losing the ranch?"

He jerked his arm out from underneath her hand. "You have a knack for tearing me down, Grace."

Her hand fisted on the railing. "What's that supposed to mean?"

"How can you not know, clever lawyer?" He could feel his old frustrations on the rise. That talk about Emmett hadn't helped. Grace had forgotten about that night at the bar, as if it didn't matter that it had ruined their friendship, had ruined his stupid youthful dreams of a life with her. "How about we call it a night? I'll come over to fence. I'll keep your secret. Deal?"

Grace held up her hand. "No way. We're going to hash this out. I have a stake in this ranch, too. It was me three years ago who talked to Haley and Dad about the home quarter."

"Sweet deal for you. You got a piece of Blackstone without having to marry into it."

She flinched, and Hawk didn't blame her. He was hurting and had lashed out at her. He opened his mouth to apologize, but Grace spoke first. "You're right. I didn't. And since I'm now in your life whether you like it or not, how about we deal with this Emmett elephant once and for all?"

"Emmett's not the problem. I never cared that he kissed you."

She cocked her head skeptically.

"Not as much as I cared that you didn't want to kiss me."

"I told you it was because—"

"Friends didn't kiss. I don't need the reminder. Fifteen years later, and I still remember. You were always up for anything, and yet when it came to us, you didn't even want to try one kiss. That's what hurt."

She drew her hand down her ponytail, a kind of self-soothing gesture that pulled at Hawk. "I admit there were times when I wondered what might have happened if I had given in."

The collapse of their friendship had torn her up, maybe not as much as it had eaten at him, but the point was that it had mattered. He caught her hand in his and pulled her close. "And now? Now that not kissing didn't work out so well? Should we try it my way this time?"

Her eyes widened in surprise, her lips, inches from his, quivered.

"Say it, Grace. Say what you have denied us for the past fifteen years."

She laid her free hand on his face, her fingers scraping his stubble. "All right, Hawk. All right."

He kissed her, holding nothing back. And she responded in kind. It took the same effort as pushing away a falling horse, but he pulled away.

"Well, Grace. What are we now?"

GRACE WAS WIDE awake when Rachelle called her at midnight for a ride back. It was almost a relief to pick them up and listen to their tipsy patter about country music and two-stepping cowboys. Anything to take her mind off Hawk's kiss.

And his question. She had not given him a straight answer, had made an excuse about pressing phone calls and paperwork. He had given a little half smile and wished her a good night. He knew she was running off.

Grace brewed a dark roast coffee for herself the next morning. She hadn't taken more than a bitter, reviving sip before Rachelle descended from on high and plunked herself down across from Grace. Grace hadn't seen her without makeup before. She had great skin, though a little green right now.

"I'll get you a coffee," Grace said. She didn't bother to offer cream or sugar. She and Rachelle had always preferred their coffee strong and black. The staff room reserved all the dark roast pods for them. Rachelle had them all to herself now.

Grace set her biggest mug, filled to the brim with the black potion, before Rachelle. "Steak and eggs now, or do you want to wait for Keira?"

Rachelle groaned and shook her head. Grace sat again, bracing herself for Rachelle's onslaught. Hangover or not, her old rival wouldn't pass up a chance to needle her about something.

It didn't take more than a half-dozen sips. "How did it go with Hawk last night?"

A rather presumptuous question. She and Rachelle had never socialized together outside of the group events, like a Christmas party or Friday staff drinks.

Grace shrugged. "Good. We sorted out issues around land sharing."

"I bet he folded."

Grace bristled. "You know, Rachelle, I settled a whole lot more cases before they went to court than in court. I can negotiate. Believe it or not, I prefer a win-win situation."

Rachelle widened her eyes. "You do know how he looks at you, right?"

Grace took a gulp of coffee, the heat nicely searing its way down her throat. "I don't know what you're talking about."

Rachelle stared at Grace as if to force a confession out

of her, and then she peered more closely at Grace. "You really don't know."

Her old office nemesis pushed aside her coffee. "Let me enlighten you. This is how he looked at me." Rachelle gave a friendly smile. "And to Keira." Rachelle's smile widened into something reminiscent of Hawk. "Now, this is how he looks at you." Rachelle's mouth shortened to a tease of a smile, her eyes softened, lingered. Yes, she had seen that look. Just before his lips had closed on hers. But all the time?

"Stop it," Grace said, and Rachelle laughed.

"It's not me you need to tell to stop."

"I think it is. If you could see that he...he has feelings for me, why did you tell him about my firing, then?"

Rachelle set her elbows on the table and leaned across to Grace. "Because I hate liars just as much as you."

Grace blinked before Rachelle's intensity. "Fine. Apparently, he's not as hung up about liars as you and me. He was more concerned about me not telling my family." Why was she confiding to Rachelle as if they were best buddies? "You really are good at getting information out of reluctant people."

"It's why I'm sitting in your office now," Rachelle said.

Her junior partner spot.

"You didn't know? I thought Keira would have told you. About a month after you left, I got my invitation."

It should have hurt. But after last night's kiss, it was only one more confused feeling in an already whirling mix. "Congratulations." It wasn't as hard to say as she thought it would be.

And from the way Rachelle's triumphant smile faded away, she knew it. "I see you've moved on to greener pastures."

Meaning Hawk. One kiss did not determine a future

together. Especially a future she wasn't sure she wanted. She wasn't ready to give up her law career and settle in as a simple B and B owner. She wanted…something more.

Who are we now?

Forget that. Who was *she* now?

CHAPTER SIX

As soon as he dropped the kids off at kindergarten on Tuesday morning, Hawk beelined for Grace's place. The Home Place. Smart to use what the Blackstone family had always referred to the old homestead as. It had a nice ring to it. Another linking together of the Blackstones and Janssons.

Of course, their families wouldn't be joined. The wild dreams of his twenty-year-old self weren't going to fall into place because he had finally kissed the woman who had got away. She had run off again, after his question. Not that he knew the answer himself. Today, he was just the guy building her a fence.

He was coming up on the straight before the bend at Irina's place when he recognized her truck coming toward him. He expected to exchange waves, but she slowed and stuck out her hand. He rolled to a stop alongside her open window.

"You're a busy man," Irina said. "I've been meaning to stop in, but I see you coming and going on the road so often I can never say for certain when you're home."

"Coming and going describes my life. What can I do for you?"

"I was just wondering if Grace has talked to you about her plans for your home quarter."

He had sold the land nearly three years ago, and Irina

acted as if it belonged to the Blackstones. "You mean the trail rides? Yes."

"You're not going to let her do it, are you?"

"I don't know that I have any objection. She sounded pretty reasonable to me."

"You would think that. You have a soft spot for city girls."

"Grace isn't from the city." Now, why say that? It admitted that he had a soft spot for her. "I'm not sure what the problem is."

"The problem," Irina said, pointing with her thumb behind her to the bend, "is that corner there." Hawk did not have to follow the backward point of her thumb to know she meant the crash site. Like the stone cairn for Miranda on the ridge, a wooden life-size horse, painted roan, stood there now, and soon Irina would set out containers of flowers where the saddle would go. "It's unnecessary. Her whole business isn't necessary. Why do people need to come out here to relax? Let us work our butts off in peace."

There was a time when Hawk couldn't have agreed more. A pre-Grace time. "I understand, Irina."

"If you did, you wouldn't sign off your support, which you plan to, right?"

Hawk nodded.

Irina lifted a folder from the passenger seat. "And that's why I'm going into town now to request to make a presentation when county sits for a second reading on her proposal. I'm making two. On my behalf. And on behalf of the ranchers' association. That's two against your one, Hawk. She might be a lawyer, but I'm meaner."

Hawk repeated the message to Grace during a lunch break. It was the first time he had stepped inside the place where he'd spent the first twenty-five years of his life since the sale. The house was already the worse for wear then, and while they had taken care to board up the windows and drain out water, a good decade of vacancy had taken its toll. When he had sold the quarter to Knut, he half expected the house to get demolished.

Instead, he stepped into a full restoration. Grace gave a tour of his old home, and he was happy to tag behind her long legs and messy blond twist of hair. She had updated the kitchen and flooring, replaced fixtures, stripped off old wallpaper and painted the walls, and installed new windows. Yet she had maintained the open concept of one living area flowing into the next. She had kept the hardwood flooring in the living room and polished over the scars. Grace had brought The Home Place back to life. He might feel at home himself here, if it wasn't a beautiful reminder of his failure to keep the Blackstone land together.

He rubbed the newel post at the bottom of the stairwell. "You kept this."

"It's smaller," she said. "I had it sanded down before applying the stain. But even now when I make the turn, it kick-starts my day."

"Yeah, I know what you mean. Now two sets of feet hitting the floor do that for me."

"Which reminds me…" She moved into a story about their latest shenanigans, and that carried them right into a lunch of burgers and homemade fries. All very friendly, but he felt a kind of frisson between them that hadn't existed before. She gave him a small, knowing smile and he realized that she'd caught him staring at her.

He cleared his throat. "I met Irina on the road," he said. "She plans to oppose you at the second reading."

Grace straightened. "But why? I followed every regulation to the T."

Hawk didn't relish gossiping about other people. But

this was Grace, and maybe some insight might smooth
things over for everyone concerned.

"Irina…is scared. Her husband left her with a daughter to raise."

"Lena, I remember her. She was a few years older than
us. I always felt like such a kid around her. Didn't she
marry and move away?"

"She did, but it was to the wrong guy. She came back
with a little girl. Amy. You met her, the babysitter. But
about a year later, not long after your mom passed, Lena
was killed out at that corner."

Grace gasped. "That is who the horse cairn in the ditch
is for. It's…hard to miss."

"Lena was riding in the ditch, and an RV came around
the bend too fast, lost control and hit her and the horse."

The aftermath of that scene still flashed through Hawk's
mind. In a quiet country, he had heard the squeal and crush
of steel from their place, a full mile away. And then the
screams of people, and what pricked up the ears of the
Blackstone horses, the scream of a horse.

While Irina rode with her daughter in the ambulance,
Russell had put down the horse and his mom gathered up
Amy from Irina's house.

"It was a hard day, that one," Hawk said.

Grace frowned. "But what has that to do with my trail
rides? They are not on the road."

"There's the issue of increased traffic. It is a dangerous
curve, if you're not used to it. But—" Hawk hesitated, unsure of opening up to Grace. She widened the blue pools
of her eyes and like a fool, he plunged in.

"Something else you might not know. This home quarter used to belong to the Sandbergs. They claimed it first.
Then, when my great-grandfather showed up a few months
later and took up the land here and to the south, the first

Sandberg sold half the quarter to him and both their names went on the title. That continued out of habit until Irina's husband died, and she sold the other half to my dad. She needed the money, yes, but she thought she was selling to a Blackstone. And then I sell it to an outsider. I didn't even let her know my plans."

"Why didn't you?"

Because he would have had to acknowledge that he had failed to hold on to the land. As it was, he had disappointed his own parents. His dad had blamed himself. *I poured too much into the horses, and left you with the fallout.* "I honestly didn't know it would bother her."

"But you are not to blame. You did what you had to do. How many times do I have to say that before you believe it?"

Every day of my life, he thought. He looked around at his old home, her new one. She had restored The Home Place—and a bit of the Blackstone legacy. He pushed away his coffee. Time to do his part. "Let me get started on the fence."

A WEEK LATER, Knut and Russell sat sideways to the dining table, their legs stretched out, and talked. They had wandered about the ranch for the past couple of hours, shooting the breeze, and had come in for a cup of coffee. The boys were outside with Amy. Hawk stayed in the background as he did household chores, trying not to appear to be monitoring his dad.

Irina pulled up. Hawk welcomed her in and she called a "hello" to Russell. And there it was, the hand over the temple, the frown as Russell searched for the right name. Knut made the connection first. "Irina. Well now."

Irina's hand fluttered to her short hair, her cheek. "Knut Jansson. Is that really you?"

Knut stood, touched his own gray hair. "It is. Hard to believe. But you haven't changed."

She came over, hand extended for a shake. "Then, you need new eyeglasses."

Russell waved to a kitchen chair. "Have a seat. I'll get you a coffee."

"I can grab that." Hawk could see from the way his dad's eyes darted about that processing a new arrival was already taxing enough. The more people for Russell to sort out, the harder it was for him to track. He hesitated and trailed off a couple of times, but Irina and Knut didn't seem to notice. The two chatted, and Russell frowned and his silence grew longer.

Grace pulled up. He hadn't seen her for more than a week, other than brief exchanges when dropping off and picking up the boys.

"Grace is home," Russell announced.

It was so dead wrong, so patently false, that both Irina and Knut turned to Hawk for confirmation. Irina's look was of disapproval; Knut's of open curiosity.

"A bit of a joke," Hawk said. "She's over here so often."

She hadn't come alone. She held the hand of a little red-head about the boys' age.

"That's Sadie," Knut said. "She's the grandkid I was talking about." As soon as she came inside, she kicked off her boots and climbed onto Knut's lap as if she had full rights there.

At least, that's what Hawk saw from the corner of his eye. He mostly had his eye on Grace. She came in like a fresh breeze, all swinging blond ponytail and fancy blue jeans. She carried a big shopping bag. "Are the boys around?"

"Outside with Amy."

She held up the bag. "I finished putting the border on the quilts and I couldn't wait to show them."

"How many quilts is that now?" Knut said. "One hundred?"

"I lost count. Natalia knows better. She insists I keep her updated. But I don't plan on telling her about these two. These are real heirloom pieces."

"You quilt?" Irina said.

"She can do just about anything," Russell said. "Right, Hawk? This one's a keeper. Not like..." His hand went to his temple. *Don't Dad. Don't.* "The other one. I forget her name." He lifted his head. "Not important, anyway."

Russell had never approved of Eva, but Hawk had made him promise not to badmouth her in front of the kids. He was keeping his promise, but his talk was making the others uncomfortable.

Grace dove her hand into the bag. "I'm not taking credit for these creations. Amos and Saul originals. The first crazy quilts off the Blackstone production line."

She spread two quilts over the dining table, and Hawk drew closer. He recognized the boys' outgrown shirts and pajamas. Cloth bunched like pebbles in places. "Amos did this one." It was big chunks of color with two-inch ridges here and there. "And this is Saul's." It wasn't bad. There was a kind of pattern there.

"The boy has an artist's eye," Grace said to Hawk. "I'm so proud of him."

He would never have thought his rowdy boys would ever sit long enough to quilt. He had thought she meant a few patches sewn together.

"Thanks, Grace."

"Believe me, my pleasure. Where—"

Amy came through the front door. "Gramma, what are you doing here?"

"Visiting," Irina said. "Is that a crime?"

"No," Amy sighed. "I lost track of the boys."

Russell made a disgusted noise. "Those boys are always running off. Don't worry. They'll come back. You chase after them, and you chase them all their life. I remember when we were that age, and gone all day."

He looked for support to Irina and Knut who were exchanging glances between themselves.

"I keep telling Hawk not to let the boys run the show." His dad was getting wound up.

"I'll go out and check again," Amy said, backing away.

"I'll come with you," Grace said. "Let's go, Sadie. I want you to meet Amos and Saul." She cast a look at Hawk, her expression clear enough for him to read. *You take care of your dad, and I'll take care of the boys.*

His dad turned out to be right, sort of. Grace with Sadie and Amy had barely reached the corrals before the boys came ripping around the house, straight out of the caragana bushes, pedaling their bikes, in hot pursuit of whatever their imaginations had created. He could see Grace and Amy turn at the screaming and start back.

"What did I tell you?" Russell looked around in triumph. "They showed up, not giving a care for the trouble they're causing."

"That's kids for you," Irina said neutrally. She turned to Knut. "I hear you have more than one grandkid."

"Two so far, and two more that feel like my own."

Irina rested her cheek on her hand. "Oh?"

Knut explained how he had two through his biological daughter, Haley, and another two with the man who used to be his hired hand and his wife. Brock Holloway. Hawk knew of him through Mateo. They ranched together, now. Hawk wished he had a partner like that. Close, family even. "Brock and Natalia, their coming together is quite the story."

Irina deepened her resting posture. "I like a good story,"

Was she flirting with Knut? Knut's eyes crinkled, and he gave Irina a soft look over his mug.

Through the open kitchen window, Hawk heard Grace call to the boys about someone she would like them to meet. They detoured to her and he couldn't quite make out her introductions to Sadie. Saul took Grace's free hand, leaving Amos to tuck himself right in front of Grace as they all moved forward together. One kid must have said something, because she stopped in her tracks, threw back her head and laughed.

If he was lucky, she would share the story later with him.

Grace must have told the boys that there was a surprise was on the dining table, because they rushed in, screaming, "Cookies!"

They were brought up short by the quilts, and then they were all over that, dragging them off the table, hiding under them, rolling in them. Everyone, including Hawk, was caught up in their antics.

His dad jumped to his feet. "Hey, watch what you're doing! You're wrecking them. Grace made them for you!"

He reached and yanked the quilt off Amos, but he must have caught hold of Amos's hair too, and Amos let out a howl.

"Shut up," Russell said and pulled on Saul's quilt. Saul spun out of it. "Look at the mess you two made. You two are nothing but trouble."

His dad had never yelled at the boys. He couldn't remember his dad ever yelling. Stern words, yes. That had been enough. This was not his dad.

Saul started crying, and Amos stared in fright at his grandfather.

His dad drew himself up sharply, and he looked about. Irina, Knut with Sadie back on his lap and tucked tight against his chest, Grace, and finally Hawk. Sudden terror welled up in his father's eyes.

His dad left the room without another word. And everybody, including Grace, left within minutes. She looked at him in sympathy, but he couldn't bear to hold her gaze.

His dad didn't come out of his room for the rest of the day. Supper comprised of food being pushed around plates, and it was the quietest bedtime since the boys had started talking. Hawk was walking past his room on his way to his own room at the end of the hall later that evening when his dad emerged. His face was pale and drawn. "You make me an appointment, okay?"

Hawk swallowed. "Okay, Dad."

HER DAD TOOK the lead up the slope the next day, with Grace a few steps behind, the task so much lighter than when she had tramped up the hill more than a month ago.

The three kids—Amos, Saul and Sadie—ran about her dad and Grace, like gophers, whizzing back to them to show off with their treasures or to tank up on the water Grace had packed. They were on their way to visit her mother's favorite viewpoint. And location of her cairn.

"They remind me of you girls and Mateo and Hawk, all running together in the summers."

"The four of us didn't often run together. It was mostly Hawk and me picking on the other two until they went off on their own."

"Well, all that time together paid off."

"For Mateo and Haley."

They had reached the outcropping of rock where she had twisted her ankle. And Hawk had rescued her. She had flirted with him, and why? Had part of her wanted to reconnect even then?

Her dad sat on a flat spot of the boulder. "I suppose it could for you and Hawk, too. You are both free to choose each other."

"Because we're both available, because we ran together when we were kids, because we're neighbors? Because it's convenient?"

Knut held up his phone and took a snap of Sadie and the boys. She was slung betweenthem. Amos had her underneath the shoulders, and Saul by her boots, as they rescued her from what sounded like a fire in the barn. Sadie waved her arms and begged them to save the horses.

"Sounds as if you've already given this some thought."

Grace seated herself on another part of the rock, an edge biting into her butt. "I might have, and that's all I'm saying on the matter."

Knut grunted. "I suppose you have a whole life in the city, still."

Grace turned away, using the kids as an excuse not to look at him. "There is that, but I'll be here often enough."

"Hard to be in two places at once. Hard for the heart to be, at any rate."

Her dad seemed to be gunning for her to move out here. To give it all up. If she did, then she would never have to confess about her firing. At least, not right away. "Would you be okay if your lawyer daughter gave up the city life and became a quilter and B and B operator?"

"What do I care what you are, so long as you're healthy and happy?"

That was about as good of an opening line to make her

confession as any. Except she couldn't be sure that living out here forever and a day would make her happy. Neither could she keep him out of the loop. Her dad and George would eventually talk. She would tell her dad once she screwed up the courage.

A sudden wind slapped against them and Knut tugged his hat down tighter. "I guess we better keep going before we are blown back down the hill."

It wasn't just the wind that slowed their steps as they climbed. Her mother's cairn gradually came into view. No longer just a blip on the ridge, but with form and shape. And remembrance.

The kids had quieted as they drew closer, perhaps picking up on the quiet of the adults. The horse trail, which once ran straight along the ridge, now took a detour around the cairn, like a loose loop in a straight stitch. How many times had Hawk ridden past? He'd kept more in contact with her mother's memory over the decade than any Jansson had.

As they approached, Grace reached out her hands and felt the boys slip theirs in. Sadie did the same with Knut.

"Dad has never taken us here," Amos said.

"He said it's too dangerous," Saul added.

"He's right," Grace said. "Under no circumstances are you two to let go of my hands. There's a drop-off here." A deadly one.

Knut approached the cairn with Sadie. She fastened her attention onto the rock arrangement. "Isn't that a cairn? Uncle and Auntie helped me put one up for Daddy where he fell into the river. Did somebody die here?"

Knut looked over at Grace. So much for a tale of pretty views. "Yes, Sadie."

Sadie twisted to look up at him. "Your wife?"

"Yes."

Saul laid his head against Grace's arm. She couldn't see his face under his hat, but from the weight of his head, he was feeling it. Amos was digging his toe into the grass.

"Okay," Sadie said. "Do you want me to get a new rock for it?"

Her dad rubbed his thumb along Sadie's hand. "I think she'd like that."

She turned to the boys. "Come on. Let's look for rocks. One for each of us."

She scampered down the hill. Amos's hand twisted in Grace's as he stretched to follow her. He stopped. "Can I? Can we?"

"So long as you come back straight to me. Got it?"

Her attention still angled to the kids, she watched her dad at the cairn. The rest of the ridge had a steep but not a deadly drop-off. It was only here at his feet, where some ancient forces had sheared off the rock, that a cliff had formed, and from then on, water and wind had worn away at the face. This horse path, formed hundreds of years ago, traversed by natives, first on foot and then on horseback, and then by settlers, had inches shaved away—until time and circumstance narrowed to one fateful second.

Hawk had discovered the body. And shot the horse.

"Did you ever speak to Hawk about—what happened?" Grace said.

"There wasn't much to tell."

Grace wasn't so sure about that. From the stillness in Hawk's frame when he'd talked about Lena's death, coming a year after her mother's couldn't have been easy. He was probably sparing her father. "Okay."

Her dad lifted his eyes from the cairn, west to the Rockies. It was an immense view. The blue sky with far ribbons of cloud, the long range of Rockies still capped with snow, blue and craggy, rounding into the grassy heave of the foothills. A harsh, unforgiving country of rough rivers and skin-stripping winds. Even now, the wind plucked at them, buffeted her, testing her footing, looking for a way in.

He raised his phone to the view and tapped the screen. So these were the missing pictures he had talked about. "I could always tell when she'd been up on this ridge," her dad said, taking another picture from a different angle. "She'd call and say 'I was up on the ridge' and she sounded as if she'd talked to God. She told me in the morning she was heading up there, and I waited for her call."

"I should have been there with her," Grace said. "She asked and I begged off."

"You still holding on to that?" Her dad lowered his phone, and wrapped his arm around her shoulders and pulled her tight to him. "You can't beat yourself over that all your life. Let it go."

"You're one to talk," Grace said. "How many years has it been?"

"Thirteen years on the day I called to say I was coming down."

"Oh." She had only remembered the month, not the day.

"And you're right. It's time both of us let her rest in peace."

"We're coming!" Amos yelled, even though she had been monitoring his progress the whole time. The kids were making their way back up the hill, slowed by the weight of their burden. Amos carried a rock the size of his head, Saul juggled two jagged ones and Sadie cradled two egg-sized ones.

Grace had them deposit their load well away from the cairn. Knut walked the kids, one at a time, up the hill with their personal offerings, taking a picture each time. Rocks in place, Grace retreated off the ridge with the kids, letting Knut have a moment alone. She glanced over her shoulder, expecting him to still be on one knee at his wife's marker. He had risen and was gazing in the opposite direction to where Irina lived.

Her father might have let go. She looked toward the Blackstone Ranch. She had avoided Hawk for so long— and avoided her own conflicted feelings for him. Maybe it was time to take her mom's advice and move on. Not away from Hawk, but to him. And face up to the one person she had always avoided—herself.

CHAPTER SEVEN

IRINA ROLLED THE wheelbarrow out of the barn, the empty metal chop pails from feeding grain to the horses clanging away, just as Knut pulled into her yard two mornings after the visit with Russell. Poor Russell. What was going on there?

As Knut unfolded from his truck, Irina paused to admire how he was every bit the handsome rancher who had stolen her good friend's heart. He looked around her spread. There wasn't much for him to see. With only her and Amy, and a tractor that worked half-time, they had scaled down to next to nothing. She might have to sell, not for lack of money but for lack of manpower.

Knut approached with a long, easy stride, messing up her heartbeat.

"Irina," he said with the same lift as he had when he had greeted her at Russell's, as if he actually was excited to see her. No wonder Miranda couldn't stay more than a week here before hightailing it back to him.

"Knut, nothing for years and now twice in three days. I'm honored." She was, too, though she passed it off as a joke.

"Ah well, since I'm down here, I might as well see as many people as I can."

"I didn't know I was on the list."

"It's a long one." His eyes lifted to the ridge that ran

along the Sandberg and Blackstone property. No doubt his beloved wife topped the list.

She stripped off her gloves. "I bet. You have time for a cup of coffee?"

"The question is if you got the time. Did I catch you in the middle of chores?"

She had the chicks to sort out and Amy's pet goat. Amy was supposed to take care of that, but she had stayed in town for a high school volleyball game. Nathan was going to drive her back out. "Odds and ends."

"I can do odds and ends. That's all they let me do anymore."

By "they," he was likely referring to Mateo and Haley, and that other boy he considered a son. "Well, in that case, I keep the shovels inside the barn."

It was also where she had the chicks madly cheeping away. "Well now," Knut said. "I should have brought Sadie along. No, better I didn't. She would stuff a couple in her pocket and bring them home."

"I might have done the stuffing," Irina confessed. "I got them with plans to do up the roosters in the fall, and winterthe hens over. But I think I just made myself work."

Irina filled their feed pen. "You want in."

Knut looked at her dog, Lulu, staring between the railings of the pen, her tail in a slow wag. "Won't she——" But Irina had already opened the door and Lulu came in.

"I thought the same myself when she barged her way in the second day. I thought they were done for, but——"

Lulu sniffed the chicks and then lay down on her side. The chicks scampered over and started using her as a jungle gym. "She's the worst dog this place has ever had. She won't bark at strangers, as if it's not polite. I swear she'd show the thief over to the gas tanks and nose out the house key."

"Whereas the one we got at home thinks he runs the place."

"Oh?" And just like that, they fell into a conversation as easy and fresh as the one yesterday at Russell's, while Knut shoveled out the old straw and chicken poo, and she laid out clean straw and checked the heat lamp. They moved on to the goats and the conversation shifted to hobby farms and the cost of everything and her hips and his back. She asked outright what he thought of Nathan.

"I don't think we exchanged a dozen words. Quiet. Good with the stock."

"Only reason Amy babysits the boys is to find time with him, and to be blunt, Sandberg women don't have a great history with choosing men. I married a gambler, my daughter a drunk and now Amy has set her eyes on some kid who can't keep his eyes in one spot. Dodgy."

"Or real nervous around the one woman who holds sway over the girl he's lost his heart to."

"If you're right, I intend to leverage that until she's out of high school with marks that'll take her to university. Hopefully by then, she can see straight to make her own decisions, and he might figure out how to look me in the eye."

Knut twisted the fork handle. "Ah well, that takes courage. Even for a man my age." His voice was soft, amused. What did he mean by— "You could ask Hawk. He's the one who hired him."

"I don't want to bother him. He's got enough to think about, what with—" She waved her hand, unsure she had read Knut's concern about Russell the same way she had.

"He's our age," Knut said quietly.

"Speak for yourself," Irina said. "But yeah, I know what you mean. That's got to be its own circle of hell for him."

"And for you," Knut said. "You are good friends, right?"

She had leaked out a few tears when she had come home

the other night. But only a few. Russell's decline would go for a stretch and best to ration out the tears. "Is what it is."

She could feel his eyes on her, and she took a deep breath, afraid she'd open the waterworks right then and there. "Listen, you here about Miranda?"

"Maybe, a little. I went to see her cairn today, with Grace and the kids."

"Best view in the country, Miranda always said."

"It's a good one," Knut said. "I could see straight down to your place here."

"Spying on me, were you now?" The notion didn't bother her. She felt protected.

"No, but it got me to thinking that I was really surprised to see you the other day at Russell's. Surprised in a good way."

She reached up to touch her hair, but her hand touched her beater of a cowboy hat. He couldn't possibly mean—

"Knut, I'm too old to be this confused. Are you making a pass at me?"

"I'm kinda out of practice myself, but I think I am."

"We live hundreds of miles apart."

"For now."

"What does that mean?"

"I don't know. I'm just not wanting to figure out the future when I'm not sure about the next few minutes."

"Fair enough. You know I don't see eye to eye about your daughter's bunk 'n bacon operation?"

"I heard. I believe you two can work something out."

"Huh."

"So...yes."

"What are you agreeing to?"

"That cup of coffee you offered."

"I can do that." Surely, by then, she would have stopped

her hands from fluttering like butterflies. The ones in her stomach were another matter.

BEFORE GRACE'S DAD left after lunch with Sadie back to the Jansson place, he hinted she might want to check into Nathan. And when she pressed him, he only said that Irina was naturally concerned since Amy had taken to Nathan.

"Maybe you could run a check on him or something."

"Dad, I'm a lawyer, not a private investigator."

"Still. You could do something through the firm, right?"

Grace bit her lip. "I'm on sabbatical. The terms of the sabbatical are that I don't conduct business on behalf of the firm."

"But this isn't on behalf—"

"Dad, just let it be."

"Everything all right, Grace? Anything you want to talk to me about?"

"Everything's fine, trust me. I already questioned Hawk about Nathan, and he's satisfied with him." Grace didn't think it wise to add that Hawk was using Nathan's dog as his chief character reference. "Listen, I will check into Nathan. And let you know."

He nodded, though his bright blue eyes—the same color as hers—regarded her for a moment longer. He held out his arms, and she stepped into them automatically. His arms weren't as thick and strong as they used to be, but he was still real and strong. Body and mind.

She began her research on Nathan the next Monday during the boys' visit. Over a snack of granola bars and milk, she asked, "Do you hang out with Nathan much?"

"We can't ever find him," Amos said. "He's with the cattle or gone somewhere."

"Him and Doxie Sue," Saul added. "His dog."

"If you see the dog, he's close by. They are both strays."

"Do you like him?"

Amos and Saul looked at each other. "I don't know because I don't know him," Amos said.

"We like you better," Saul said, as if the issue was a popularity contest.

She brought the boys home a half hour earlier than usual. Sure enough, when she pulled up, Doxie Sue barked from the doorstep. Seconds later, Nathan was coming out the door, Amy on his heels.

Nathan sidled off. *Oh no, you don't.* "Uh, Nathan, is it? Hawk asked me to give you a message." She looked over at Amy. "You okay with the kids?"

She was unloading the kids early, but this was important for Amy and the kids. Amy nodded, clearly not happy but resigned. When they had disappeared inside, Grace turned to Nathan, who was looking at the silent door.

"I don't have a message from Hawk," she said, "but I do have questions for you. Care to walk with me out of earshot? Say, over to the corrals?"

He stilled, except for his eyes, which darted about for an escape route. Where did he think he could go? He had no vehicle, not even a horse.

Doxie Sue decided for him. On her own, she began a leisurely trot toward the corrals. He followed, and she fell into step beside him. "How did you meet Amy?"

Nathan pulled his cowboy hat lower. It had bits of straw and grass on it and a hole in the front brim. It looked as if he had stolen the home for a family of mice. "She babysits for Hawk."

"That doesn't answer my question."

"Me and the dog slept in her barn one night, and before I could leave the next morning, she came upon us."

"Not your usual dance or bar or our-parents-are-friends kinda meet," Grace said.

"I told her I would go, but she asked if I wanted work and said that her neighbor needed help. And then she brought me here."

They were at the horse corrals. Doxie Sue shimmied under the railing and began sniffing at dung in the corral. After apprising the new arrival in the pen, the mares returned to grazing.

Nathan faced her. His eyes were dark brown, a bit like Hawk's. "I work hard. I like it here."

"I bet you do, but no one knows you, Nathan. That's the problem."

"My boss doesn't mind."

"And you don't give him trouble, which is exactly what he doesn't need more of. Me, however, I made a career out of causing it."

He gave her a quick, hard look. She called him on it. "And I bet you're hoping I go back to causing trouble somewhere else."

He had the decency to flick a smile. "I honestly don't mean any harm. I'm grateful for the place to sleep and food and work."

Sometimes the direct question was the best. "What's your last name?"

"Smith."

Grace crossed her arms.

"It's true."

"Are you a suspect in a crime, Nathan It's-true-my-name-is-Smith?"

"Not really."

"Not really an answer."

"I stole some money from my stepdad, but not as much as he's taken from me."

"Fair enough. I'm going to assume from your current living situation that it wasn't enough to count."

He gave a single sharp nod.

The boy was unusual. She could imagine his appeal to Amy. Poor, troubled boy with a soft spot for animals. What was there not to like?

"I won't give you trouble," Grace said, "but if you ever feel like running off again, let us know. Maybe we can give you reason not to. Deal?"

He looked over to where Doxie Sue and the mare had lain down together. "Deal."

GRACE WAITED UNTIL late in the evening, when Mateo might finally be putting his feet up, before calling him.

"Okay, what did I do wrong now?" Mateo's question was only half-joking. True, she gave him the gears, never for her sake she liked to think.

"Nothing yet. And that's why I'm calling you. So you don't do something that you think you have to do."

"Okay. I don't know how you got into my head, but go on."

"I don't want you to buy the rest of Hawk's breeding stock."

"Well, we agree there, because I don't really want to buy them. It's mostly to help him out."

"It won't help him."

"Hawk might argue that point. How do you know his mind so well?"

"Because I've known him for longer than you."

"I knew him for the past six years. When you weren't around."

"Yes, I know. I have faults—thanks for pointing them out—but not when it comes to Hawk. You just said that you are only doing it to help him out with money. Is that what it comes down to?"

"And it would expand my operation. It wouldn't be just me buying them up. I'm partners with Will Claverley, right?"

Grace knew Will from her childhood. A good guy, one who would do the right thing. So long as she could persuade Mateo, then he would persuade Will.

"Okay, I know why you want to buy the horses. Tell me why you don't."

"Because he's lost enough. The land, which is like losing his home, he's reduced his cattle herd—and then there's Eva and the money paid out to her."

"What happened there?" Grace said. "And yes, I'm snooping."

She heard the crack of a can open, and Mateo mutter a thanks and then—lovely—the distinct smooch of her sister's lips on Mateo. "I dunno, Grace. She always seemed like kind of shell-shocked. Quiet, and would start at every sound like a baby calf. A few times she came outside and kept looking up at the sky as if expecting something to fall on her. I guess she wasn't made for the ranch."

She didn't sound at all like Hawk's type. You had to be a special breed to make it as a rancher's wife in this country. Tough, independent and never lonely. Like all the Blackstone women. Love must have mushed his brain.

She touched her lips. What had happened to his brain when he kissed her?

"I don't want him to lose any more, either. How about I buy the horses instead?"

"They are not cheap."

"I've got money set aside."

"How much?"

He grunted when she named the figure. "That's good down payment, but I can give him a better offer."

"Withdraw it."

She could hear Mateo suck back on his drink. "I'm not going to withdraw my offer. You pitch yours to him and let him decide. What's so wrong with that?"

She was coming off as bossy and interfering. Exactly how she had treated her coworkers, and look how well that had worked out. "You're right," she said. "There's nothing wrong with Hawk looking at two offers instead of one."

"Whoa, did Grace Jansson just admit she's wrong about something?"

Grace let him crow for a bit more, before interrupting. "But—"

Mateo sighed. "Of course there's a *but*."

"But, like it or not, we're family. And it doesn't make sense for us to treat this like a business deal."

"You're saying that we should combine our money and present/Hawk with a single offer?"

"Not exactly." Grace fumbled to explain her half-formed thoughts. "I mean, Mom considered the Blackstone Ranch like a second home, and I'm living on the land, too, and in their old house—" She stopped. Explaining to Hawk had gone easier. "I just think we're all family. Hawk included."

"Uh-huh. In your family scenario, what's Hawk to you?"

"I don't mean family family. I just mean family in a general sense."

"Uh-huh. Like how Haley and me are family?" In the background, Haley gave a whoop and then dissolved into giggles. She said something that had Mateo burst into laughter.

"Haley said that she sees Hawk as a brother-in-law. She wants to know if you view it the same way."

"What are...? I never... I don't mean... That's not right." Grace tried again. "I'm only concerned about coming to an arrangement that benefits us all."

She swore Mateo snorted beer out his nose. "I bet you are."

On principle, she liked to get in the last word, but he and Haley were impossible to reason with in their current state. She ended the call with them still laughing.

CHAPTER EIGHT

HAWK HAD HIS arm up a heifer's birthing canal when Grace came alongside the calving shed. Her flashlight cut across the heifer and him, and then slanted onto the straw-piled ground.

She shouldn't be here. It was tricky enough with heifers on their first calving, without strangers about.

"Can I help?" she whispered.

That was enough for the heifer to decide to lie down. He yanked out his arm in time, just as he was about to unhook the problem hoof. The calf was trying to come out front knees and head at the same time.

He hoped the glare he shot her way was answer enough. She winced and he could see her flashlight bob away, in the direction of the house. Why was she even here at nearly eleven on another night as chilly as their last night-time chat more than two weeks ago?

On his knees now, Hawk reached inside the heifer to continue his work. He hooked his hand on the hoof and eased it forward. There. The second front hoof followed-more easily. And just in time, as the heifer heaved herself back up. Now the calf was in position, the heifer seemed to have fresh energy, and Hawk had little to do except watch as the calf's head and front legs emerged. He broke the calf's landing. Now he just had to hope the heifer accepted the calf. Some heifers took to their calves right away, and a few never did.

A few were like Eva.

"Can I talk now?"

Hawk spun around. Grace had switched off the flashlight, her voice coming from the metal side of the shed. Clearly, what she had to say couldn't wait, in her mind. Still, getting calf and cow together was more important.

The heifer had turned to see her baby, but there wasn't any nosing or licks. She just stared. "She's yours," Hawk said. "Get on with it."

He took a handful of straw and rubbed the calf's nose and mouth to free it of the afterbirth. The calf started and shook its head. The heifer gave a soft moo and leaned forward. A good sign. Hawk stepped back to give her a chance to take over. The heifer sniffed the calf and then licked. Hawk blew out his breath. He'd let them alone for a short while and check back to make sure the newborn was suckling.

In the meantime, there was Grace to deal with. He tilted his head around to the back of the shed. There was a stiff breeze Grace must have stood in the entire time. She definitely had something to say. Likely, the twins had got her going.

"Sorry I interrupted," Grace whispered. She edged closer to him, just like the night they had kissed. It was her style. She wore a puffed vest over a sweatshirt, and a toque. Her arms must be freezing. May the first had come with a frost warning.

"Is it the boys?" he said.

"What? No, they're fine. I mean, I assume. I haven't seen them since dropping them off. Why? Did something happen?"

Hawk closed his eyes briefly. "No, just trying to figure out why you tracked me down when it's going on for midnight. I assume that it's something that can't wait until daylight."

"Well, it could, but you're hard to track down. I mean, you are always out here, it seems."

The same complaint Eva had made, as if cowsworked a neat nine-to-five schedule. "Still have forty-three left."

"How many have calved?"

"The other two hundred and thirty-seven."

"That's a lot."

"Some didn't make it." Seven calves and two cows.

"Oh. I'm sorry."

"The way of it. Look, I still have to see that the heifer lets the calf feed before I can go inside and grab a few hours of sleep before I start again. What would you like?"

"Mateo and I talked—and he indicated that he's open to the family concept of investment when it comes to your breeding stock."

"Family concept of— English, please."

"It's like you said. We're a messy family, but still family."

She stood close enough for him to loop his arms around her waist, pull her against him, give her some of his warmth. "Grace, we kissed. We are not family."

"Okay, so that area of relations is still a little soft, but generally, when it comes to the ranch, we can all agree that it would be better if the horse breeding was kept here, right?"

"This 'we' include Mateo?"

"Yes. If you could keep the horses, he doesn't mind. Call and ask him."

Great, his ex-employee was bailing him out. "I'm not calling at this time of night. Anyway, I believe you. It's just that—that I need the cash, Grace."

"How much?"

When he named the sum, her eyes darted back and forth and then settled on his. "Okay. I can swing that."

"So now I'm your charity case, instead of Mateo's."

"It's not charity. I want a stake in the horses and boarding for my trail horses. That includes feed and grooming, too."

"Horses you don't have. You're just saying that to make me feel better."

"Do I look like someone in the business of making people feel better?"

Cold to the bone, tired to the bone and his pride ground to the bone, and yeah, she made him feel better. Or, maybe gave him reason to do better. "What kind of stake do you want?"

"What are you offering?"

"Half."

"Done."

She was within striking distance of a kiss again. From the other side of the back wall, he could hear a bleat from the calf. "I have to check on her," he said.

The calf was up on wobbly legs and the heifer was licking its flanks so hard that the calf stumbled a little. Ready for the next step. Hawk nudged the calf forward and hoped that the heifer put two and two together. The calf ducked its head and took hold of a teat. The heifer took a step forward. The calf lost hold, but it was persistent and tried again, and this time, the heifer let it suckle. Her head dipped. Good.

He headed for the house. Grace fell into step beside him. "Well?"

"I'm not deciding anything at a quarter to midnight."

"Are you at least interested?"

Yes, he was interested. Not in her money, but in her. In her being on this ranch, in his life, at his kitchen table, there at the end of the day. But he had long ago given up on that dream, and her return had ignited a spark of hope that he was forever trying to stamp out. And here she was again, on a chilly May night, throwing heat on it again.

And yeah, he wanted to keep the horses. She knew that, too. Was she doing this for his sake? Did she…care about him? Or was he just setting himself up for another heartbreak?

"I'm interested to know what we are, if you say we're not business partners and I say we're not family."

This time, her eyes shifted back and forth without settling on his. Fine. He didn't know the answer himself, only what he wanted it to be. "Good night, Grace. We'll talk again."

Friday was always a tricky day for childcare. Neither Grace nor Gemma had them, and Amy was still at school. Usually, Hawk shifted more of the workload to Nathan, while he focused on the boys.

But this Friday, there was the Pincher Creek horse sale. Big enough to draw in horses and buyers from both sides of the border. He had already decided not to attend. He couldn't afford any stock, and what stock he had, he'd promised to Mateo. Or Grace, should he take her offer.

Then, at the breakfast table with his dad, Nathan and the boys, he got a call from his Montana buyer. He wanted to know if Hawk was selling there, and when Hawk said no, he said come on down anyway and we can talk. Meaning there might be a future sale in the works. He couldn't miss this opportunity.

"I'll be there," he said, with no idea how to make that happen.

"That was Grant Sears," Hawk said to his dad. Russell frowned and nodded, and Hawk could tell he didn't recognize the name.

Nathan perked up. "From Montana?"

"Yeah, he's coming up to the Pincher Creek horse sale. You know him?"

"No," the boy said and then shrugged. "I mean, I know of him. Who owns a cutting horse and doesn't know him?"

Nathan dug into his porridge. He was the only person Hawk knew who could eat porridge by the bowlful, layered with whatever was on hand. Today it was frozen berries and walnuts. On other days, days when calving had gone hard the night before, he'd seen him shake instant coffee granules onto the steaming oatmeal. The kid was strange, but man, did he know animals.

"He expects me at the sale today but—" Hawk looked at the boys.

"We can come," Amos said.

"Me, too," Saul said, as if dividing the two of them was ever an option. It would be like using a knife to split a puddle.

"I can't bring you boys," Hawk said. "Too long to sit."

It would also signal to Grant that he didn't respect his time. He could make the boys mind for maybe a half hour, but that would hardly be enough time to catch up on where Grant had vacationed over the winter.

"Do you know if Amy's got school today?" The teachers might have booked a Friday off, as the joke went.

Nathan shook his head. "No, she has two exams today. I haven't seen her all week."

Right. And he couldn't ask Nathan. There were still a dozen cows expecting and two heifers any day now.

Grace. He could ask her. He could ask her outright as a favor or...

He tapped her name on his phone.

"Why are you calling me when I haven't finished my first coffee yet?"

He explained his situation, and before he could properly finish, she said, "Sure. I have guests checking in tomorrow, but tonight's guest canceled. It's meant to be. When do we leave?"

Had he really thought Grace would make it easy? "I meant the boys would stay here, and I would just go."

"But why do we have to miss out on the fun?"

"It won't be fun. A lot of standing around."

"Not my first rodeo, not my first horse sale. Besides which, I'm in the market for a few trail horses. You can be my expert eye."

Which meant bringing the horse trailer. "I don't know if they'll have riding horses there. It's for cutting horses."

"I'll take my chances. I'll pack up sandwiches and snacks for the road. Make sure the boys fill up their water bottles. They like lots of ice."

Grace beside him on the hour-and-a-bit drive and the boys behind in their seats. They would pile out and everyone would think they were one big, happy family. The real kind, not the mixed-up one Grace went on about.

And when she slipped into the truck passenger seat an hour later with the kids in the back, it felt so much like a family he had to grip the steering wheel to remind himself that it was all wishful thinking. Grace slipped waters into the cup holders in the truck console. "I packed a thermos of coffee, too."

"They have a concession stand at these things," he said.

"Which comes with lineups. This way, we eat on our schedule. Tell me, what's the story on this buyer?"

Hawk threw the truck into gear and they rolled away, hauling the horse trailer. "His name is Grant Sears. A year before the boys came along, I visited the Sears ranch in Montana. Not overly large, but top-notch. The animals were treated like royalty, and the hands had no less than a dozen years of cowboying experience apiece. Then he came up and saw the Blackstone Ranch, and we did business together. He likes my mares, and I like his studs. He doesn't like the actual foaling end, but he's picky about what mares his stallions cover. Which is good for me. That means he asks for higher stud fees, but if I give him a stallion, then I will see that back easy, because he'll automatically buy it."

"Wouldn't it be more efficient for you to have the studs, too?"

"Eventually, yes. But this works for now."

"But you have to depend on a guy in Montana this way."

He might as well admit it. "I depend more than I like on too many people, Grace." He turned to her and added, "And you're at the top of my list."

She set her hand on his shoulder. Her touch constituted a violation of the distracted-driving law. "Good thing I'm so dependable."

Her voice had a teasing lilt, like when he'd carried her to her doorstep back in March. He couldn't leave fast enough then, but now... He offered his hand palm up and she slipped her hand from his shoulder into his waiting hold. He spoke softly so the boys couldn't hear. "You're my good thing, Grace."

"Would you rather," Amos said loudly from the back, "be a horse or a goat?"

"A horse," all three said together.

"Would you rather," Saul said, "live on a mountain or in a valley?"

They settled into the road game, and Grace eventually drew away her hand to pour coffee, but Hawk didn't mind. On the road with Grace and the boys, there was no other place he'd rather be.

"WHAT DO YOU THINK?" Grace said to Hawk, as she rubbed the neck of an eight-year-old roan through the railing of a selling pen. The boys were beside him.

"She's good. But fancy, for just a trail horse. I know the ranch she comes from. They sell cow horses and ropers."

"Out of my league, you're saying."

"I'm saying she'll sell for more than your needs."

Grace didn't care. She simply liked this horse. The moment Grace had started circulating among the pens, the mare had snickered at her and given her head a toss, as if to say. "Come over here. Let's talk."

"Could you use her, too?"

"That's not the point. You could get two decent riding horses for the price of her."

"But maybe I could expand to include guests at your ranch. On special days like when you're taking the cattle out to pasture or rounding them out."

"I'm not letting strangers around the cattle. That's a flat no."

He was right. Too dangerous. The mare turned her head to nuzzle Grace's hand. "Oh, come on, Hawk. I can't just let her go."

"She looks good to me," Amos said.

"Son," Hawk said. "You don't buy a horse because it looks good. You buy for how the horse will fit into the program. And she doesn't."

"What's your program?" Amos said to Grace.

Grace avoided Hawk's eye and said, "This horse."

Hawk shook his head. "Why am I even here?"

"There you are."

Grace turned to take in a rancher about her dad's age in a crisply pressed shirt and jeans, with a spotless hat and cowboy boots. He looked as if he was dressing for the part, except that the lines around his eyes and his thick hands proved that he was the real deal.

Hawk took the outstretched hand as if they were old friends. "Grant. Good to see you."

Grant nodded to Grace.

"This is my—" Hawk seemed stuck, and she couldn't blame him. It was easier to say what they were not. "This is Grace," Hawk said, "and my boys. Amos and Saul."

They exchanged greetings, after which Grace took her cue to leave with the boys. *Time to let the men talk,* Grace grumped to herself. She led the boys over to the picnic tables near the concession stand and fished out their sandwiches.

"I see our husbands found each other." Grace looked up to see a woman about the same age as Irina sit across from her. With her were two girls about the age of the boys. The girls assessed the boys. Saul offered each of them a cookie, leaving himself with none. Amos sighed and gave his brother one of his.

"What do you say?" the woman said to the girls.

"Thanks," they said to Saul.

"I'm Deb, Grant's wife. You must be Hawk's wife. I heard you had twin boys."

Amos shook his head. "This isn't our real mom. This is Grace."

Deb blushed and squeezed her eyes shut. "I'd apologize, if it weren't for the foot in my mouth."

"It's okay," Saul said. "She's like a real mom."

Deb and Grace exchanged quick smiles. The older woman reminded Grace a lot of her mother. The same easy humor, the same perceptive eye, the same long legs.

"This is Amos and Saul," Grace said. "My favorite five-year-olds in the whole world."

Amos rolled his eyes and Saul grinned. Deb introduced her grandkids as she drew out plastic food boxes and opened them up. The older of the two rolled grapes across the not-too-clean table surface. Before Grace could intervene, the boys snatched them and popped them into their mouths. To their credit, they thanked the girl before Grace had to prompt them. A little proud moment to share with Hawk later.

"I understand Hawk and Grant are business partners," Grace said.

"Unfortunately, yes. I'm trying to get Grant to retire, but it's harder work than ranching, I swear."

"Have a kid ready to step up?"

"Both my son and daughter, and their spouses. We couldn't ask for a better transition, but Grant can't seem to let it go. He told me on the way up that he's just here to take a look, and then we get here and he takes a checkbook out of the glove compartment."

"Do people still take checks?"

Deb sighed. "The auctioneers will take Grant's. He's a known quantity."

Unlike her. She was good for the money, but she'd never thought to ask about how the money was transferred. "So, he came with an eye to buying one?"

"Oh yeah. A stallion from the Cross C Ranch. It has lineage from Metallic Cat. He's quality, but he'll need training before he can go into the arena, and our ranch is not geared up for that right now."

But Mateo was. And no borders to cross to breed with Hawk's mares. And didn't Hawk say that getting his own stud was part of the plan?

Deb threw up her hands. "Of course, there's no talking Grant down once he gets something stuck in his head."

"Oh yeah?" Grace said distractedly as she thumbed through her contacts. "I'm sorry, but I have to make a call."

Much to Hawk's surprise, Grace, with the boys, joined him ringside for the auction. Amos sat beside him, Grace was on the other side and Saul tucked tight on her left. From her bag, Grace produced a tablet for Amos and she gave her phone to Saul. They automatically opened up apps and got to playing, the noise muted.

She winked at Hawk. "Normally, they only get fifteen minutes when I'm catching up on emails, but today is a treat."

He couldn't begrudge her the break. "I've done that myself."

They weren't buyers, but they were sitting in the buyers' rows. "We should move back," Hawk said, "since we're not buying. Unless you still want that roan?"

She shook her head. "You're right. She's too expensive."

"You actually listened to me?"

She shot him a bright smile. "I listen more than you think. But can we stay? The boys are comfortable."

She was right, let sleeping dogs and quiet boys lie.

When the Cross C stallion was brought into the ring, immediate tension ran through the buyers. The horse was the highlight of the show, and for good reason. A bay, the stud circled the ring, his head high and with a light, athletic step that marked him as champion material. Grant had agreed earlier to give Hawk access to the horse. Maybe, one day down the road, he might be able to bid on a quality horse like this himself.

The bidding started. Grant Sears and another buyer Hawk didn't recognize raised their bidding cards. Hawk's head was half-turned toward them when from the corner of his eye, he saw the flick of a bidding card.

It was Grace. The auctioneer acknowledged her card, and raised the bid.

"What are you doing?"

"Shush." Grace waved her hand at him. "I'm trying to concentrate. These auctioneers really do talk fast."

"You can't do this."

"Why not?"

"I told Grant I wasn't bidding against him." Not in so many words, but he had assured his stud supplier that he was sticking to his mares.

"You're not. I am." She raised her card again.

Hawk risked turning in Grant's direction. The older rancher was shooting daggers at him. "Grace," he said through gritted teeth. "This is my reputation."

"I didn't know, okay? And this is in play. I need to get this right or I'll never hear the end of it from Mateo."

"Mateo is in on this?"

"As if I know the first thing about this. Mateo already knew about the sale and the horse. He wants to do the training, and yeah, maybe he'll breed down the road. This has nothing to do with you."

Amos had picked up that Grace was bidding on the horse in the ring, because when the auctioneer acknowledged Grace's card on the next round, he gave a whoop and fist pumped the air.

Hawk took hold of his arm. "Not a sound, boy."

Amos shrank down. Hawk himself felt like doing the same under Grant's glare. "You do this, and Grant won't allow his studs to cover my mares."

"I'm sure you can talk to Mateo about that." She was determined and nothing would change her mind.

The third buyer had backed out, and now it was down to Grant and Grace. They were bidding ten grand above the top price Hawk had expected. The Cross C owners were leaning forward. How much money did Mateo and Grace have, anyway? Their pockets couldn't be as deep as Grant's. And he was rich in US, not Canadian, dollars.

Then, from the corner of his eye, he saw Deb touch Grant's arm and speak to him. When the raise came back to Grant, he shook his head and kept his card down, though from his stiff back, he didn't like it.

"Sold to Grace Jansson of Pavlic Ranch." She had used the name of Mateo's ranch then, salvaging his reputation somewhat, though he doubted Grant would see it as anything other than a partnership between Grace and the Blackstone Ranch.

Right after the auction, Grant marched straight for Hawk. "There's the law, and then there's the spirit of the law," he said bluntly.

Grace had gone to make payment, and the boys were stuck tight to his side at his order. Hawk couldn't agree more with Grant, but they had both assumed that Grace was with Hawk, while she, as always, had acted independently.

"I spoke for myself," Hawk said. "And she acted on her own."

"Did you know what she had planned?"

"If I deny it, would you believe me?"

The older man opened his mouth to counter when his wife came alongside him, two little girls trailing behind. "You know, Grant, not getting your way every day is not a bad thing. Aren't you on about the grandkids sharing?"

"With each other, not with others," Grant burst out.

Deb laughed. "The last thing we need is one more horse."

She acted as if buying the horse was a lark, which maybe for them, it was. She steered Grant away. Now he could focus on dealing with Grace and her new purchase.

THE TRIP BACK from Pincher Creek was as silent as Grace had expected. She had decided not to make a peep until

Hawk spoke first, and he didn't seem too intent. Instead, he drove a good ten kilometers under the speed limit, no doubt in honor of the precious cargo.

Her new purchase rode quietly in the back, and she rode quietly in the front. For once, he could do the talking. Amos and Saul were nodding off in the back, their heads bobbing like unstrung puppets.

"You know where I'm going to keep him?" Hawk said suddenly, making her start.

"You've got lots of pens."

"None good for a stallion. Not of his quality. I can't have him getting in with the mares."

"What does it matter? Don't we want them breeding?"

"I don't know. That might be a question for Mateo. Or do you two have it all figured out?"

"Don't blame Mateo. He didn't know until I called him from the sale, but he had half thought of coming down himself. It became a kind of no-brainer for us."

"And neither of you cared to clue me in."

"Mateo did, but I wanted to surprise you."

"Surprise me with what? The cost of feed, a new pen, another animal to groom and ride?"

"I will pay for that, okay? Besides, the horse needs more training, so Mateo will probably take him, anyway. Hate me or not, this is the right thing for all concerned."

He finally turned his eyes from the road. "Wasn't it that kind of thinking that got you fired, Grace?" His voice was light, but with a thread of taunting.

"I got justice for my client."

"And lost your job and your reputation. Was it worth it?"

"No," she said, "it wasn't. But this is."

"This is just you turning me into one of your cases. You should go back to lawyering. You got what they call in the arena a lot of *try*."

"I've got more than try. I pulled it off."

Hawk shook his head, sighed. "That's exactly what I mean."

"Can you not just say 'Look, Grace, I don't entirely approve of your tactics today, but you got us a quality horse that I can build an outstanding future on. Thank you. And oh, thanks for taking care of the kids, too'?"

"So, you did buy it for me? Not for you and Mateo?"

"What difference does it make? You and Mateo have a partnership already."

"And you just got yourself a buy-in here, and I never agreed to any of it."

"Is that the problem? You wanted to be consulted?"

"Yes, Grace, yes. Didn't you say that I'm part of this big family you keep on about? I like to think that I can be open-minded. You don't have the same confidence in me."

He was right. Once again, she had bullied her way into his affairs, made assumptions about him and dragged them into a fight. She pressed her hands against her thighs. "I'm sorry, Hawk. I should have talked to you."

He didn't say anything, but she thought his grip on the wheel eased a bit. It gave her the courage to add, "I have a world of confidence in you, Hawk. That horse in the trailer behind us proves that. I believe in your breeding. I believe you know how to get the best out of horses. I know it's in your blood. You are the one with no confidence."

His grip tightened right back up. "You're right. I don't. Not anymore. Not with you around, pointing out how I don't supervise the kids right, how I should get Dad treatment, which, by the way, is happening next month, and then I find out from Nathan that you've been asking him questions. You've been gone all my life and now— now you decide to show up and take over. What gives you the right?"

They were approaching the highest hill of the ride that lifted them to the top of the foothill overlooking their valley, and the horse adjusted to the sudden steep incline, his motions rippling through to the cab. While Hawk was attuned to the horse, Grace twisted in her seat to check on the boys. They were both out like a light, their heads against the headrests on their booster seats. Each had their fingers touching their dad's cowboy hat in the seat between them.

Today she had more than babysat. She had mothered them. Fed them, wiped their faces, reminded Saul to avoid biting on his loose tooth, consoled Amos over not having any loose teeth and kept her mom radar on at all times. They hadn't seemed to mind one bit. They'd followed along and taken her hand from time to time as if she really was their mom.

It was a role she had jumped into. And today, she had jumped again into a partnership with Mateo on a horse. And she could concoct whatever excuse she wanted about good investments and interest in the kids, but at the heart of the matter, she had wanted to help the man sitting stony-faced beside her.

Because she cared about him, maybe even... No, she wasn't ready to go there yet.

But she was eroding Hawk's belief in himself. She had gone too far, and she didn't know how to stop herself.

They descended the long hill into their home valley in silence. At the turn into Blackstone Ranch, Hawk turned on the flashers and pulled the unit into Park. "I'm still waiting for an answer."

She turned in her seat to face him. "I don't have the right. I screwed up, Hawk, but that's what I do. I push, I interfere, I act before I think. I'm not the good thing you said I was. And you probably regret saying that now."

He reached across and took her hand. "I don't. A good

thing isn't perfect. I'm still annoyed with you, but I have to admit I'm excited to drive this horse onto the Ranch. It's a big deal that would not have happened if you hadn't acted."

"So I'm forgiven?"

"I don't have a choice, because the alternative means you're not part of my life, and I couldn't forgive myself if I let that happen again."

His dark eyes had warmed and settled on her lips. Was he aiming to kiss her again? Last time had ended in a question she finally could answer. "I think I know who we are now, Hawk."

"Yeah?"

"A couple of good things."

He grinned and lifted up their hands, bringing hers to his lips. "I'll buy that," he said, "any day of the week."

CHAPTER NINE

HAWK WATCHED THROUGH the open barn doors as the boys ran ahead of his dad to Katzmobile's pen. Since the horse's arrival three days ago, his dad had come out in the mornings to feed the stallion a carrot or apple while the boys observed. The small ritual helped repair the rift between his dad and the boys after his explosion two weeks ago. The psychologist's appointment wasn't until next month in early June. Another month of keeping a close eye on him...and then what?

"You'll be run off your feet with your foal by then," Hawk said to Paintbrush. Her milk bag had swollen in the past few days. She was still a little early, but calendars were only a suggestion when it came to animals—and humans. The twins had been born six weeks early by an emergency caesarian. That threw Eva further into a depression that she had never fully recovered from.

Another layer of remorse. Grace wasn't the only one who was pushy. He could see himself in her.

No, he could see himself *with* her, but he would wait for her to make a move. He could tell from the forced cheer in her voice that she missed her job, and he had learned his lesson from Eva not to hope others could change for you. Or even that they should.

Impulsive, stubborn, headstrong, outspoken. That was Grace, and he didn't want her any other way, except experience had made him cautious. If she made a leap into a relationship with him, he had to make sure that she looked first, for both of their sakes. And the boys'.

Her move was slow in coming. He had dropped off the twins yesterday for their usual Wednesday, and she had transferred them immediately into her vehicle for a day at the Calgary Zoo. She had dropped them off with a wave, and a quick exit. Of course, she had a right to her own life.

His phone rang. Mateo. "Good time to talk?"

"The mare can wait until we're through before she foals, I guess."

"That close?"

"In a day or so, I'm thinking."

"A little early." Mateo's voice had lowered in concern. He had still been on the ranch when Paintbrush had lost her first foal And even though she had delivered a healthy prizewinner fifteen months later, every pregnancy was now considered high risk.

Hawk looked over at Katz. "The baby probably wants out to see Blackstone's latest arrival."

"How's he working out?" Mateo's voice held an edge of deliberate lightness.

"Getting fat on carrots and apples. Dad has taken a shine to him."

"Then, he must be worth it."

"Time will tell."

"I guess Katz was a bit of a surprise, from what I hear."

"Yep."

"I told Grace to run it by you, but you know her."

"I do."

"Haley and I talked, and if Katz is too much, we can trailer him up here. I'll start on his training after the crops are seeded. And we can work something out with the mares going forward. I already told Grace that."

"And what did she say?"

"You haven't talked to her?"

He wasn't about to get into the state of his relationship with anyone, especially with the man married to Grace's sister. Mateo must already feel pulled in more directions than hair in the wind. "Just want to know what I'm walking into."

"She actually agreed to let it be whatever you and I decided." Mateo laughed. "She must not be feeling well."

So, she had listened to him. It didn't make him entirely happy. What was wrong with him? He didn't want her interfering with his life, but when she withdrew, he moped.

"Are the other horses a combined offer, then? You and her, like with Katzmobile?"

Mateo made a clicking noise, like to a horse. He also made it when about to unload his opinion which he'd done now and again as Hawk's hired hand. "Listen, for all Grace and I give each other the gears, she has a point about all of us coming together on the horses. You take good care of the horses, and we'll help out with whatever costs you got coming your way."

"How about I tell you what those costs are first?"

But Mateo didn't hesitate when Hawk told him. "Much what I expected. I'll transfer money in the next day or two."

The boys had left Katz's pen and were coming toward him in the barn. His dad didn't seem to have noticed, his attention fixed on the Blackstone's latest equine acquisition. Or maybe his mind had wandered off completely, while he just stood there.

There was his family before him, and yet Mateo was calling him into a wider one. He couldn't refuse, for the sake of the boys. And for the sake of the hope of a future with Grace.

"Thanks, Mateo. It means a lot."

The next morning, Hawk found Paintbrush pacing in

her stall, her tail up, ready to foal. He felt the same rush from a year ago, not as intense as when the twins were born, but up there.

An hour later, his dad came in and shook his head. "She's not right." Her flanks were heaving, and she was in a full sweat, yet no progress.

"I'll give her another hour."

His dad gave a single nod and left. At the end of the hour, Hawk whipped out his phone and called the vet.

"I'm already on my way," Ryan said.

"How—"

"Grace Jansson called. She had gotten a call from Russell and contacted me for him."

His dad couldn't remember what he ate for breakfast some days, but still knew horses.

Between Ryan and Hawk, they worked to turn the foal. "I am not," Ryan said, pushing on the mare's flanks, "going to let you lose another one."

And he kept his promise. The foal dropped a half hour later. A male who immediately fell under maternal licks and nuzzles.

"I'll wait until both are on their feet before I go," Ryan said. "Grace will like the news."

She would.

"Useful neighbor to have."

"She is that."

"I have to admit that going around the ranches, you get their opinions on all kinds of topics, and that B and B came up more than once."

"Let me guess. No one was in favor."

"Somebody paints the fence a different color and everyone notices. Wait, what have we here?"

The foal was struggling to his deer-like hooves, the mare neighing soft encouragement. And then, one step, two, three and he had reached milk. Hawk experienced another rush, a tingly one that had come a year ago. Another special one. A winner.

Hawk took a picture and attached it to a text to Grace. Thanks for making the call.

Now, if she would just call him.

LEAVING HER GUESTS to relax in the living room, Grace drove over that evening, and with Amos and Saul, tiptoed into the barn.

"Are you sure it's safe for us to go in?" Saul whispered to Grace.

"I'm sure." After all, Hawk himself had sent her a text invite to say she could take the boys along with her. He had gone on the quad to repair fence in the pasture. Next week, Amos said, they would move the cattle to pasture. Meaning into her quarter of land.

There was the little beauty, tucked tight against her mother's side. The mare tensed at the sight of their peering eyes, but she didn't rise.

"It's okay, Mama," Grace said. "We just want to see your new baby."

"Rest up," Amos added. "You'll be having another one."

The mare's ears twitched, as if she had different thoughts. "How do you know this?" Grace said.

"Dad said so, and he's always right about these things."

Whatever Hawk lacked in confidence, his son made up for by the bucket. "Does the baby have a name?"

"Grandpa does the naming," Amos said. "And he said he doesn't know."

"And you can't keep asking him, Amos. It upsets him." Saul looked up at her. "We are not to upset him."

"Then, we won't. We have loads of time yet."

Despite their chatter, the foal's head had grown heavy and now dipped to the ground. "Is he okay?" Saul whispered.

"Just sleeping. How about you show me this roping you are practicing?"

Amos was gone like a shot, and Saul followed, after looking up at Grace for her permission. "Shoo, I'm right behind you."

Grace was trying, and failing, not to laugh at the boys when Hawk returned on his quad. He parked in an open lean-to and came across to where they were taking turns roping a calf dummy.

"The deal is," she explained to Hawk, "that whoever gets it roped first gets one more cookie than the other."

"Cookies? I don't think I have any on hand."

Grace lowered her voice out of the boys' range. "You do ever since I brought a batch over."

"Huh. Still chocolate chip and oatmeal?"

She nodded.

"And still about as big as your face?"

"More like the boys' faces."

"Huh." Hawk turned and headed for the barn.

She could have told him the foal was fine, but she also understood the urge to see for himself. But he reappeared immediately with a rope, much longer than either of the boys'. He started swinging the loop, and the boys started hooting as if he was a big-time country star. And wowza, but he looked it. Grace aimed for nonchalance as she leaned against the fence.

"So," Hawk said to the boys, "I hear cookies are up for grabs."

"You can't do it as close," Amos complained. "That's not fair."

"Move it away then," Hawk said, loop still circling.

The boys each took an end of the calf dummy and carried it off, placing it only about twice the distance from where it originally was.

"Easiest cookie you'll ever earn," Grace said.

"You want to up the ante?"

"Yeah, I place the dummy."

She thought herself clever when she and the boys tucked it behind a fencing panel, with only the dummy's fire-log head visible. She and the boys stepped away.

Hawk adjusted his footing and let loose. The rope uncurled through the air and snagged the head, as if drawn there by a magnet. The boys gazed at their dad as if he walked on water. Grace clamped her jaw shut. She wasn't behaving much better.

And from his lazy grin, he had read her mind. "Would you like to see that again?"

To their loud agreement, Hawk got the rope whirling above him. Like the boys, she fixed her sights on the dummy, so when the rope sailed around her shoulders and tightened at her elbows, she was completely unprepared. The boys laughed and pointed.

"Oops," Hawk said. "I missed."

"Some males around here obviously don't value my cookies," Grace said, trying to recover her bargaining power. The rope tightened a little more. Not so snug she couldn't wiggle free if she tried. Which he must know. Yet she chose to remain tied to him. Which she hoped he also knew.

"I got her now," Hawk said. "You boys run in and load up your plates."

They didn't need to be told twice.

"And don't forget I get one more than you two," he called after them.

"We should not leave them alone," Grace said. "Can we stop with the immature games now?"

"Nathan's inside with Dad. We're good." Hawk held the rope with one hand and took out his phone from the other. "I don't know. This looks pretty good."

"Don't you dare take a picture." She stalked after him, and Hawk gathered up the slack in the rope. With a foot of rope between them, he slipped his phone into his hip case.

She could make out every hair on his stubble, the faint laugh lines at his dark eyes. The way those dark eyes focused entirely on her.

"All right," she said. "You got me where you want." Or where she wanted him. "Now what?"

Hawk leaned against the railing. "Oh, I don't know. Let's consider the possibilities."

Laughter rippled through his words. Just like the Hawk of old. He didn't look the least tired or depressed, like when they met months ago.

"I could hitch you to the railing and go in for some bedtime milk and cookies. And I might remember to come out before I go to bed myself."

"Hawk, don't make idle threats. I know you will come back."

"Because I'm a decent guy?"

"Because of all the screaming I'd do."

"I suppose I could gag you."

If he tried that, she'd bust free. "You mean like what we did to Haley when she was nine, and we were old enough to know better?"

"Mateo found her, I remember. And I thought I was safe because I was leaving to come back here the next morning. But he must've walked the mile from his place to yours, got into my room and emptied a fresh cow pile into my backpack."

"Ew. How did he get away with that?"

"I wasn't there." Hawk's eyes settled intently on her. "Remember?"

She did. "You spent the night in my room. We talked the night away."

"Almost. I fell asleep on your bed and stole back before anyone got up. That's when I smelled what he'd done."

Grace made the connection. "And that's why we couldn't find your backpack. That's why we found it buried in the garden the next year. We thought Mateo and Haley had done it. But you had!"

"Only thing I could do is pretend he hadn't gotten back at me."

"Is this what—" she gestured at her strung-up arms "—this is about?"

"I have been feeling as if I'm at the wrong end of the rope this past while with you."

She looked across to where the stallion had his gaze pinned to the mares in the far pen. "You called it. I'm pushy, and I like getting my way."

"You like deciding what's good for people, and then going full bulldog into delivering it, whether or not they approve."

"I have a hard time going halfway on anything. You included."

"I've always wanted what's best for the ranch since the day I was born. Question is, what do you want, Grace?"

"I consider our families connected, and I want what's best for us all."

"But what's in it for you, Grace?"

"Because I live here now. I need to make a fresh start."

"Couldn't you just find another job as a lawyer? Start up your own business around here? Why the ranch, Grace?"

It wasn't the ranch she wanted, but him and the boys.

Except they came with the ranch. He should know that better than anyone else. "There's already a law office a half hour away. The market's saturated."

"Word is he's about to retire. Interested in buying him out?"

A legal business with established clients. Close to The Home Place. And to him and the boys. Except, was he testing her? Seeing if she would choose him over her career, again. There was only one answer to that.

She loosened the knot and wriggled free from the rope, but didn't back away. "I'm interested in you, Hawk. In your boys. In us finding a way for a couple of good things to build a life together." It felt so good getting that out.

Hawk lifted her chin, his dark eyes searching hers. She met his scrutiny full-on. She had nothing to hide.

"I really want to believe you, Grace."

"You can."

He smiled, more of a sad twist of the lips. "I saw the way your eyes lit up about the law office. You might want me, Grace, but you also want your old life back. You know how to reconcile the two?"

He had her. "Isn't this an 'us' problem, Hawk?"

He shook his head. "You know how long I waited to kiss you?" He didn't wait for her answer. "Since I was sixteen. Four years. That morning when I woke you were beside me, asleep. I was tempted to try for a kiss. I didn't in case you woke up and punched me in the face. And two, I wanted you awake for it. But I waited. Because I always wanted you to know that you could trust me."

Four years—since she was fourteen?

"Point is, I've always wanted you, Grace. There was a time when I'd given up on that dream and pursued others, but now we've got another chance. Only, you can't change who you are in order to make someone happy. Eva and I twisted ourselves into pretzels to do that, and only made each other miserable. I'm not doing that again, and neither should you, Grace."

The evening chill stole up her spine. "So...you're breaking up with me before we've even got together?"

He gathered up the rope in even loops. "No, Grace. I'm not going anywhere. I'll be here, whatever you decide to do. I'm only asking you to be sure. For everyone's sake."

"But I don't know what that is."

Unexpectedly, he grinned and tossed the looped rope over a railing post. He wrapped his arm over her shoulders. "Whaddaya know? Grace Jansson is thinking before doing. Let's celebrate with cookies and juice."

She leaned into his warmth. "Might as well. I don't have a better plan."

HAWK RUBBED WILDROSE'S neck two days later as they took the east exit out of the barn. "Happy Mother's Day." She had last foaled three years ago, and he had kept her open since then for working on the ranch. He'd already given Paintbrush an apple by way of recognition of the day. Across the wide Eden Valley, the early morning sun spread down the hills and across the valley floor, spreading up to the Blackstone Ranch.

He often came here to set his day right along with the rising sun, and today, he would start with the most awkward part. He took out his phone and called his ex-wife.

Eva answered on the sixth ring, her voice low and groggy.

"Sorry to wake you," he said, though calling at a more reasonable hour didn't always guarantee her wakefulness, either. She never kept a regular schedule.

"That's fine," she said. He could hear the rustle of sheets as she moved about. "Are the babies okay?"

Eva still called them that, even to their faces. Amos would scowl and Eva would look hurt. Neither understood the other.

"They're fine. Only, it's Mother's Day."

Eva moaned. "And what would you like me to do about that?"

"I could bring them into the city for a quick visit, I was thinking. We could go out for a burger or an ice cream. I could stay with them, if that makes it easier."

"Oh, Hawk. To what end? To remind them their mom is absent every other day of their lives?"

"You are still their mom. That hasn't changed."

"No, but I wish for all of our sakes, it would."

That cut. He would never forgive himself for pressuring her into a choice she didn't want. She had loved him, and he used her love to persuade her to give him a family. Because then they would all be happy. "There's no chance, then?"

"No chance of what? That some future Mother's Day I will be bright and cheery, or that someday I will wake up and have the strength to be a mother? I want that more than anything else, and I'm getting help now. I'm seeing a counsellor and on medication. But I don't know how long it will take."

"Okay," he said. "I'll let it go. You doing okay?"

"Meaning, do I have enough money? Yes, I'm doing fine. I even have a part-time job now, so you can cut back on your payments next month."

A reduction in payments required courts and lawyers, and then, what if she relapsed? "Let's see how things go, Eva."

"You're probably right. I could slip off the edge at any moment, right?"

She had read his mind, and maybe her own.

"Listen," she said, "the best thing you can do for our boys—for all of us—is find them a mother. A real mother. And get yourself the wife I couldn't be."

His gaze sailed over the slight ridge separating his place from The Home Place. "I want the best for you, too."

"I know," she said softly, but with a hint of strength he hadn't heard before, "but I am responsible for making that happen."

She had released him from any lingering guilt, and in the new sun, his thoughts flew to Grace.

Not that he would show up at her place today with the boys. She probably had her B and B guests, and anyway, Mother's Day couldn't be easy for her. Even for him, and he'd had time to say goodbye to his mother. He couldn't imagine a sudden death.

It had been hard enough to come upon Miranda's body like that.

But hadn't Grace shown up for him when he needed help with the boys? What kind of person let her spend the day alone, remembering her mother?

If he was interfering, Grace could set him straight. He opened his phone again as he took his shades out from his jacket pocket and slipped them on. "What are you up to today?"

"Making an omelet for three fine moms who are here on a retreat while their husbands are holding down the fort. And then I'm off for a hike. Up the ridge."

Short for "going to see her mother." He wasn't far off.

"Care for some company? Me and the boys. Dad, too, if he's up to it. We could take the horses up."

She didn't hesitate. "Sure, come in a couple of hours."

All four were at her door on the dot.

As they threaded their way through the trees, Hawk's dad turned in his saddle to Grace behind him, "There were Mother's Days where it was snowing. You couldn't see from here to Hawk." Hawk had chosen the lead position to keep ahead of the boys. "Remember that, Hawk?"

Hawk couldn't, not because it hadn't happened, but that he had never pinned the May snows to a specific date. "I remember, Dad."

"Not like today," his dad affirmed.

Today differed completely from any other Mother's Day Hawk had ever experienced. And it all had to do with the rider at the back. Grace was mostly silent as they switchbacked their way up the ridge. Probably thinking about her mother.

Her first words when they dismounted at the top were for the boys. "What did you two not do last time you were up here with me?"

"We didn't go past the trail by ourselves," Saul said.

"And what are you going to do this time, Amos?"

"I will wait for an adult to be with me," Amos said. He didn't even push it. "Can we have snacks now?"

She tapped her lip. "Hmm, give me something for them."

Amos looked around and darted off farther back down the hill. Saul hung by Grace's side, his eye on the backpack where the snacks were. That wasn't like Saul. A deal was usually a deal with him, and he didn't argue the point.

Saul took Grace's hand and tugged on it. She bent her head to him, and like a dating pro, he swept in with a kiss on her cheek.

Grace snapped straight. "Saul! You little trickster." But she was grinning, big-time.

Saul eyed her backpack. "I gave you something."

She looked across at Hawk, her face glowing under her hat. "No arguing that."

She gave up the goods, and Saul sat happily down with what turned out to be a full-size cupcake.

"Amos is going to howl when he finds out all it took was a kiss," Hawk said as she joined him. His dad had walked farther along the ridge, a long way from the edge, thankfully.

"But I'll have one more pretty rock for my collection. Besides, I think he would bring me a sack of rocks, if it meant avoiding a kiss."

"That's him. I get one hug a day, at bedtime."

"You poor cowboy," Grace said. Her voice was teasing, but then she stepped close beside him. "How are you doing?"

She glanced at the cairn of Miranda by way of explanation.

"Shouldn't I be the one asking you that?"

"I was always so wrapped up in my sadness, and then in Dad's and Haley's, that I never thought about what it must have done to you to…find her."

She stood as close to him as the other night, her eyes soft on his. "I'm sorry," she said.

"It was…a long time ago."

"Thirteen years, but some things you don't forget."

He glanced over at his dad who was riding his horse down the ridge. He would follow along the trail there and cut back where the hill opened into a gully. It was a good Sunday riding trail. Saul with his cupcake was going off to Amos, no doubt to gloat over his brother.

"Do you want to see where… I found her?"

"Only if it's not too much."

Normally, it was, but if it could give Grace some peace, he could do it. He took her hand, and they stepped to the edge. Thirty feet below, a rocky ledge jutted out of the rock face. "There."

"I was on Wildflower. You remember her?"

"Wildrose's mom. The horse that could read minds."

"Yeah. She stayed put, and I lowered down on the rope. I kept hoping that maybe she was just unconscious, but..." He couldn't finish.

Grace squeezed his hand. "Thank you."

Now that he had started, he couldn't stop. "The horse was farther down. Still alive, but in a full sweat. Both legs broken. All I could think about was Dad's rule—don't let an animal suffer.

"I climbed up using a rope, took the rifle back down. The thing is, I forgot what the rifle shot would do to Wildflower. She galloped away, not far, but far enough to pull the rope out of reach. No cell service, so I ended up walking through brush in the gully nearly a whole mile before I could climb back out and to her.

"By then it was pitch-black, and it was enough to come back with the news. We couldn't do anything about Miranda until the next morning."

Realizing his hold on her hand had grown tight, he released it. "Sorry. I guess it wasn't that long ago in my memory."

He looked away to steady himself, but then Grace closed the space and wrapped her arms around his middle, pulled herself tight against him. He didn't question it, and dropped his arms around her.

Holy. He ached to have her this close to him for the rest of their lives, but he couldn't force it.

Amos was steaming up the hill, slowed only by a rock the size of his hat. Hawk nudged Grace to look. Amos dropped his offering at her feet. "Saul gave a kiss and Dad a hug, but I brought the biggest and the best. What do I get?"

Before Hawk could cut in with a sharp word about manners, Grace crouched down before him. "I will grant whatever food wish you want."

Amos scrunched up his face. "Anything?"

"Anything that is within my power to provide."

"Then, I want hotdogs and potato chips and cookies and root beer. At The Home Place."

"All right, I can manage that."

"Today?"

Grace twisted to look up at Hawk. "Can you spare him?"

Amos shook his head. "No, with Dad. And Grandpa and Saul. All of us together."

"That's a pretty big demand," Hawk said, giving Grace an out.

Amos pointed. "And that's a pretty big rock."

Grace grinned. "You know, Hawk, your boys have me all figured out. Kisses and pretty big rocks are all it takes to win me over."

She was, he liked to think, dropping a hint like a rock on his foot. The trouble was he didn't trust that she knew her own mind. Patience, he told himself, still aching for her.

CHAPTER TEN

GRACE WAS OF two minds when Hawk called her a week and a bit later to ask for her help on cattle-moving day. She wanted to help Hawk, but working cattle was not her thing, and all that went with it. Like needles and castration clippers. Like separating worried mamas from their calves. Like tagging calves. She had only ever attended one at the Jansson Ranch. After that, she had been more than happy to let Haley and her mother and whatever hired help or neighbors they rustled up do the dirty work, while she cooked the huge, postwork meal dull as that was.

"Sure," she said. "I can watch the boys and barbecue steaks."

"The boys are at school that day, much as Amos disagrees. And I'll have a roast in the smoker for most of the day. I need you at the corrals, helping out."

There was never a better time to tell him that she chose a clean office over manure-riddled corrals. "All right. When do you need me?"

Hawk was up on Wildrose when she returned from dropping the boys off at school. Both Amos and Saul had pouted the whole way there, neither pleased that once again, they had been excluded from important ranch work.

In the far pen, Katz was on high alert, his gaze fixed not on the mares this time, but on the herding of cattle, the shouts, the dogs skimming the ground to get behind a straggling cow and calf.

Everyone wanted in on the excitement, except for her. But she couldn't let Hawk down. She had told him her interest lay with him, and now was a chance to prove it.

At the corrals, he tossed her a pair of gloves. Gardening ones with grips on the palms. They looked a few years old. His mom's, she guessed. Angela said leather gloves made her hands sweat too much.

"Irina is up at the chutes, tagging. If you could help with the gate."

To stand in one spot suited her just fine. Even if it was next to her father's girlfriend. Her dad had not returned in the past month. Or at least, not to stay with her. Haley reported that he had gone off on some mysterious road trip to a mountain lodge a couple of weeks ago, at the same time Amy said her grandmom was gone for a few days. Grace was tempted to ask straight up, except she wasn't sure she was prepared for the answer.

Irina avoided eye contact herself, and maybe it was to get away from her that Irina asked if she wanted to take over.

"I don't know how to do it."

"Your dad never showed you?"

"More that I never showed any interest."

"Yet here you are today."

Grace couldn't help but look over at Hawk working the cattle. Irina chuckled. "I see. Anything for a good cause."

"It's not that." Not that, entirely. "I hate hurting them."

"Do they look bothered?" The ones released back with their moms didn't look rattled. They flicked their newly tagged ears and stood calmly beside their moms.

"How about I watch for now?" As in forever.

"All right." But that didn't stop Irina from showing her how the female part and male part of the tag fit into the clamp, and then how to grab hold of the ear about a third of the way or so from the headand one, two—snap. Done.

It couldn't be any worse than what Nathan was doing with the castration snips. Irina's phone rang. "It's Amy," she said and handed Grace the clamp. "Over to you."

"But—" She looked around. Nathan had finished with the calf and the day help was guiding the into the chute.

She fed in a tag and leaned over. "He owes me big," she muttered. One, two and— The calf jerked as she hit home.

She sent it loose and pulled up the lever to let the next one in. Irina was still on her phone, and Grace refilled the clamp. When Irina got off, she waved to Hawk. They talked over the fence, and Irina left.

What?

"Her bull got into the neighbors'," Hawk said. "She has to deal with that."

"But you can't leave me here."

"Why not?"

"Because—" If she explained herself, he would give her an out, and she would have failed him. She gave her clamp a menacing chomp, chomp. "Fine. I always wanted to add bovine ear piercing to my list of skills."

After a twenty-minute noon break for everyone to bolt down sandwiches and pickles, Hawk and his crew resumed on fresh horses. Back at the chutes, Russell joined Grace at the gate after she said she needed someone there to back her up. It was also a way to monitor him.

"You want me to go get the boys?" Grace asked Hawk as she released the last calf.

Hawk shook his head. "Their aunt agreed to bring them out later. Along with her kids. I said we'd feed them."

Right, the roast.

Hawk tilted his head to her. "I was thinking baked potatoes."

She got his point. "I'm on it."

"Dad can show you where everything is."

Russell led her into the basement that served as an enormous storage room. Boxes were stacked to the ceiling and three deep. Tables, chairs, the old family couch patterned with a dusky brown-orange design of watermills now seated old lamps, a wall clock and pictures of horses. Curtains draped over more boxes and a TV. "This is from when I moved in a while back," Russell said. "Angela and I had a house in town. Hawk sold off some of the stuff and the rest we put down here."

A year of unpacked boxes? Then again, Hawk had worked himself to the bone to build a future. He didn't have the time to sort out old things. She spotted a set of boxes marked Clothes and then a name behind them. Dad, Mom, Hawk.

"Those go back twenty, thirty years ago. Angela thought they were too old and out of style for the secondhand shop, and she couldn't bring herself around to chucking them. Go without once, and you think twice about throwing things out."

He shrugged. "But I suppose you can't let things take up space." He snorted. "I guess that applies to people as well."

"Oh, Russell—"

He waved a hand. "Don't mind me. This way to the food."

But Grace hung back at the boxes. What if she used the clothes to make a memory quilt for Russell? The boys had started to piece together a few squares for their Grandpa's quilt, but they could incorporate new fabrics.

"Russell? Do you mind if I take the boxes? I'm always looking for quilting fabric."

He shrugged. "Have at 'er. I'll tell Angela you took them." He frowned at the boxes, as if seeing them for the first time.

"The food?" she prompted.

He waved his hand in annoyance. "Where it always is."

"Sure, of course, how about—"

"I'm going back upstairs." He pushed past her, she heard the floor creak above her as he crossed over and down the hallway to what she presumed was his bedroom. She quickly gathered up vegetables, and hurried back to the kitchen. She stepped into the hallway and from behind a bedroom door, she could hear Russell muttering.

Good, he was okay. Well, as okay as he could be.

From the kitchen window, she watched the dogs, hired hands on their horses and Hawk, now back on Wildrose, after an afternoon of rest, release the herd into the pasture that overlapped onto the home quarter, her quarter. It was a quiet enough event. The cows and calves were allowed to choose their pace, the horses and dogs only there to make sure that they headed in the right direction. The veteran lead cows set the pace, their young calves forced to keep up or get left behind.

This was the part she would have liked. Riding alongside Hawk, talking about the day, going over any problems. Not making supper. Gone from taking on city hall to figuring out how to get lumps out of gravy.

She caught herself. This resentment was what Hawk had warned her about. He was right. She did miss the law shop, and she had driven past the Diamond Valley law office, curious.

But she couldn't bear to give up on Hawk and the boys. Yes, there were working moms and wives the world over, but maintaining a law business was not a nine-to-five job. There were no half measures, just like with ranching. All-in or nothing.

She was taking potatoes from the oven when the crew filed in and used the mudroom to wash up. Hawk appeared with the boys, and Gemma with her girls, and directed them to the house bathroom. He turned on the tap at the kitchen sink and applied dish soap.

"Looks good, Grace. How can I help?"

"We need more chairs, and is there any way to make that table bigger or set up another one?"

"On it."

As if setting up a meal for a crew was an everyday occurrence for them, Hawk and Grace had the table set, serving bowls filled and roast carved in under fifteen minutes. Everyone took a seat. Except for Russell.

Hawk came from the hallway and gave a single headshake to Grace. Right, she would make a plate up later. "Time to eat."

Nathan reached for the bowl of carrots but pulled back when no one else moved a muscle. Grace glanced over at Hawk, who suddenly looked as if he had to shoot a horse.

"I guess we'll say grace first."

Grace remembered that it had always been Angela who said it at every meal. She had never seemed like the religious type, considering the language she got into when moving cattle. But saying grace was an ironclad rule, and the crew here knew that.

Hawk couldn't seem to push it out. Russell must have said it last year, and now he didn't even trust himself to sit at the table.

"Oh," Grace said. "I guess that's my cue." She bowed her head. "Heavenly Father." It was Angela's standard greeting. And then she pretty much ad-libbed the rest, covering gratitude for the weather, help and food. She finished with Angela's piece. "Bless this food to our bodies in the name of Jesus Christ. Amen."

"Amen," Nathan said ahead of the others, his hand already on its way back to the carrot bowl.

"Thanks," Hawk said into Grace's ear. "It threw me there for a bit."

"You're welcome," she whispered back. "I'm used to thinking on my feet."

"Grace, can you cut my meat?" Amos, beside her, asked.

"Say please," Saul said.

She cut both of the boys' meat, and when she turned back, Hawk was talking to one of the hired hands about where he would next be cowboying, as if the fact she was sitting in the spot Angela had always taken, occupying the traditional seat of the rancher's wife, taking on the role of grace-sayer, meant nothing.

Except, as she settled back into her seat, Hawk hooked his foot under her ankle and left it there for the rest of the meal, as if it was a natural thing to do. She didn't pull away, but when the cowboy turned to her and asked what she did when she wasn't at the corrals, she said the first thing that came to mind.

"I'm a lawyer."

She snuck a peek at Hawk, but he chewed on his meat as if she hadn't said anything surprising.

It was Doxie Sue skimming underneath the corral fence to Katz that alerted Hawk to Nathan's proximity. He turned as the boy joined him at the railing.

"Your dog going to give him trouble?"

"Hardly. She's just making her rounds for the night." Less for her to patrol since turning the cattle out to pasture two days ago.

"I always wondered. Back in November when you first came, I'd see you two walking around here."

Nathan looked to where Doxie Sue was drinking from Katz's horse trough. Ears perked, Katz snorted. Doxie Sue gave a dog grin and trotted off. "Yeah. It was hard to stay in one place then. I'm pretty settled now."

"Amy helping with that?" Hawk had promised Irina that he would keep tabs on the boy when Amy was over. *It's in both our interests that we make sure that boy can be trusted.* Other than coming from south of the border, where half the ranchers in this part of the country could trace their ancestry from, there didn't seem to be anything to fuss over. He got up, did his job and called it a night. He had to be the most boring young adult Hawk had ever met.

Another shy smile. "She is. That's, uh, why I wanted to talk to you. She has her graduation next Friday, and she has asked me if I would go with her. And I, uh, said yes."

Hawk smiled. At his graduation, Grace had been his date Though they had not called it that, because hey, they were just friends. But she had played her part and come in a tight, knee-length dress. Blue to match his shirt. Their moms had been talking, apparently. A sheath, Grace called it. He produced a wrist corsage, only because his mom had instructed him to do so. A pale white carnation will do, she said. But the florist had easily upsold him into a white rose with little, foamy flowers and a blue ribbon. Grace's blue eyes had widened at the sight. It was the best purchase in all his eighteen years, and she gave him the best night of his life.

"Have you got a suit?"

"I ordered one online. I used your dad's credit card. I paid him back right away but the thing is…as you know…" Nathan scratched his head "I was hoping…and I'm willing to work it off…"

"Spit it out."

"I was wondering if I could borrow your truck."

"You can't take Amy's?"

"She and her grandmother share it, and her grandmother

wants to drive back right after the grad dinner, but we were hoping to meet up with her friends later. And then I would want to drive her back. Especially if there's drinking."

"And if you are drinking?"

"I don't drink. I don't do drugs." There was such bitter vehemence in his voice that Hawk believed him.

"And I take it you have a license?"

"I do."

Hawk hesitated. As much as he wanted to show confidence in Nathan, the truck was his means of transportation for the kids. He could point Nathan to his dad's beater pickup, but that wasn't the vehicle to arrive in for a date. "All right, then. Only condition is that I keep Doxie Sue as collateral."

Nathan stiffened and then relaxed as he registered Hawk's grin. "Agreed. This is the one time she's not coming with me."

The boy walked away with a definite lift in his step, drawing out his phone as he did. No doubt to text Amy the good news.

Oh, to be young and in love.

He remembered that time well, thinking that Grace might come to love him, too. It hadn't worked out for him then. Now Grace bowed her head and asked for the blessing, as all Blackstone females had done, and showed up to do a job he knew she didn't like. For him.

Yet she still called herself a lawyer.

He would have to wait to see how this all turned out.

"Do you want chocolate chip oatmeal cookies with your tea?"

"You could persuade me," Grace's former boss answered from the comfort of the leather recliner in The Home Place. George had called her three days after the cattle move to ask if she had an opening on Monday. He wanted to do something quick and special for Hilda. It turned out that it was their forty-third anniversary, and he had been on the cusp of forgetting. Grace hoped that his call meant that he had also forgiven her.

Hilda, in the chair beside him, smoothed her hand over one of Grace's quilts. A seascape one, inspired by her trip to the Caribbean a few years ago, back when she had more money than she knew what to do with.

"This is beautiful," Hilda said. "Who knew you had such talent?"

"I wouldn't call it talent," Grace said, "It's just sewing small squares into big squares until you have something you can sleep under or hang on a wall."

"You sound like Hilda here," George said. "She's always downplaying everything she's ever done. You know she sang in a band when I met her?"

"Oh, George. That was so long ago."

"And not so long ago. They fronted for the Stampeders. You know them?"

Grace vaguely recalled that the Stampeders was a Canadian rock 'n roll band from the '70s still played on classic rock stations. "Wow, that's a big deal." She set a plate of cookies on the coffee table, and George immediately helped himself.

Hilda tapped her husband's knee. "She's just being polite. Our little band didn't make a recording. Everyone left for ordinary lives. I exchange texts with the lead guitarist about our kids and grandkids." Hilda smiled at Grace. "Raising a family became our business. Not like you."

George studied his cookie, as if counting the chocolate chips. Had he not told his wife about firing her?

"Your sabbatical looks good on you," Hilda said. "Will you still want to come back to the firm?"

George gave another hitch in his chair. "I certainly hope so. We would certainly miss your other talents at the office."

Okay, what was he trying to tell her? She would cover for him, if only to avoid a marital dispute.

"George was reluctant to bring you on at first. Since we are all family friends. But I told him to try you, and it has all worked out."

George had lied to Hilda to not disappoint her. He shot Grace a sheepish look.

"That it has," Grace said. "I am where I'm supposed to be."

Hilda frowned, and Grace hastily added, "For now. This has been a great experience."

"Well, I know the firm has missed your experience there. Right, George?"

"Just on one or two accounts," George said. "There have been some personality conflicts."

Rachelle.

Hilda laughed. "That's putting it mildly. Not everyone has your level of persistence, Grace, to get the job done."

It was only when Hilda left to pack that George leaned in to explain. "Rachelle took on a land-use litigation soon after you left. You remember that fellow with the housing development?"

At Grace's nod, George continued. "He had a friend with a similar problem. Stymied with housing permits and paperwork. He said that you were the one to talk to. Except you weren't there, and Rachelle was. She said she had worked side by side with you, that she knew the case inside and out... Anyway, I didn't question her too much. I am not in the office every day. But it turns out that wasn't the case?"

He raised a questioning eyebrow, and Grace said,

"Rachelle helped out here and there, but really it was Keira who knew the most. Rachelle is bright, though. What's the trouble?"

George sighed. "The city brought documents to discovery that set her back. Hilda thinks I should ask you to assist Rachelle, but she doesn't know the history between you two."

"She also seems to be unaware of my employment status at the firm."

George gave another hitch in his chair. "She and your dad. Your dad called me back when it all…happened. He asked me point-blank if it was true that you were on a sabbatical or if you had done something to get yourself fired over."

"And like Hilda, you couldn't stand to disappoint him. I don't blame you. I did the same. Nobody in my family knows. Except for Hawk."

"Hawk?"

"My neighbor. Who Dad bought the land from. We're family friends. I guess you two never met."

"Different circles. So, he's not really quite family, then?"

"What? No, did I——" Grace replayed what she had told George, who, ever the legal wit, had not missed her slight slip. "I suppose I think of him as family." Despite his claims to the contrary.

"I'd like to offer you your position back."

Back. Back to everything that she had lost. Four months ago, this would have been a dream come true. But now— "Why the change of heart, George?"

George swept cookie crumbs from his lap, eyes down. "I—I may have overreacted. I lost a good lawyer that day. I should have considered other options, first."

"A suspension?"

"I hear from Keira you're calling it a sabbatical. That's a better term."

Grace looked out the front window to the hill that separated her place from Hawk's. His cows grazed there now, calves in tow. "It kinda feels like one. I think you gave me the break I couldn't see to give myself."

"And now you can come back. I know you sold your place, but Hilda and I have a little downtown apartment that's vacant right now. You could stay there—rent free—for the first few months until you find something of your own."

"But—I live here now."

George frowned. "But this can't be all that you had planned for your life. It's so different. And there's no need to get rid of it. You always planned to have both places, didn't you?"

"Yes, but that was before—" Before Hawk.

Grace gestured to the rise over which Hawk's spread lay. "I invested in the neighboring ranch. In horses, actually. Hawk breeds them. I committed to helping him see it through." She had done nothing of the sort. Why was she trying to talk herself out of the position she had once been ashamed to lose?

Man, she hated pacing the edge like this. She had never lacked direction as she did now.

"Can you see yourself coming in part-time, maybe until Christmas, and then we'll revisit it? By then, this case will have worked its way through the system."

"If Rachelle and I haven't clawed each other to death before then."

"She'll be fine. I talked to her."

"I can't imagine that went well."

"Her pride is secondary to the firm's reputation. My problem with you was internal."

"Look, I behaved horribly, George. I'm still pretty bull-headed. Ask Hawk."

"That man's name has come up an awful lot. How come you never mentioned him before?"

"Oh well, I moved to the city, we grew apart, he married and had kids."

"He's married," George said.

"Not anymore."

"So it is what I'm thinking."

"No—I mean—not entirely—"

A truck came up the lane. Hawk. What was he doing here? He drove past the kitchen window and parked. Grace turned to George. "Ah well, speak of the devil, here he is."

From where she sat, she couldn't see him approach the back door. George could, and his eyebrows shot up. "Well now, another piece of evidence to support my case."

Graceleaned in her seat to see what her old boss was talking about. There was Hawk, holding something unexpected.

Flowers.

THE LAST TIME Hawk had bought flowers was for Eva on the birth of the twins. She had stared at the colorful profusion and then had turned her head away, as if the sight offended her.

In the grocery store this morning, he had decided to give it another try. He couldn't say he wanted Grace to stay and then not demonstrate his sincerity. A different, smaller bouquet and for a different woman. But the reaction was only slightly more favorable.

Grace opened the door, her smile wavering. "Hawk. This is a surprise." She looked at the orange lilies as if they were weeds.

"I happened to be in the neighborhood." He extended

the flowers to her. "I thought I'd give you more than my thanks for helping with the cattle."

She took them, glancing over her shoulder. "You shouldn't have."

"I know. I was halfway here before I remembered the boys broke your vase." He held up a pair of flowered rubber boots. "I had put these behind the back seat way back when. Castoffs from Gemma's youngest daughter. Four sizes too big and the wrong colors but I figured they'd do in a pinch for the boys. Eventually. In the meanwhile..." He'd never passed along so much useless information in his life.

She took the boots and the flowers. "Uh, come on in. I have guests."

He had seen the Lexus parked outside, but by then, he was already up the lane and he couldn't exactly retreat without it looking bad. The door was only half-open; she wanted him to skedaddle.

He edged backward. "Sorry to—"

"So, this is Hawk." An older voice boomed behind Grace.

Grace's eyelids fluttered, and she gave a faint gasp. Hawk had never seen her this uncomfortable since Miranda had caught her in a lie about her whereabouts with Hawk when she was thirteen. She opened the door wider to show a man about his dad's age. He wore pressed jeans and a crisp dress shirt and canvas boat shoes. He looked like a man deliberately dressing to appear casual.

"Hawk, I'd like you to meet George Davis. George, this is my neighbor, Hawk Blackstone."

George and Hawk shook hands. The guest seemed genuinely pleased to see him, so why was Grace so anxious for him to go?

"I'll put these in water," she said.

A woman came down the stairs, looking as pressed and

neat in a pale yellow outfit as George did. "We need to get moving if we're going to keep our tee-off time." Her bright eyes skimmed Hawk.

"This is Hawk Blackstone, Grace's neighbor and investment partner," George said. "Hawk, my wife and minder, Hilda."

He smiled at Hilda, and wondered why Grace had shared their business arrangement with a guest.

Grace must have guessed he'd be thinking that. She had filled the boots with water and was arranging the daisies and lilies. She had her face down over a lily when she said, "George is my old boss from Calgary."

The man who had fired her. Yet now they were all smiles and looking cozy.

"What's this about 'old boss'?" Hilda said. "As in *former*?"

Grace's hands fluttered over the flowers. "I misspoke. This sabbatical thing throws me off."

George sighed. "Don't cover for me, Grace. A man's got to fight his own battles." He turned to his wife. "I fired Grace back in February. It was a mistake, and I just asked her to come back."

Hilda set her hands on her well-pressed hips. "Confessing to a lie is no way to celebrate forty-three years of marriage. At least, you did the right thing and brought her back."

Grace was leaving. Again.

She waved a bit of leafy branch. "I haven't agreed to go back."

He had a chance. The flowers were perfect timing.

"Anyway, you let me know soon what you'd like to do," George said and turned to Hilda. "Ready to go?"

"The suitcases are just inside the bedroom door," Hilda

said and turned to Hawk. "Good choice of flowers. Showy but not imposing. Roses are a tad obvious."

"I was thinking that myself," Hawk said. "I don't want her assuming that I'm easy."

"Our Grace always did like a challenge," Hilda said. "I suppose it's a battle now between you and my husband to see who wins her devotion."

George returned, an overnight case in each hand.

"Let me see you off," Grace said, and to him, "There's coffee on the go. I'll be back."

Hawk watched the protracted farewell from the wide kitchen window, coffee in hand. He texted Nathan to say that he would be at least another half hour. He had a few questions that needed answering.

Grace's step on the old porch steps was heavy and she leaned against the door after closing it behind her. "For the record, he only made the offer about five minutes before you pulled in. I expected this to be an apology stay on my part, a kind of rebuilding of the bridge that I had blown up. I didn't realize that my old boss had other intentions when he accepted my invitation."

"Okay."

"And don't ask me what I'm going to do, because I don't know what to do."

She slumped at the dining table. He rose and poured her a coffee. Black.

"Thanks," she said when he set the cup in front of her. "And thanks for the flowers. You really didn't have to."

"I know," he said. "That's why I got them."

"Huh." Gone was the flirty Grace he'd carried to the door when she'd injured her ankle. Her renewed job offer had shoved aside any romantic notions about him she might have had.

"I take it he wants you to go back to work sooner than later."

"Yeah, I guess Rachelle—you remember her?—she has made a mess out of an account. The client is a friend to the guy whose case ended up getting me fired. Essentially, I'd be going in to clean up her mess. And after, to carry on."

Her voice was carefully neutral.

Stay. Stay here with me. He looked over at the flowers. One of the lilies had a broken petal, jutting out from the others.

"What do you think I should do?"

"I think," he said, "you should do whatever makes you happy."

Grace rubbed her thumbs over the stenciled letters on her cup, Quilters Patch Things Up. "Being a lawyer made me happy. Doing this—" she gestured around "—makes me happy, too." She paused. "Our—arrangement makes me happy. But if I go back to the city, something has to give."

Something and somebody. Hawk looked out the window of his childhood home, to the hills beyond. His cattle were there now, grazing. This year's calves tucked close or, as he watched, bucking in the late May sun. He kept his eyes on them as he said, "I'm the last one to tell you what to do. Look, you made a great life for yourself somewhere else. And this is my life. I'm not moving from here unless the bank drags me off."

She gave a thin smile. "You're not changing."

"That's who I am, Grace. I stay because land stays. You—" he stopped and looked up to the ridge. "You're the wind, Grace."

"Loud and noisy and creator of migraines?"

"Strong enough to knock a man flat." He could admit

to that easy enough. It was the next part that choked him up. "And always on the move."

She twisted her mouth, not disagreeing. He reached across the table and pulled one of her hands into his. "I'm not going anywhere, Grace. That wasn't so great for us fifteen years ago. I'm hoping that this time, it's different."

He wished she would tell him she knew her mind, and that she was with him all the way. Kiss him hard and tell him don't be a fool. Instead, she nodded. "Okay."

Walking back to the truck, he turned to see her at the flowers, trying to tuck the lily petal back into place. *Leave it, Grace. What's done is done.*

CHAPTER ELEVEN

WHEN RACHELLE'S CALL came through, Grace was tempted to ignore it. "But that's not our style, is it?" she said to the cairn.

Grace had come to visit her mom to clear her mind. The wind ripping straight over the snow-tipped Rockies was trying its best as it whipped Grace's hair about, but not even the wind could wipe away an miraculously clear cell signal.

"Where are you?" Rachelle asked in response to Grace's greeting. "It sounds as if you are in a wind tunnel."

"Wait a minute." Grace walked down off the ridge and ducked behind the shelter of the boulder. "Better?"

"Better."

Grace braced herself against the hard rock curve and waited.

"How's your handsome cowboy doing?"

Really well without her, it would seem. It had only been a week to the day since their conversation, and he had acted neighborly and no more when he dropped off and picked up the boys. Saul had wondered about the flowers and Grace had only said that a friend had given them to her. It was true, and less messy.

"He's doing fine."

"Has he made a move yet?"

"Rachelle, is it really my love life that you are calling about?"

"It's just small talk."

Hawk's cattle were resting in the afternoon sun. The calves were gathered here and there in groups, one or two cows watching over the nursery while the others grazed farther afield. "Rachelle, we have never done small talk. We raced each other to the water cooler, rather than talk around it."

She laughed, and it sounded genuine. "We had so much fun together, Grace. You've got to admit it."

"It was, until it wasn't." It had taken months out here—and, as her gaze traveled to Hawk's place, other dreams—for her to realize it. "Neither of us are team players, Rachelle. First, I paid for it, and now you are."

"George didn't pull any punches when it came to my recent…performance review."

"He only gave me the big picture, but I know you—I know us—enough to fill in the details."

"I will tell you anything you want. You're still covered under the nondisclosure, right?"

"Yes. I don't think George would have said anything if I wasn't. But don't start. You know me well enough that if you go into the details, I will want to help, and George said he would give me time to decide."

"If we had time, I wouldn't be calling you."

Rachelle probably was under the gun. "Look, Grace, I'm out of my depth here. And the worse thing is I don't care. I mean, I understand that money and livelihoods are involved, and for that reason, I should care. But there's no justice involved."

Grace could have easily argued the point. Families and the pursuit of a fair living were crucial, but she got Rachelle's point. "You miss criminal law."

A cow walked her slow, ponderous way over to the nursery and nosed a calf.

"Yeah, I do. Except there was no money in it. I have just finished paying off my student loans. On to car loans and a line of credit."

Grace's father had supported her through her university training. Some of that money had come from her mother's life insurance. Another reason for the guilt over her firing.

But now she could sweep away her guilt. She could return as the glorious rescuer.

A calf stood, gave a shake and moved to the cow's full bag, its ears waggling, the yellow tag visible. Likely one she had put in. She had forged a life with Hawk, and he was as open to her as the land before her.

She couldn't give that up.

"I'll tell you what, Rachelle. I will consult with you on this case. You still lead it, but send me the files on the firm's email and I will review it. Okay?"

"I'd rather you took the lead, Grace, even though it kills me to say it. I'm willing that I pay you as the lead, too."

But that would mean driving to Calgary almost daily, that would mean giving up her days with Amos and Saul, that would mean telling Hawk that she had chosen career over him.

"You asked me how it was going with my cowboy? The reason I'm saying no to you, Rachelle, is because of that cowboy. Do you understand?"

"I've seen him. I understand the attraction."

"It's more than looks." She didn't realize until she had come back exactly how good-looking Hawk Blackstone was. She had always just seen him as Hawk.

"I know. Like I said, I've met him. If that's all you can do, I accept your offer. Be prepared for your inbox to start groaning under the weight of my emails."

Be prepared, Grace thought as the call ended, *to get even busier.* She rose and climbed to the ridge, and the wind slapped her across the face. Always on the move, Hawk had said of her.

"Not this time," she said. "I'm staying put."

Because she wanted it all—Hawk, the boys, her B and B—and her old career. Maybe if she only practiced as a consultant that would satisfy her lawyering itch. Maybe she didn't have to make a choice.

First, she had to prove that it could be done, before telling Hawk.

GRACE CAME EARLY the next Day, Wednesday, to pick up the boys so Hawk could get on the road to make the psychologist appointment in Calgary. His dad assumed she was coming, too, and grew agitated when Hawk explained Grace was staying behind with the boys. Grace switched gears. The boys were going on another road trip.

He wished she was sitting beside him now in the office, instead of in the waiting room with his dad and the boys. The psychologist had run the tests and was giving Hawk the depressing results.

"Early-stage dementia, you say?" He looked out the psychologist's fourth floor view of another brick building much like this one.

"Well into that stage."

"Can he remain at home?"

"For now, yes. But if it gets so he's not safe for your family or himself, then you will need to make plans. You will know."

Hawk didn't think he would know. He felt as confused and uncertain as his dad must feel on a daily basis.

"He had an outburst about a month ago with the boys. Yelled at them. Which is not like him. And then he's having trouble naming a foal. Last week, he left a gate open." Doxie Sue's barking had alerted them to Katz head bunting the fence alongside the mares. That could've gone sideways fast.

The psychologist frowned. "I, well, I don't know about that…"

Of course, he wouldn't know. None of the literature on dementia addressed unusual behavior for a rancher.

"But anything that he wouldn't normally do is of concern. It's a question of severity and frequency." He paused. "Other than you, does he have any other supports?"

The woman out there with him right now. But how long would that be for? She'd mentioned her plan to assist Rachelle on the case, but that she wasn't taking the lead.

Hawk didn't believe Grace would take the back seat for long.

And even if she stayed, she hadn't signed up for long-term care of a dementia patient.

"I'm it. What can I do to help him?"

"I thought I could bring him in now and we could chat together. I would like to leave you with a plan."

The psychologist left to invite his dad in, and Hawk could hear his dad's voice rise in response. What now? His dad had seemed calm enough when he had rejoined them in the waiting room after the testing. Grace had sat beside him, their arms touching from elbow to wrist, even as his dad had stared blankly down at the gray floor planking. The boys had amused themselves with a box of Legos. No doubt a little freaked out by the formal setting, they had behaved better than he could have hoped.

The receptionist offered to watch over the boys, while Grace came in with his dad. The psychologist placed extra chairs and Grace took the middle one, Hawk and his dad on either side.

The psychologist pulled the pin fast on his diagnosis.

His father nodded and then kept nodding as if his neck was on a spring.

Grace took a notepad from her bag. A large, leather one, the kind she might use in a courtroom. "I have a few questions, if you don't mind."

The psychologist invited Grace, in her casual clothing and braided hair, to ask away.

"What is the best diet for Russell?"

"I'm not sure. I'm not a nutritionist, but I would think a healthy diet is preferable."

Grace, Hawk noted, didn't even bother writing that obvious reply down.

"What therapies are available for the slowdown or reversal of the condition?"

"There are therapies to provide comfort and support. Studies are always underway, of course."

Meaning, there was nothing.

"Russell lives in the Foothills County. What services are there to support him?"

"I'm more familiar with Calgary and area."

"Diamond Valley, the town near us, is part of the Calgary metropolitan region."

"Is it? I didn't know."

Grace waited, her pen hovering above her still empty pad. Russell had stopped with the head-bobbing and now sat with his head lowered.

"I could check a few sources. I suggest you contact the health services there."

"You are part of the health services, and I am contacting you." She spoke with a kind of chummy humor. For his own sake, the psychologist had better not be fooled.

"I'll email you suggestions."

"Lovely." Grace took out a business card from her bag, her lawyer card. As she wrote her email on the back of it, she said, "I'm especially interested in any training care-givers can receive."

The psychologist looked at Hawk. "For you?"

"And me," Grace said.

Both Hawk and Russell turned to her. Grace didn't seem to register their surprise, but handed the psychologist her card. "Ignore the email on the front. That's my business email. The one on the back is my personal one."

She continued with a whole battery of questions about home care that Hawk would never have thought to ask. He might have taken it as a sign of her commitment to his father and him, but with her return to the firm, he was now just confused.

Between his dad and the boys, he didn't get a quiet moment with her for the rest of the outing. He resorted to a text, while the boys had a post-supper play in their corral.

Thanks for your offer to help with Dad going forward. But don't feel obliged. I know you are busy already.

She replied within minutes. I'd rather be busy in body than in my brain.

He couldn't exactly refuse her help, when his own dad stood to benefit. Okay.

How's your dad?

In his room with his photo albums. Your dad gave him the idea. He went outside and came back in and said he'd taken a picture of Picasso. I thought it was just him but then he tells me that's what he's calling the foal.

I like it!

Hawk's thumbs hovered over the phone. He wished she was here. Typing took too long and stalled his brain.

I like it, too.

After a quick wave of typing dots, How are you doing?
He couldn't unload on her when she was already doing so much. Okay.

Liar. Even knowing it was coming, it had to hurt. I feel all shaky inside.

The woman who had streamed out questions felt shaky? He typed, Maybe a little down.

Do you want me to come over?

Yes! If you want.

She pulled in ten minutes after he had put the boys to bed, and out under the early June evening, they leaned together on the railing and talked as he had not talked to anyone since he had roped her. They talked so long that finally he slipped his hand into hers and asked, "Tell me the truth about that night with Emmett. Why didn't you give us a chance?"

SHE LOOKED DOWN at their joined hands, her chest squeezed at how good it felt. "I was scared," she whispered. She shot him a quick look, and he raised his eyebrows. "I know, the great Grace Jansson scared, right?"

"Was it something I said?"

"It was the look on your face. Shocked, as if I kicked you in the gut."

"That's what it felt like."

"Kissing Emmett was easy," she said. "But you and me, if we had kissed, I don't think I would have had the strength to break away and become a lawyer."

"I wasn't against you becoming a lawyer. I was against you doing it without me in the picture."

"But, Hawk, back then, you filled so much of my picture." He frowned, as if he still didn't get it. She lifted her hand, palm to him, about six inches from his face. "You were like that hand. I had a hard time seeing around it."

Hawk took her raised hand and kissed her palm. She automatically closed her hand, as if capturing it. He smiled softly. "You know, you could have said something to that effect. I might not have felt like pile driving Emmett every time I drove past the bar."

"We didn't date, if that's what you're asking. I left for university the next week." Now it was Hawk's turn to tell the truth. "Then again, you could have visited." *You need to move on. He has.* Her mother's words.

"I might have, if your mom hadn't passed."

"How so?"

"It was two years after you had gone to university. An eternity back then. She was saddling up to go on a ride. That ride."

He swallowed. "She said that she'd asked you to come out, but you had 'made up a stupid excuse with a hole the size of a barn door,' she said."

"I didn't want to see you. It would have felt too...awkward."

"Miranda—your mom thought as much, but I remember her swinging into the saddle. 'But don't worry, Hawk, she'll come around. You'll see.'"

They both looked up to where a rim of orange light

still lit the ridgeline. "Last words she said to me," Hawk whispered.

The ridge blurred and Grace blinked hard. "But after that, it seemed the hope kind of passed with her. You didn't comeback this way, and I made up my mind that I had better grow up and get on with living."

"Last time I talked to Mom, she told me I needed to get over it, because you had. I assumed she meant you were dating."

"I did date, but more because it was something to do on a Saturday night and all the girls I went with felt the same way. It didn't mean I was over you. But after your mom passed, and we still didn't see each other, I kinda put a foot down on my feelings. And now I guess I'm lifting my feet again."

"And here I am, with your boot prints all over me."

He grinned, and that gave her the courage to bring up another touchy topic. "I have to say it, Hawk. Eva doesn't seem like a natural choice."

"You mean she isn't a bit like you?"

"Yeah, I guess so."

"She isn't. I knew it wouldn't be easy, but that somehow made it more worthwhile. Opposites attract, and all that. I figured I could succeed with her where I'd failed you. But I couldn't pull her out of her depression, and with you, it's the opposite problem. I can't hold you back from taking on life, not that I care to. But it leaves us in an impossible situation."

He looked so defeated. She tugged on his shirt and he turned from his contemplation of the ridge to her. "Hey, if you couldn't make me stay, then no one could have."

His eyes warmed. "You're just saying that to make me feel better."

"If the truth makes you feel better, then yeah."

His arm slipped around her waist and she let him pull her close. It was an awkward embrace against his side instead of his front. "You still scared?" he whispered.

Her insides quivered and she couldn't draw a full breath. His lips were right there. She shifted to face him, sliding her hands over the plane of his hard back.

"To death," she said, and then kissed him anyway.

CHAPTER TWELVE

THEY HAD BROKE apart at Doxie Sue's barking as she and Nathan crossed over to the bunkhouse. Hawk had reluctantly let Grace go home. He'd expected to pick up from where they left off, after the weekend, when her guests left, but on Sunday, Mateo called and wondered if he and Haley could stop by during their two-day stayover with Grace. They were also trailering down two mares Mateo had picked up at a horse sale, suitable for Grace's trail riding.

Mateo pulled in two days later while Hawk was still wrangling the boys into pajamas.

All bets were off now that Ma-ta-to had landed. He hefted them both into his arms and mock-carried them to his truck. "I'm taking you back with me. I need help back on my ranch."

"You have to ask Grace first," Saul told him, limbs dangling. "She's expecting us at her place nine o'clock tomorrow morning."

Mateo turned to Hawk who was watching from the porch steps. "Your dad doesn't have a say?"

"Yes," Amos said, "but they team parent us."

"First," Hawk said, "I've heard of that term. Grace teach you it?" Did she really think of herself as a kind of parent to his children?

"She said it's for kids with two parents in different places."

Which should describe him and Eva. Hawk didn't know whether to be worried or hopeful at their distinction.

"I had better hold off taking you two back then," Mateo said. "At least, until tomorrow."

"Can we show him Picasso?" Saul turned to his dad.

"And then straight to bed."

"I will," Saul said and poked his brother who gave a reluctant commitment.

Mateo brought them back to set them on the porch steps. "Get socks and boots on. And then we'll go."

"Leave your pajamas on," Hawk added.

Mateo shot him a grin as they pounded back inside. "Team parenting, eh? We had that down when they were still in diapers."

Hawk lifted his hands, palms up. "No argument here. You couldn't wait until tomorrow to see the horses, I take it?"

Mateo leaned on the porch railing. "I came to get the inside scoop on you and Grace. You have no idea how much fun Haley and I are having at her expense."

"What is Grace telling you?" Long talks at fencess aside, it might be useful to get some insight into her thinking.

"As if she would show her hand," Mateo said. "I was hoping you could give us leverage."

"Now, how would that help me?"

"Ah, so you are after her?"

The boys shot through the door. "C'mon, Mateo," Amos said. "He's out in the barn."

From there on in, it was all about horses, which suited Hawk fine. He didn't much want to talk about Grace yet, not with everything so new between them and it just as likely to blow away like the dandelion puffs at his feet.

The next day, Mateo arrived bright and early to saddle

Katzmobile. The horse was sold as a performance cutter, but a horse behaved differently for every rider. As a treat, Hawk let the boys watch, which meant foregoing their usual Wednesday with Grace.

"I've been expecting your call," Grace said to him. "I've got Jonah and baby Jakob here to be an auntie to. Just don't let Mateo talk you into anything."

From behind her, Hawk heard Haley call out, "Like having a third kid. Trust me."

"Is there something that I need to know?" Grace said, clearly to her sister. "Sorry, Hawk, I got to go. Have fun."

Mateo certainly intended to. He had already enlisted the boys' limited help to drag out the pulley system for training cutting horses. "You don't know what this is?" he was asking Amos. "You set it up along a fence and then you run a flag up and down it. The flag is the cow. And the horse chases it."

"A game for horses?" Saul said.

"And the rider. Here let's get this up." Mateo glanced up at Hawk. "This is fun, isn't it?"

He and Grace had kissed again, he had a promising foal in the pasture nearby, his boys were happy and healthy, and his ex-employee and now partner had come to share the day with him. Hawk lifted the other end of the pulley system. "I've had worse."

The pulley erected, Mateo saddled Katz, inspecting the stallion as he went. "Grace had a good idea, I admit."

"It was, though I can't say I liked the way she went about it."

Mateo eased the halter on Katz, adjusting the bit. "That's Grace. She barrels to the end, like a stampeding bull, because she thinks she knows best. It will get her in trouble one of these days."

Grace still must have not told her family about her firing…or her rehiring. Hawk pretended interest in the boys as they dared each other to balance on the railing with no hands.

Mateo interpreted his silence differently. "Of course, you hold a different opinion of her."

"I agree with you, and I hold a different opinion."

Mateo led Katz toward the corral. Hawk walking alongside. "She's not Eva," Mateo said quietly. "She won't come apart on you."

I was scared, Hawk. I was scared that I wouldn't have the strength to leave.

She was Grace, and that was trouble enough.

Katz and Mateo were a dream team on the flag. His dad came out and leaned beside Hawk on the railing, while Hawk was inside on the pulley. "I might be losing my mind, but I still know beauty in motion when I see it."

"He rides the tiger well," Hawk said and his dad pushed up his hat.

"You remember me saying that?"

"The day you came back with the first horse."

"I thought so," his dad muttered. "I thought I said that."

"Hold," Mateo called and Hawk let up on the pulley. Mateo came over. "We don't need to train so much as we just need to get acquainted. I can still get him in a few shows this season. I could even try for the Stampede. Only a month away but they might have a cancelation."

"What will you do with Risky B?"

"Show them both. The better they place, the more we can ask by way of stud fees, and Risky B's foals."

"You talk to Grace about this?"

"Can you see her saying no?"

He couldn't. "I say we show them as much as we can in the summer, then next April, Katz can cover Risky B.

If she takes, then we can still show her over the summer and she can foal here. You can board Katz over the winter."

"Sounds good," Mateo said. "I'll start making calls to get them in shows."

Hawk saw a hiccup to their plan. "Two horses, twice the hauling."

"You bring Katz, and I'll bring Risky B."

"That'll mean days away from the boys and—" He broke off, aware of his dad next to him.

"And me," his dad said. "I can't be left alone with the boys anymore. I might leave them on the stove and boil them dry."

Mateo looked uncertainly between the two of them. Hawk wasn't sure how much Grace or Knut had divulged to Mateo and Haley, and out of respect for his father, he wasn't about to get into it. "I will need a few days heads-up, at least." Hawk said. "To arrange for care."

"Grace will help out," Mateo said. "She already does."

"The shows are usually on the weekend, Grace's busy time."

"If she sees it as you being part of the business she invested in, I'm sure she can be persuaded."

Persuaded into playing rancher's wife. "I don't like putting her in that position."

Mateo swung off the saddle. "You know you can't talk her into doing anything she doesn't already want to do."

"You should ask family first," his dad said.

"I was thinking the same thing," Hawk said. "There are people around on the weekend at Gemma's. The boys will have more fun."

His dad frowned. "I meant Grace."

Gemma had done more than enough when it came to her nephews. But to ask Grace… He wasn't so much afraid that she would refuse him, but that she would accept it out of obligation, and resent him for it later. That, he couldn't live with.

"I'll think on it," he said.

How infuriating.

Grace had invited Hawk and the boys for supper together at The Home Place, where Mateo dropped plans for how they were going to show both Katz and Risky B this summer. Her dad and Sadie had also come, but they had gone over to Irina's. Grace felt as if she had a teenage son ditching his family for his girlfriend.

"Who will cover for the boys?" Grace said.

The two men both dropped their gazes to their steaks and baked potatoes. "We haven't got that one figured out yet," Hawk muttered.

Grace raised her hands and pointed her index fingers to her head. "I'm sitting right here." She turned to Amos and Saul, Saul to her right and Amos across the table at Hawk's right. "Your dad might need to be away a few days here and there over the summer. You okay to stay with me?"

Amos turned to Hawk. "Why can't we come with you?"

"Amos, you're brilliant," Grace said. "We can come along." It would be fun. They could take in the show. Do a little bit of touristy stuff, depending on where the shows took them, camp or grab a motel…

"What about your guests?"

Shoot, she had forgotten all about them. She was booked pretty well solid throughout the summer. Word had got around, thanks to her contacts in the legal community. "Let's not get the cart before the horse," she said. "We don't even have any show dates confirmed yet."

"Worse comes to worse, the boys can come up north to stay with me," Haley said.

"But that'll make you busy when you're already taking care of the outside work," Hawk said.

"Brock will handle that," Haley said.

"Which is to say," Grace said to Hawk, " we've got you covered. What I don't understand is why you wouldn't think we did."

"You got a lot on the go, Grace," Hawk said quietly. "And I don't want the boys and me making your life harder."

If by *hard*, he meant more purposeful, then the Blackstone males were the hardest thing she had ever undertaken. All four of them. "Busy isn't harder."

"So it's all settled then?" Mateo said.

"It's all settled," Grace said before Hawk could answer, but Mateo turned to Hawk.

"I guess we have a plan," Hawk affirmed. He sounded more resigned than supportive.

She had promised Rachelle to forward case recommendations by that night, but she wasn't in the head space for legalese until she had sorted things out with Hawk.

The boys were camping overnight in the living room with Sadie, so Grace suggested they try out the trail mares while checking the cattle. Hawk shrugged his agreement but led the way to the pen where she kept the horses. He ran a hand over their backs and legs.

"Don't you trust Mateo's judgment?"

"Don't you make sure your tires are inflated before driving?" Hawk said as he laid the saddle pads on their backs.

"Who does that?"

Hawk gave her a dry look and reached for one of the two saddles in the shelter he had renovated when he'd fixed the fence two months ago in April. Mateo had brought down all the gear. When not annoying, her brother-in-law was thoughtful and generous, way more than she was to him. Which was annoying. "They come with names?"

Grace pulled down the second saddle, the weight yanking at her shoulders. "The one with the white patch on the haunch is Sage, and the bay is Willow."

"Good names." Hawk swung his saddle onto Willow's back and took hers. "You remember how to cinch a saddle?"

Not really, it turned out. One more thing to get on top of.

The sun was still high enough, light cutting up the west side of the pasture and daytime heat warming her bare arms and her denim jeans. Hawk turned in his saddle. "You want to get the horses into a trot?"

She would have been up for a gallop but changed her mind as she bounced, trying to catch the rhythm of the horse's gait. How had she gone full gallop when they were kids?

They slowed the horses as they began the climb across to the upper pasture behind The Home Place. Already her place looked tiny, the vehicles pulled up outside like toys. She thought she could see two figures moving to Irina's truck.

"Do you think that's Dad and Irina?"

"I'd say so," Hawk said without looking. He must have already spotted them.

"Great," Grace said, suddenly feeling grumpy. "Another wedding in the offing."

"But they've only been seeing each other for a couple of months."

"Dad proposed to Mom after only two months. I'm expecting the hammer to fall any day now."

"You don't like her?"

"I don't know her. Other than she kicked up a fuss about a dozen extra vehicles on the road a week and abandoned me to stapling the ears of innocent calves. Dad comes down to see Mom, and hooks up with Mom's friend. What's going on there?"

"I think it's called closure, Grace."

Something gentle and sad in his voice turned her to him. His lips moved as he counted calves. She'd not interrupt that process.

"There's probably more down by the creek," he said at last, and started that way, expecting her to follow.

He had always assumed she would follow and had always assumed right. She glanced down the hill one more time. Her dad was getting into the passenger seat beside Irina.

She urged her horse after Hawk.

Calves were bunched along the sides of the gulch, the majority along this side but a few peppy ones had crossed the shallow creek. Most were curled into tight, hair-covered rocks. A few stood quiet, staring curiously at the intruders.

Hawk's lips were moving again, and Grace decided to join the game. When he looked done, she called over to him. "I got fifty-seven."

Hawk pointed across the creek. "Did you get the two under the bush there?"

She hadn't. "I guess that's why you're the cowboy. Is that all of them?"

He nodded.

"Then, you ready to tell me what's really bothering you? Why don't you want me involved in the business?"

"It's not that. It's—you, Grace."

Grace sucked in her breath. Word for word what George had said. "I'm pushy, right?"

"You said you cared about my family and I believe it. And you care about the ranch itself. And maybe about me."

"Correct on all points."

"The thing is, I care, too. You are more than this ranch, Grace."

"By *more*, you mean my career as a lawyer?"

"If you didn't want to do the work, you wouldn't have signed up for it."

He was right. Hadn't the sweaty work with the calves, in part, spurred her to take on the assignment? She'd come out tonight to give him support, to let him know that he could count on her. And he had pinpointed that she couldn't be held to one place. Nor did she want to.

"Look, you might be overthinking this. I'm ready to take care of the twins, because that's important work, too. I like to think that we are good for each other."

"You jumped on it, forgetting your own business here. And you might need to make some choices."

"What are you saying, exactly?"

"I guess what I'm saying is that you can't do it all, Grace. You're one person trying to be a bunch of people, someone for everyone. This whole B and B thing is for your mother, and she's been more than ten years gone. That's not fair to you."

She hadn't seen it that way. She had seen it as making peace. "But I can handle it all. I'll prove it to you."

"You will cut yourself into smaller and smaller pieces, and the thing is—"

He shifted in his saddle and looked away.

No way. "Finish what you start, Hawk Blackstone."

He slowly turned to her. "Because, Grace Jansson, I don't want pieces of you. I want all of you. That was the deal."

His dark eyes on her were like just before they kissed. Except he was a full body length from her and didn't look inclined to close the distance. "That's asking for a lot."

"I'm not asking, Grace. I don't want you to give up your life for me. I want you to feel that your life is with me. And the boys. You don't have to be everything to everyone, least of all to me."

She looked down and picked a brush bristle from the mane. She would give the mare a good brushing later. After her report to Rachelle, before babysitting the boys, between her B and B guests. She could handle this. "I don't," she whispered, "know how to be anything else."

His silence was reply enough. He was immovable. Like the land. And like the wind, she was going every which way, set to blow things apart. Including herself, if she wasn't careful.

GRACE SENT HER email to Rachelle and peered at the computer clock. 11:49 p.m. "Eleven minutes to get to bed before I turn into a pumpkin." Her mom used that line on her and Haley when they were kids. They'd never believed her, but neither did they risk it.

She sent a text to Natalia. Brock's wife felt more like a friend than family, probably because they both had lives outside the family. Natalia was a partner in a growing franchise business, had a family of two young ones, a cowboy husband and also traveled internationally. She had it all, and never had to choose.

Hey, Nats. I was hoping to get your input on something both personal and professional. Could we chat tomorrow?

Grace set down her phone, not expecting a reply at this late hour. Her phone buzzed.

Now is good for me.

"Aren't you supposed to be sleeping?" Grace said when Natalia picked up.

"I could say the same to you."

"I had work to do, and with Dad and Haley and the kids here, now's when I have peace and quiet."

Natalia laughed. "And thank you for taking them. I'm using the time to catch up on some paperwork. What's up?"

Grace didn't know how much to divulge to Natalia. She couldn't ask Natalia not to tell Brock, though she didn't think it would go beyond him. At any rate, she would have to risk it. She really couldn't figure this out on her own.

"I guess I want to know… Well, how do you juggle everything in your life?"

"*Juggle* being the operative word. I have gotten so used to dropping the ball, especially since Daniel was born. If it wasn't for Brock, I would have walked off the deep end long ago."

"You're saying that behind every successful woman, there's a good man." Was Hawk that man for her? It wasn't as if he had offered to help her out. Then again, she helped him because he was already going flat-out.

"In my case, oh yeah. Things coming hard and fast for you?"

"You could say that. The B and B is booked through most of the summer, I have the Blackstone boys twice a week, I bought shares in a horse, and the sabbatical with the firm is a wash because they need me to take on a case as a favor. And oh yeah, I promised the boys we'd make a quilt for their grandpa's birthday in November."

"Wow," Natalia said. "At least, you don't have to worry about taking care of a husband."

Grace hesitated for too long, because Natalia immediately pounced. "Or are the rumors about you and Hawk true?"

"We're not married or engaged." They had not even gone on a single date. That was just how busy they both were.

"Then, what are you?"

Two kisses and a few long conversations, that's what they were. "Not quite together and not quite apart."

"Ah, I remember those days with Brock. A bit...tense, then?"

"He's left it up to me to decide if we should be together. I know he still has hang-ups from his ex, so he doesn't want to push me into a relationship I'm nervous about, but he seems to think that I need to give up my career if we are to make it work out here with him and the family. And I don't want to have to make that decision. I want everything, like you."

"I have everything I want, but I still had to give up what I thought I needed. And as a guideline, everything connected to Brock and family I have kept my greedy hands on."

"Yeah, but Hawk is not like your guy. He can travel with you, and Mateo picks up the slack. I'm the one helping Hawk out. There's no time for just the two of us."

"So why did you go on sabbatical, Grace? It sounds as if you needed a break from the work. Could it be that in your heart of hearts you were already looking for a change?"

"I... Well, uh, maybe so. Maybe you're right."

"But then you took on more work. So, were you really?"

Maybe it was the late hour but Grace couldn't think fast enough. "The thing is that I was fired from the firm for good reason, and now I'm trying to make up for my past mistakes."

"Oh wow. That's the first I heard of that. I'm sorry."

"It's the first time anyone has heard about it except for Hawk."

"I won't tell, either. Besides, it sounds as if it might come out in the wash, anyway, if they came to you for help."

"That's what I'm hoping, but it's not a one-time deal on my boss's part, and tonight, well, I kinda lost track of time working the case. That speaks tons about how I still love law, right? I don't know what to do."

"Yeah, that's a tough one."

"Natalia, you're supposed to tell me what to do," Grace said.

"And if I knew, I'd tell you. But past midnight, I'll put it this way— Where do you want to be at the end of the day?"

With Hawk. With the boys. With an interesting case to tackle tomorrow.

She wanted it all and she could give it her all. She would find a way to strike a balance. *I'll show you, Hawk.*

CHAPTER THIRTEEN

HAWK MEANT TO drive past the house on his way out with Katz loaded in the trailer, but at the sight of Grace on the porch with the boys waving him off, he stopped.

One last goodbye.

"Did you change your mind?" Amos said.

"Can we come?" Saul said, finishing off the direction of Amos's question.

"Not a chance," Hawk said. "I came to make sure Grace is okay with me leaving you two alone with her."

"Why wouldn't she be?" Amos said.

"Exactly," Grace said. "Why wouldn't she be?"

Man, she looked good. Her light hair wrapped up in some kind of knotted bun, with a pink fitted shirt and her bare legs in denim shorts and sandals. All summery and fresh smelling. The knots in his stomach, all twisted up like her hair, eased off.

"I don't know. I feel guilty. Going off and leaving you to handle it all by yourself. A few hours is one thing, but bedtime is a whole other rodeo."

"First, I'm not alone. Nathan's here with his trusty dog. Those two count for four people right there. Irina and Amy are also around."

"And there's us," Saul pointed out.

Grace winked at Hawk. "And there's the boys. Question is, how are you going to make out with only Mateo to help?"

"All right, then. I should be back late tonight."

"No, you won't. You're staying the night. Mateo booked the last room at the inn."

"He moves fast. Seems as if it were only a couple of weeks ago that we were talking about showing them."

"That's because it was. Two-and-a-half, to be exact. Now, hurry, go, we're fine."

"Go," Russell said, from the doorway. "Have fun, but not too much." He used to say that to Hawk when he was a teenager. Had his memory lapsed? And then— "Give Mateo my best."

Hawk let out his breath. Grace followed him to his truck.

"Don't spend all of your time thinking about me," she said.

Hawk took in her outfit again. Her toes were painted the same pink as her top.

He walked towards the back of the trailer, Grace following, until it stood between them and their audience on the porch. He kissed her, not for long but enough to kick up his heartbeat.

"I do nothing but," he said and then left quickly, while he still could.

That kiss carried him through the rest of the day, through a two-hour trip to Lethbridge and the show itself. Things were working out. He and Mateo had a strategy to keep the breeding program in place, thanks to Grace. His life had changed for the better since the boys had brought them back together. He could have a fresh start.

If she chose him. Because as much as she said she could handle it all, she couldn't. Nobody could. In the end, she would have to choose.

And it was on him to give her every reason to choose

him and the boys. Something more than three kisses and a broken lily.

Mateo and Risky B in the arena were like two old-time partners. The cow—really a yearling steer—didn't stand a chance as they separated it from the others and halted its return, finally driving the yearling to a standstill. The audience sent up an appreciative applause, and Hawk drew in the sight of people giving it up for the horse he had helped bring into the world.

He spotted Grant Sears sitting with his wife, and an idea popped up. He stepped along the bleachers until he drew even with them. Grant looked up, first in passing, and when recognition set in, his mouth twisted down.

"Good to see you again, Grant." Hawk nodded to Deb. "Hello."

"I saw the horse you bought out from under me was a last minute addition. I had to see what I got cheated out of."

"Just to be clear, Grace—and Katz's trainer—bought her. I was as surprised as you."

"Where is he being stabled?"

"My place."

Grant gave a grunt. "Even better deal for you. You got yourself a free horse."

"It's working out so far," Hawk admitted. "I'm anxious as you to see him perform. Mateo hasn't been able to get as much training in as he has with Risky B."

"That mare's a fine horse. Not selling her, is he?"

Grant's wife patted his knee. "Remember that you left your checkbook at home."

Hawk worked to keep his shrug casual. "Too bad. I was hoping we could do business. One-on-one."

"What did you have in mind?" Grant's words were out even as his wife placed a staying hand on his arm.

"Mateo and I are partners now." Grace, too, but he

didn't want the mention of her name to rile Grant. "And we plan to breed Katz and Risky B. She would foal spring after next."

"That's more than eighteen months out," Grant said.

"But not unusual to be investing that far ahead."

"You want me to put money down on something that might not even happen?"

"Money held in reserve, Grant. I'm not here to rip you off. I'm here to give you an opportunity. See it as a kind of apology."

"An apology I pay for? How much?"

Hawk named a figure. "If you take her right at birth."

"I'm too old to work a horse all day long."

Music to Hawk's ears. "If you like how Mateo handles the horse, then we can come up with a different fee. He trains and shows. Sort of pay as we go."

"And what if I want him showing across the States, instead of around here?"

"Mateo shows into the States."

The announcer called in Mateo and Katz, and the pair entered the ring. Katzmobile was clearly up for the show, perhaps a bit too much. He had spirit all right. Mateo paced him back and forth a couple more times than he had with Risky B, and Katz seemed to relax into the job at hand. They split the herd and spliced off a set of five before working them down to one, and then it was game on, as the white yearling sought to return to the herd. Katz held him fast, but a sudden dodge left Katz back on his haunches for a split second too long and he raced across the arena to cut off the yearling in the nick of time. The cow gave up right after, but Katz had nearly lost it for them, and the judges would see that loss of control.

"He needs work," Grant said shortly. "How long has Mateo been working him?"

"Last two weeks, mostly."

"Huh."

Hawk didn't want him dwelling on Katz's less-than-stellar performance for too long. "As Mateo said, 'You can control the flame, so long as one's there.'" Mateo had said nothing of the sort, but it sounded better coming from a trainer.

Grant's wife watched Mateo and Katz exit the arena. "He has a wife and kids, and a ranch of his own, right?"

"They're...ambitious."

She fixed her gaze on him. "Like you and Grace."

Hawk dodged. "We all make for a great team. You could be part of it, Grant."

The horseman's mouth worked, as if he was chewing on a wad of tobacco. "All right, let's do this." He reached inside his jacket, and Deb leaned back.

"Remember, no checkbook?"

"No book," he said and pulled out a single blank check. His wife sank and Grant gave a rare grin. "You really didn't think I'd leave home without one?"

"READY TO GO?" Amos shoved his head between Grace and her computer screen, his thick, black hair going up her nose.

"Not if you keep getting in the way," she said, pushing his head aside. "How about you and Saul go find Grandpa and see if he wants to come with us?"

She had promised them a trip into Diamond Valley for ice cream, once she had sent off an email to Rachelle. Her frazzled colleague had bombarded her with urgent questions, and the answers demanded careful consideration.

Grace heard the boys clatter down the porch steps of the Blackstone home and race each other to the corrals. She had a clear eye on them. Now for the first bit of peace all day. "The litigation between the parties," she muttered, re-reading, "finds its precedent in the matter—" Her fingers and brain settled into the work, her thoughts finally coalescing after a day of keeping up with demands of twins who absolutely did not stop. They even vibrated while they ate.

"Finally, please instruct—" Truck doors slammed and Grace looked out the window to see Russell get in the driver's seat of his truck. The boys' heads barely cleared the dashboard.

"No, no, no, no, no."

The truck motor started and was pulling away as Grace yanked open the front door. "Russell, wait for me!"

But he was already heading down the lane. Shoot, shoot! Russell was having an off day. He had wandered aimlessly about the house, and once, she had found him standing in the lane, looking up and down. "I came to get the mail," he said when she joined him, "but I must have got the days mixed up."

Mail was no longer delivered but arrived at a community mailbox. "I hardly remember myself, Russell. You want to join me and the boys for lunch?"

And now he was driving down the same lane with the boys. There were no booster seats. At the end of the lane, she saw who she thought was Saul look out the back window at her.

The truck jerked onto the main road and Saul's head sank out of sight. Grace tore to her car. She would follow them into town, or maybe persuade Russell to pull over, and everyone could transfer into her car.

"Please, please be in your right mind."

No one had warned the kids not to get in the vehicle with Grandpa because Russell himself had said the day of his diagnosis that he wouldn't drive on the road, and he wouldn't drive with passengers at all. That had seemed enough. But she and Hawk should have warned the boys, regardless.

Hawk. She reached for her phone and then stopped. No use calling him. He could do nothing, and if she could get to Russell, there was nothing to worry about. Maybe there was nothing to worry about anyway. Maybe the Russell of old would surface for the next half hour and she would catch up to them at the ice cream shop.

She caught up with them at the bend before Irina's place. About two hundred yards ahead of her, she watched Russell brake for the bend and keep driving straight off the road and down into the ditch, stopping only after he smashed into the horse cairn.

Grace pressed on the gas and then slammed to a halt on the shoulder of the road, parallel to Russell's truck. The horse memorial was decapitated, the head in the ditch grass, and Irina's saddle of daisies and pansies hung in the truck grill. Russell sat slumped, his head on the wheel. She could see nothing of the boys.

"Please, please, please," she whispered and ran through the tall-grass ditch, the blades binding around her legs. The driver's door opened and Russell's leg flopped out.

"Russell!" She reached his side. He gave her a glazed look, and beyond him were the kids. Amos had one hand over his eye and another over Saul's mouth where blood outlined Amos's fingers. Saul stared ahead, as if his eyes were pinned open. Neither was crying. Shock, probably. Or ranching life had vaccinated them against the sight of blood.

"Are you okay?" Grace said. Stupid question when they clearly weren't.

"We hit here," Amos said, patting the dashboard. "My eye, his mouth."

She didn't see any bruising on their heads but— "Did either of you at any time fall asleep, even for a short while? Your eyes close?"

Amos and Saul shook their heads. "Why would we fall asleep," Amos said, "in the middle of an accident?"

"Do you feel dizzy?"

"No," Amos said and Saul shook his head.

"Feel like throwing up?"

Same response.

"Can you see okay? Nothing looks blurry?"

Negative. No point calling 9-1-1. The nearest ambulance was an hour away, and the injuries—thankfully—were minor. But she would run them to the clinic, just to be sure.

"You tell me if any of that changes, okay?"

"I forgot," Russell whispered. "I forgot I wasn't supposed to drive on the road." Wetness appeared in his eyes and he passed a hand over his face. "I thought I'd get the mail with the kids. We've done it before."

A quad gunned across the pasture from Irina's place. She cut the motor and yelled, "Don't touch the fence. It's electrified."

Grace waved to her in understanding, and Irina gunned for the fence box that housed the battery. At least, Grace assumed that was what she was doing. "Boys, did you hear that? Irina's fence is electrified. Stay in the truck."

Saul pulled away his brother's hand and fresh blood spilled from his lips. Oh God. Amos clamped his hand back over his brother's mouth.

"Hold tight. I've got a first aid kit in my car." By the time she returned, Russell was leaning on the truck box. From the way he sagged, Grace was pretty sure he wasn't wandering anywhere.

Irina brought the chugging quad up and turned it off. "The power's cut. How's everybody?"

"Conscious," Grace said. "Shaken." Herself included. "I'm just going to look at Saul's mouth." She took Russell's place behind the wheel. "Are you going to let me, Saul?"

She had to pry Amos's stiff hand away from his brother's mouth. Blood had dried around his mouth, even as more pooled inside his lip. She spotted a box of tissues on the floor of the cab and tugged out a few. She wrapped her arm around Saul and leaned him forward. "Spit."

It was a mess of blood and spit and…two teeth. "Wow, what a way to lose your loose tooth," Grace said, injecting more cheer than she felt. "Can I take a peek?"

Saul opened his mouth, and Amos, like he had with the computer screen, stuck his head between Grace and his brother to get the first look.

"You got two knocked out," Amos turned to Grace. "Did you see that?"

What she saw was a bruise swelling around Amos's eye. "You look as if you got in a fight," she said.

"Really?" Amos scooted to the side-view mirror to check it out, while Grace used the Amos-free space to lean over Saul's mouth. Two definitely gone, the gap there like a baby's.

Tears welled up in Saul's eyes.

"Don't worry," Grace said. "Those were your baby teeth. Adult ones will come soon enough, and they'll be bigger and better."

Saul pointed at the windshield. "We hit the memory horse."

A pansy with its purple-and-white face lay on the trunk hood. Irina stood beside Russell, both of them staring silently at the destroyed horse.

"Yeah, that happened, but what really matters right now is that you and Amos and your grandpa are okay."

Saul's eyes flooded with tears. "Grandpa forgot how to drive."

"Nobody quite knew that, Saul. It's not your fault, okay? Accidents happen."

Another accident she didn't prevent. And this time, she was in charge. She had thought she could handle her career, her B and B business, and take care of active kids and a disabled elder. One day in, and she had blown it. What if something worse had happened?

She sorted through the first aid kit to see if there was anything to patch them up with. "Here, Amos. I found an ice pack." She cracked the plastic barrier to activate it. "Hold it against your eye. It will reduce the swelling."

"But I want it to get huge."

Hawk did not need to see his son sporting a big whopper of a black eye. "Trust me, you don't. Get it on there."

He and Grace had a split-second staring contest, with her having the advantage of two healthy eyes. Amos clapped on the pack, and then, because cowering before a brush with serious injury was not his style, he asked, "Can we get out now?"

Grace slid out and helped the boys down, though the little bale hoppers could handle themselves. It seemed important to have live contact with them.

"It's that bend. It's been nothing but trouble," Irina was saying to Russell, as the boys left the vehicle. She was leaning on the truck box, beside Russell. He was facing the inside of the truck box, whereas she was staring down at the horse head, its single visible painted eye staring back. She turned to the boys as they came out. "You two are having a bit of an adventure."

Amos lowered the ice pack. "I got a shiner."

Russell turned to take in his grandson, and he winced

at the sight of the bruise and Saul holding the bloodied paper towel to his mouth.

"He lost two teeth," Amos reported.

Russell dragged a shaky hand down his face, and Grace quickly added, "One was already loose and the other is probably a baby tooth, too. That's all. They are both alive and well. Any damage to the truck?" Grace said, to distract everyone from the human injury.

Russell hung his head. "I hope it's totaled, so I never turn a wheel again."

Grace and Irina exchanged swift gazes. Nothing so robbed independence in the country as not being able to drive. Saul mumbled something behind his wad that only Amos deciphered.

"Saul wants to know if that means bicycles, too?"

It wasn't all that funny. Its humor only lay in its seriousness, but it broke up the adults, and even the corner of Russell's mouth cranked up.

"I suppose so long as the only motor driving the wheels is myself, I'll try it," he said. "If I even remember how."

Grace took his arm. "We can just leave the truck here for now. I'll take out the registration, and we'll lock it up. Tomorrow is soon enough to deal with it."

Meaning when Hawk got home. Russell picked up on her train of thought. "You'll tell him, then."

"Sure, I can do that," she said brightly, as if she'd only be passing on the normal day's events.

Russell pulled himself up straight. "I'm sorry, Irina, for what I did here." He gestured to the broken wood and scattered flowers.

Irina shook her head. "It's about time it got taken down. I just didn't know how to go about it. So, thank you, Russell." She gave his arm a squeeze. "You always were a good friend to me."

Russell gave a nod that looked like a spastic jerk of his head and turned for Grace's car.

"Irina, if there's anything—"

"Go on. You have your hands full. I'm okay, but I think I'm calling your dad tonight."

Grace stretched out her hand to the boys. "Come on, boys. We're all going to the clinic to get checked out."

Saul mumbled something to Amos whose eyes widened. "Wait a minute. Does this mean we don't get ice cream?"

THE NEXT MORNING, Hawk rolled in shortly after breakfast, which suited Grace just fine. She had called him last night from the clinic after the three Blackstones passed physical inspections. She had confirmed that there were no signs of concussion, but she would monitor for signs as per the doctor's instructions, that Russell was completely uninjured, and that they were going home right after a stop at the ice cream shop. In typical Hawk fashion, he'd listened, asked a few questions and then spoke to the boys. Amos and Saul chattered on about the headless horse and bloody teeth and how the doctor didn't even know how to saddle a horse, and what flavors of ice cream they wanted.

"I'm so sorry," Grace said for what felt like the hundredth time when she took the phone again, and for the hundredth time, Hawk assured her it wasn't her fault.

But it was. Hawk had left his father and his sons in her care, and she had let him down. Now that he was back, she couldn't look him in the eye, and was glad when she slipped away and didn't have to try any longer.

Not that she could avoid him forever. He had texted her to say that he would like to come over in the evening, when Amy and Nathan could watch over the household. They had set a time, and she had come onto the porch to watch the laneway.

Instead, she heard the clip of hooves and the soft rattle of harness. Hawk had come through the backyard past the fence, past the two trail horses.

"Thought I'd combine business with pleasure," he said, dismounting Wildrose. "Checked on the cattle and the fence. Both are holding up."

"Good to hear," she called to him. "Do you mind parking your transportation on the other side of my lawn to avoid having to shovel anything she drops from her exhaust?"

Hawk obliged, giving her time to take a few deep breaths to steady herself. By the time he joined her, stretching his legs out beside hers, she felt a little less shredded. In fact, his presence went a long way to repairing her unraveled state.

"I had to resew a square twice today," she said. "I put it on upside down the first time, and sideways the second. The accident last night rattled me," she said in a rush. "And of course, here I am, stuck with bits of your dad's old clothes around me, cut and pinned and sewn together."

"I gathered that from the way you tore out of the house this morning." Hawk wrapped his arm around her shoulders and pulled her in tight against him. She should resist and not let him think that whatever they had going on could continue. But she softened against him, anyway.

"I'm sorry," she whispered. "I am so sorry. If I had been more careful, it wouldn't have happened. I should have been watching."

"You're not the first one who has apologized today. Dad, of course. I don't think he ate at all today. Even Amos and Saul apologized for not checking with you first. And then Irina called to say that she was just sorry about the whole mess, and that I was to call her anytime, if I needed help."

Grace forced herself to straighten away from him a smidge. "I'm the only one who should be apologizing."

"How do you figure that?"

He actually sounded confused.

"Do you know what I was doing when your dad drove off with the kids? I was answering an email from Rachelle. I was working when I should have been with the kids. Yes, I meant to follow them outside. Yes, I sent them to Russell, and I didn't think he would drive away. But the point was, they weren't my priority and they should have been."

"We all got work to do, Grace. It could've happened to anyone. It happened to me. Remember why we met back in March?"

"I do, and do you remember what you were doing when I called? Yeah, buying groceries for the family. Do you know what I was doing? Taking care of myself. I was more concerned about getting my reputation back than the welfare of your kids."

"You have spent days and days with my kids. I'm not going to let you beat yourself up about an event that came right in the end. By the way, Saul's teeth are fine. He should have two shiny white teeth in a couple of months. Ahead of Amos, likely."

"About the time Amos's shiner will disappear." Grace rubbed her arms at the memory of their little mutilated faces. "I don't know if I can do this, Hawk."

Tension entered his arm and corded around her shoulders. "How so?"

"You asked me to make a choice. And at first, I didn't think I needed to. I could have it all, I thought. I ignored you, ignored my own instincts, and your family paid for my arrogance. I won't jeopardize the safety of your family again. You are right. I can't do it all. I have to choose."

"What if I told you I changed my mind?"

"I would tell you to change it back again."

Hawk smiled. "How often is it I ever change my mind about anything? You should call this a win." His arm tightened around her. "You're scared, is all. Don't make a decision out of fear. That's not you."

"I am only scared that I will do it all again. And the thing is, I really don't want to give up my law career."

"Then, don't. We'll make it work."

She twisted away. "How can you say that, Hawk? You were already stretched to the breaking point when we met. How can throwing my career and this—" she gestured to The Home Place "—little business here into the mix possibly work?"

His jaw set. "I don't know. It just will."

Except it wouldn't. His dad was only going to get worse and the boys would still be boys.

And what if—

"Hawk, do you want more kids?"

He looked at her warily. "I wouldn't call it out of the question."

Kids. Career. Side business. Ranch. Ailing parent. Grace shook her head. "No, Hawk. I can't do it. It's all or nothing for me. And I really tried all, so I guess—" she spread out her hands "—it's nothing."

CHAPTER FOURTEEN

NOTHING.

The word clanged in Hawk's brain as he rode back to the ranch in the falling light. That was what it had all come down to. Nothing. Back to pre-Grace times. Except now it was worse because there were traces of her everywhere. His boys depended on her for a place to go. His dad, too. And she was now part of his business. They might be over, but she remained wound into his life in a way that Eva, his own ex-wife, would never be.

He had thought she would be the one, because she had always been the one.

The fact of the matter was that they had both tried, and in the end, it wasn't enough. No remorse this time, the way it was with Eva.

Still, it was a short sleep that night, and Grace pressed on his mind like a hot rock the second consciousness kicked in. No. He had pushed his way through a breakup before and he'd do it again. It had rained the previous night, a rare peaceful one without a whole pile of thunder and lightning, and Hawk stepped with his cup of coffee onto the porch. The smell of rain and damp earth and grass, and everything with a sheen. Grace would get the same morning. He remembered the view from The Home Place. Through the trees and up the hill. The cattle would be up there. They both could see the same ones.

The front door opened on a squeak. His dad stepped out,

coffee in hand. He walked over to the rain gauge perched out over the edge of the railing. "Three-tenths."

"Enough to keep the dust down for a day or two," Hawk said.

"Not enough for the pasture."

"Yeah. I'll talk to Nathan. We'll get them moved in the next week or so."

Russell took his chair. It was a padded office armchair on wheels. Not exactly fitting for Western porch decor, but then again, his dad never had cared for what other people thought. "If you find me trying to help, you have my permission to tie me to this chair and roll me off the stairs."

It was the first year his father would not take part in moving the cattle into the far pasture. "I hope it doesn't come to that."

"I'm saying it, nonetheless. And while we got a quiet moment here, I'm also giving you permission to boot me off the place."

His dad had his dark eyes locked on Hawk. There was no confusion, only unflinching clarity. The same look he'd given Hawk when he had turned Blackstone Ranch over to him right after he'd married Eva.

"Dad, I can't do that."

"Yes, you can. You need to think of the boys. I'm a loose cannon, son. That accident was God's fair warning."

Grace had said much the same about her limitations. The accident had been about everyone finding out what they couldn't handle. All about giving up.

His dad leaned forward, the wheels rolling backward on the planking. "If I was a horse, you'd shoot me and that's the truth."

"Except you're not," Hawk ground out. "You're my dad and the kids' grandpa."

His dad sat back and then slapped the arms of his chair.

"That's the truth. It isn't for a father to make his son choose between him and his own sons. I need to find a place to park myself. Away from you and the kids. You can all get on with your life, especially now—" he thumbed over his shoulder toward The Home Place "—that Grace is in the picture."

"That's—that's not an issue."

His dad shook his head. "I saw her at the accident. She was scared, and I made her that way. She's too good of a girl to go around worried sick about what I'm going to do next."

"Dad, listen. You don't need to worry about what she thinks. It just doesn't matter." His voice broke on the last word, and he looked down at his scuffed boots.

His dad rose from his chair. "Look at that. I'm wrecking your life, son. And I won't have it."

AMY HAD COME over late morning to watch the boys, which gave Hawk time to go with Nathan to check fence prior to moving the cattle. And she agreed to take the boys on Mondays and Wednesdays for the rest of July and August, with Gemma taking them on Tuesdays and Thursdays. In the fall, they would be in first grade, and with their aunt taking them after school, he would have the day care program largely handled.

He and Nathan had settled on Thursday next for the move. Amy would help, Nathan assured him. In fact, Amy came up more than once during their long afternoon together, which was something, given Nathan hardly ever said anything.

"You're going to be one mopey kid when she goes to university in a couple of months."

They were out behind the barn where it looked down over the valley, the spot where Hawk had come up with the stupid idea that Grace might want to become a mother to his boys. It turned out that Nathan did his dreaming out here, too.

"We'll make it work. She's less than two hours away."

The same distance he and Grace would have had to deal with at their age. That hadn't worked. Hawk didn't have the heart to tell him that time and space were enemies of the heart. He would find out soon enough, and who knew? Maybe they would be the exception.

"You have any plans to move with her? Get a job in the city?"

The boy flinched. "I have no plans to walk concrete. Unless... I mean, you still want me?"

"More than ever. That's the thing. I can't pay you much more than I am now. But I'm hoping that'll change in the next year or two. I'm working with Mateo to build up the horse breeding and the cattle. Maybe another thirty head or so next year. I was thinking we could settle on a number of cattle, and you could have a cut of whatever they sell for."

It was as if he'd handed Nathan the full check from the sale already. "Yeah, I'd like that. I could do that."

"But if something happens to a calf, that's not on me."

"I get it. That's life. I was thinking maybe, what with you building up the cutting horses, and I've seen it done and you've said yourself how useful Doxie Sue is and, well, maybe—"

"You got to break yourself from going tongue-tied every time you want something."

Nathan let out a breath. "I was hoping to go into the dog training business for cattle with Doxie Sue. I have some experience, you know. And I've heard where you can sell a trained dog for upwards of six grand, and even the ones that don't make the cut, there's still a market."

Hawk gazed across the blue-and-green sweep of Eden

Valley. There was a vehicle twinkling jewel-bright far down the main road. Likely on its way to Kananaskis Country, the playground for urban dwellers. It had always given him a kind of perverse lift to know that he lived where urbanities dreamed of going.

"You're thinking of a package deal? One horse and a dog."

"One horse, two dogs."

Hawk smiled at the boy's enthusiasm. "One horse, two dogs, three hundred head of cattle."

Nathan grinned. "That's a perfect tagline."

"Now we just need a name for the company."

Nathan scratched Doxie Sue behind the ear. "Ah, we can just market it under Blackstone Ranch. I'm okay with that."

"That's not right," Hawk said. "You deserve to make a name for yourself."

"No. Makes more sense that I just ride on your name. Nobody knows me from that post there. I'd rather have the money than the name."

It made sense but not for a boy with his quiet drive. Hawk wasn't going to push him. It was enough that he had one good worker and yet another partner to add to his business.

A business partner, when he'd hoped for a life one.

"What do you mean we're not going to Grace's?" Amos gave Hawk a mutinous glare across the breakfast table. Monday breakfasts had become upbeat affairs as the boys anticipated a day with Grace, but today was decidedly different. Grace had not specifically said that the boys' regular visits were over, but he figured this was part of the "nothing" deal. His dad had taken his coffee and toast out to his porch chair and table, no doubt to duck the storm that was about to let loose inside.

Saul used his finger to spread the saskatoon berry jam on the toast. Hawk had opened up the special treat this morning to make the news about Grace go down easier. "Do you mean not on this Monday or all Mondays?"

"All Mondays."

Saul's finger punched through the toast. Amos let out a howl. "But why?"

"She's just got really busy, son. She's back to working at the firm and she still has her guests coming and she has her own family, too."

"But we're not a trouble," Saul said softly. "She said so herself."

"You're right. It's just that she can't manage all fronts, and something had to give."

"And now we only have Wednesdays," Amos said. He crunched on his bacon. He liked his bacon crispy and Saul like his soft. Hawk had made it exactly according to their individual wishes today.

Saul licked his finger. "I will have to work really hard Wednesdays on the quilt." He leaned closer to Hawk. "We're making Grandpa a quilt for his birthday."

Hawk swallowed coffee. He'd already gone through nearly a pot on his own and it wasn't even eight in the morning yet. "This affects Wednesdays, too."

Hawk braced himself for Amos's howl of outrage. Instead, his firecracker son hunched his shoulders and stared down at his bacon and eggs.

Saul gripped his seat, as if he might topple from it. "We're never going to see her again?"

"You just don't see her on regular days. You can still see her now and again, I suppose. Maybe for a horse ride. Or lunch. Something like that."

"How about half days? Like just the mornings or just

the afternoons?" Saul must be desperate. He didn't usually wheel and deal. Amos's eyes hadn't shifted from his food.

"No," Hawk said. "That won't work."

"Why—" Amos spoke faintly "—why don't you like her anymore?"

More, why didn't she like him? Or why didn't she like him enough? "It's not that, son. I like her fine. She's a good person."

"You say the same thing about Mom. That's she a good person, but you don't visit her."

"That's because your mom wants a life separate from us. That doesn't mean I think she's a bad person. Lots of good people don't hang around me," he tried to end on a joke.

"So," Saul said quietly. "It's me and Amos she doesn't like anymore."

"Not at all," Hawk said. "She likes you both very much. Remember she took care of you with the accident? Remember she gave you cookies? Heck, she's the one who asked if you boys would come stay with her during the days I am away."

"But now she hates us," Saul shouted. "First Mom and now Grace. Why? What's wrong with us?"

Hawk stared at Saul and then at Amos who seemed to have shrunk further. It was as if his sons had switched personalities. "Hey. There is nothing wrong with either of you. Ever."

Amos still had his head down, but Saul faced Hawk. "Why don't they want us, then?"

Hawk and Eva had both agreed that the twins should never feel as if they had failed as children. *Blame me,* Eva had said, *if the subject ever comes up. God knows it's true.*

"Your mother has...problems that make it difficult for her to be the kind of mother she knows you deserve to have. It's as if there is a part of her missing that's good with children."

Amos set his head on the table. "She's missing the mom part."

"Is Grace missing the mom part?" Saul said.

"Well, she's not a mom," Hawk said, "so that's different."

"So you're saying that she doesn't have the part, either?"

"I... I don't know, to be honest."

Saul dipped his head. "Me and Amos think she does. I've been with Auntie and she's a mom, and I've been with Irina and she's a grandma and Grace has the mom part."

"Her mom part is this big." Amos threw out his arms and then set his forehead on the table. Dramatic but effective.

Hawk had thought that the twins were reconciled to it just being Dad and Grandpa. They'd never really asked for more, and Hawk figured that their Auntie gave enough of the female warmth to round out their family life. Yeah, he had looked to Grace to become a mother to the boys, but he hadn't considered that the boys, too, were also checking her out as mom material.

"Tell me, months ago, when you went over to The Home Place, was that because you had heard about Grace living there and you wanted to see if she...had a mom part?"

Saul looked over at Amos, but his head was still on the table. "The place had always felt like ours. And then she came, and it still felt like ours. We weren't looking for a mom part."

Amos lifted his head an inch. "Not at first." He lowered it back down.

Saul bit his lip and nodded.

It wasn't just losing Grace. It was losing hope for a mother who showed up for them. "Listen and believe me, it's not either of you. She's walking away from me. Blame me. The thing is, you two and me and Grandpa, we're a family package, right? There's no picking one but not the other. And I proved the deal-breaker. I was the one who was too much."

Amos's head shot up. "What doesn't she like about you?"

All the things that made him who he was. To give up any of them would lessen him, and oddly, lessen him in her eyes, too. But it wasn't just that. The fact of the matter was that he had no room in his life for hers, too. He could contribute nothing to her work life, and even her own family supported his ranch life, too. He brought nothing to the table for her.

He waved his hand and shrugged. "Oh, you know, I guess I'm a little too much ranch, is all."

Tears zigzagged down Amos's face, and at the sight of his brother coming apart, Saul's eyes flooded, too, and he clapped his hands over his face. "But, Dad," Amos said, "there's nothing wrong with that."

"I know, son. There is nothing wrong with any of us."

And that was the hardest part.

NINE O'CLOCK ON Monday morning, and Hawk still hadn't dropped the boys off. A full hour past his usual drop-off time. She checked her phone again for a missed call or text.

She gave it another ten minutes and then texted him.

Is everything okay? Just waiting for you and the boys.

Ten more minutes passed before her phone chimed a text.

They are with Amy now. I understood our previous arrangement is over.

What? She called him and he didn't pick up until after the fifth ring.

"That wasn't my understanding," Grace said. "I understood our arrangement, our—that we were over, but not the boys and me."

She heard a door open and swing shut, and he answered in a lower than normal voice. "I don't see how that would ever work, Grace. I get you care for the boys, and let me tell you this morning, telling them they weren't going over to see you, was rough. What if you are off next week to the city? At some point, you won't be around for the boys on a regular basis, and they might as well get used to it. If you don't want all-in, then it isn't fair that you pick what you want. Not fair to the boys and not fair to me."

He was right. Let's face it, getting close to the boys was the way she had hooked herself into Hawk's world. She didn't trust herself to keep her relationship with the boys separate from hers with Hawk, because it hadn't worked before. No, breaking with Hawk also meant breaking with the boys. At least, ending the same special closeness they'd developed over the summer. They would return to just being neighbors. She looked over at the quilt for Russell's birthday. She and the boys had cut up their Grandpa Russell's denim vest, and Grace had made good use of a flannel shirt she had remembered from a camping trip with Hawk. They hadarranged them into squares, and were ready to start sewing them together.

"Okay," she whispered. "I understand. Give my best to the boys."

Hawk sighed. "I'm not saying that to them now, not after I just got through the tears."

She had walked out on the boys as surely as their mother had, and left Hawk to patch their little hearts together again. And she could do nothing to make the matter better.

"Look, I know you are still part of the business, Grace, but I would really appreciate it if you kept your distance for the next while. Just let things cool down a bit. All right?"

There was nothing to do but agree. She hated Hawk had to pick up the pieces after a breakup she had initiated, but she needed to back off.

She was packing up the quilt squares when she looked out to see a horse rider coming down the backside of the hill from the Blackstone Ranch. Hawk? No, the sit in the saddle wasn't him.

A few more hundred yards, and she recognized Russell.

Had he wandered off with no one knowing? She got her answer when Russell dismounted at the horse. "Morning, Grace. Let me make a call before I forget."

He held his phone away from his ear and shouted into it, "I'm here safe and sound." He paused. "Yes, she's looking at me right now." He held the phone up to her. "Say something, will you?"

"Hello. I'm with Russell. I'm the luckiest woman in the world."

Russell grinned. "You got that?" he yelled into the phone.

He slipped the phone back into his jacketed shirt. "There, that's done. Nathan's a good boy."

Nathan? "I thought that was Hawk. Does he know you are here?"

"No, he doesn't. But I told Nathan to tell him if he asks. Hawk's got enough on his mind."

Not the least the fallout from her decision to leave him. "Can I get you a coffee?"

"I'd rather talk first."

"We can do both. Have a seat." She waved to the patio seat on the front porch.

"You know Angela wanted one of these sets for years,"

Russell said, lowering himself into one. He moved stiffly, as if cranking himself down like a machine. "And I said any old chair would do. Why fork out for a set? But I was wrong. We could have afforded it, and she deserved it."

She couldn't comment on Russell's treatment of his wife. They had been married for thirty-eight years, thirty-eight more than she had the courage to enter.

Russell tapped the wood arms, drumming up a fast tempo. "I want you to do something for me. Help find me a place that'll take me in."

This was sudden. And completely out of her wheelhouse. "Have you talked to Hawk about this?"

"This has got nothing to do with him. It's me taking care of myself and asking for your help to do that."

But she had given Hawk her word that she would stay away from them. "Fair enough. It's just that I don't want it to seem that I'm going behind his back."

"You're not. We're just doing what Hawk finds hard to do. Besides, you two aren't together, am I right?"

"We aren't. It's just that I don't want to cause any more trouble in the Blackstone household. I know that our breakup has disrupted things enough already."

"You, too, will get back together again, don't worry. He'll come around."

Practically the same words her mother had said to Hawk before the fateful horse ride. Grace squirmed in her seat. "I'm the one that started it all, Russell. I guess the ranching life isn't for me."

He gave her a sharp look. "It's because that accident scared the willies out of you, isn't it?"

She licked her lips. "Listen, it was building for a while and the accident just put it in perspective, that's all."

Russell studied her. "All sorts of perspectives out there, believe me. Some you can choose, some—" he touched his temple "—you lose control over. And today, I'm thinking clearly. By tonight, my brain could get scrambled again. Will you help?"

She didn't want to be the one shoving Russell into an extended care facility. But, if it would give him peace of mind, if it would help Hawk through this transition, then she really ought to help out the man who during the summers of her childhood had welcomed her into the very home she now lived in.

"All right," she said. "Let me get my laptop and we'll see what we can come up with."

CHAPTER FIFTEEN

GRACE DROVE RUSSELL to the extended care facility in nearby Diamond Valley. Except with no appointment, they only received vague answers and pamphlets. But Russell was "firing on all plugs," as he put it, and informed the staff he intended to visit with an old friend and offered a name. The two men visited, though since his buddy was deaf, they mostly shouted at each other.

"Now, let's go on a little walk," Russell said after a half hour, his voice noticeably hoarser. They still couldn't see much. Most doors were closed, and partly opened doors only gave a slice of a dresser, a mirror and a bedside table. But there was one unoccupied room, and they snuck in. A single bed, a dresser, a narrow built-in closet with plastic hangers. A window gave a view of a lawn and an outdoor patio, where an elderly woman in a wheelchair was nodding off.

Russell flattened his lips. "She was a grade behind me in school."

He pivoted and left. Outside, he scowled back through the main glass doors into the lobby of the extended health care facility. "The rooms are a little small, aren't they?"

The room wasn't that much smaller than his current one at the ranch. It was just that he wasn't expected to actually live in it full time. "Hard to tell," Grace said noncommittally.

Russell blew out his breath. "Well, that's that. First step done."

"You want to go home, then?" Three hours had passed, and by now, Hawk probably knew that his dad had gone off with her. She was tempted to text him and let him know all was well. Then again, he could work a phone, too.

"I'm hungry. Let's eat. My treat." Russell didn't wait for her but headed across the lot. "Russell, I'm parked over here."

He rerouted himself. "See? It's starting to go. By night, I might as well check myself into that room."

The restaurant Russell chose was the local favorite spot. It served breakfast all day, and breakfast included steak. Russell nudged her elbow. "You see what I'm seeing?" He lifted his chin down the aisle to a booth at the back. There was Irina, and sitting across from her was a man based on what she could see—a shoulder in a plaid shirt. But then he presented his profile.

"Dad."

"I thought so." Not waiting to be seated, Russell headed straight for them, forcing Grace to trail behind.

"Knut, you lost again?" Russell spoke to her dad as if nothing of the awkwardness from their last meeting had ever happened.

Her dad turned at Russell's voice, and his eyes connected with Grace's. "Russell. Grace."

"I didn't see you at Grace's this morning. You just get in?"

Knut and Irina exchanged private looks. Very private looks. Wasn't this awkward? And it just got more awkward when Russell said that he and Grace had just come in for a bite to eat, and what could her dad and Irina do but invite them to sit with them?

Irina shuffled over for Russell and Grace slipped in beside her dad. Perhaps the two lovebirds had already eaten, but no such luck. Through the meal, Grace listened to her dad drop in various "we were planning on" and "we took in." How long had he been visiting Irina's without telling her?

"Sounds to me as if you've been logging quite a few miles on your truck," Grace said.

"I'm getting to know the road well enough," he said and winked at Irina, who colored right up. Grace's chicken salad tasted like straw, and before Russell could reach for the dessert menu, she asked him if he would like to go home.

"I'd like some apple pie first," Russell said. He had stayed remarkably lucid through the meal. Everyone easily smoothed over a couple of glitches.

"Pie and ice cream sounds good," Irina said, and turned to Grace. "If you prefer to go, we can take Russell home afterwards." Another "we." The new normal. She had to call Haley and get the update.

She was about to take her up on the offer when she remembered Russell's horse who was hopefully having a friendly get-together with Sage and Willow.

"You ride her back," Russell said. "Hawk can give you a ride home."

Except she had promised Hawk to stay clear of the place. On the other hand, he might forgive her if he knew his dad was having a rare day out with old friends.

She called Nathan and arranged for him to meet her out in the horse pasture beyond the Blackstone buildings. She would walk back.

But it was Hawk who came out to meet her. The wind was rippling his T-shirt as he stood next to a salt-block stand, hands shoved into his front pockets.

"I am trying to keep my promise here," Grace said quickly, as she dismounted. "I arranged for Nathan to meet me."

"I told him I'd take care of it. He has better things to do."

"Than deal with me, right?"

Hawk moved to adjust the stirrups on Russell's horse. Her long legs had fitted into Russell's well enough, but Hawk required extra inches.

At his silence, she said, "Your dad came to me."

"I know," Hawk said. "Nathan told me right after he got the call from Dad."

"I asked him if he had talked to you, and he said that he was taking care of his own business and would I help him. I couldn't refuse him, Hawk."

"I get that," he said and went around to the other stirrup. He couldn't seem to leave fast enough.

"He's having a really good day. The facility shook him up a little, but seeing my dad and Irina at the restaurant is making his day."

"That's good." Hawk was back to his old communicative self.

"How are the boys? The bruising and the teeth?"

"Good." He swung into the saddle. "Thanks for bringing back the horse."

That was it? He was just going to ride off. "Look, Hawk, I am trying here, okay? I understand we need space, but I can't help if our lives overlap now and again."

Hawk briefly closed his eyes. "You still want everything, don't you? My kids, my dad, my business—everything about me, except me. You walked away when we were young because I scared you. And now you're saying I'm too much to handle, but you still want to be in every part of my life. What's so wrong with me that's still got you running?"

"I'm not running," she said.

"Like the wind," he said, and rode away.

She watched him, his back straight and sitting right

where he belonged. She began the trudge back to The Home Place. He might think she was the wind, but right now she felt heavier than stone.

THE NEXT DAY, Grace's dad invited her over to Irina's for a lunch before he headed north to the Jansson Ranch. It was so weird that her dad's girlfriend was at once his dead wife's good friend and her prickly neighbor.

"You sure you want me there, or are the both of you just trying to be polite?"

"None of us are too good at being polite, so I guess we really want you here."

She arrived to the sight of her dad pushing Irina in a wheelbarrow as she sat cross-legged and held on to the sides. Her dad was carting her over to a small pen fenced off with chicken wire, and as Grace walked up, she saw the couple dozen chicks inside. They were gaining the flat gloss of adult feathers, but they still had baby cheeping voices as they plucked the green grass. Her dad parked the wheelbarrow and held out a steadying hand to Irina as if she were in a carriage.

"Aren't they pretty?" her dad said. "Have you ever seen them so red? Pretty as a roan. Irina says the roosters get blue feathers."

Her dad had never given two hoots about chickens, much less the state of their feathers. He was just in love with Irina, and everything she loved. Something like she was with Hawk. Except she didn't love him. No, she did. But loving him was just too overwhelming.

A truck sounded on the gravel lane. "Amy," Irina said. "She brought the boys over to help with the chores. Something for them to do."

Grace wished she could disappear. She actually considered ducking behind the shed, but the twins would recognize her vehicle.

"Dad," Grace said in desperation, "I'm trying to avoid the boys. To not upset them."

"Why would you upset them?"

"Because of Hawk. We're not...together."

"Grace!" Amos tore toward her, Saul on his heels. Grace meant to greet them casually, but her knees gave way and she met them with a hug. They were both so bony and bouncy. Amos had a bit of egg stuck to his shirt and Saul sported a streak of purple marker up his arm.

Saul drew in a deep breath. "You still smell like cookies."

She smacked a kiss on his cheek. "You say the nicest things. Let me see your teeth."

Saul displayed the gaping hole. It seemed to have healed nicely. "And, Amos, your bruise is as blue as a rooster feather."

The boys shifted over to the chicken pen, sitting on their haunches to observe the pecking and peeping. Grace crouched, too, to observe the boys. Amos had picked up a cat scratch, and Saul had peeling skin on his ears from a sunburn. Amy finally said, "C'mon. The goat waits for no one."

Amos bit his lip. "But we want to be with Grace."

"Chores first," Grace said. "I promise I won't go without checking in with you. Deal?"

And they were off. A week away from them seemed like forever.

"Now," her dad said, "what was that all about?"

"Oh," Grace said, "remember how I used to babysit the kids a couple times a week? We got along well, but then things got busy for me and it just wasn't working out."

"You don't look busy," her dad said.

"I am," Grace said, aware of the scrutiny from both her dad and Irina. "I took time out of my hectic schedule to come here to see you."

"Grace Miranda Jansson," her dad said gently, "you look as if a breeze might break you to bits. What's going on?"

"I'll go make sandwiches," Irina said.

"Why bother?" Grace said. "Dad will just fill you in later. You might as well stay and hear it firsthand."

"But that means I get extra time with him before he leaves." Irina gave her dad a flirty smile. Honestly, it was all very sweet except for how it only highlighted what a mess her own love life was.

Her dreamy-eyed dad watched Irina walk to the house.

"In answer to your question," Grace said pointedly, "what happened is pretty typical. Hawk and I were moving into a relationship, but then Russell's accident made me realize I didn't have the guts for all this and told him so. Now we're back to just being neighbors."

"Irina said you handled yourself pretty well."

"Of course I'm good in a crisis. It's after it's all done. I'm still making quilts, and Mom has been gone for more than a decade, for crying out loud."

Knut looked off to the bend in the road. "I helped Irina haul the wood horse back here. She didn't want it there anymore. We both agreed that with people leaving us, there's no recovering. There's just making peace, and that's daily. She said everybody carries loss of some kind, and it isn't right to expect random drivers to take on hers as well."

"Look, Dad, I'm really glad for you and Irina. I am, even though I sound like a grump. I'm jealous, okay? I wish I could find your peace."

"You still making that quilt with the boys?" She had told him about Russell's birthday gift during a phone conversation.

"I don't get to have them anymore. Hawk wants a clean break, and I don't blame him. The sad consequences of my decision, I guess."

Her dad watched a young rooster drink water. "Seems to me that making a quilt with the boys wasn't really about you getting over your mom. Sounds to me as if you were piecing something together with the boys."

Grace hooked her fingers on the chicken fencing. The bite of the wire suited her mood. "You might be right, but it hardly matters now. I'll have to finish it myself before Russell's birthday in September."

Knut studied his boots. "Hawk's just trying to protect them."

"Why do you think I got involved in the first place? I wanted to help as a friend and a neighbor, but when I wanted to pull back on us, he pulls the plug on everything. And I'm being the unreasonable one? I'm good for them. Why can't he see that?"

"I don't know that he doesn't see that," Knut said, "but he's always been sweet on you, Grace. This can't be easy for him."

"He doesn't need to worry about me banging on his door."

"I don't think," her dad said softly, "you got this far in life by not banging on doors. You just can't get scared by what's on the other side."

But she was scared. Scared of disappointing Hawk. Scared of not being there for those who needed her, and then not doing enough when she was there. And then when she had gone all-out in her work, her boss had rejected her anyway. And then she had run, too scared to tell others about her rejection.

Why are you running from me, Grace?

It's not just you, Hawk.

"Dad, I didn't go on sabbatical. George fired me."

Her dad lifted his arm into a hug, and she threw herself against him. "I called George back in February when you left," he said against her hair. "You taking a sabbatical so suddenly didn't sound right, but George didn't say otherwise, and I thought maybe you were looking for a break."

"I was scared that you would be disappointed in me."

His arm tightened around her shoulders. "I'm not disappointed in you, Grace. I'm sadder that you were too scared to tell me and held it all inside."

Grace breathed in her dad's old familiar smell in his shirt. "I talked to Hawk about it."

"And was he disappointed?"

That talk had led them to their first kiss. "No."

Her dad eased his hold. "Well then. I guess there is a door you don't have to be scared to open." He looked at the house. "And there's another one. With sandwiches on the other side."

She didn't need sandwiches. But Amy would be along soon with the boys, and there was the sweetness of her dad and Irina to take in. "Then, let's bang away."

"YOU AND NATHAN are on to something with dogs," Mateo said to Hawk, as Doxie Sue darted after a straggling cow and calf. They were riding behind the herd as the nearly three hundred head and eighteen bulls moved from the lower pasture to the higher pasture. Hawk had postponed the cattle move for a few days so Mateo could be part of it. He had brought down the trailer to haul Katz back to the ranch for deeper training.

"Nathan says one good dog's worth three horses," Hawk said, his eyes on the twins. Off to his side, they were riding double on Greta, thrilled to be coming on their first ride, even if it meant staying well behind the herd. Amy and Nathan were up ahead, flanking the herd to keep them moving through the draw. "Cheaper, too."

"But trickier to ride," Mateo said, giving Katz a rub on the neck. "Unless, we're in the arena, isn't that right?" Mateo had wanted to test Katz in his outdoor element, and nothing wrong with an extra person on the drive.

"You know, Nathan's almost a worthy replacement for me," Mateo said, grinning.

"He's fitting in," Hawk said. "I thought I was doing him the favor by letting him work here, but I think I'm getting the better end of the deal."

"How's that going to work with Amy? She might steal him over to Irina's."

"I don't know," Hawk said. "I think Irina has her eye on stealing your help."

Mateo twisted in his saddle. "You mean Knut?" At Hawk's nod, Mateo said, "Haley and Grace had a long discussion about it the other night. And then they held a conference call with Natalia on the subject. Knut might make a move."

"Isn't he attached to his grandkids and being a great-uncle?"

"That's what I said, but apparently Knut promised Sadie trips down here no less than four times a year, each with at least one visit with the twins. He'll probably take Jonah and Jakob, when they get older, too."

Mateo's sons and Sadie running wild with his boys, just like him with Grace. "First I heard of this."

"That's just the speculations of three women and one girl. Though four pretty determined females." Mateo leaned to look past him to the boys. Even though they were mostly out of earshot, he lowered his voice. "So what's the deal between you and Grace?"

"What did she say?"

"Only that you two weren't together."

"She's got it right."

"And you're okay with that?"

"I guess I have to be."

Mateo snorted. "You don't have to be anything that Grace tells you to be. The only way I can handle that sister-in-law is to get right back in her face. You should know that."

"I don't like getting in people's faces. That strategy has backfired for me."

"And what did I say about that?"

"Grace isn't Eva. I know that, but I'm the same in both cases. I tried to make Eva fit my ideal. I'm not about to do that to Grace."

Mateo swatted his hat at a persistent horsefly. "You scurried down your burrow like a badger, Hawk. When has that ever worked with Grace? She takes on everyone when she figures the fight is justified. Haley, her father, me. I haven't seen her have it out with Natalia. Yet. We would worry about her mental health if she didn't."

Hawk thought of how she had gone head-to-head with the boys about everything from baths to coordinating tops with bottoms to applying sunscreen. She didn't let up.

But she had with him. Stopped dead in her tracks and walked away.

"She knows where I am," Hawk said.

"And you know where she is," Mateo said. "Take the fight to her."

Hawk didn't want to talk about this anymore. "We need to catch up." He called over to the boys. "You ready to kick it up a gear?"

The twins had only recently learned how to handle a trot, although Greta didn't care for the strain on her eleven-year-old heart.

"Are you ready?" Amos said to Saul behind him, and they were off. Sort of.

"How about you go on ahead with Katz?" Hawk said. "Let him show off. I'll stay back with the boys. We can bring in the stragglers. It'll give the boys something to think about."

Mateo seemed about to say something, probably to do with Grace, but Hawk pretended not to see and turned Wildrose toward the boys.

Greta didn't last more than ten minutes before she lapsed into a walk. "She won't do what she's told," Amos said.

"She's old," Hawk said, as he always said when the boys complained about Greta. "Be glad she's carrying your butts at all today."

"You can lead a horse to the trough," Saul said, "but you can't make her drink."

Amos twisted in his saddle. "What are you talking about? There are no troughs around here."

"It means," Hawk said, "that you can show people the way out of their troubles, but you can't make them do it."

"That's not true," Amos said. "You make me and Saul do things we don't want to do all the time. Grace, too."

"I didn't mind doing things for Grace," Saul said. "They never lasted long. When can we see her again?"

"If she leaves for Calgary, you'll miss her even more."

"But we already miss her, and she isn't even gone. It doesn't make sense to miss someone when they are right here."

"I miss her cookies," Amos said. "And I'm sure they are there in the jar, too."

"I miss her riding with us right now," Saul said and offered his brother a slices of apple from his plastic baggie.

Amos took the biggest one and crunched down. "How

can you miss her when she's never helped move cattle before? This is the first time for us."

"She's helped move cattle before," Hawk said before thinking. "A couple of times when we were older than you, about thirteen or fourteen." Hawk and Grace had been were up where Amy and Nathan were now, the summer heat sweating them up as they turned ornery cattle, calling each other out, egging each other on.

"So you miss her, too?" Amos said.

There was something in his voice, as if asking permission to feel bad. His breakup with Grace was affecting them, even worse than with their mom. "Yeah, I do."

Saul stretched out his arm with the baggie. "Want one, Dad?"

He edged Wildrose over and took one. "Thanks, son."

"They're okay," Amos said, "but—"

"Not as good as cookies," Saul finished.

CHAPTER SIXTEEN

GRACE STEPPED OFF the elevator onto the carpeted hallway, turned the corner and kept moving, as much as her tight skirt and heels would allow. In the seven months away from the law firm, she'd forgotten how to walk in heels, and her toes and calves screamed at the unusual punishment. Still, the hot August sun had tanned her legs and arms nicely, and she'd worn a white sleeveless dress to show off a bit. First impressions mattered.

She couldn't fall flat on her face again. She and Rachelle had worked together via email, but Rachelle had suggested a face-to-face with the client. "I really need him to see that you are on board," Rachelle said.

Grace pushed open the mahogany doors with the name of the firm in a steel-and-brass installation mounted on the nearby wall. There were already two clients waiting, but neither seemed to be the one Rachelle was representing.

"Good morning," she said to the receptionist who looked new. "I'm Grace Jansson. I'm here to see Rachelle."

A familiar face popped around the corner. Keira. "Grace! No one told me you were coming."

"Rachelle asked me to come in. I'm here for a meeting."

"Oh." Keira's smile dimmed. "This isn't a social call?"

Grace had been so focused on making a good impression at the firm that she'd forgotten that Keira had never seemed to care about that. "Not right now, but um… How about I take you for lunch?" There, quick recovery.

"Great, I'll see who else wants to come."

Was she expecting Grace to pay for everyone? If that was what it took for her to get their forgiveness, then fine. It wasn't as if she planned to buy any more horses.

"And I'll go see Rachelle."

"Right, she's in—" A look of pain crossed Keira's good-hearted face.

Grace wrapped her hand around the strap of her computer bag on her shoulder. It felt a bit like taking hold of reins. "At the end of the hallway, on the right?"

Keira gave a half laugh. "Yeah, that one."

Past five doors, past colleagues she had composed apology letters for and then discarded because they had come out either flaky or formal. A door opened on her left, and out came Devon with his perpetual frown.

"Oh, sorry," he began and then recognized her. "Grace. Wow. Good to see you. I've been meaning to call you." His excitement looked genuine. "Any openings at your place? My fiancée and I are looking to get away."

"I'll text you my website," Grace said. "No weekends available until September, unless you want to come out in the middle of the week. Lower rates and it includes a trail ride."

"Horses? I'm in. You still have my number, right? Text me the earliest date. Better yet, call."

A second door opened. "Is that Grace?" Out came Diana. The twenty-three-year veteran of the firm had guided Grace through her earliest cases. The apology note to her had not gotten beyond the opening.

Diana wrapped her in a hug. "Oh my gosh. Keira said you were alive and kicking, but look at you with a real tan. And did the sun do that to your hair? You look gorgeous."

Did they all suffer from amnesia? Didn't they remember that her bullying had damaged their corporate team? Only the promise of a lunch together, with coworkers vying to pay for her, extracted her from their clutches and down the rest of the hallway to Rachelle. She waited outside her door, her arms crossed, her mouth upturned in a slight smile.

Grace recognized that smile from their Zoom meetings. It came just before she pointed out something Grace had overlooked. "You didn't expect to run the welcome-back gauntlet."

"I'm not exactly back. I'm just…here." Grace took a seat across from Rachelle who swung into the deep leather chair that had once been Grace's. It was the same chair that she had specially bought for herself when given the promotion.

"You look good in my chair," Grace said. "Honestly."

"It feels as if I'm sitting on tacks," Rachelle said.

"It's a big seat to fill," Grace said, for the fun of it.

Rachelle narrowed her eyes. "Oh really, Grace, you're not as fat as you think you are."

That was a good comeback. Grace waggled a finger. "You want help or not?"

Rachelle flipped open a folder. "Yes. I worked on this mess until two in the morning . What do you think?"

Grace barely had time to jot a couple of notes before Rachelle's computer dinged that the client's arrival. "Okay, I'll go get him." Rachelle stood and pointed to the empty seat. "You take it. Please. It'll look better."

Maybe there were tacks in the seat, because it didn't feel as comfortable as it used to. And when the client's damp hand met hers, Grace could barely stop from squirming. He was nothing like the one Grace had successfully defended. Her client had talked about keeping promises. This one talked about how to get out of them. What had Rachelle been thinking by taking on this sleazebag?

Once the meeting was over and Rachelle had shown him out, Grace popped out of her seat and back into the harder chair. The office door clicked open and Rachelle entered. "Well, what did you think?"

"I think he's scum, and if there's any justice in the world, they will toss our case out."

Grace expected Rachelle to come back firing. Instead, she dropped her head into her hands. "I knew it. We're hooped. I'm hooped."

"Rachelle, this is not like you. Why?"

Her reply came muffled through her hands. "Because his case was like yours. And if I could win this one, I would have earned this stupid seat of yours. And yes, I know, it was not a good reason, but it was what I thought I had to do."

Rachelle dragged her hands away from her crumpled face. "The fact is that I've always envied you, Grace. You are so good at everything you do. After getting fired, you sailed out and opened up a B and B the next day, and that took off."

"It was not exactly the next day, and my dad bought that land for me. I have had lots of help you didn't get, Rachelle, and yet you are in my seat."

"And who's the complete wreck here? No one knocks on my door and wonders where we should go for lunch. You, you even landed a cowboy with kids to boot."

Her perfect life according to Rachelle. "Not exactly. That went…sideways."

"How?"

"Despite what you think, I'm not good at managing everything. I decided that I'd rather reestablish my career than take on the responsibilities of man, kids and ranch."

Rachelle's crumpled face widened into shock. "Are you

out of your mind? You gave up all that for—" her hand swept around the room "—for this?"

"I missed it." Except now that she was here, it was the people she missed the most, and her good name among them, which, apparently, if their warm greetings were anything to go by, she had not lost.

Rachelle shook her head. "You shouldn't be here. You should be back at your home place, begging that cowboy to ride double with you forever. There are loads of ways to scratch the lawyer itch."

Like taking over from a retiring lawyer in Diamond Valley? "Not as easy as you think."

"Yeah," Rachelle said, "but remember that you make hard things easy."

Missing Grace. It could be the name of a cheesy show, but it described the state of the Blackstone household through much of August. Saul drew pictures of a tall, yellow-haired woman with big blue eyes. Amos drew pictures of cookies and grids that he explained were quilts. Russell kept setting out an extra coffee cup and then muttering, "I thought she was coming over." As for himself, he wasn't sleeping well, and he kept looking at his phone for messages. What did he expect? He'd told her to stay away, and wouldn't you know it, she was actually listening.

Only Nathan didn't seem perturbed. He came in for meals, especially if Amy was over babysitting, and Hawk usually hauled the boys somewhere to give them a few minutes together. Nathan didn't spend too long with her, and rejoined Hawk soon enough. Once given the green light on dog training, Nathan had come up with new projects from renovating an old granary to working up the lawn south of the house for a vegetable garden. He didn't have to, Hawk thought, but the boy seemed driven to prove his place.

It was during one of those downtimes after lunch that Hawk had the boys in the side pasture with Paintbrush and her foal. Doxie Sue had joined them, finally comfortable after all these months to let Nathan out of sight.

"Don't chase him," he told Amos, who was trying to pet Picasso.

Amos kicked the dirt. "But Saul got to touch him."

"Saul didn't stomp over as if he owned him."

"But we do own him."

"Only on paper," Hawk said. "Mostly they are partners."

Amos didn't seem to buy it, his mouth turned down as he watched the foal high step back to his mama's side.

"Hey," Saul said. "Company."

Sure enough, a wide truck, dark gray and kicking up road dust, rolled up the lane. No one he recognized. Doxie Sue tore away toward the vehicle, barking. Her barking of general announcement with her tail up changed suddenly as the driver and passenger emerged. Her barking ceased, her tail went into a brisk wag, and she scampered over to the passenger's side. Out stepped Grant and Deb Sears. Why were they here?

"I know that lady," Amos said. "She gave us pretzels and cheese crackers at that horse sale. She and Grace are friends."

As if his longstanding relationship with the Sears counted for nothing, one he'd had to repair after Grace's stunt at the horse sale. Grant got right to the point as soon as Hawk was in hearing distance. "Deb wanted me to call, but I figured you could kick me off the place if you didn't want me here."

"Of course not, Grant. Good to see you."

"I got kind of curious about where that horse of mine was going to be raised, so I thought—"

"Grant, tell me, do you recognize this dog?" Deb had rounded the hood, Doxie Sue at her heels.

Grant's face lit up. "It can't be. Doxie Sue?"

In response to her name or to Grant, Doxie Sue came right over and slipped her head under Grant's open hand.

Grant frowned at Hawk. "You bought my horse, *and* you took my dog?"

Before Hawk could answer either charge, the door to the house opened and Nathan stepped out. He stood on the porch with his feet apart and his hands shoved in his pockets. Amy stood behind him, waving her arms about, as if not knowing what to do with them.

"Nate!" Deb said. "That you?"

Nathan walked slowly down the porch steps. "It's me."

"Have you lived here the whole time?"

"More or less."

Grant turned on Hawk. "And you didn't have the decency to tell us?"

"He didn't know," Nathan said. "I didn't tell him I came from your ranch. I just said I came from Montana."

Hawk felt much like when he was on a horse set to spook. Grant and Deb looked genuinely perplexed. Amy still looked as if she were trying out her arms. She *knew*.

It made sense that Nathan shared his secret with Amy. Had Grace known? No, she would have told Hawk. He could always trust her to be honest with him. He wished she were here right now. In this episode of *Missing Grace*…

"Amy," Hawk said. "Aren't you planning to take the boys down to the creek?" The low waters of late summer created a quiet wading area behind The Home Place. He and Grace had spent many a lazy afternoon there when kids. During much better times.

Amy seemed reluctant to move.

"I'll see you later," Nathan said to her, with its implied meaning of "I got this."

"Sure. Come on, guys. Time to pack up."

Amos and Saul knew where the real excitement lay, and hesitated. Hawk pointed to thehouse. "Git." They shuffled off, their heads coming up when Amy mentioned snacks to pack.

The door closing behind them, Hawk said, "That'll give us a good quarter-hour to square this away. Nathan, what's going on here?"

"I didn't lie to anyone."

"You stole my dog," Grant burst out.

"She's not your dog. She's mine. Her mom was mine. You sold all her pups, and they were excellent dogs. They had potential, but youwouldn't let me train them. I gave up half a month's salary so I could keep her. You remember that. She's mine."

"That is true," Deb said quietly. "But, Nathan, you just…left. You sent a text, so at least, we didn't call the police. It was just cold. You'd been with us, since you were a boy."

Nathan scuffed the dirt. "Eleven. I came with Mom when I was eleven."

"And we gave you a place and covered expenses when your mom's wages couldn't."

"She hated every minute there," Nathan mumbled. "It's why she left. Her and her loser husband."

"Ranching's not for everybody. But it's the only thing we got to offer people," Deb said quietly.

Wasn't that the truth? It was the only life he could offer Grace. And she hadn't wanted it.

"You liked it," Grant said. "You were on the horses and out with the dogs. Why did you leave and come right to another ranch anyway? What's this one got mine doesn't?"

"And don't say 'Amy,'" Hawk said. "You didn't know her before you came here."

Nathan looked at him, and then blinked and turned away, as if Hawk was a bright object. "You, actually," he said.

Grant sent Hawk another blistering look. Hawk raised his hands in defense. "Listen, I came to your place once years ago. I don't think I even remember seeing you there."

"I was just a kid then." Hawk didn't point out that the fifteen-year age gap still made him a kid. "I was out in the barns when Grant introduced you and I picked up on the name, Blackstone. That was my mom's name before she married my dad, you see."

"What? You think we're some long-lost relatives?"

"We are. I told Mom to ask you about them, but she said what was the point of that and that *Blackstone* was common enough. And then I heard you tell Grant about how your people came up here from Montana, because it was a big family and the boys went off in all directions. But there are no Blackstone Ranches down in Montana anymore, so I thought maybe, you were the last of them, so I thought... I thought I'd go check you out."

"It's possible." His dad had come out onto the porch and was listening in. "Granddad talked about coming up from Montana. It wasn't even Montana then, just wild country. Here, there were Mounties and the law. He could lay claim and not have to worry about another rancher shooting him off the property. I'm not saying it is. I'm saying it could be." His dad turned to the door. "Let me see if I can find a few pictures."

Another Blackstone. Hawk faced Nathan. "Why didn't you just say that to me day one?"

"Because then he'd have to admit that he ran off," Grant

said. He frowned at Nathan. "I could have made proper introductions, given you a reference."

Nathan touched Doxie Sue's head as she sat tucked against his leg. "Because you would have made me leave her behind. And that wasn't happening."

"Oh, Nathan," Deb said, "I wish you hadn't thought the worst of us."

Grant leaned against his truck door, embossed with the Sears brand and the company name, Sears Cutting Horses. "I might not have been the most...benevolent of employers, but I didn't think anyone would have chosen to run off."

"I suppose I could have handled things differently," Nathan mumbled.

"I'd say," Hawk said, which the best he could come up with. Grace would have so much to say and to so many people.

"But things seem to have worked out," Deb said, looking around at the corrals. "You seem to have met a girl."

"Amy," Nathan said. "We're actually getting married."

Hawk must have made gulping noises, because everyone, including the dog, looked at him anxiously. "Did this all happen when I was out with the boys?"

"No, it's been a couple of weeks."

A couple of— "Does Irina know?"

"No, we were keeping it a secret."

"Then, why did you tell?"

Nathan looked sideways at Deb as if she were another, overbright object. "It's hard to keep secrets from you, Deb. Another reason I had to leave so quick."

Amy came out onto the porch, wrangling boys and bags ahead of her.

"They know," Nathan said to her. "About us."

She closed her eyes. "Now we'll have to tell Grandmom, for sure."

"We'll do it, tonight."

"Know what?" Amos said.

"They're getting married," Hawk said. "To each other," he added just so everything was clear.

"Oh," Saul said. "Does Grace know?"

"I don't think that—"

"We'll tell her on the way from Irina's," Nathan said. "She'll want to know."

"That Grace who bought the horse out from under me?" Grant said.

"That Grace," Deb said, shooting her husband a warning look, "who operates a lovely B and B close by and might just have a room available tonight. If we ask nicely. Hawk, you wouldn't happen to have her contact info, would you?"

Deb had given him an opening. "I'll tell you what. Let me call her."

"And I have to sit on this for how long?" Grace squirted window cleaner onto the front of the dining room window and applied elbow grease. Fly specks always stuck as if glued on.

"At least, until tomorrow," Hawk said through her speakerphone. "Do you think you can hold on?"

He spoke dead seriously, so seriously she knew he was joking. Had he forgiven her? Was this out-of-the-blue call his way of reaching out to her?

"No guarantees. I may call up random people just to get the news out of my head. I mean, wow."

"Yeah, not every day you discover your hired hand is some cousin. Dad's gone off to find old pictures to show Nathan."

"So he believes it?"

"It's so bizarre it must be true." Hawk paused. "I don't

mind if he is. He makes a good fit here, and if he's family, all the better."

"The Blackstone legacy grows."

"And then their marriage joins the Blackstones and Sandbergs together."

"They're so young," Grace said. "And they haven't known each other for a full year. How do they know what's good for them?"

"I'm sure Irina will have the same questions."

"And you don't? No words of wisdom as Nathan's older, experienced cousin?" Grace stepped back to examine her work. There, all little fingerprints gone. Those boys. She blinked at the sparkling surface. Empty and boring.

"They are young," he said quietly, "but that doesn't make them wrong."

He was talking about them fifteen years ago, wasn't he? "Who am I to talk? Thirty-four, and I haven't figured anything out." There, an admission that maybe with him, she had got it wrong.

"I got two years on you, and I'm no better."

So, he was admitting to uncertainty. Was that an opening for her?

"Hawk, I was thinking—"

"Not the only thing—"

They both stopped at the overlap of their voices. "Go ahead," he said.

"No, you. You called." She just needed a moment to settle her nerves.

"Any room at the inn? Grant and his wife were looking for a place to stay."

He hadn't called to shoot the breeze, to connect, to talk her back into his life. Grace swallowed. "He's not still sore with me about buying Katz out from under him?"

"He's gotten over it. I think. Maybe sleep with one eye open tonight, just in case." Again dead serious.

"A cancellation came this morning, so send them over when you're done with your visiting. How long, do you think?"

"Not until later. Maybe after supper. He's here for the horses."

"What? You're not selling them, are you?" It was none of her business but—

Hawk breathed out. "I guess I never got around to telling you. He bought first rights to buy the foal from Katz and Risky B, if that happens. I arranged that at the show, just before Dad's accident. Then after the accident—"

Right. They broke up, and that had sucked the air out of their business partnership, too.

"Mateo knows. I assumed he would have told you. I'm sorry."

"It's okay, Hawk. I didn't keep you in the loop about buying Katz. Let's call it even. You've got enough on your plate, what with the Nathan drama now."

"Yep, meanwhile back on the ranch..."

The conversation was teetering back into the familiar. Now or never, she thought.

"I went to—"

"I suppose I—"

Another stop. "Your turn to go first," Hawk said.

Grace found a fingerprint she had missed. Beside it, she smeared her thumb against the glass. "I went to the office the other day," Grace said. "Rachelle wanted me to go over that litigation. It was the first time I had seen everybody."

"And how did that go?" His voice was neutral. Because he really didn't care? Or cared but couldn't show it?

"It went well in a way I didn't expect," she said. "I was hoping for a way back into the firm through this case, and to gain back their trust. Only they were all excited to see me. They seemed to have forgotten, or it mattered less than I thought. They took me out for lunch and it was like old times."

"Good to hear." Still neutral.

"George was there, too. You remember him?"

"Yep."

"And I mentioned that there's a lawyer retiring in Diamond Valley, and George asks if I want to open up a second office and I said that it might be too much, and then Diana—she's been with the firm the longest—says that she's looking to go half time, and how about we share hours? And I said that I would think about it."

Several beats passed before Hawk said, "Don't keep me in suspense, Grace. What did you decide?"

"I haven't. It would give me flexibility. I could choose clients. Still be a lawyer and run the B and B and—help out. What do you think?" Her grip on the bottle was so tight it hurt.

"Sounds as if you're the one with a full plate. Not sure if there'll be room to…help."

"I plan to close the B and B over the winter, and the firm will handle the setup of the office. I will have loads of free time. There are only so many quilts I can make. I like to be busy. I think… I think I found a way to have it all. If you like."

A burst of voices rose from Hawk's end. "Hey, they are all back from the tour of the yard. I should probably go."

"Okay." She waited for him to say something about how they could talk later. Then again, she had offered herself up before and then pulled back. Why would he believe this time was different?

He would have to be an idiot to try a third time, and she would have to be an idiot to expect him to.

CHAPTER SEVENTEEN

TWO WEEKS LATER in early September, Grace stood beside her mother's cairn. "Happy birthday, Mom. Fifty-eight today."

The sky was in vast motion. Wind stretching and building clouds. A stiff breeze battered at her windbreaker. She had better come off the ridge soon, before the wind knocked her off.

"One misstep is all it takes," she muttered to herself and her mother. To lose your life. To lose your chance. The way she had with Hawk. He hadn't called back. Amos and Saul had come over a few times on quick visits, once when Knut was down with Sadie. Amy delivered them, never Hawk. She could have a piece of the boys, but not him.

And she had kept busy. August was her record month for the B and B. If she could pull it off this season, then each should get easier. She already had a few bookings for next season. This week, George would sign off on the Diamond Valley office. Her business life, as always, roared on.

She came down from the ridge to lay her head just below the cairn and stretched out her arms and legs to gaze starfished up into the churning sky. She would lie here for a few minutes and then head back.

Her first Friday night without guests. Weird. She had nothing to do and nowhere to go. "Mom, I really blew it."

Her cell phone buzzed. Hawk.

"You alive?" he barked.

What a question. Wait, his binoculars. Was he watching her? She pushed up onto her elbows. "Yes."

"Then, tell the boys to turn around and get back. Now."

"What?"

"Look at—" His cell call dropped. It was a wonder he had even made the connection. She sat up and looked toward the ranch. There, coming across the browning pasture were the boys on the back of Greta. And it was no gentle walk. They had her at a full trot. And they were bareback with just the halter on.

Hawk's number flashed up again but then dropped before she could swipe it open. Never mind, she knew what to do.

The boys were still coming at a full trot, so she hadn't far to go down the hill before they met. Saul held the reins. They were pale and they must be freezing in their T-shirts.

"All right, what's the panic?"

"Dad had the binoculars," Amos said, "and he saw you on the ridge and he said that you were going to fall off—"

"He said," Saul interjected, "that you had better get off before you fall off, but he wouldn't let us see."

"Then he sets them down and goes back in the barn. We look—and you were just lying there!"

"We call him and he looks and he says you're okay, that you are just lying there. But who lies there for that long?"

"And you decided to check things out for yourself."

"It was mostly Saul," Amos said. "He needed help getting the halter on, and then I came, too."

"You lost your mom," Saul said quietly. "And I didn't want to lose…you."

"Oh, Saul." She stripped off her lined jacket and settled it around Saul. Then she took off her sweater and pulled it over Amos's head. She was down to her shirt and the stiff wind bit at her skin.

"Listen, I am okay. And I deeply appreciate that you two risked life and limb to come to my rescue. But we all need to get home, okay? There's a storm coming, and your dad is worried about you two."

"He's going to kill us," Amos said.

Saul nodded. "Probably." He opened his fanny pack and took out three store-bought cookies, and handed them around. Grace couldn't say no.

"You shouldn't have come up here by yourself," Amos said. "It's dangerous."

"It is, if you're not careful," Grace said. "But I wanted… My mom's birthday is today. And I wanted to check in."

"Are you going to leave something there?"

"We should put up another rock." He moved to slide off Greta and Grace pushed him back up.

"Not today. Go home."

Saul leaned over and handed her a cookie from his baggie. "Here, give it to your mom."

"Sure, I'll do that. Now, git before I'm in trouble with your dad, too."

She watched the backside of Greta and the boys recede back toward the ranch. Greta wasn't losing time. Down by the corrals, she thought she could make out the lean frame of Hawk.

Well, that little drama was over. She thought of polishing off the cookie herself. No one would know. Unless Hawk had those binoculars trained on her.

Anyway, she couldn't lie to the boys and some cruising raven might appreciate the handout. She retraced her steps back up to the cairn.

"Here, Mom, a cookie. I'll see you again. Miss you."

She stood and turned to leave. Her boot caught on the rocks gathered during the summer visit with her dad. She stumbled, her arms windmilling.

"No!"

Her last thought before tipping over the edge was that at least the boys hadn't seen her go.

BUT HAWK HAD.

He threw down his binoculars and raced for the quad parked next to the barn.

"It's out of gas," Nathan said, coming out of the barn. "What's going on?"

Hawk pivoted, and wolf-whistled to call Wildrose over. "It's Grace. She's fallen off the ridge." His breath caught. He couldn't say more, and he didn't need to. By the time he saddled Wildrose, Nathan had crossed to open the far gate. "I left the binoculars down by the corrals," Hawk said on his way through. "Keep an eye up there in case I need help. And watch the boys."

They weren't more than five minutes away on Greta. "I don't care what kind of lie you come up with. Don't tell the boys anything."

Nathan nodded and Hawk only slowed when he drew alongside the boys to tell them to stick with Nathan, and then he set Wildrose into a full gallop. He couldn't have lost her, not like this. She had to be okay.

But accidents happened all the time. A mother. A daughter.

Why not Grace, too?

I think I have found a way to have it all. If you like. But he hadn't believed her. Or his luck. It had seemed more real that she would leave than that he, too, could have it all. And now, right before his eyes, she had vanished.

Please, not for good. Wind tore at his clothing, had taken his hat long back. Wildrose's breathing came in hard, jolting pants. *Let her live, let her be alive.*

"Come on," he urged. They were approaching the steepest part now, and Wildrose slowed. Hawk could run just as fast, but he needed the mare in case he had to lift Grace up.

"Grace!"

Was it the wind or his own wishing, but was that her calling to him?

He couldn't take it anymore. He halted Wildrose and swung off, making for the ridge.

There she was, thirty feet below him on the same ledge where he'd found her mother. Kneeling, her face turned up to him, dirt all up her front and on her face. Alive.

"You were spying on me with those binoculars," she said, the wind whipping away her voice, so her words arrived in pieces to his senses.

Hawk looked at the roiling clouds and took a long breath. Then he turned to the ranch and gave a wave and a thumbs-up signal. That should be good enough. "I apologize. How about I forget what I saw and head back to the ranch?"

"Sure," she said. "And then explain that to your boys."

He squatted. "You really think that I would only haul your butt up because of what the boys might think of me?"

"Okay, you have a conscience. Could demonstrate it at your earliest convenience?"

Hauling up a living being who could brace herself and help the process was a sight easier than...before. He uncinched the rope from her middle and gathered it up. His hands were shaking as bad as she was. Cold pebbled her arms, and her bottom lip was trembling.

He wasn't aware he'd moved to her, but suddenly she was flat against his chest, his arms wrapped tight around her. And he had no thought of letting go anytime soon.

"What happened?"

"My foot caught, and I slipped. I mostly slid and grabbed at whatever until I landed on the ledge."

"You hurt?"

"Major grass burn, bruised ribs and I grabbed a thistle on the way down, so my hands feel as if they are on fire. The whole front of me feels on fire."

His front did, too, but for a different reason. Wildrose whinnied, her ears flicking. "Hold on, we'll go soon."

"There's a storm coming," he said into her hair. Her very prickly hair. He tugged out a sagebrush twig.

"I had noticed that. Can I bother you for a ride back to my place?"

That would require moving, loosening his arms around her, and he wasn't ready for that yet. "I saw you go over and my heart stopped beating."

She didn't say anything, her arms folded against his chest.

"I have pretended with you, Grace. I pretended it was up to you, if you wanted to make a go of it with me."

Her reply came muffled. "You said that you wanted to be with me."

"Sure, I said it. But what happened when you got scared and left? I got scared, too. I didn't go after you. I nodded my head and let you go."

"That was the deal."

"That was a rotten deal." He rubbed his hands up and down her back. She was cold, and they should go. But he wasn't going to let her go until he had finished.

"You know why I look for a missing calf, even though I've got hundreds? Part of the reason is money, but a bigger part has to do with not letting a creature suffer. What I did to you was let you suffer because I didn't want to take responsibility for you."

She shuddered against him. "That's a tad dramatic."

"No, I was always great at taking on responsibility. Unless it came to us. I let you go and called it giving us freedom, the right to choose. I could have compromised on everything else, except you. I should have chased you, Grace. Fifteen years ago and when you broke it off after the accident."

She lifted her dirt-smudged face to his. "But you said I was like wind and couldn't be caught."

He could feel her ribs under his hands, her heart beating against his chest. Grace, alive and in his arms. "And yet here we are with a storm about to break. I'm not letting go."

"It wouldn't matter if you did, because I'm not going anywhere."

Her mouth was inches from his. "I've got one more thing to say."

Her blue eyes widened. "Say it."

It was the most natural thing to say in the world. "I love you, Grace Miranda Jansson. You were always my best friend. Now you're my neighbor and business partner. And I aim to make you my wife one of these days."

Her arms slid around his neck. "Make me, you say?"

There was that same light in her eyes that had him since he was five. "Is that a dare?"

She ran a finger down his cheek. "Yeah, it is. I love you back just as hard, Hawk Blackstone. If you accept the dare, I'll make sure you win it."

Hawk grinned and lowered his head, getting a head start on the challenge.

Meanwhile, back on the ranch, Nathan hastily lowered the binoculars. He had done that as soon as Grace was in Hawk's arms, but Amos and Saul insisted he keep checking, just in case. Not that he'd seen much with Hawk's checkered back bulking up the view.

"Can we look now?" Amos said.

"Is Grace still okay?" Saul said.

Nathan pocketed the binoculars and spun them toward the house. "She's very okay. Your dad's okay. He'll bring her home soon."

EPILOGUE

GRACE OPENED THE door to The Home Place, bringing with her the rush of the April winds.

The stink hit her. The cake. She raced to the oven. "Haley!" she yelled. She opened the door and out billowed a wave of heat and smoke. The wedding cake, a simple form cake Grace had popped into the oven two hours ago, looked like a giant charcoal briquette.

The smoke detector shrieked, and her sister pounded down the stairs, carrying baby Jakob in her arms. Jonah peeked out at his aunt from behind the safety of his mom. "Jakob's teething and Jonah bumped his head—"

Grace tilted the pan to her.

"Oh. I'm so sorry." Haley opened her phone. "I'll call Mateo."

"He's busy enough helping Hawk get the chores done so they can dress for the wedding," Grace said, waving a towel under the detector to clear the smoke and shut off the noise.

"He'll know what to do," Haley said with quiet confidence.

There was only one thing to do with this cake. Grace flipped the smoking brick out the back door for whatever hardy wildlife was up for the challenge. She lifted her gaze to the ridge. Through the bare branches of the early April trees she could make out the cairn on the ridge. "I hope you can come, Mom."

Hawk had the solution. "He said there's an extra package of cake mix left over from the boys' birthday in October that hasn't expired," Haley said. "Natalia's whipping it up."

"She's a godsend. Thank God Brock married her."

"Yeah, she's the good sister we never had."

Grace snorted. "Hey, it's not me that nearly burnt the house down. Come on, let's get the decorations up. There's less than two hours to go."

A frantic two hours it was. Texts flew back and forth between The Home Place and the Blackstone Ranch, the load lessening once Natalia and Sadie arrived with Irina and Amy. Between swapping out toddlers and babies, the women arranged hair, and wiggled and zipped into dresses. Haley caused another minor emergency when her dress, perfectly fine two months ago, couldn't accommodate her baby bump. Grace opened seams and basted in quilting fabric. For the same reason, she would be opening the seams on her own dress for Nathan and Amy's wedding in late August.

The men pulled in, and Grace heard them assemble in the living room. She picked out Mateo's and Brock's voices. George, who had a special one-day license to act as marriage commissioner, and the single female voice of his wife, Hilda. Nathan spoke with her dad and Russell.

At the top of the stairs, Grace cocked her ear to Russell's voice, deep and raspy. It sounded strong and centered. She had plowed through mountains of research, and had instituted a new diet and mental therapies for him. Russell still lived at the ranch, and could keep a routine easily enough. Last week, when Irina came over for last-minute alterations on her dress, the topic had turned to Russell.

"You have saved his life," she said flatly.

Surprised, Grace pricked her thumb on a pin. "You are...okay with me, then?"

Irina played with the spill of blue faille. "I have grown okay with the entire world, since your father came along." She looked up at the ridge. "Though I will never compete with her, I suppose."

Grace repeated something she had overheard Hawk tell Amos about a school rivalry with another boy. "No competition if you don't enter."

Irina released a long breath. "You're right. Wise words."

But now, among the rumble of voices downstairs, she couldn't make out the speaker of the wise words. She peeked out the upstairs window to the driveway below. His truck was missing. Where were he and the boys? She couldn't do this without them.

Just as she turned from the window to fetch her phone, in he rolled. She allowed herself the quiet pleasure of watching him and the boys assemble themselves. For the quick dash to the house on the cool spring day, the boys just wore the suits she had bought them in early November for a similar occasion.

He was wearing her favorite shirt. A dark, bright blue under a black suit jacket. Nothing more satisfying than a cowboy dressed up, holding a cake server. He glanced up at the window and pointed her out to the boys, and they waved as if she had just arrived back from a long trip. The boys ran to the house, but Hawk lingered and shot her another look she understood. She touched her lips.

"Are we ready?" Natalia said quietly. The five women glanced at each other, and then at Sadie and the babies.

Irina gave a brisk nod. "Let's do this." They lined up and proceeded to the living room.

The men and boys were already in their assigned places, so it was only a matter of the females settling into place.

Amos and Saul opened a spot between them on the otto-man for Sadie. Jonah followed her and sat at her feet. Haley sat beside Mateo with Jakob on Mateo's lap. Beside them, Amy nestled next to Nathan. Brock and Natalia with baby Daniel took one end of the second couch.

Hawk sat at the other end and Grace claimed the open spot next to him. He drew her left hand into his lap, the one with the wedding ring. True to his word, Hawk had proposed marriage in early October and they'd married in January in a ceremony not much different than this one.

"Did you tell Haley?" he whispered.

She shook her head. "I want to tell Dad first."

The news of a grandchild due in the fall would be her special wedding gift to him. Then together, they'd tell Russell.

Her dad stood near the fireplace, his eyes on his bride who came to stand beside him with the bouquet. They both looked wonderstruck.

"Welcome," George said, "to another special gathering."

And there had been so many in the past few years, Grace thought, as she glanced around the room. Mateo and Haley, then Brock and Natalia, Hawk and herself. All of them happily married. What were the chances of that happening?

And for her dad, to happen twice in one lifetime?

Hawk laced his fingers in hers and squeezed, her ring hard in their hands. He knew the odds. She squeezed back, and along with her family, attended to the words of abiding love.

* * * * *

WESTERN

Rugged men looking for love...

Available Next Month

A Lullaby For The Maverick Melissa Senate
The Rancher's Reunion Lisa Childs

....

Fortune's Convenient Cinderella Makenna Lee
The Cowgirl Nanny Jen Gilroy

....

LOVE INSPIRED

Training The K-9 Companion Jill Kemerer
The Cowboys Marriage Bargain Deborah Clack

6 brand new stories each month

WESTERN

Rugged men looking for love...

MILLS & BOON

Keep reading for an excerpt of
THE INNOCENT'S ONE NIGHT SURRENDER
by Kate Hewitt—find this story
in the *One Night With The Italian* anthology.

CHAPTER ONE

Laurel Forrester burst from the hotel room like a bullet from a gun, aiming for the lift down the hall. Her breath came in tearing gasps and she stumbled in the heels she wasn't used to wearing—stupid, sky-high stilettos her mother had insisted on.

She heard the sound of the door to the executive suite being wrenched open behind her and then heavy footfalls.

'Come back here, you stupid little—'

With a mewling gasp of terror, Laurel put on a burst of speed, racing around the corner. The gleaming black doors of the lift shimmered ahead of her, a promise of freedom.

'Wait until I...'

She closed her mind to Rico Bavasso's threats and stabbed the button for the lift with a shaking finger. *Please, please open. Save me...*

Bavasso came round the corner, moving swiftly for a man pushing sixty. Laurel risked a glance back and then wished she hadn't. Three diagonal cuts slashed one of his lean cheeks, where she'd scratched him, blood oozing down his face in crimson, pearly droplets.

Please, please open. If the lift doors didn't open, she didn't know what she'd do. Fight for her safety, for her life. Go down kicking and screaming, because go down she would. Bavasso might be older but he was big, strong and angry, and she was five-foot-four and just a little over a hundred pounds soaking wet.

With a glorious ping the doors opened and Laurel threw herself inside, bruising her shoulder against the far wall before she scrambled upright. She pushed just about every button she could, anything to get her away from the hell that had erupted with Bavasso's demands and grabs, his insistence that he would get what he'd paid for. What her mother had promised him.

Bile rose in Laurel's throat at that memory and she choked it down. She didn't have the luxury of memories or even thoughts in this moment. This was about basic survival. She pushed the 'door close' button repeatedly as Bavasso stumbled towards the lift, a smile of triumph curving his cold mouth, his glowering face thrust forward. His bow tie was askew, his tuxedo shirt straining against the buttons as he reached one hand forward to keep the doors from closing. Laurel shrank back against the lift wall, her heart beating in her chest like some wild, winged thing.

'I've got you, you little slut.'

Laurel kicked off one of her wretched stilettos and swung it at Bavasso's grasping hand. He let out a howl of outrage and yanked it back, his palm impaled by the dagger-sharp heel. The doors closed and then the lift was soaring upwards and Laurel was safe, *safe*.

She let out a sob of both terror and relief, her senses overwhelmed by what had happened—and what had almost happened, but thankfully hadn't. Her trembling legs felt weak and watery and she sank onto the floor, drawing her knees up to her chest as shudders wracked her body. *That had been so close.*

But she wasn't out of danger yet. She still had to get out of this hotel, out of Rome. Bavasso had her handbag in his hotel room, as well as his security detail waiting down in the foyer. Laurel had seen them when he'd been playing baccarat, standing around like stony-faced gorillas, eyes darting around the casino floor, looking for threats. And now she was one.

What would he do? Over the last two days' acquaintance he'd been sleek and charming, although admittedly paying her more attention than she'd have liked, considering he was her mother's latest love interest. He also seemed arrogant and entitled, and she feared he might not let this lie. And what about her mother? Was Elizabeth safe? Would Bavasso turn on her—or had she really been part of it all along, as he'd implied? *I'm only taking what your mother promised me.*

Surely not? Surely her mother wouldn't have sold her off like a cow at auction? With another cry Laurel covered her face, the tumult of the evening too much to bear. She should never have agreed to come to Rome, to play a part so she could get what she wanted. And yet she had. She'd weighed it up in her mind and she'd decided it was worth it. One last favour and then she'd finally be free. Except she wasn't free now. She didn't feel remotely free.

The doors opened and Laurel lifted her head, shrinking back, half-expecting Bavasso to be there, waiting. But, no; the lift opened directly into what looked like a private suite, twice as elegant and spacious as the one Laurel had just fled.

She scrambled to her feet, pulling on the hem of the short sparkly dress of silver satin that had also been her mother's choice. *Bavasso wants to see a lovely young woman in her prime, not some dowdy wallflower. He's a discriminating man, Laurel.* Now she was afraid she understood all that had meant.

Laurel knew she couldn't stay in the lift; the doors would close and then the lift would start heading down again, back to Bavasso or his goons, somewhere she definitely didn't want to be. Cautiously Laurel took a step out, onto a floor of polished black marble. Floor-to-ceiling windows were visible in every direction, giving a panoramic view of the Eternal City, lights shimmering in the darkness.

Modern-looking sofas of black leather and gleaming chrome were scattered around, the soaring space lit only by a few minimalistic table lamps, so it took Laurel a stunned second to realise there was someone in the room with her.

A man stood at its centre dressed in black trousers and a charcoal-grey shirt that was open at the throat. His hair was black and cropped close to his head, his eyes a piercing grey, the same colour as his shirt. His arms were folded, emphasising impressive biceps, and everything about him radiated power. Control. *Danger.*

Laurel's breath hitched and she froze where she stood, dawning realisation, relief and fear colliding inside her with an almighty crash. *Could it be...?*

Then he spoke, a voice like molten silver, pitched low. His tone was both authoritative and sensual, winding around her shattered senses, pulling them tight.

'Hello, Laurel.'

She gave a little gasp of surprise even though she'd known, deep inside, that it was him. That it had to be him. The awareness she felt of him didn't make sense, considering they were near strangers, yet she wasn't surprised by it at all.

'Cristiano.' She let out a little laugh of relief; the adrenalin still coursing through her body made her feel shaky and weak. Or maybe he was making her feel shaky and weak, standing there like a rock-solid pillar, arms still folded, face expressionless in the dim light. 'Thank God.'

He arched one dark slash of an eyebrow, his gaze travelling to her tiny, torn dress. 'Things get a little out of hand?'

Laurel glanced down at her dress, an embarrassed flush sweeping over her along with all the other overwhelming emotions. The dress was practically indecent, a spangled slip that revealed far too much thigh and cleavage. One of the straps had torn from the bodice, so the dress gaped even more. She wasn't even wearing a bra, only a tiny scrap of a thong. And, from the hard look in her stepbrother's eyes, Laurel suspected he knew it—and wasn't impressed.

She took a deep breath, trying to gather her scattered wits. Her head was spinning from everything that had happened, and her legs still felt weak. She longed to sit down, to *breathe*, to figure out how she'd got here and what on earth she was going to do next. 'I didn't even know you were here.'

'Didn't you?'

'No, of course not...' Laurel frowned, belatedly registering Cristiano's cool tone, the look of mocking censure in his iron gaze. And then she remembered the last time she'd seen him, ten years ago, when she'd been a silly four-teen-year-old to his manly twenty-three, and when she'd practically thrown herself at him as part of a stupid teen-aged dare.

'I don't even know where I am,' she said, trying to smile, but her lips didn't seem to be working properly. They just wobbled.

'You're in the penthouse suite of La Sirena. My private home.'

'Oh.' So she'd pushed *that* button? But how had she been granted access? 'Well, I'm glad the doors opened up here. Very glad.'

'I'm sure you are.' There was a note of sardonic amusement in his voice that Laurel felt too scatter-brained to understand at the moment. It sounded as if he was referencing something she was meant to know about and didn't.

Unless he was referring to her stupid schoolgirl crush all those years ago. Laurel doubted that. She doubted her one clumsy attempt at a kiss—he'd pushed her firmly away before she'd so much as made contact—had stayed in Cristiano's memory for more than a millisecond. He'd been that unimpressed.

'Do you mind if I clean myself up?' she asked. 'I feel...' Dirty. She felt dirty. But Cristiano didn't need to know that. He was already looking at her as if he thought she was, a realisation that made heat scorch Laurel's face once more. She knew she was wearing a slinky, slutty get-up, but did he have any right to judge her? Although, considering her actions tonight, perhaps he did.

'Be my guest.' Cristiano gestured towards a corridor that led to the suite's bedrooms. 'You'll find everything you need in one of the bathrooms.'

'Thank you,' Laurel answered, her tone turning a bit haughty to cover her confusion—and her guilt. If she could have picked the circumstances in which she ever saw her stepbrother again, these would not have been them. Not by a million awful miles.

Was it just the way she was dressed or was there another reason he was being so cold? Not that they'd ever had much of a relationship, or one at all. Her mother had been married to his father for three years, but in that time Laurel had only met Cristiano twice. Once after the wedding, when he'd had a blazing argument with his father, Lorenzo Ferrero, and then stormed out. And the second time when he'd come home for some reason and she'd attempted, in pathetic, girlish naivety, to impress him.

Six months later Lorenzo had divorced Elizabeth and Laurel and her mother had high-tailed it back to Illinois, with nothing but a pocketful of jewellery to fund Elizabeth's often exorbitant lifestyle. Ferrero had had a watertight pre-nup, and her mother did like to spend money…

Cristiano was still staring at her, arms folded, the emotion in his silver eyes fathomless. What had she expected him to say? Do? He'd never expressed any familial concern or even interest in her before.

She was a stranger to him, or near enough to it, just as he was to her—or should be, except for the fact that out of idle curiosity—or perhaps, shamefully, something a little deeper than that—she'd followed his exploits on social media and scanned the many tabloid articles about his playboy lifestyle. She'd always been fascinated by this man who had loomed on the periphery of her life, dark and powerful, when she'd been an innocent teenaged girl emerging shyly from her chrysalis of gawkiness into uncertain womanhood.

It truly stunned her that she was in his penthouse now, although she supposed, if she stopped long enough to think rationally about it, she shouldn't have been that surprised. She'd known the hotel where they'd met Bavasso was owned by Cristiano. She just hadn't expected actually to see him.

Cristiano's mouth curved in a smile that held neither humour nor warmth. His eyes glittered like burnished mirrors, reflecting nothing. 'You said you wanted to clean yourself up?' he prompted.

'Yes.' Laurel realised she was staring but it was hard not to stare at a man who was so starkly beautiful, so arrogantly attractive. The silk of his shirt clung to his well-defined pectoral muscles and the narrow trousers emphasised lean hips and powerful thighs. But beyond the impressive musculature of his body was the aura he possessed, the lethal authority and latent sexuality he emanated from every perfect pore—and that was what made Laurel stare. And not just stare, but *imagine*, shadowy, vague thoughts and images that danced through her mind, awakening longings that been dormant for her whole life. Thankfully they remained shadowy, falling back and leaving a streak of restless heat in their wake.

Staring at him now, taking in the arrogant tilt of his head, the dark, winged eyebrows, the sculpted mouth formed into a hard, hard line—he looked just the same as he had ten years ago. Perhaps he was a bit more muscular now, a bit more powerful. He'd made his own millions in the last decade, she knew, in property, casinos and hotels, at the highest end of the market.

He'd also, according to the tabloids, had dozens and dozens of mistresses—Hollywood actresses and European supermodels who graced his arm like the most expensive accessories, and, if the papers were to be believed—and Laurel suspected they were—were discarded after a matter of days.

It seemed incredible to her that she'd actually tried, in a clumsy, desperate way, to make him like her gawky teenaged self. The realisation made her cringe even now—especially now—yet surely Cristiano didn't remember that? He'd swatted her away like a fly.

Just the memory made flustered confusion sweep through her and quickly she turned away, afraid that Cristiano would see her uncertainty. He'd seen too much already, starting with this skimpy dress.

'Thank you,' she mumbled again and then, not wanting to prolong her agony, she hurried down the hall.

CRISTIANO WATCHED LAUREL scurry down the hall like a frightened rabbit. A sexy frightened rabbit, wearing far too little clothing for his comfort, and only one shoe. He turned away, his jaw tightening, the flare of sexual attraction arrowing through him annoying him further. He hadn't expected to feel it quite so strongly, especially now that he knew what she was like.

When he'd seen Laurel Forrester swan into La Sirena this evening, dressed like a hooker and on the arm of a man who made his skin crawl, he'd felt shock slice through him. It was ten years since he'd last seen her; she looked a whole lot more grown up now, yet he'd recognised her. Instantly.

That second of stunned amazement had morphed into a deep, sick disappointment that settled in his gut, a leaden weight that was absurd, because if he'd had to think about it for a second he'd have known Laurel would be just like her mother—a craven, amoral gold-digger playing for her best chance. She'd shown her true colours at just fourteen years old, after all, and heaven knew the apple didn't usually fall far from the tree.

Which was why he had been so determined to cut off all his ties with his own father. The last thing he wanted to do was make the mistakes Lorenzo Ferrero had, chasing after some ridiculous and ever-elusive happily-ever-after and becoming increasingly more desperate to find it. Letting himself be used, hurt and humiliated, and for what? An amorphous emotion that didn't really exist, or at least shouldn't. Love.

Cristiano strolled towards the window, shoving his hands deep into his trouser pockets as he mused on what lay in store for Laurel…and for him. He'd watched her on the casino floor, draped on Bavasso's arm, her attempts at flirting cringingly over the top and obvious. She might be many things but what she definitely wasn't was a good actress.

Bavasso, of course, had lapped it up and demanded more. A lot more, apparently, because after Cristiano had left the floor he'd stayed by the bank of security cameras in his flat, watching her, waiting—but for what? He was acting obsessed, which was stupid, but he hadn't been able to keep himself from doing it.

He'd told himself it was because of their past—because he knew her mother was a thief and he had no intention of letting her fleece any of his customers, even one as unpleasant as Rico Bavasso. He'd told himself that, but he didn't completely buy it.

Then everything in him had frozen and clenched hard when he'd seen her leave the casino floor, Bavasso holding her hand, practically dragging her towards the lifts. But she'd gone. She'd been *smiling*. For some reason that smile had reached a vulnerable place he hated the thought of even possessing.

Cristiano didn't know what had happened upstairs in the hotel suite but he could guess all too easily. Still he'd stayed by the cameras, which was why he'd seen her running for the lifts, as if the hounds of hell were chasing her—or just one lascivious one. Whatever game she was playing, she'd decided not to see it to the finish. And, while Cristiano certainly believed in a woman's right to say no whenever she chose to, it didn't change his opinion of Laurel Forrester one iota.

On the cameras he'd watched her hit all the buttons, including the one for the penthouse. The lift doors to the penthouse were always locked, but with one flip of a switch Cristiano had sent Laurel straight up to him.

And now here she was.

The only question that remained was, what was he going to do with her?

He narrowed his gaze as he looked out of the window, the Colosseum lit up at night, a beacon to the city. He'd brought Laurel up here because she'd needed rescuing and he was a man of honour.

But honour only extended so far. And now, with the lift doors locked again, the only person Laurel needed rescuing from was him.